Welcome to the adventure

Where loyalty matters, magic runs deep, and nobody stands alone.

3

LISA CASSIDY

THE WYVERN'S CRY

THE INKWEAVER ARCHIVE

BOOK 3

TATE HOUSE

A catalogue record for this
book is available from the
National Library of Australia

National Library of Australia Cataloguing-in-Publication entry

Creator: Cassidy, Lisa, 2024 - author.

Title: *The Wyvern's Cry*

ISBN (paperback): 978-1-922533-16-6

Subjects: Epic fantasy fiction

Series: *The Inkweaver Archive*

First published in 2024 by Tate House

Cover artwork and design by J Caleb Designs

Map artwork by Chaim Holtjer

Also by me

The Mage Chronicles
DarkSkull Hall
Taliath
Darkmage
Heartfire

~

Heir to the Darkmage
Heir to the Darkmage
Mark of the Huntress
Whisper of the Darksong
Rise of the Shadowcouncil

~

A Tale of Stars and Shadow
A Tale of Stars and Shadow
A Prince of Song and Shade
A King of Masks and Magic
A Duet of Sword and Song

~

The Inkweaver Archive
The Nameless Throne
The Dreadwater Gate
The Wyvern's Cry
The Unleashed Storm

Contents

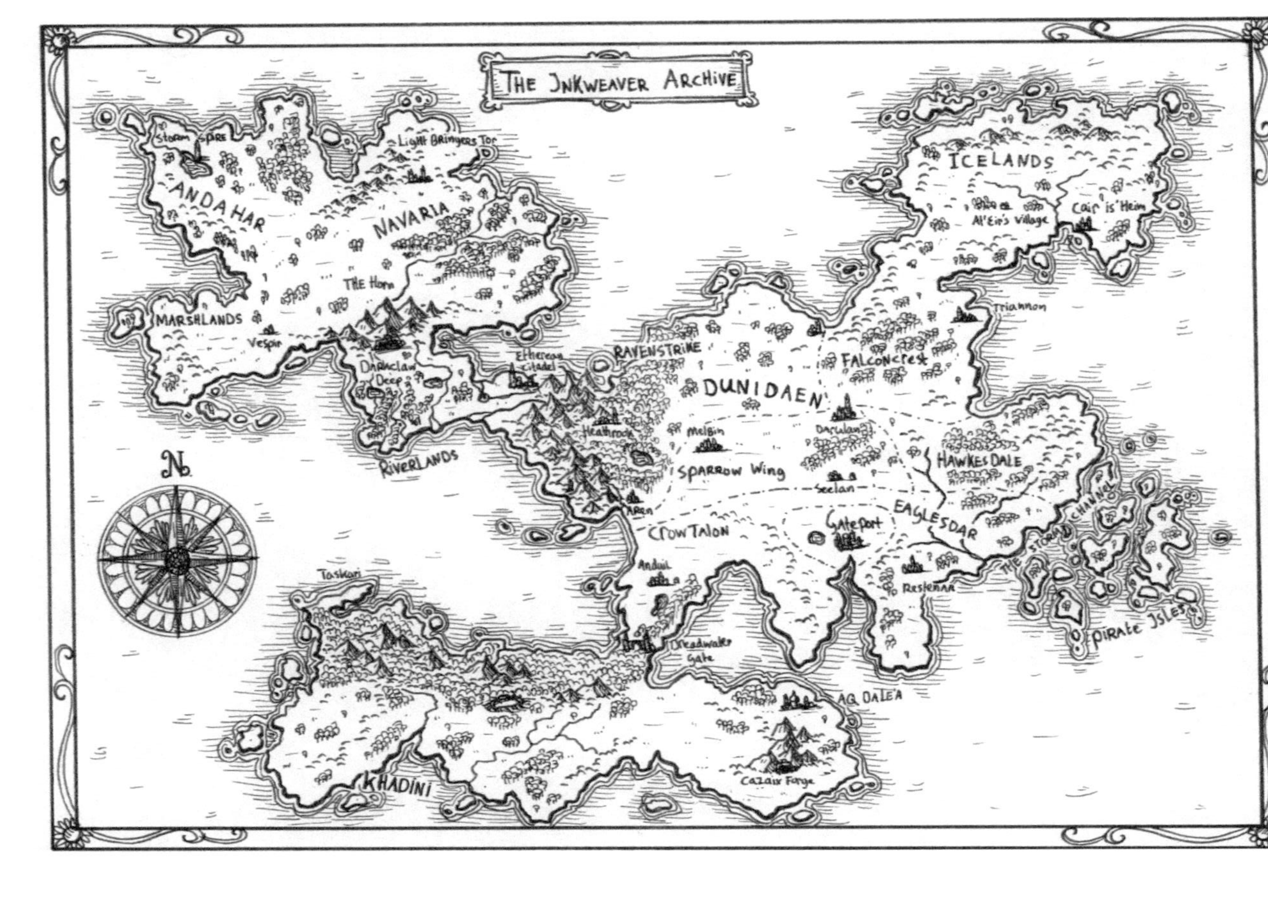

The Inkweaver Archive
Storm Spire
Light Bringers Tor
ANDA HAR
NAVARIA
ICELANDS
Al'Ein's Village
Cair is'Heim
The Horn
Triannon
MARSHLANDS
Vespir
RAVENSTRIKE
FALCONCREST
Draxclaw Deep
Ethereon Citadel
DUNIDAEN
Heathrode
Melgin
Draculaw
HAWKESDALE
RIVERLANDS
SPARROW WING
Seelan
EAGLESDAR
N.
Aren
CROW TALON
Gateport
Taskari
Anduil
Restemaa
THE STORM CHANNEL
Dreadwake Gate
PIRATE ISLES
AG DALE'A
KHADINI
Cazaix Forge

Chapter 1

The maddened roar of an ice bear echoed across the snowy plain.

Six warriors circled the bear in a blur of constant motion, a short sword in each hand, long snowy braids tied back so they wouldn't get in the way. Sensing it was becoming penned in, their prey reared on its hind legs to trumpet its fury and affront. The warriors looked the size of ants in comparison.

Arya Ravenstrike held her position equidistant between the warriors at her left and right, breath frosting in the icy air, feet moving as if in a dance. Hunting an ice bear was a team effort, all warriors in the team operating as if tied to a single piece of string. Attempting it any other way was a death sentence.

The bear crashed back to all fours, and the ground shuddered with the impact. Lowering its head, it ripped out a snarl and *lunged* at the warrior directly in front of it. Despite its size, the bear moved dangerously fast, its massive jaw opened wide to reveal long yellowed incisors. In the second before those fangs found their target, a flurry of snow spun off the ground and into its face, blinding it. It yowled, shaking its head, and the warrior danced in and slashed his blade deep along the bear's neck before spinning away again.

The bear screamed. Bright red blood dripped to the snow. The wound wasn't deep enough to kill—thick fur had stopped the blade cutting too deep—but enough to injure.

The warriors kept moving, light on their feet, keeping their quarry contained. Growing frustrated, the bear swung and charged the warrior to Arya's left. He swung his blades, slicing inches from the creature's nose, but it was undeterred, the pain making it frenzied. Lowering its head, it kept coming.

The warrior shouted, and an impressive cloud of ice and snow swept into a whirlwind around the bear's head. It growled in frustration and lifted a paw to try and bat away the stinging pieces of ice. Red streaks of blood stained the snow from its bleeding wound, spattering every time it shook its head.

The distraction allowed another warrior to close in, swinging both blades. Her first strike missed, but the second slashed across the white fur of its nose. The bear squealed in agony, but in its maddened state, it continued to close rapidly on the warrior closest to Arya, the focus of its rage. Arya readied to intervene, knowing her fellow warrior could never outrun an ice bear, even an injured one. She couldn't summon ice and snow like her companions, but she could—

Instead of retreating, though, the warrior planted his feet before the on-rushing bear. Unafraid. Ice and snow whirled, but it was no longer having any effect. His blades looked pitifully inadequate compared to the size of the beast coming at him.

The bear swiped viciously with claws the size of knives. The warrior ducked and lashed out with his sword. Blood sprayed from the bear's right paw, but the pain only increased the bear's frenzy. It roared, striking out again, and the man dodged, barely avoiding the blow. As he moved, he slipped on a patch of ice and fell.

Arya had already started running.

As she did, the other four warriors moved in concert, closing the gap she left, ceding her the assist to the warrior in trouble. The bear reared up as the man under it tried to roll away. Arya dashed in under his claws. Blue metal gleamed as she drove her cazaix sword deep into the bear's heart before yanking it out. Blood sprayed, hissing in the cold air, and she managed to leap out of the way as the bear fell heavily to the snow, dead.

For a moment she stood there, catching her breath, marvelling at the size of the beast. Then, she shot a taunting grin in the warrior's direction. "You're getting slow in your old age, At'eir."

He rose to his feet, quick and graceful. "And you have a death wish. You should have waited for the team to close in."

"If I'd done that, you'd be dead. You weren't getting up fast enough to beat an ice bear." Still filled with the adrenaline of the fight, Arya shifted on her feet, eager for more.

The other four warriors gathered, all with a nod of acknowledgment for Arya's kill. The youngest of them spoke, head bowing deferentially towards At'eir. "I'll go and summon the others, Er'fin," he said, using the Icefolk word for prince.

At'eir nodded. "Be swift, At'hur. We've strayed closer to Ce'Garn territory than I'd like, and I want to be gone before his patrolling warriors stumble across us. At'near, you and At'urn will patrol the area while we wait."

They'd left the rest of the tribe's hunting party back at their camp. It was the job of At'eir and his handpicked warriors to bring down the bear, but many more hands would be needed to skin and dismember the enormous creature and then transport the meat and fur back to the tribe's village. Arya glanced up at the sky—if the clear weather held, they should have the job done by nightfall. Then they could set out at first light for the village. The meat and fat of the beast they'd just killed would provide enough food for At'eir's tribe for a month. All in all, a successful hunting trip.

At'hur sprinted off. Icefolk warriors hunted on foot and could travel at a swift run for hours with ease. Their endurance and skill with their twin short swords were beyond anything Arya had seen in Dunidaen, and her Raiders had been *very* good. She understood why. Survival in the Icelands relied almost entirely upon two things; hunting enough food to keep everyone fed and having proper shelter from the severe weather. It was why most of them lived in close-knit tribes rather than large towns or cities—both food and shelter were scarce resources.

"You're the one with the death wish if you think the five of us could fight off a Ce'Garn war party," Arya spoke to At'eir. Although the prince spoke fluent Dunidae, Arya had learned Icefolk language over the past three years, and now communicated easily with him and his warriors in their own language.

Living in an environment with such scarcity of resources also meant competition between tribes was vicious. The queen of the Icefolk sat above the tribe leaders in much the same way the Dunidaen High Warlord sat above the State warlords, but the queen's control over her tribe leaders was more tenuous than the High Warlord over his warlords.

"I am the son of the Icefolk queen. Even Ce'Garn would not dare to attack me outright," At'eir said.

She conceded that. "It must be nice to have such security."

"Is that a note of envy I hear?"

She laughed bitterly. "I'm no ruler, At'eir. Nor do I desire to be one."

He gave her a look like he thought that was a lie, if only to herself, but all he said was, "No, you'd rather hide away from the world here in the Icelands."

"I'm not hiding. You and your mother offered me safe haven," she snapped. "It's bad enough having the Etherean on my back without you nagging me too."

"You will always be welcome among my people." At'eir spoke with solemn formality, an odd diversion from his usual amiable mien. "We Icefolk have always been allies of House Stormrider; my grandfather swore fealty to yours. That doesn't mean the Icelands is where you belong."

"I am hunted by the Nightstalker and his nazal and I don't have the means to protect myself against them," Arya said wearily. This wasn't the first time they'd had this discussion, and it exhausted her every time. "Not to mention the High Warlord's bounty on my head. I have no choice but to hide where they cannot find me."

He let it go there. He usually did. She was grateful for that, at least. "You will be returning to the Etherean citadel soon?"

She nodded. Full winter had almost arrived in the Icelands, and it got far too cold then, even for Arya, who'd grown up in northern Ravenstrike winters. "I'm going to freeze if I just stand here. I'll do my own sweep of the area. Whistle if there's trouble."

At'eir nodded and Arya took off at a jog, glad to be moving again. Even in those few moments of standing still her body had begun to grow uncomfortably cold. By the time she and the other two warriors returned to the Icefolk prince, her roving gaze caught movement on the horizon. She pointed. "At'hur returns."

They both spotted the blood spattering At'hur's furs at the same moment, and ice and snow crunched under their boots as they shifted into a run. The other warriors closed in behind them, swords drawn. Arya was relieved to see At'hur didn't seem hurt, just deathly pale and shaking as he stumbled to a stop before them.

"What happened?" At'eir demanded. "Where are the others?"

"Dead, Er'fin." The young warrior swallowed. "All at the camp are dead."

Arya looked at him in confusion. The forested territory where they'd made camp—along the Icelands' southwestern border with Dunidaen—had its usual array of predators, but nothing an Icefolk hunting party couldn't handle, even if they weren't all elite warriors.

"Killed by what?" At'eir demanded.

"I don't know, Er'fin. Blood was everywhere. And..." A shudder went through At'hur. "I couldn't recognise some of them."

At'eir's jaw tightened, startling blue eyes turning ice cold. "We go at speed," he snapped.

"Er'fin!" The response was resounding.

And they ran.

Arya trailed At'eir and his warriors as they moved swiftly across the hard-packed snow. The furs they wore helped them blend with their environment so well that if it weren't for the footprints they were leaving in unbroken snow, she'd be in danger of losing them if she dropped too far behind.

Pushing hard, they reached the top of a ridge before plunging down the tree-covered slope on the other side. At the bottom, they leaped a frozen stream without breaking stride and emerged onto another snowy plain. Above them the sky was a faded blue, the weather clear and calm. That calm would only be temporary, though. Just like in the Diamondfang, bad weather could blow in at any time.

Directly ahead was the hazy outline of the forest where they'd left their camp. In tacit agreement, the warriors ahead of Arya drew their blades and increased their pace. The trees closed around them, cutting off much of the blinding white light of the plains. As soon as her eyes adjusted, Arya reverted to the scanning soldier's gaze she'd perfected as a young Raider stationed at Icecliff Fort. They came upon the camp quickly.

Arya slid to a horrified halt, boots skidding in the ankle-deep snow, her eyes taking in the bodies of their hunting party, the blood-streaked snow, the wounds, the—

Her stomach lurched, and she was glad she hadn't eaten in hours. They'd chosen a large clearing for the camp, big enough for twenty Icefolk and four large tents. There wasn't a single spot of snow that wasn't reddened.

She'd seen this before.

A presence curled in the back of her mind, one always with her, shivered into awareness. "*Coming.*"

"Arya?" At'eir was looking at her oddly. "What is it?"

"Wraiths." She forced the words out. "Wraiths did this."

Those icy eyes flashed. "The creatures from Andahar that invaded Raven-strike nine years ago?"

Arya nodded as her stomach heaved again, and despite her best efforts she emptied what remained of her meagre breakfast onto the bloodied snow. Nauseas sweat slicked her skin and her hands had begun trembling. She took several deep breaths, blinking, trying to dispel the images, the memories, forcing their way into her mind. She wasn't in the Ravenstrike townhouse. She was in the Icelands. With At'eir.

They were—

Shadow rippled in the trees nearby and Arya leaped to her feet, crying, "Beware ambush!"

At'eir and his warriors were good. Deadly good. And so, they were already in fighting position, twin blades lifted, ice and snow lifting in a protective flurry around them, when the wraiths launched themselves out of the trees surrounding the clearing. They swarmed en-masse, a hissing darkness of claws and insatiable hunger. Arya lifted her sword, eyes widening as she read how many there were. Enough to dim the light in the clearing to almost full night.

They were horribly outnumbered.

"Go for the eyes!" she bellowed. "That's the only thing aside from fire that will kill them. Use your magic to keep them away from your faces so you can see well enough to go for the eyes."

Before she'd finished speaking, she'd lost sight of the Icefolk warriors in a cloud of teeth-filled darkness. The high-pitched hissing tore through her ears, mixing with the grunts of battling Icefolk warriors and the screams of wraiths as they died.

Her long cazaix blade was too unwieldy for this.

Arya sheathed it and as she did, she found her anger, her *hatred* of the Nightstalker's monsters, and reached for her magic. It came to her easily, and she brought her hands together as a focus for the electrifying power rising inside her. Sparking blue energy lit them up, and with a roar of her fury she pulled her palms apart and released the banked-up force.

Magic exploded around her, pulverising anything in its path for a metre-wide circle around her. The darkness lifted, the wraiths dying too quickly to even scream. But it wasn't enough. One of At'eir's warriors was down, another swaying on his feet, and there were still too many wraiths. Arya drew a breath, ready to draw upon her magic again, even though she'd already burned through most of her reserves.

A roar ripped apart the afternoon.

Arya's head snapped up, energy flooding her, a vicious grin spreading across her face. The sound echoed again, challenging, angry. Even At'eir's hardened warriors cowered. The trees surrounding the clearing shook. The wraiths hissed in fear.

A wyvern's cry.

"Get back!" Arya shouted a warning. "Get clear, into the trees!"

Elendryl was a golden blur as he dropped out of the sky, landing in the centre of the clearing, wings outstretched, balancing easily on his two powerful legs. He reared over them all, taller than an ice bear, fearsome fangs displayed as he screamed another challenge, then his serpentine head swung around to tear into a pack of wraiths. Fangs ripped through red eyes and the creatures couldn't get a purchase on his iron-hard scales. His barbed tail whipped back and forth, tearing through wraiths and their little red eyes. And the claws at the tips of his wings swiped and ripped relentlessly.

The wraiths' dying screams made for an almost unbearable cacophony of noise.

Arya ran for At'eir, letting loose another surge of magic to clear the wraiths around him before dragging him backwards, to the trees at the edge of the clearing. "Stay!" she bellowed. Then, one by one, she went to each of At'eir's warriors, helping them fight off any wraiths still clustering around them, before drawing them to safety as her wyvern tore the rest of them to shreds. She and At'near carried the fallen warrior between them to safety.

And then they were all dead.

Silence fell, the bloodied snow now coated with the greasy ash of dead wraiths. And in the middle of it all stood a golden wyvern, fury still vibrating from him, a snarl ripping from his throat.

"Remain still and quiet while he calms down." Arya spoke loudly as she crossed to Elendryl.

His head lowered at her approach, and she pressed her palm against the scales along his nose. "*Calm, my friend. All is well now.*"

"*Danger.*" The thought was still hot with anger.

"There was. It is no more. I am safe now."

He visibly settled at those words, and she pressed her forehead against his scales. Their bond settled around them, edged with the triumph and violence of battle, yet underpinned by affection and trust.

"Victory," she murmured.

Chapter 2

Several minutes later, once she was confident Elendryl had calmed enough not to snap at anything that moved, Arya stepped away with a final stroke of his neck. *"You should return to your hunt. You'll be hungry after all that fighting, and we're safe here now."*

"Hungry." He agreed, but added: *"Close."*

Reassured by his promise to remain nearby, Arya turned to At'eir as the wyvern lifted out of the clearing, enjoying the looks on his warrior's faces as they watched him. They'd seen Elendryl from a distance many times now, but they'd never had cause to fight together until the wraith ambush.

"I never thought to see it. Another true Sky Lord," At'eir said in awe.

"I'm nothing close to it," she said sharply. "Not yet anyway. And maybe never."

He wisely left it at that and made a sharp gesture for his warriors. They spread out to check the fallen bodies of their hunting party, hoping for survivors. The one who'd fallen was back on his feet, limping from multiple gashes in his leg. The grim silence hanging over them deepened as it became clear there were no survivors. Arya stood, head bowed, as At'eir kneeled by each of his fallen tribe, gently closing their eyes before murmuring a few words, hand over heart.

When they were done, At'eir glanced at the sky before looking at Arya. "You've noticed the wind change?" he asked, and she shook her head. She hadn't yet learned to notice the minute changes in weather that the Icefolk were able to. "A blizzard comes. We'll need to shelter here for the night. There isn't time to make it back to the village."

She nodded. "Do we have time to burn your people?"

"Not if we are to get a shelter set up in time. It will be done after the storm passes." His voice was heavy with sorrow. "We'll recover whatever supplies we can and move somewhere close by."

The small group worked hard against increasing winds to dig down into the snow at the base of a large tree, before laying a sheet of tarpaulin across the top. Arya cut sturdy branches that the Icefolk used to bolster the entrance, giving them a way out as the snow inevitably built up. By the time the blizzard arrived, they were packed tightly together in the makeshift snow cave. While the work had distracted them from their grief and shock, there was nothing else to dwell on once they were hunkered down with the wind shrieking and howling around them.

Ayra had lost Raider shield-mates before, knew the ache of grief they were feeling, and said nothing at the silent tears that tracked At'hur's cheeks, At'near's slumped shoulders and downcast gaze, or the way At'eir's jaw was clenched so tightly it had to be painful. Others had glazed eyes, like they were still picturing seeing their fellow tribe members bloodied and torn in the snow. Her own mood was dark. She was familiar with most of At'eir's tribe, and their grief was bringing back terrible memories.

"Er'fin, do you think the wraiths were sent by the Nightstalker?" At'hur mumbled, barely audible over the screaming of the wind. He sat hunched, hands clasped tightly as if to stop them shaking. "And how did they even get here?"

Terror flinched through Arya. She'd been trying not to think about that exact question. To be in the border region of the Icelands, the wraiths had to have come through Dunidaen. Specifically, through Ravenstrike State and into Falconcrest.

At'eir gave Arya a sympathetic glance. "The last message my mother received from High Warlord Crowtalon did not mention any troubles in Ravenstrike or Falconcrest. You know that, Arya. Just as you know that he made a formal agreement with her and the Khadini emperor at the last State Council to notify us immediately if Dunidaen did experience any trouble with the Nightstalker."

Arya's shoulders bowed as grief and guilt twisted so tightly inside her she struggled to take a full breath. It was a weight she still couldn't carry.

The last State Council.

When Thiara Ravenstrike and her husband had been brutally murdered mere hours before winning the High Warlord vote. When Arya had murdered Mathas Crowtalon's chief advisor in a fit of rage in full public view. When she'd barely escaped the Nightstalker and his nazal hunter with her life—forced to leave behind everything and everyone she loved. And then, after all that, finding out ... her hands were shaking, breath choking, and she tore her thoughts away before they could go back down that well-trodden path of torturous grief and guilt.

At'near, sitting beside Arya, tried a joke, "How much did the High Warlord offer for Arya this time?"

All glances turned Arya's way. She ignored them. Mathas Crowtalon, High Warlord of Dunidaen, had put a very hefty price on her head. If not for the Icefolk loyalty to her Sky Lord House—and their dislike of Mathas—she would not be safe here.

"A promise to negotiate trading concessions in the Winter Sea," At'eir said.

Arya's head shot up. "Mathas Crowtalon is willing to redraw the boundary lines to give you the exclusive fishing zone the Icefolk have been after for decades?"

"He's willing to *discuss* it." At'eir said. "If we capture you and ship you straight to him in Gateport."

Arya wondered what Falconcrest State thought of that. They currently controlled the exclusive rights to fishing in the western half of the Winter Sea, an area the Icefolk thought belonged to them. It had been a friction point between the two countries for generations.

"Why does he want you so badly?" At'hur asked. Still pale, his question seemed to be an attempt to distract them all from heavier thoughts.

"He thinks it will keep Dunidaen safe from invasion if he hands me over to the Nightstalker," she said.

As newly crowned High Warlord four years earlier, Mathas Crowtalon had made an agreement with the Nightstalker to hunt any potential Sky Lords inside Dunidaen's borders. Arya Ravenstrike was the only named target so far—something she sought an update on every time the Icefolk queen received a missive from the High Warlord—which meant nobody had yet identified the other four. But the Nightstalker's patience would not last.

Clawing fear followed the grief and guilt. Her family was still being hunted, and she wasn't there to protect them. She *couldn't* be there to protect them. Distance was the best way to keep them safe. And not just her Sky Lords and her Ravenstrike family, but her deepest, most terrifying secret, the thing that would undo her completely if the Nightstalker learned of it. The thing she'd been running from for three years.

Everything she did now. Every breath she took. It was about protecting that secret.

"Which brings us back to the wraiths," At'eir said soberly. "There are only three months until the next State Council of warlords. Almost four years and Crowtalon has nothing to show for his promise to the Nightstalker."

"You think the wraiths might be a scouting party for invasion?" At'near sounded sceptical. "Scouting for what? Beyond this forested region along the border, they'd have limited range and nowhere to hide out on the open plains."

Arya shivered. She remembered when wraiths and shadowhounds had crossed the Diamondfang nine years ago, how she and her fellow Raiders fought them back. Not *her* Raiders anymore. Her teeth gritted with the force of grief and loss that rose up at that reminder.

Elendryl roused in the back of her mind, sensing her distress, but familiar enough with it by now that he settled after realising she wasn't in danger. She took heart from his presence so close, well-fed and curled up under a layer of snow, his inner body heat all he needed to protect himself from the cold.

At'eir cast another glance in Arya's direction. "My mother and I, and Elder Salyarin, knew the agreement Mathas Crowtalon made with Dunidaen at the last State Council would not hold forever. Maybe the Nightstalker is finally reaching the end of his patience."

Arya chewed on that, not for the first time. Why *hadn't* the Nightstalker made good on his threats? Was the fact he now had a firm ally in Dunidaen's High Warlord holding him at bay? War was costly and dangerous … perhaps the Nightstalker felt he didn't need to risk it while he had Mathas Crowtalon hunting Sky Lords on his behalf. That line of thinking was plausible, but it didn't feel quite right. A powerful Sky Lord with an iron rule over his country was at a clear advantage in war with a largely magic-less population. And if he truly saw Arya and her Sky Lords as an existential threat, then the longer he left them alive, the stronger they grew, and the more of a threat to him they became. Her temple throbbed, thoughts circling endlessly without a solution.

"Whatever the reason for their presence, the wraith pack we faced today could destroy an entire village," At'near said. "And we cannot rule out more nests of wraiths in the area."

"Elendryl and I will fly over the border region as soon as the weather clears and make sure there are no other nests," Arya offered, beyond glad for something to do. Some action to take. "If there are, we'll clear them out."

"Thank you, Arya, that would be of great help. We will travel to Cair Is'heim with speed to bring news of the attack to my mother." At'eir spoke of the Icelands capital, the only permanent city in the country. "If the Nightstalker is planning invasion here, he'd be a fool to attempt it with the Icelands winter looming, but we need to be prepared for spring."

Arya frowned. "Why come for the Icelands at all? Your magic combined with your elite fighters and harsh terrain mean it would not be easy to win, even on Xaphistryl's back."

"Not easy, but doable. Our ability to weave the snow and ice is nothing compared to the Sky Lord magic he wields, and our numbers are not large," At'eir said. "I take your point though. There's nothing for him to gain by taking the Icelands, except territory."

"Inhospitable territory at that," At'near agreed.

Arya's head came up. "It *would* be an easier staging point for invasion of Dunidaen than trying to get his army over or under the Diamondfang mountains."

At'eir shook his head, long braids rustling. "He still has to get an army here. The north sea is frozen until spring, yet the ice isn't thick enough to risk marching an army over. He'll have to wait for the melt and send ships to attack our western coastline."

"The wraiths could be scouting for that eventuality?" At'hur suggested.

"Why wraiths? Why not trained scouts who can map territory?" At'near asked.

Silence fell. After a moment Arya spoke. "After Elendryl and I have searched the border for wraiths, we'll head straight for the citadel. The Etherean should know about this too."

The er'fin and his cousin shared a look, but it was At'eir who spoke. "We will be sad to see you go, but know you are welcome back next spring, Arya Ravenstrike."

Arya wondered whether they'd be facing an invasion by then.

***

The blizzard blew itself out in the early hours before dawn, and they emerged from their half-buried snow cavern to a landscape covered in white. Arya helped At'eir and his warriors as they trudged through deep snow to their old camp and spent hours digging out the bodies to be burned in the Icefolk way. They worked in silence, the warriors' grief a heavy counterpoint to the fear and dread lurking in the pit of Arya's stomach. By the time the pyre was lit, and smoke curled in the sky, she was desperate to be gone.

The er'fin approached Arya as she was buckling up her pack, half smiling at the sight of Elendryl snapping at the snow a short distance off. Her terrifying wyvern apparently liked the sensation of icy snow in his mouth.

At'eir told her, "At'near will go straight to our tribe's village to carry the news of what has happened, while I will head directly to Cair Is'heim."

"What of the ice bear?" Arya knew how critical the felled creature was to the survival of his tribe.

"At'near will lead a party to it after she has returned home. We can only hope the body is still there." At'eir managed a smile. "I am sad to be parting from you again."

Arya reached out with her left hand, palm facing outwards. He did the same, pressing his left palm against hers and they bowed their heads; the traditional Icefolk farewell. "Thank you once again for giving me safe haven, Er'fin."

He straightened. "You are always welcome here. A pretender may sit the throne of Andahar now, but we Icefolk hold true to our oaths of allegiance. My mother would be disappointed if I did not do whatever I could to assist you and your House."

"I hope the day comes when I can repay that allegiance." Arya stepped backwards and slung her pack over her shoulders. "If Elendryl and I spot anything untoward on our patrol, I'll find you."

He smiled. "Then I hope not to see you again until spring. Safe travels, Arya."

"And you, At'eir."

Elendryl's head came up as she crunched through deep snow towards him, and delighted anticipation shivered through them both. Ensuring her pack was firmly secured on her shoulders, Arya climbed onto Elendryl's back, using his bent leg as a stepladder of sorts.

It took only a moment to settle into position at the base of his long neck, sinking into the only gap between the razor-sharp spines running down his back—as if it were tailor made for his rider—legs resting against his powerful shoulders. The direct contact connected them both to a sensation of rightness they could never achieve when apart.

With a final wave to the Icefolk, Arya braced herself as Elendryl took two lunging steps forward and launched himself into the sky. She watched in awe as ground dropped away beneath them. Icy wind burned her cheeks and whipped though her hair. The thrill of flying with Elendryl was some-thing she'd never grown accustomed to.

Still, the momentary joy faded as quickly as it had come.

The events of the previous day had shattered the fragile peace that months with the Icefolk had given her.

The Nightstalker was making a move.

She could feel it in her bones.

Chapter 3

For several hours Arya and Elendryl flew low over the forested treetops of the southwest Icelands border but saw no sign of wraiths. Arya was initially concerned they might miss a nest amidst the thickest forested areas, but Elendryl gave a vigorous body-length shake when she shared her worry with him.

After adjusting to the sudden movement—their intimate bond meant she knew his every shift before he made it, making the chances of falling slim—she asked indignantly. *"What was that for?"*

"Smell," he sent.

"You can smell *them?"*

Her doubt must have been obvious, because he sent a snippy. *"Bad smell,"* then stopped talking to her for a while. Not that the two of them *talked* as such. Elendryl didn't communicate with words or sentences. It was a combination of sense and feeling and images, an instinctive language developed over four years together. While Arya often still spoke to Elendryl aloud, the fact they didn't need to use words meant communication could be lightning-quick and made working or fighting together seamless.

As clever as he was, though, her wyvern wasn't human. He was an aggressive predator with all the instincts of one, and Arya needed to be constantly aware of that when they were around others. If he thought she was in danger, nothing but her command would stop him destroying everything in his path to get to her. And his definition of her being in danger included someone breathing wrongly in her direction. *Or* her feeling a spike of pain when stubbing her toe.

Eventually, as the sun lowered towards the horizon, Arya was confident they'd searched every inch of border territory without crossing into Falconcrest State. "*I think we're clear.*"

Elendryl sent back a confident assent before sending a questioning image of the Etherean citadel.

Arya sighed. "*Yes.*"

He circled upward until they reached a high altitude, then turned southwest towards the Diamondfang, home of the Etherean citadel. They travelled along the north-eastern coast of Dunidaen, using the coastline to navigate, though staying high enough in the sky that nobody below would see more than a dark speck if they happened to look upwards.

They flew until well after nightfall, and then Elendryl brought them down along an isolated section of the northern Falconcrest coast, only a few miles east of the Ravenstrike border. He hunted his own dinner—livestock if he could find it without being spotted, or less satisfying, wild rabbits or other warm-blooded creatures—while Arya chewed on supplies from her pack, and then they curled up together to sleep until dawn.

They were aloft again at first light, and after several hours, the hazy outline of the Diamondfang range came into sight. Thick cloud enveloped them as they weaved between looming mountainsides, but Elendryl was undeterred. The wyvern had learned his way unerringly around these peaks and valleys over the past years.

The higher they went, the thinner the air grew. Elendryl didn't seem bothered by it, but Arya's breathing became laboured, and light-headedness engulfed her. The first time they'd made this trip, she'd suffered from terrible altitude sickness for days. Each time she'd travelled since it had gotten easier, but it still took her a full day or two to adjust.

The Etherean home was not built for humans.

Arya reckoned it wasn't long after midday when they broke through the cloud cover and the graceful spires of the Etherean citadel came into sight. Despite having seen the vista many times before, she still stared in awestruck fascination.

The home of the Etherean, a winged people, was so high that most of the time it sat above the clouds hugging the lower mountaintops. The citadel clung to two of the highest summits of the Diamondfang and spread out across the lower peaks encircling them. Sun gleamed off its graceful marble towers.

The southern face of the tallest mountain dwarfed Elendryl as he glided towards the yawning entry that was the formal entrance into the Etherean city. Several stories high, it was easily large enough to admit a wyvern.

He flew inside and landed with a jolt in an enormous cavern. Arya looked up as a group of three Etherean flying above called out a friendly greeting—though they smartly didn't try to come any closer. She waved back, watching them as they swooped out into the sunlit skies. "The Dunidae have no idea what beauty lives so close to them," she murmured.

Elendryl snorted in contempt.

Then she imagined what someone like Mathas Crowtalon might do to the Etherean if they came to his notice by stepping outside their borders, and she shuddered. He hated all magic-wielders with a passion, and he wasn't the only Dunidae who felt that way.

Brushing off her grim thoughts, Arya dismounted and stroked Elendryl's neck affectionately before bidding him go in search of good hunting and then rest. After returning her affection with a gentle nudge of his nose, Elendryl took off. The elder had told her that this citadel had once been a waypoint for Sky Lords travelling to and from Andahar, either to Dunidaen, Khadini, the Icelands, or other lands that lay beyond. The old, unused wyvern stables had been re-opened with enthusiasm on Arya and Elendryl's arrival three years earlier. Once he gorged himself hunting today, her wyvern would return there and be treated like a king—from a safe distance.

Giving herself a shake, Arya began walking, boots echoing loudly in the cavernous space. It took several minutes just to reach the other side, where a wide set of stone steps led upwards into the city proper. Despite hard-won elite physical fitness from her months hunting with the Icefolk, the thin air meant Arya struggled climbing the endless stairwells—there for young

Etherean whose wings weren't strong enough to fly yet, those that were injured, and the elderly—toward her destination. Regularly she had to stop to catch her breath and let her light-headedness settle.

She struggled to the top of one stairwell only to be almost bowled over by a group of three winged children, no older than four or five, pelting madly after each other, laughing and shrieking. Her gaze tracked them, her thoughts far away, the joyful note of their laughter driving shards of glass into her chest.

Finding herself still staring long after they'd vanished from sight, Arya shook herself, turning and forcing herself to continue on. She eventually emerged into an open-aired corridor, this one holding a series of guest rooms, one of which was hers whenever she stayed.

Panting, heart galloping as if she'd sprinted all the way, Arya closed the door and immediately began stripping off her Icefolk furs and underlayers. It had been over a week since she'd had a chance to wash or change clothes, and she went straight to the small tub sitting in the corner of her room. On her first visit, she'd been astonished to learn that Etherean engineers had worked out a way to pipe water up from hot springs under the mountains—it was only lukewarm by the time it travelled all that way, but it was a damn sight better than washing in ice cold water.

She scrubbed her skin and hair, then after a quick dry-off rummaged in the closet for the comfortable breeches and shirt in warm wool that she usually wore in the citadel. As a final layer, she belted on a thick quilted robe and slid her feet into wool-lined short boots.

Time to go and see Salyarin.

***

An icy breeze ruffled Arya's drying hair as she crossed a narrow suspension bridge between two graceful towers. Several Etherean flying overhead waved or called down greetings, which Arya returned politely. The warrior that stood guard at the double-doored entry to the residence of Elder Salyarin, leader of the Etherean, gave her a nod of greeting. "Arya Ravenstrike, welcome back."

She tried to mask her too-fast panting, but suspected she'd failed by the amused glint in his eye. "Thanks, Rithil. Is the elder in?"

"He is. Wait here, and I'll let him know you're seeking an audience." Rithil's bright scarlet wings rustled as he opened the door and ducked inside.

Arya wandered over to the floor-to-ceiling windows on the eastern side of the entry foyer, gaze drinking in the view. The elder's tower was the highest structure in the citadel. Today, the low-lying cloud gave the citadel a mysterious air, offset by the bright sunshine above.

Behind her, the double doors creaked open, and instead of Rithil, the silver-haired elder himself emerged. It struck her then, as it had several times over the past years, how similar the Icefolk and Etherean were, even though the Icefolk had their own language and the Etherean shared a language with the Dunidae. Both races were tall, with striking white hair no matter their skin colour, and an ability to survive in the coldest of environments. Though the Etherean had wings, of course, and were shockingly thin by human standards—an adaptation to help their wings hold them aloft, she supposed. And both races had magic, though it differed in type.

Salyarin wore a silken green robe, and his powder-blue wings were folded neatly behind his back. In all the years she'd known him, he'd never looked a day older. She wondered about Etherean longevity but hadn't wanted to appear rude by asking directly about it. "Arya Stormrider. Greetings."

Immediately she was on the defensive. "I've asked you not to call me that. My name is Arya Ravenstrike. That name is all I have left of my family. It is who I am."

"My apologies, Arya." He sounded like he meant it. "You've returned earlier than I expected. Is all well in the Icelands?"

She took a deep breath, trying in vain to fill her lungs and dispel her frustration with him. Damned altitude. "Unfortunately, not. Yesterday a nest of wraiths near the Icelands-Dunidaen border ambushed our hunting party and killed most of them. Er'fin At'eir worries they might be a precursor to an Andahari invasion."

Salyarin's only visible reaction to this news was a rustling of his wings. "And what do you think it means?"

"I have questions, as does At'eir, not least of which is why only one pack of wraiths, and why were they lurking in the forest on the Icelands border?" Arya said. "But whatever the answers are, I wanted to warn you as soon as possible."

Salyarin stepped up to the window beside her. "I appreciate the warning. But we both know that neither the Icelands nor this citadel will be the first target of an Andahari invasion."

Tense silence settled between them.

"That may not be true," Arya said eventually, outlining the discussion she'd had with the Icefolk about the Icelands being a better staging point for invasion of Dunidaen.

"Even if you are right, Dunidaen must be warned."

"I hope you're not suggesting *I* should warn them," Arya said. "Mathas Crowtalon has put a bounty on my head, not to mention the nazal still hunting me. You're the one who tells me I'm not ready to survive an encounter with one of those monsters yet." And if that were true, she didn't dare go near them, especially not the monster who'd killed Thiara Ravenstrike, who had the ability to get inside her head and see her thoughts. A shudder rippled through her—every time she thought of the nazal, she remembered that they'd once been Sky Lords. Now they were stronger. Darker. Incredibly dangerous.

"And it can't be us, for similar reasons. The Etherean haven't stepped foot outside the Diamondfang since the border closures decades ago, and I don't intend to risk my people by doing so while Mathas Crowtalon rules Dunidaen. If the Nightstalker invades through Dunidaen, he will hit Ravenstrike first." The elder spoke with a calm that rarely failed to stoke Arya's temper. "You must warn Warlord Ravenstrike, at least."

"Rorin won't want to see me anymore than the High Warlord will. I was the reason his parents were murdered." She spoke as evenly as she could, though it took too much of an effort, and she suspected Salyarin wasn't fooled. "Perhaps Chiarn could go."

After four years, none of Arya's guilt had faded. Thiara Ravenstrike and her husband had died because of Arya, all her hopes and ambitions in ruins. Arya had ignored repeated warnings about the level of threat the nazal posed, thinking in her arrogance that she could keep everyone safe, and instead the creatures had murdered two people she loved. She was sure they must hate her for what she'd done.

"Chiarn cannot go, you know this. And even if he did, you are the only one who could gain an immediate audience with the Ravenstrike warlord. You are the only one he will listen to. Arya, it is your duty."

"Elder—"

"Listen to me for once in your life!" He cut across her protests. "If Andahar invades, it could be swift and without warning, and with a powerful Sky Lord riding a wyvern at the head of its army. Dunidaen needs to be warned in time to gather its strength to face this threat."

"And what of the nazal hunting me, waiting for me to step foot back in Dunidaen?"

"It has been almost four years. The nazal is not in Ravenstrike, Arya. Stop making excuses." He was resolute. "Besides, *you're* the one who keeps telling me that your only purpose in life now is destroying the nazal."

"And I *will*," Arya hissed. "I *will* avenge Thiara Ravenstrike's death. But I won't make the same mistakes again. I will not face them until I am strong enough to win without putting more people I love at risk." Or risking the Nightstalker learning anything about what had happened after she'd fled Gateport that night. A shudder went through her at the very thought. But she couldn't tell Salyarin that.

The elder sighed, as he usually did when faced with Arya's rage and guilt. "I have taught you all I can about your Sky Lord magic. You cannot hide here or in the Icelands forever. And if Andahar invades Dunidaen without warning, the people you love will die first."

Arya stared at him, Salyarin's words cutting through all her denials.

The elder pushed his advantage. "Maybe you're not strong enough to face a nazal yet, but this is your chance to get some measure of revenge. Forestall the invasion; thwart the Nightstalker's plans."

Her jaw tightened until her back teeth ached. "If I do as you say, then I need your help."

He looked at her warily. "What kind of help?"

"Information. If the Nightstalker invades, either with wraiths and shadowhounds, or a human army, how will he do it? The Diamondfang is impassable for all but a small, lightly burdened force. The pass over the top can only be traversed in summer, and even the underground road forms a chokepoint if that's the only way in or out."

"The underground road was the main passage under the mountains for trade and travel between Dunidaen and Andahar, but it wasn't the only one. The foundations of these mountains are riddled with tunnels—most branch off the underground road. Some were used by smugglers, others formed shortcuts to make the trip faster. The Nightstalker was alive when those travel routes were open. He knows of them."

Arya's gaze narrowed. "When I mentioned the Nightstalker using the Icelands as a staging point for invading Dunidaen, you looked highly doubtful. Why?"

"To stage from the Icelands, the Nightstalker would have to invade across the north sea after it melts in spring," Salyarin said. "Andahar always had a formidable naval force, drawn primarily from the riverfolk. But they sided with House Stormrider during the Nightstalker's war and were almost wiped out in the aftermath. The Nightstalker is a vengeful man. He has ships, and no doubt sailors to crew them, but not riverfolk. The Icefolk queen has a stronger navy. Andahar would struggle to land its army on the Icefolk coast, or Dunidaen's."

Arya snorted. "If we were talking of human navies, yes, but he and Xaphistryl alone could do untold damage to Dunidaen's or the Icefolk's ships. Unless…"

Salyarin gave her a questioning look.

"If Dunidae or Icefolk ships were crewed with Hawkesdale Longbows carrying cazaix-tipped arrows, and there were enough of them ... we could shoot Xaphistryl out of the sky."

"For that, Dunidaen and the Icelands would need an alliance with Khadini so they could source the cazaix needed," Salyarin observed.

She let out a breath, thinking. Dunidaen hadn't mapped the tunnels under the Diamondfang, and even if they had, the mountainous territory was dangerous, even to those trained to operate in its environs. The three Raider forts; Icecliff, SheerRock, and Windfall were the first and only line of defence. If an invading force captured the forts, they'd be able to march unimpeded into Ravenstrike State.

If the Nightstalker was confident of getting his army through the Diamondfang using the tunnels, then he *would* come that way. Breaking Ravenstrike's forts would be a challenge, but an easier one than moving his army by sea and facing the full Icefolk army and navy.

It was the decision any good general would make. Desomer's barking laugh echoed in the back of her mind. "You're right, he'll come through those tunnels," Arya said eventually.

Salyarin was silent, letting her think.

Eventually Arya sighed. Since coming to the citadel three years earlier, she'd let Salyarin teach her what she needed to know about her magic so she could protect herself and stay hidden. Or at least, everything he *could* teach her. But she'd fled the citadel to the Icelands as often as she could. She'd ignored the rest of what Salyarin wanted from her. Not asked questions about her Andahari heritage beyond learning her magic.

She didn't want to know. Because it didn't matter. She wasn't what Salyarin wanted her to be, what At'eir and his mother thought she could be. She never would. She'd made too many mistakes, and the Nightstalker had a strength and power she could never match, even if she tried.

But now ... if Dunidaen was facing an invasion, then their generals needed to know more about the enemy they faced if they were going to win. So, she gritted her teeth and forced herself to ask, "Why did the Nightstalker murder the Stormrider House to steal the throne?"

Salyarin let out an amused huff. "That's a story long in the telling. Do you want to try a simpler question?"

"I..." She corrected herself. "*They* need to understand the way his mind works. What makes him tick. That's the best way to effectively counter a superior force. And you and I both know the Nightstalker riding Xaphistryl with shadowhounds and wraiths behind him, not to mention human soldiers, is a superior force."

Salyarin fixed her with a look that said he could read right through her but obliged. "All right, but don't forget I was a child when it happened. I learned what I know from my mother who was elder at the time and not present for these events. She learned of it all through reports, intelligence, diplomatic meetings."

"Yes, I get it," she said impatiently.

"Lucius Nightstalker was the youngest of your grandfather's Sky Lord *caidre*—his predecessor was killed in a freak accident when your grandfather was a much older man. As is tradition, a wyvern was born shortly after. Her chosen rider was Lucius, a scion of House Nightstalker. He was only sixteen at the time."

"How does it work, that magic? Where do the wyverns even come from?"

Salyarin lifted an eyebrow. "How is knowing that going to help your generals win a war?" He lifted his hands in surrender at the look on her face. "Those are secrets held close by the Andahari Houses. I doubt any beyond a select few of House Inkweaver know them."

Arya pivoted. "Why did a sixteen-year-old Sky Lord turn on his king?"

"A Sky Lord *caidre* operates as a single unit. The shared bonds are key to both its survival and strength." Salyarin paused when Arya lifted a hand unconsciously to her chest, uncharacteristic sympathy filling his gaze. "I'm sorry, I know how it must affect you. I wish there was another way."

She looked away. Her *cairdre*. The threads she'd once felt, tying her to Chiarn, Essa, Darmanin, and Leanir. The first thing Salyarin had taught her when she'd arrived three years earlier was how to mute them.

Because they also linked her to the Nightstalker. It was how he'd been able to exert such control over her when she was close by. How his nazal—with their own twisted Sky Lord bonds—had been able to use that thread to sense when she used magic and track her. What they would be able to use, through her, to find the others in her *cairdre*. With those bonds muted, her *cairdre* was safe, and the nazal were unable to track her through her magic use. But it had meant shutting down awareness of Darmanin and Essa. She had no way to tell whether they were well, or hurt, or sick or...

Arya wrenched herself away from those thoughts and returned her gaze to the elder. "You're saying the Nightstalker somehow undermined the unity of my grandfather's *caidre*?"

"Not intentionally, at least not in the beginning. Lucius fell in love with one of his *cairdre,* Mariel Windspinner. There was a battle ... Lucius put the rest of the *caidre* at risk when he left them in the midst of it to protect Mariel. Afterward, your grandfather forbade the union."

"I can see how that would impact the unity of a magically bonded unit," Arya said. It would affect any kind of military unit that relied on shared trust for survival.

"The Nightstalker and Windspinner obeyed their king's command, but a year later, Mariel was dispatched on a mission with Deerin Daystormer. She was badly wounded and almost died. Lucius was furious. He hunted down the Daystormer and killed him for failing to protect her. When Mariel recovered and heard what he'd done, she renounced him. That proved the final straw. Lucius murdered Mariel in a rage, then turned on the other Sky Lords and finally your grandfather."

"How?" As interesting as that story was, Arya needed to know the specifics. "You've told me the Stormrider ruler is the strongest of their Sky Lord *caidre,* and I know from experience we can use the *cairdre* bond to compel the others. I could see how Lucius might have defeated his fellow Sky Lords if he attacked them one on one, taking them unawares, but how was he able to kill his king?"

"Nobody knows. Just like nobody knows how he was able to obtain multiple Sky Lord magics." Salyarin hesitated. "Mariel had a child before she died. A baby girl, Nyasa."

Arya's breath hissed out. She'd known Darmanin was from House Night-stalker, but it was more than that. He was the Nightstalker's grandson.

"Mariel must have feared what would come, because she had the child before confronting Lucius and renouncing him," Salyarin said. "If you are going back to Dunidaen, you must be careful of Darmanin."

The grief Mariel must have felt at giving up her child rebounded through Arya like a slap, but she pushed those emotions aside with an effort, fo-cusing on Darmanin instead. "You told me all those years ago that I had to protect him, not be careful of him."

"It *was* important he be protected, just like all the other potential Sky Lords. Not just for his safety, but so that he didn't grow up twisted like his grandfather."

Arya looked away. It was an interesting tale, but she couldn't see any-thing in it that would help them combat the Nightstalker. "I don't know what you think I'm supposed to accomplish. All these years of you nagging and nagging me, and you've never *ever* addressed my fundamental ques-tion."

"Arya, I—"

"I don't have a cohesive and bonded *cairdre*, even if I wanted to try and re-take my grandfather's throne. I have a mercenary assassin who would kill me if given half a chance, a singer who is afraid of everything, a woman who has no desire for war, and a Dunidae warlord who will never walk away from that position. None of us come close to matching the Nightstalker's strength in magic, let alone his skill in wielding it, and it will be years before our wyverns are grown enough to challenge Xaphistryl." She held his gaze. "So, tell me, Elder Salyarin, what is it that makes *me* capable of defeating the Nightstalker, when all others in my family failed?"

"And that, as always, has been the wrong question," he said quietly.

"And the right question is?"

"What happens to the world—and all the people in it that you love—if you don't?"

Chapter 4

She had to go back to Dunidaen.

It was the last thing she wanted. But she had no choice. Shoulders so heavy they were literally bowed, Arya returned to her quarters. She rounded the corner to the sound of music drifting on the icy air. The door to the room beside hers was open, the source of the music. Arya paused at the entry, unsurprised to see Chiarn lounging on a pile of cushions, one hand idly strumming a lute. Several Etherean were gathered, smoking and drinking, an air of conviviality filling the space.

"Arya!" Chiarn greeted her with a raised glass before downing its contents in one swallow. His cheeks were flushed. Eyes bright. So, he was drunk. Again. The musician had spent as much time as Arya under the Etherean's tutelage during the past three years. Even drunk, his blue eyes danced with fire magic, and it was no longer possible to mistake him for anything other than a magic-wielder. "You're back earlier than expected."

She leaned against the doorframe, arms crossed. "I thought you'd be gone by now."

Chiarn had been dreaming of his wyvern with increasing frequency for almost two years. Remembering how insistent Elendryl had been on coming to her, Arya often wondered how Chiarn had held his bonded wyvern off so long.

He rolled his eyes. "I'll go when I go. And don't look at me with that disapproving air. It's not like there's anything else to do here but drink."

"Do you know where he is?"

He didn't reply, mouth a tight line.

"If you leave it much longer, the danger to—"

"Leave it. You're not the boss of me." An edge to his voice now, a bitterness that was never far beneath the surface. "I'm not risking my neck searching for a wyvern, the mere existence of which is only going to put me in even more danger."

Arya sighed. Part of her wished she'd never brought Chiarn here. He was safer, certainly, but it didn't change his desire to stay as far away from magic and Sky Lords as it was possible to be. Or ignoring the existence of his wyvern. "Then why don't you just ask him to come here? I'm astonished he hasn't already insisted on it."

He looked away. "He doesn't know where I am. I won't tell him. I don't want him here."

"Yes, you do," Arya said softly. "You're just refusing to admit it to yourself."

Chiarn rolled his eyes, then leaned over to refill his glass and take a long, insolent swallow. The Etherean gathered in the room were growing uncomfortable, wings rustling as they tried not to make it obvious they were listening to this exchange.

Aware of that, and the fact she had no energy for this argument anyway, Arya shrugged and pushed off the door. "Suit yourself. I'm leaving tomorrow. Not sure when I'll be back."

"Where are you going?"

"Like you care." She snorted and left.

***

Arya barely slept that night, with what felt like every muscle in her body tight with anxiety. She gave up on sleep in the pre-dawn darkness, shoving off the covers and working through a series of stretches and strength exercises, pushing through the difficulty of exercising while barely able to suck in enough air until she was sweat-soaked and gasping.

After a wash, she dressed in a quilted long-sleeved tunic and matching breeches in a deep blue. Midnight-blue leather boots finished off her attire. The material was woven by the Etherean; lined in wool, it was lightweight and warm without being restrictive. She coiled her hair in a braid at the base of her neck, then buckled on a swordbelt. To this she attached her cazaix sword, these days sheathed in plain grey leather that matched her belt. Then, she stood before her mirror, trying to summon the resolve to take a single step outside the door.

Nobody in Dunidaen was going to welcome her.

There was now no mistaking that Arya was a magic-wielder. Three years of spending winters at the Etherean citadel learning her magic had seen to that. Her indigo eyes glimmered with banked magic in a way that no normal human's did. Physical maturity—she'd reached her twenty-fifth year six months earlier—had sharpened her features. The hours of flying with Elendryl, of learning to shift her body on a hairsbreadth of warning, meant she moved with unusual grace; able to grow utterly still or flicker nto movement quicker than thought. There was something unmistakably *other* about her now.

She looked nothing like the Ravenstrike general she'd once been. The blood-red and black were no longer her colours to wear. Now she was apart from them, whether she liked it or not. And she *didn't* like it. She didn't want it. She just wanted to be a simple Raider at home in Heathrock.

But it wasn't her home anymore. She had no home.

"Stop procrastinating," she muttered, turning away from the mirror with an effort. Her whole life before that night in Gateport, she'd never once let fear rule her, yet these days it shadowed everything she did, making her feel heavy and slow, as if she were constantly walking through sand. She hated it, but didn't know how to fix it. Didn't think she *could* fix it, not after what she'd done.

Arya opened the door and walked through it, every step an effort of will.

***

The commander of the Etherean army waited for Arya in the entry cavern. Elendryl was on his way, a golden presence pulsing in the back of her mind.

Cirilla's lilac wings hung loosely at his side, and he smiled politely when she reached him. His mouth began forming the word 'Lord' until he remembered her frequent reminders not to call her that, and switched it to a simple, "Arya. Good morning."

While Arya knew the names and faces of the guards that rotated through protecting the elder's quarters, she'd deliberately keep her distance from the Etherean, spending most of her time at the citadel either with Salyarin learning or on her own. She wanted no more close bonds that could be torn from her in heartbreaking agony. She and Cirilla had spoken in passing, but something about him had always irritated her—a barely hidden condescension in the way he spoke to her. She got the sense he didn't like her much. Or didn't approve of her.

"Has Elder Salyarin given you the news I brought?" she asked.

"Yes. He also said that you travel today to warn Dunidaen?"

"That's right," she said, then, made uneasy by the lack of concern in his voice or expression, she continued, "Commander, if the Nightstalker invades, this citadel technically stands between Andahar and Dunidaen. He may not wish to leave an enemy at his back."

He offered another bland smile that made her itch. "I believe we are safe here. It would be more effort than it's worth to march an army this high. The altitude sickness alone would kill many of them."

"True enough. And your warriors can fly, which is an advantage in some situations. There aren't many of you, though." The Etherean army numbered no more than two thousand, a paltry force. "If the Nightstalker rode Xaphistryl up here you *would* be in trouble. It might be time to consider expanding your army, increasing your training, preparing to defend against a wyvern attack."

"We are not a violent race, Arya," Cirilla said, a pointed note in his voice. "We are healers. Our army is intended only for self-defence."

Elendryl swooped through the great arched entry to land on the marble. *"Ready?"*

Arya turned back to Cirilla. "I don't think the Nightstalker cares much about your noble ideals of self-defence, Commander. At least think on my suggestions. None of us know the Nightstalker's intentions for certain."

He bowed his head. "Good luck in Dunidaen."

***

Arya and Elendryl flew low through the peaks and slopes of the Diamond-fang, weaving their way southeast to Heathrock. She'd thought long and hard during her sleepless night about whether to arrive on Elendryl's back or leave him hidden and approach on foot. The sight of a wyvern would terrify the Dunidae, but Arya's appearance was going to mark her as a magic-wielder anyway. Ultimately, she'd decided to return as who she truly was. There was no point hiding her identity any longer. And if the Night-stalker was coming for them, best the Dunidae start getting accustomed to the presence of a wyvern. Even so, her dread and anxiety grew with every mile travelled until Elendryl abruptly banked and began circling higher.

"Go back?"

"No, keep going."

"Scared." He sounded confused. *"Danger?"*

"A little bit of danger, maybe. But we have to go."

Reluctance came back in response. His instinct to protect her overrode everything. He wanted to take her someplace safe instead of continuing on.

"It's all right," she promised. *"You and I are going to have to do a lot of scary things together. Let's start getting used to it."*

"Together." He sent the word with a warm combination of affection and determination.

She smiled, leaning forward to press her gloved palm against the shimmering golden scales of his neck. His whole body shivered in response, and he dived with purpose, seemingly taking her resolve to face scary things with abandon.

Soon after they flew through a gap between two lower peaks and found the dark canopy of the Wraith Forest laid out below. From there, Arya guided her wyvern out to the south of Heathrock castle, not wanting anyone in the city or on the main roads leading toward it to see a wyvern in the skies.

Too soon, they crested a lower peak and there was Heathrock castle, the seat of Ravenstrike, perched alongside a large frozen lake. Tears welled in her eyes and her chest closed over so fiercely she couldn't draw a breath. *"I'm okay, Elendryl. I'm okay,"* she said hurriedly. *"It's just been a very long time since I was here."*

She received a little shiver of warmth in response.

And then Elendryl lifted his head and let loose his wyvern's cry.

It was challenge and greeting and reassurance for her all wrapped up in an echoing roar that could surely be heard for miles around.

"Elendryl!" she chided, but only half-heartedly.

Her wyvern circled Heathrock's walls far enough out they weren't in range of Raider arrows, before landing on the main road outside the castle's main gates. As his taloned feet hit the cobblestones, he kept his wings spread wide, head high, teeth bared, challenging anyone who might think to attack. She doubted they would. While nowhere near the size of Xaphistryl—yet—Elendryl made for a terrifying sight.

For a moment it felt as if she were simply returning home from patrol, as she'd done hundreds of times before. And then pain burned through her with a fierceness that made her gasp. She wasn't returning from patrol, and she couldn't expect the same warmth and welcome she'd once enjoyed.

Elendryl let out a low growl, mouth opening wider to reveal his long fangs. He'd seen the flurry of movement on the walls that their arrival had caused. Raiders lined the battlements, bows drawn and knocked, resolute.

"Stay," she murmured, sliding down from his back and keeping a palm pressed against his scales.

"Protect," he protested.

"If there is danger, I will call, I promise."

By the time she'd taken about ten paces away from Elendryl, the gates were swinging open, and a full shield raced out, galloping towards her. It was an impressively quick response, and she hadn't expected it.

"Shit!" Arya only had time to look at her wyvern and tell him to "*BE STILL!*" before the shield was surrounding her, its unfamiliar captain bellowing at her to raise her arms in the air and drop to her knees.

She did as they bade, wincing as knees crashed into cobblestone, half certain she was about to be filled with arrows, but the Raiders were disciplined enough to hold fire when she didn't make any threatening moves. "Don't go near the wyvern," she said loudly but calmly. "He won't attack if you stay clear of him."

Elendryl growled low in his throat. She could feel his rising anger thrumming through her. If even one of these Raiders got trigger happy, her wyvern was going to tear them all apart. "I'm not here to hurt anyone," she tried. "You can put your bows away."

The captain demanded, "Who are you and what do you want?"

Keeping her hands in the air, Arya risked lifting her head and glancing at the faces surrounding her. One or two she recognised, and her shoulders relaxed a little. "I know it's been a while, but have I really changed so much that none of you recognise me anymore?"

A long silence greeted her words, and they echoed back to her on the cold morning air. Then, into the silence came the sound of running boots, and a familiar voice snapping out. "What's this about a wyvern landing on—"

The shield moved their horses back enough for another Raider to stride toward Arya, though none lowered their bows. He came to an abrupt halt as soon as he saw her.

Laskin was exactly as she remembered him. Weathered brown skin, short-cropped salt and pepper hair, stocky frame, an air of steadiness that settled around him like an old cloak. The rush of gladness that swept through Arya had her voice shaking as she spoke. "Please tell me *you* recognise me, old man?"

"Arya?" He rubbed his eyes. "Lass, is that really you?"

She smiled uncertainly. "Yes, Laskin, it's me."

"You look..." The veteran Raider's eyes were suspiciously damp, and for a long moment they simply stared at each other. But then he cleared his throat, straightened. "All clear," he bellowed. "Weapons down. Back to guard duty. Now!"

The Raiders on the walls lowered their bows before shuffling back into position, but not without frequent wary glances between Arya and the wyvern still perched on the road behind her. The shield surrounding her reluctantly turned their horses and rode back through the gates, again, with plenty of looks over their shoulders.

"Come inside." Laskin gestured, and Arya clambered to her feet, relieved to have made it through without Elendryl eating them all. Two guards remained in position at the gates as Laskin and Arya walked through, hands on the hilts of their swords as they glared distrustfully at Elendryl. She hoped her wyvern would heed her instruction to be still. Laskin's expression changed as a myriad of questions seemed to go through his head before he settled on, "Where in raven's balls have you *been*?"

"Away," she said. "I thought that was safest."

He scowled.

Ahead of them, the main doors of the castle swung open. And then, for the second time in the space of minutes Arya froze, tears welling, her chest so tight she couldn't breathe or speak.

Rorin Ravenstrike strode down the front steps, signing furiously in Laskin's direction. "*Captain! Was that a wyvern's call I just heard? Is that why the guards are massing on the walls by the—*"

And then he saw Arya.

Rorin stopped mid-stride, shock spreading over his face. She drank in his tall, rangy form, messy blonde hair and merry blue eyes. He looked older than she remembered, a man more worn than his twenty-two years would dictate.

Her heart tripped in her chest. Her brother. It had been so long.

"*Arya?*" A slow smile crept over his face. "*Arya, is it really you?*"

"Hello, Rorin."

He broke into a run, sprinting across the remaining distance between them and crashing into her so hard they both went staggering backwards, only Arya's balance keeping them on their feet. And then he was lifting her, spinning her around. She clung to him fiercely, tears pricking at her eyes as she buried her face in his neck, his familiar scent and warmth overwhelming. He seemed so happy to see her. Wasn't he mad?

He let her go eventually, dropping her back to her feet as unceremoniously as he'd picked her up, grinning from ear to ear, his eyes as damp as hers. *"You finally came back. Why did it take you so long?"*

Her smile faded, and she looked at him warily, still unsure of her reception. "I honestly didn't think I'd be welcome."

He frowned. *"What? Why would you think that?"*

She looked away, eyes dropping to the ground until he began signing again.

"Really, Arya, I..." Rorin's words trailed off and his eyes widened as he finally noticed Elendryl through the open gates. *"So, it* was *a wyvern's call we heard? Half the castle is cowering in terror thanks to you."*

"His name is Elendryl."

He grinned. *"He's magnificent. Laskin, will you go inside and let everyone know we're safe."*

Laskin saluted and left, with many backward glances. Her gaze followed him as he went up the steps and disappeared inside, heart aching. "Rorin, you shouldn't have come charging out here like that! What if it *had* been Xaphistryl?"

He shrugged. *"This is my home. If it was under attack, I wanted to know."*

She choked a laugh. Her brother, always with the cheerful dismissal of danger. "It's so good to see you."

"And you." He gripped her shoulder hard, tears in his eyes. *"I've missed you so much."*

"Arya!"

Her head snapped up as another Raider came sprinting out the front doors, tall and lean, dark eyes alighting on her with joy. "Arya! It's really you?"

"Taze." She met him halfway and he threw his arms around her with only slightly less enthusiasm than Rorin had.

"You're home," he murmured into her hair. "Finally, you're home."

She hadn't expected this. Not any of it. Arya looked over his shoulder at more movement from the entry, recognising Peemla instantly. She did *not* recognise, however, the child Peemla carried at her hip. Arya froze. The woman's eyes were bright as she hurried over.

"Laskin said you were here, he said … oh Arya, you're really here." Peemla handed the child to Rorin and stepped forward, arms wide to hug Arya, before halting awkwardly, probably realising they'd never hugged before. Arya couldn't stop herself though. She stepped away from Taze and wrapped her arms around the chamberlain. It had been years since she'd experienced affectionate physical touch and the sensation was making her unsteady, almost drunk on it. Even so, as they hugged, Arya couldn't stop her gaze going to the child in Rorin's arms.

"It's good to see you Peemla." She cleared her throat and turned to Rorin and the child, fighting with everything she had to keep her voice from breaking. "Who is this?"

"*Arya, meet my son.*" Rorin's eyes glowed as he looked at the child. He had a cap of blonde curls and his father's faded blue eyes.

"I think you'll find he's *our* son," Peemla said, reaching up to stroke the boy's hair. "His name is Anjurin, Anji for short. Say hello to your aunt Arya, Anji."

"So, you two…?" Arya said faintly.

"Got married," Taze finished, smiling widely. "Right after Rorin was confirmed as warlord of Ravenstrike. This little munchkin is almost three."

Almost three. Arya stared at the toddler, trying to fight down the fierce surge of guilt and grief that swept through her at the sight of Rorin's son. Her gaze was glued to him, his blue eyes, the pudgy cheeks—

"*Arya?*" Rorin's signing brought her back.

"Sorry." She shook her head and smiled at the toddler. "Hello, Anji."

The boy looked at her solemnly for a moment, then stuck his thumb in his mouth and turned his face into his father's shoulder.

"*I think he likes you.*" Rorin chuckled. "*Come inside. Lunch will be ready soon. Taze, would you let the general know that Arya is here and have him make sure the Raiders don't get too overexcited about the wyvern?*"

"Warlord." Taze saluted and strode off with a passing smile for Arya.

"*I'm not sure we have a stable big enough for a wyvern,*" Rorin said ruefully.

"Elendryl can look after himself." Arya assured her brother, then glanced down the road to where her wyvern waited, suspicious and ready to pounce if an enemy leaped out at her. "*Go and hunt. I'm safe here,*" she told him.

"*Close,*" he promised. Then everyone stared as he spread his wings, took two lunging steps, and soared into the sky. Arya's gaze went to the walls, where the Raiders were also staring ... some had knocked bows despite Laskin's orders, all had shoulders stiff with the tense alertness of a solider ready to fight.

Peemla began leading them towards the castle, and Arya fell into step, something drawing her gaze upwards to one of the higher-floor windows. The one she remembered as the warlord's office.

Essa stood at the glass, looking down on them.

Arya's heart did a funny little skip as her eyes settled on her friend's familiar brown curls and blue dress decorated with sunflowers. She lifted her hand in a wave. Essa didn't respond.

Arya turned to Rorin and Peemla, suddenly feeling horribly awkward and out of place. Both had seen the exchange. "Rorin, maybe I shouldn't..."

"It's not what you think," Peemla said. "Essa is well, and she's a marvellous chief advisor for Rorin. But she still carries a lot from that night. And when you never came back..."

"I couldn't," she told them. "But I understand if I'm not welcome here anymore. I won't stay long, I—"

"*Arya, you can stay as long as you like.*" Rorin's signing was so emphatic she could barely read it.

"Will the Raiders and your staff be all right with a wyvern and its rider staying here?" she said. "I don't want to cause trouble for you."

"*They'll be fine.*" He waved a hand, but Ayra didn't miss Peemla's dubious glance at her husband.

Rorin passed Anji to Peemla and wrapped an arm around Arya's shoulders. "*Come on inside. Everything will look brighter after a good meal.*"

Arya hesitated before following, nowhere near as certain as Rorin about her reception. Her gaze scanned the walls again, instinct making her wary; the Raiders on guard still looked calm, though they kept glancing down at her.

"Arya, the Raiders are fine. Because it's you. Look."

She looked where Rorin pointed, where more Raiders were trickling around from the northern side of the main castle, where a path led to the barracks and drill yards in the southwestern corner. There were many faces she recognised among them, including those from her old Icecliff shield. They were gathered in a huddle, pretending not to be watching what was going on in the entry yard.

Tentatively, she raised a hand in greeting.

The gathered Raiders promptly lifted their hands in matching greetings. She stilled in shock. She'd expected fear, hostility. She'd ridden in on a wyvern, of all things. But then the shock faded, replaced by guilt and shame.

She didn't deserve such a welcome.

Chapter 5

Rorin led them into the large castle kitchens rather than the family's formal dining room and they took seats around a rough oaken table. Just like they had so many times before. Only, Essa wasn't there.

Arya hesitated. "So Essa is well then? She and Dar?"

"*They are.*" Rorin assured her.

Arya looked down at the table. Peemla reached over and touched her arm in silent support. The kitchen staff moved efficiently as they always had, and soon a spread was laid out. Taze appeared soon after, flashing Arya another delighted smile.

Rorin signed. "*Where have you been all this time?*"

"I moved around a lot to stay ahead of the nazal," she said, then, wanting to change the subject. "Have you had any problems with the Nightstalker? I know about the agreement he made with Mathas."

"*So, you've kept yourself well informed while moving around?*" Rorin gave her a pointed look.

"We've been vigilant ever since that night," Peemla said softly. "Essa lives in fear that they'll come for her one day and that we'll be hurt in the process. It has been hard to convince her to stay here and not disappear like you."

Arya winced, even though Peemla had spoken without remonstration. "Rorin and Essa told you everything about us then? I'm glad."

An awkward silence fell. Arya ate sparingly, appetite non-existent, while watching Rorin try, mostly unsuccessfully, to get Anji to eat his lunch. It was hard to look away from the little boy. Shame curdled in her stomach, making food even more unappealing.

Taze caught the direction of Arya's look and chuckled. "Anji prefers playing with his food to eating it."

"He's beautiful." Arya supplied. She had no idea what one was supposed to say about children, but her words were true.

The next awkward silence that descended was broken by the sound of the bells ringing to announce an arrival at the front gates.

"*Are we expecting anyone?*" Rorin looked at Peemla and Taze. "*Essa didn't mention a visit.*"

Both shook their heads.

"*It seems to be a day for uninvited guests. Riter, go and see who it is, will you? And keep them out of the kitchens while Arya's here. Have them wait in the reception room then come tell us who it is.*"

On Taze's translation, Riter saluted and ducked off.

"*Taze is my bodyguard, translator, and personal advisor all wrapped into one these days,*" Rorin explained off Arya's questioning look. "*Between him, Essa, and Peemla, I am a fortunate warlord.*"

"What brings you back to us, Arya?" Taze asked, then hesitated and added, "As glad as I am to see you, I get the feeling you wouldn't be here if there wasn't a compelling reason."

Arya pushed her plate away. "You're right. And I don't dare stay long—I know about the bounty on my head and how much of a problem it will be for you if the warlords find out you're sheltering me here."

Peemla snorted. "Nobody here is betraying your presence to anyone outside the household, Arya."

"*She's right,*" Rorin said when Arya opened her mouth to protest.

She sighed. "To be honest, I didn't expect to be welcomed here. I came because I had to."

"*Why?*" Rorin asked, genuinely confused. "*You're family.*"

"It was *my* actions that led to your parents being murdered," she said. "*I* destroyed two of the most important people in my life, in *our* lives. I put all of us in greater danger. You should hate me, Rorin."

"*But I don't,*" Rorin said gently. "*It wasn't your fault. You didn't kill them, Arya.*"

"I was arrogant and careless with our lives." She shook her head. "Essa isn't wrong to blame me."

"*She doesn't—*"

Arya cut him off. "There's a possibility that the Nightstalker plans invasion. Soon. That's why I'm here."

Rorin shrugged. "*That's always been a threat.*"

She frowned at his casual dismissal. "A nest of wraiths attacked an Icefolk hunting party near the Falconcrest border last week. It could have been a scouting force."

"*How do you know that?*" Rorin asked in surprise.

"That's irrelevant. Rorin, Andahar is stirring."

"*How did the wraiths even get there? We've had no reports of wraith attacks in Falconcrest. And our regular patrols of the underground road and the pass show no sign of wraiths or shadowhounds—or anything else—crossing the Diamondfang.*"

"We don't actually get any messages from Falconcrest these days," Taze said with a pointed look in his warlord's direction.

Arya was taken aback. "Rorin, I wouldn't have come if I didn't think this was serious."

Crisp bootsteps sounded along the passage that joined the kitchens to the main Heathrock entry hall. Annoyance crossed Rorin's face. "*I told Riter to—*"

But his words trailed off, the annoyance turning to warmth, as the visitor reached the kitchens and stepped inside, Riter hovering helplessly behind him. Arya froze, staring at the man in shock.

It was Darmanin Crowtalon.

But this was not the boy and young man she'd grown up with. This man was ... she wasn't sure she had the words to describe it. He'd obviously been riding hard, for his short raven hair was tangled, and several days' worth of stubble covered his jaw. The light grey eyes Arya remembered so clearly betrayed no surprise at seeing her seated in Rorin's kitchen. He commanded the attention of the room without thought, and even Rorin, his equal, looked ready to spring to attention. She remembered Salyarin's warning, and a little shiver of unease rippled through her.

"*Dar!*" Rorin crossed to him with a welcoming smile, and the tension vanished in a blink. Darmanin shook Rorin's hand with genuine warmth, though his expression remained shuttered.

"Hello, Rorin. Peemla. Taze." He shifted his gaze to Arya, then. She was suddenly and vividly reminded of the intense conversation between them on the night she'd fled Gateport. "Arya. You've finally returned," he murmured.

She cleared her throat, trying and failing to achieve a normal tone of voice. It came out somewhere between strained and stilted. "Hello, Dar. It's good to see you."

"And you." He bowed his head slightly.

"Warlord Crowtalon, please sit down." Peemla issued quick orders to her staff to bring Darmanin a mug of ale and replenish the food on the table.

Taze smiled a greeting, "We weren't expecting you until tomorrow at the earliest."

"I rode fast after receiving a rather odd missive," Darmanin replied, turning his attention to the Raider by the door. "I have three shields of Lances coming behind me. Have barracks arranged for them at once."

Riter nodded and left.

Arya watched the exchange with astonishment. Riter had responded to Darmanin's order with an alacrity unheard of for a Ravenstrike Raider when being spoken to by another State's warlord.

"You were in the middle of something when I arrived." Darmanin took a mug of ale from one of the servants, then sat, as comfortable as if it were his own home. "I assume you were discussing whatever compelling reason brought Arya home."

He'd been there minutes, and yet already determined that she'd come with a purpose. The arrogance of it made her temper spark, but it died quickly. Her heart was too heavy for anger. "I came with a warning." She relayed to him what she'd already told the others.

Darmanin's eyes remained on her while she spoke, taking the occasional sip of his ale. "That's very interesting in light of the message I received from Ranier before leaving Anduil."

"You're in contact with Ranier?" she asked sharply. Leader of the criminal Shadeweaver gang that was a plight on Dunidaen trade and law, Ranier was an incredibly dangerous man. He was also Essa's father, Andahari, and a member of House Inkweaver.

Darmanin ignored the question. "He's had concerning reports from Shadeweaver camps in the Wraith Forest. Nothing substantial, but enough to make him contact me. Shadeweavers out hunting alone going missing, odd sightings and sounds within the forest, that sort of thing."

"Why would Ranier reach out to tell *you* that?" Taze sounded as suspicious as Arya felt.

"Unclear. He asked for nothing. And he certainly wasn't telling me out of a sense of altruism. As always with Ranier, his motives are his own."

Arya turned to Rorin. "Ranier hasn't spoken to Essa about this?"

"*Essa hasn't heard from her father since you spoke with him after returning from the Dreadwater Gate,*" Rorin said. "*Odd sounds and a single pack of wraiths near the Falconcrest border do not add up to imminent invasion to me.*"

Darmanin nodded in agreement. "Still, we need to ask why the wraiths were in the Icelands, and whether they're also in the Wraith Forest again—the source of Ranier's unease."

"The last time wraiths and shadowhounds crossed the border, they were hunting us," Arya said bluntly. "And if the Nightstalker is doing it again, then he no longer cares about any agreement he has with Dunidaen. And it won't be just wraiths and shadowhounds coming through the Diamondfang."

Rorin sighed. "*The mountains are massive. How would Andahar even get an army over them? Wraiths and shadowhounds are one thing, but if the Nightstalker wants to take Dunidaen as his own and hold the territory, he'll need soldiers and supplies.*"

"I can tell you that." Arya related what Salyarin had told her about the tunnels under the Diamondfang.

Darmanin frowned. "Rorin, I'd like to stay a few days longer than planned. We can discuss this further and decide the appropriate response."

"*You know you're welcome to stay as long as you like.*" Rorin rolled his eyes at Darmanin's formality. "*Arken will make sure your Lances are looked after, and some more joint training might be good too. Now, Arya's home for the first time in almost four years. I say we ask the staff to cook a celebration dinner.*"

Arya glanced between Peemla, Taze, and Darmanin, seeing none of the enthusiasm present in Rorin's voice in their faces or bearing. She didn't feel a drop of it either. After a moment, Peemla rose with Anji. "It's time for this one's afternoon nap."

Darmanin rose too. "My Lances won't be far off. I should be at the gates to greet them."

"If Lances are coming, I can't stay," Arya told Rorin when he was gone.

Rorin chuckled silently. "*If you think Darmanin's Lances are going to betray him anymore than Raiders will betray you, you're sorely mistaken. Stay the night at least. I know it's hard, and complicated, but I've missed you. Please.*"

She'd missed her brother too. So much. "I'll stay the night."

Chapter 6

When Arya had lived at Heathrock, it had been tradition that the general of Ravenstrike's army joined the family for dinner, and so she wasn't surprised when Arken Rosenthal arrived at the dining room at the same time as she did. As if by instinct, he moved to salute, then dropped his hand awkwardly. "I'm not sure how I should address you," he admitted.

"You don't hate or fear me? You know what I am now."

He gave a little shrug. "I do not."

A smile curled at her mouth, and she offered her hand. "Arya is fine. It's good to see you, Arken. Your Raiders' response to my arrival on a wyvern this morning was incredibly fast and disciplined. I was impressed."

He was visibly startled, and a tentative smile crossed his face. "Thank you for saying that. I think we both know how difficult it is for you to return home to find me in charge."

"Not as difficult as you might think," she said, and meant it.

He let go of her hand and straightened his shoulders. The general's cloak he wore looked good on him. The younger son of a powerful vicelord, Arken's looks, charm, and competence had always made him a natural successor to General Desomer—until Thiara Ravenstrike had brought Arya Nameless into the household. "You should know I'm not planning on standing aside for you now that you're back either."

That prompted the first genuine laugh Arya had had in a long time. "Fair enough, General."

"Arken," he corrected, albeit a little stiffly. "There was always respect between us, if not liking, and you do not need to address me by rank."

"Thank you, Arken." She managed a smile to lighten the mood. "Shall we go and eat?"

Dinner was a strained affair despite Rorin's best efforts and the delicious meal, with the warlord and Taze working hard to keep the conversation flowing while Peemla was distracted by getting Anji to eat and Darmanin remained distant and brooding.

Essa didn't join them.

After they'd eaten, Peemla took Anji up to bed and Arken left quickly, presumably driven away by the awkward tension. Arya found herself alone with Rorin, Taze, and Darmanin. It was familiar, but not the same as she remembered. Things had changed so much. Grief threatened to swallow her whole.

"*You look different, Arya*," Rorin said, breaking the awkward silence.

"I know," she said. "It's another reason I was reluctant to return. I am too obviously a magic-wielder now. I doubt feelings on that have changed in Dunidaen during my absence."

"*It's not just your appearance.*" He hesitated. "*You're different from the Arya I remember.*"

"That's because I'm not her anymore," she said shortly, failing to keep the bitterness from her voice. Part of her was aware of Darmanin's cool stare from down the table. He'd been civil at dinner but hadn't once addressed her directly.

"Where have you been all this time? In Andahar?" Taze asked.

She shook her head. "I spent the past three years dividing my time between Er'fin At'eir's tribe in the Icelands and the Etherean citadel." Discomfited and off balance, the words came out without thinking, and she cursed herself, because of course Darmanin would pick up on...

"You disappeared almost four years ago. If you've only been in the Icelands three years, where were you before that?" he asked.

Arya shrugged, trying to keep her face and voice casual. Deep down, desperation clawed at her. They couldn't know about that first year. Nobody could. They couldn't even *suspect* that she— "Moving around a lot." Her frantic thoughts seized on the perfect change of subject. "It was when I finally felt clear enough of the nazal hunting me to go to the Etherean that Salyarin taught me how to properly hide myself from them."

"How?" Darmanin demanded, leaning forward.

"You remember the threads connecting us, the ones I accidentally pulled on the night the nazal attacked Warlord SparrowWing's son, Amius?"

"I do, but they faded after you left. One day, I woke and realised I couldn't feel them anymore." Darmanin trailed off as realisation crossed his face.

"*Is* that *why Essa thought*—?" Rorin started signing, but abruptly broke off.

"What did Essa think?" Arya asked sharply.

"She thought something had happened to you, that you might have been killed." Taze's words were quiet but resounded through Arya like a ringing bell.

"Is that what you thought too?" Arya swung her gaze to Darmanin.

His mouth tightened. "It crossed my mind."

She hadn't thought. Hadn't realised. All she'd cared about was making them safe—from her *and* from the Nightstalker and his hunters. She swallowed, hiding the trembling of her hands under the table, "A Sky Lord *caidre* is connected to each other, and to their leader, the ruler of Andahar. But for me there is an extra bond. It connects me to the Nightstalker."

Fear rippled over Rorin's face. "*That explains how the Nightstalker was able to compel you when he was close by, but how can the nazal track you?*"

"The nazal were once Sky Lord potentials. The Nightstalker didn't kill them all like we thought. Some he twisted into monsters bonded to him, and through him, to me. It's how they could find us when we dreamed of our wyverns. Our magic was shouting to anyone connected to it when we had those dreams. The same applied whenever we used our magic. The nazal could feel it through their bond with the Nightstalker and recognise our magic."

A silence fell as the three men processed this information. Rorin rubbed his temples. Taze glanced at him, looking worried. She understood how they felt. Her body still shivered with horror at the thought of what the Nightstalker had done to those Sky Lord potentials.

"You muted the bonds between us somehow, didn't you?" Darmanin guessed. "That's how you hide from them."

"Exactly. Salyarin told me it was the only way he knew of to keep us hidden."

"Can you teach us how?" he asked eagerly.

"No. Only I can do it. As the *caidre* leader." Arya shifted uncomfortably. "You four are only connected to each other through me."

The expression on Darmanin's face made it extremely clear what he thought about that. Rorin stifled a smile.

Taze frowned. "But if a Sky Lord *cairdre* is a single bonded unit, how is it that you have another bond to the Nightstalker?"

"I'm honestly not sure. Technically, as rightful heir, his magic should be under my control. But it's not. He's warped the Sky Lord magic somehow, made himself *caidre* leader of any Sky Lord that is born."

Darmanin's expression turned even colder. "Which means he could control us like he can you?"

"Through his connection with me, yes." She let out a breath. "I'm sorry to bring this trouble to you. I know it's not what you want to hear."

"*I truly am glad to have you back.*" Rorin reached over the table to take her hand. "*I missed you.*"

"I missed you too," she said, and meant it.

Darmanin rose abruptly. "It's late. Rorin, I'd like to get started early tomorrow. The sooner we deal with this unpleasantness the better."

Rorin nodded, resigned. "*We'll all meet in my office directly after breakfast.*"

"I'll see you then." Darmanin left without another word.

***

Arya lay on the bed in her old quarters for hours, fully clothed and unable to sleep, staring into the darkness. At midnight, she gave up and rolled out of bed.

"*Okay?*" Elendryl roused.

"*I'm okay. Can't sleep is all.*"

"Close." He assured her, sending her an image of the mossy hollow he was curled up in, the walls of Heathrock visible through a gap in the trees.

After pulling on her boots, Arya went to her old closet—now empty—and slid aside the door in the back. The passageways behind the walls were pitch black, but she remembered them as if it had only been yesterday they'd frequently scrambled between each other's rooms.

She made her way unerringly through the dark, turning without hesitation and coming to the back of another closet. With a deep breath, she slid it open, and stepped inside before pushing through the hanging clothes. The faint scent of perfume emanating from them told her she'd come to the right place. Before going through the closet door, she knocked twice.

"Come in, Arya."

Arya opened the door with a click, stepping into a space lit by the crackling fire in the hearth. "You kept this room."

"I always loved it in here." Essa nodded. She was curled up in bed, a book in her lap, two candles for extra light flickering on her bedside table.

The sight of her was like a punch to Arya's stomach, all the breath seeming to leave her in a soundless gasp. She wanted to leap across the room, she wanted to shout, she wanted to ... but she did none of those things. Instead, she stayed where she was. "Hi, Ess."

"Arya."

"Ah, good." Arya cleared her throat. "So, I'm not the only one who has no idea what to say."

A flicker of a smile in those eyes. "And not the only one who can't sleep, apparently."

Arya looked away. "I didn't expect to come home to a welcome, yet that's what I got from Rorin, Laskin, Taze, even the Raiders. I expected anger and blame, so if that's how you're feeling, Ess, then I—"

"You are not to blame for Thiara and Matte's deaths." Essa's voice shook and Arya was astonished to see tears glistening in her eyes. "*I* am. I was there, Arya. I'm a Sky Lord. I could have done something, but I didn't, I didn't do anything. If I had just—"

"No!" Arya's voice resounded through the room, at once commanding and desperate, and Essa stopped, mouth dropping open. "If you had tried to face the nazal that night, you would have died. And I could not, *cannot*, live with losing you too. Do you understand me?"

A weighted silence fell, interrupted only by the crackle and spit of flames.

"I thought you had died," Essa whispered. "When the bond went quiet, I thought…"

"I'm so sorry. I didn't realise what it would feel like to you and Dar." Arya tried to explain. "But with the bonds muted, the nazal can't track you. I did it because it was the only way to keep you safe."

It was the wrong thing to say. Essa's green eyes flashed, all the tears gone now. "I *am* angry, Arya. Not because I blame you for the deaths of Rorin's parents. But because you don't get to unilaterally decide to never come home because you think it protects me. That is not your right. Decisions about my safety and protection are, and always will be, *mine!*"

Arya dragged in a shuddering breath. "I am the leader of our *cairdre*. That makes me responsible for all of you, whether any of us like it or not."

"That doesn't mean you can make decisions about me without talking to me first." Essa sat up straighter, book sliding away, forgotten. "If you had talked to me, I would have told you that I understood your desire to stay away, but that you were wrong. That Rorin needed you, badly. That *I* needed you to help me. That I wanted to learn my magic so that I could fight next time the nazal threatened somebody I loved. But I couldn't because you were gone, maybe even dead. And we would never have known what happened to you. Do you have *any* idea what that felt like?"

The words, fiercely spoken, hit Arya like a million shards of glass slicing into her skin.

"I *am* glad, that you're alive and well." Essa spoke softly now, clearly drained. "But I'm so angry and so hurt, and I don't know how to … I need space. And time. Could you please go?"

"I'm so sorry, Ess." Arya whirled and left, this time going through the room door rather than the closet.

The door clicked shut behind her, the sound making her flinch.

She started walking, aimless. The corridors were dark and quiet. Eventually she came to a halt at the steps leading down into the great hall of Heathrock. It was filled with shadows and memories. Some of the happiest times of her life had been spent in this hall; playing pranks on the staff with Rorin, or enjoying the sumptuous Winterfest dinner put on by Peemla every year. She'd missed the last three Winterfests, missed the birth of her nephew, missed so much.

Was Essa right—had she been wrong to stay away? Maybe, but if they all knew what she'd done after Gateport, how she'd ... Arya's hands curled into fists. No, there would be no welcome then. She crossed the empty hall, boots echoing on the stone floor, before coming to a stop at its opposite end. This spot was where the Winterfest tree would stand in a few months' time. Memories flooded her; the five of them chopping down a huge tree every year, laughing and throwing snow at each other.

Arya had been alone before; her whole life before she was fifteen years old had been lived with nobody but herself to rely on. Then Thiara Ravenstrike had taken her in and given her a family, and for a few years Arya hadn't been alone. She'd been loved.

Now, though, she felt like an outcast in a place that had once been home. It was like putting on an old shirt she'd grown out of that didn't fit anymore.

Unable to be within the castle walls any longer, Arya abruptly turned on her heel. She took a back entrance out of the kitchens and emerged into the bitterly cold night. Her Etherean clothing kept her from freezing, but she welcomed the discomfort of the icy air as a punishment. Her boots crunched through the hard-packed snow as she let herself out a side gate and walked around to the edge of the lake towards a place she'd been many times before.

Nimbly, she made her way out onto a high rocky outcropping on the lake's edge and clambered up it. On reaching the top, she sat at the edge, arms crossed over her knees.

And there she sat, watching out over the lake, until dawn's light lit the horizon.

Chapter 7

They gathered the next morning in Rorin's office, around the long table near his desk. Essa had joined them for breakfast, and much to Arya's relief after the night before, she was friendly, although distant. Arya's relief was short-lived, though.

The moment she stepped into the warlord's office, what had once been Thiara Ravenstrike's space, Arya was deluged with memories. How many times had she met with her warlord in here, planning Thiara's rise to High Warlord? And instead, she'd been brutally murdered right as she'd been about to realise those dreams. The bitter tragedy left Arya unsettled, desperate to leave. Everyone else seemed fine, though, and she supposed they'd had nearly four years to let the ghosts of Thiara Ravenstrike fade. This was *Rorin's* office now.

Once everyone was settled, Arya spoke first, needing a distraction from the memories. "Rorin, how many Raiders can you draw upon swiftly if needed?"

Rorin shrugged. "*Maybe five thousand?*"

Arken cleared his throat. "I can have three thousand ready to deploy in two weeks. Ten days if we push hard."

Arya glanced at him, impressed. That was comparable to when she'd led the army. "I assume the remaining seven thousand are dispersed between barracks across the State? Seven shields at SheerRock and Windfall forts and ten at Icecliff?" She waited for Arken's nod, then turned to Rorin. "That's not enough. You need more numbers here, near Heathrock, ready to respond fast if invasion comes."

"Arya, I love you, but you've yet to convince me that we are facing an imminent invasion. I can't afford to pull Raiders from all over Ravenstrike to man the forts."

"Why?" she asked, frowning.

Rorin gave a frustrated sigh and sent a pointed glance in Darmanin's direction. *"Maybe if Crowtalon stopped aggravating Falconcrest, I could take Raiders off my eastern border. As it is, they're likely to invade if I do that."*

Arya snorted. Falconcrest invade? That seemed an exaggeration, yet nobody in the room reacted to Rorin's comment with disagreement or surprise. She looked around the table. "What am I missing?"

"Warlord Falconcrest didn't take it kindly when my Lances killed a shield of his Aggressors several months ago," Darmanin said.

"You did *what?*" Arya straightened, staring at him in shock. Relationships between States had never been frictionless in her time as a Raider, but warlords hadn't come close to killing rival States' soldiers out of hand.

His expression tightened into implacability. "They'd crossed the Crowtalon border without permission."

Essa sent him a pointed look. "Dar was responding to Warlord Falconcrest's suggestion to the High Warlord that import tariffs on lumber travelling between States should be increased."

Arya rubbed the bridge of her nose. She was still missing something. "I get that lumber is Crowtalon's primary export, so presumably Falconcrest was having a dig at Dar, but last I checked warlords didn't go about murdering soldiers because a fellow warlord proposed a policy they didn't like."

"Last you checked was four years ago." Darmanin's voice was ice cold granite, sinking the table into a tense silence.

Rorin began signing. *"After the Aggressors were killed, the High Warlord sent a shield of Defenders to investigate the deaths. Dar rode out with his Lances and refused to allow them into Crowtalon."*

"In response, the High Warlord issued a decree that each State must allow a Defender shield to be based in its capital. That was nearly two weeks ago," Essa added. "Eaglesoar accepted with some whimpering, Hawkesdale was furious, and SparrowWing stalled while Darmanin stopped Defenders travelling through Crowtalon to get to SparrowWing. They haven't gotten to Ravenstrike yet because we're the furthest away, but we're going to be facing a tough choice soon."

"*You'd think all this would make Hawkesdale and Sparrow Wing allies.*" Rorin rolled his eyes. "*But they're just as furious at Darmanin for provoking Mathas' response in the first place.*"

"All in all, the stability of Dunidaen is somewhat precarious at the moment," Essa summed up.

"You make it sound as if I am causing chaos for no reason," Darmanin said. "Enough instability will see my father dislodged from his position. Then I can take his place."

"And what possessed you to think instability in Dunidaen was a good idea with the Nightstalker just over the border looking for any excuse to take this territory as his own?" Arya snapped.

Darmanin crossed his arms over his chest and sat back. "We'll be in a much better position to face an invasion if my father is not High Warlord."

"And you think the Nightstalker is just going to politely wait for Dunidaen to sort its politics out before coming for you?" she demanded. "Or do you think he'll take advantage and strike while your army is in disarray."

"Why hasn't he yet, do you think?" Arken spoke up, diffusing the building tension. "I ask because I'd like to understand why you're so certain of invasion, Arya, especially if it's only the Sky Lords he wants."

Arya tore her gaze from Darmanin. "The Nightstalker is incredibly powerful, but he's also smart enough to know that Dunidaen, Khadini, and the Icelands allied together could be a strong enough force to defeat him. Until now, I think that has been enough to convince him that invasion wasn't worth it."

Arken nodded. "But you think the existence of you and your Sky Lords changes the odds for him, even though it hasn't in the past?"

"A full Sky Lord *cairdre* presents an existential threat to the Nightstalker, or, at the very least, a threat he can't afford to ignore." Arya remained far from convinced. "His nazal hunters have killed or captured all Sky Lord potentials over the past fifty years, but I'm different. I've managed to evade him, as have my Sky Lords. The longer it takes him to find and kill us, the stronger we grow, and the greater threat we pose."

"But how does invading Dunidaen help him destroy you?" Arken asked.

Arya took a breath, paused, let it out. "That's a fair question, General." She used his title deliberately. He'd identified a key assumption in her logic and was making her address it. "The Nightstalker doesn't trust your warlords, or their ability to find me and the Sky Lords—and that doubt has been borne out. I think he will decide to undertake the hunt for us himself, and he can do that far more easily in territory he controls."

Rorin's signing was unconvinced. "*Mathas Crowtalon is doing everything he can to hunt the Sky Lords the Nightstalker wants. What would the Nightstalker have to gain from invading now?*"

"Everything." Essa's voice cut through the room as she spoke for the first time. "Because if he invaded Dunidaen right now, he would win."

All heads swivelled to the chief advisor.

Essa continued. "You think he doesn't keep any eye on events across the world? That he doesn't have spies reporting to him? Dunidaen is increasingly unstable. The Etherean are in hiding. Khadini looks inward with an emperor that cares nothing for his neighbours. None of us are anywhere close to allying against him. As it is, he can pick us off one by one, and then he controls *everything*. One *cairdre* would no longer present a threat to him. Nothing would."

Darmanin shook his head. "We don't know that he cares anything for taking more territory."

Taze cleared his throat into the tense silence that fell. "You always had good instincts for this sort of thing, Arya. What are they telling you now?"

"Maybe invasion is not imminent—but it *is* coming. You can expect an advance force of wraiths and shadowhounds, terrifying and vicious creatures most Dunidae warriors have never faced before. And when that happens, you've got barely five hundred Raiders spread across three forts to stop them. Of course, you could warn the other warlords and have a combined army waiting for them as a second line of defence, but that's not going to work, because Darmanin has managed to get all the warlords furious at each other."

Rorin looked sober. *"I can't risk invasion from Falconcrest by withdrawing Raiders from the border right now, but bring me solid evidence that the Night-stalker is sending his army to take Dunidaen, and I will act, Arya. My word on it."*

"If you permit, Warlord, I can begin making preparations now, in the event a rapid deployment of the Raiders is needed," Arken added.

"Permission granted," Rorin signed.

Arya let out a breath. They both trusted her and her judgement. Her shoulders felt abruptly lighter. "I'll go into the Wraith Forest, speak with Ranier. Learn exactly what's been happening. From there I'll go into the underground road and explore the tunnels Salyarin told me about. If there is any sign of a scouting force from Andahar, you'll have your evidence."

Darmanin rose from his chair. "I'll come with you."

Arya shook her head. "I'll do better alone."

"And how are you going to get a meeting with Ranier? I can send a message that will reach him today, meaning we can leave first thing tomorrow." He crossed his arms over his chest. "Or you can go hiking around the Wraith Forest searching for him while he evades you from sheer spite."

Arya wanted to turn and ask Essa if *she* could get a message to her father, but didn't feel like she could ask anything of the woman right now. She'd asked for space. Arya would give it to her. And she didn't have the energy to argue further with Darmanin. "Fine."

"Fine. I'll go and send the message now."

The door slammed behind him. Rorin let out what she suspected was a strangled laugh. Essa rose without a word and followed Darmanin out.

Arya stood too, shifting her glance between Rorin and Arken. "Thank you both."

***

Uncomfortable inside the stone walls of the castle, Arya sought fresh air and space atop the outer walls. The Raiders on guard gave her a nod of acknowledgment but otherwise left her to herself.

"*Okay?*" she sent to Elendryl. His presence in her mind was quiet, indicating all was well, but she reached out anyway, wanting the reassurance of their connection.

He sent a shiver of reassurance back, followed by, "*Coming soon?*"

"*I'll be leaving tomorrow first thing.*"

He was pleased by that and withdrew with another mental tap of affection.

Movement to Arya's left signalled Essa's approach. The chief advisor leaned beside her against the battlements. As usual, she was wrapped in multiple layers against the cold, her face peeking through a furred hood. A slight pause, then Essa asked, "You really wanted to stay away so badly?"

"I didn't think you'd want me here." Arya's jaw clenched, and she tried to fight back the tears welling in her eyes.

Essa rubbed at her forehead, some of the frustration fading from her eyes. "It hurts that you would think that of us. But I suspect I would have felt the same in your position."

A silence fell between them. It wasn't entirely uncomfortable, but it wasn't the easy, contented silence they'd once shared either. Eventually, Essa spoke into it. "There's something I should tell you."

"What is it?"

"My wyvern was born almost three years ago. It took some time for her to reach me, but, well, she's here now. Her name is Alletryl."

"Here?" Arya stared. "Where? What colour is she?"

"She's green, like a deep river, with brighter emerald under-wings—colours I couldn't replicate painting if I tried." Essa sighed in awe before sobering. "She's well hidden in the Wraith Forest. I'm the chief advisor to Warlord Ravenstrike. I can't be seen riding around on a great big wyvern."

"Does Rorin know?"

"He knows, but he's never seen Alletryl. I think it's better that way." Essa paused, and a smile tugged at her mouth. "It really is the most wonderful thing, isn't it?"

Arya matched her smile, thinking back to the time she'd first met Elendryl, and how his presence made her life so much better. "It is." Her smile faded. "How will we ever unite Dunidaen without hiding everything about ourselves, Ess?"

"I don't know," she admitted. "Stay safe in the mountains, Arya."

***

After another night of little sleep, Arya was dressed and waiting in the entry courtyard at daybreak the following morning. Half of her was desperate to leave and escape these walls, while the other half never wanted to leave again.

Elendryl swooped low over the walls to land in a rush of air in the entry yard. Shouts echoed from the Raiders posted along the walls, but they sounded more surprised than afraid. None lifted knocked bows today. She went straight to the wyvern, running a gloved hand over the scales of his lowered head and earning a growl of pleasure. When Darmanin came down the steps, Elendryl's head snapped up, and his snarl rippled through the air. The Crowtalon warlord halted immediately.

"Elendryl, you weren't formally introduced, but you remember Darmanin?" Arya spoke aloud. "Dar, this is Elendryl."

Darmanin bowed his head gravely. "Elendryl. I am pleased to meet you."

Elendryl's serpentine head snaked forward. He opened his mouth, baring teeth, but Darmanin remained still. The wyvern huffed a breath and withdrew. "*Fine,*" he grumbled.

Arya stifled a grin. "He says you'll do."

Darmanin merely nodded. The implacable expression he'd worn since arriving yesterday hadn't softened once in her presence. She inwardly let out a sigh. Rorin appeared then. Elendryl didn't react at all to the warlord coming straight over to give Arya a warm hug. *"Stay safe, Arya. I don't want to lose you so soon after getting you back."*

"I'm sorry I stayed away so long," she murmured.

"Don't do it again?"

She wasn't sure if she could promise that. "I'll do my best."

Darmanin hefted his pack, looked at Arya. "I propose hiking the first part of the journey. The meeting place I suggested to Ranier is only accessible on foot."

"Works for me." Arya agreed. Elendryl hated it when she rode anything other than him. *"Watch from above?"* she sent to her wyvern.

Rorin stared, eyes wide, as Elendryl spread his wings and launched himself into the sky. Every Raider head on the wall turned to watch him go. She stifled a smile of amusement.

"Rorin!" Taze called from the steps as he came down. He brandished a piece of parchment in his hand, and the note of urgency in his voice had them all turning towards him.

"Something wrong?"

"This just flew in with a messenger bird from the Terren garrison." Taze passed the note to Rorin. "Peemla's gone to wake Essa and I sent a Raider to fetch Arken."

"What is it?" Arya and Darmanin spoke at the same time as Rorin read the note.

"A unit of Defenders has arrived on the southern border demanding permission at the Terren garrison to enter the State." Rorin signed, jaw tense. *"Commander Dirke is stalling, but he needs a decision immediately."*

Arya's first instinct was to change her plans, stay, work alongside Rorin to figure out the best response to send. Her thoughts were already considering whether to bolster the Terren garrison, or move troops to—

That wasn't her job anymore. It was Arken's. Her chest squeezed painfully.

"You can't let them in. My father can't be allowed to set a precedent like this." Darmanin said.

Arya rounded on him. "And Rorin can't afford to start a skirmish with Defenders, or Aggressors backing them up, right now."

"*I am standing right here, and I am warlord.*" Rorin signed angrily. "*I will handle this. But Arya, if you're going to bring me proof of invasion, you need to do it fast. I can't stall the border situation forever.*"

"I'll do my best," she promised, already feeling the urgency weighing on her. Impulsively, she leaned forward to hug her brother. "Good luck."

Then she turned and walked away without looking back.

Chapter 8

Darmanin took the lead as they headed into the Wraith Forest, their boots sinking into deep snow. They'd only hiked a half hour or so when they emerged into a large clearing and Darmanin slowed to a stop.

"Is this the meeting location?" Arya asked.

Elendryl abruptly dropped from the sky, landing in front of her with a gust of air and letting out a challenging roar. "*What is it?*" she asked. She couldn't see a threat anywhere.

"We're safe. Stay calm." Darmanin took several strides into the space between Elendryl and the trees on the far side of the clearing, a hand reaching outwards towards Arya's wyvern, as if to hold him back. Elendryl snapped at the hand, but made no attempt to attack, or to stop Arya when she walked forward to stand beside his head, one hand reaching up to idly stroke the cold scales of his neck.

And then she froze.

Another wyvern stepped out of the trees ahead. Her scales were as inky black as Darmanin's coat when he was in shadowhound form. Smaller than Elendryl, she nonetheless had the same powerful neck and tail, razor-sharp spines, and fearsome teeth. Her taloned wings were the same black as her scales, but their undersides gleamed sapphire where they reflected the light off the snow.

She bared her teeth at the sight of Arya, and her head snaked upwards to snap at Elendryl. He reared back in startlement before he let out a warning growl. The female wyvern didn't cower, not even close, but she didn't make any further aggressive moves.

"Well," Arya remarked, tearing her eyes from the wyvern to look at Darmanin. "Aren't you full of surprises."

Darmanin gave her an unreadable look. "Arya, this Zaphirdryl."

"Elendryl and I are glad to meet you, Zaphirdryl." Arya bowed her head and received a contempt-filled snort in return. "How long have you had her, Dar?"

"Two and a half years," he said. "She lives here; she and Alletryl hunt together sometimes, *when* they're getting along."

"She must hate being forced to be apart from you so long."

Zaphirdryl huffed, as if in agreement. Her eyes, deep yellow like Elendryl, glared in her rider's direction.

"You know I cannot bring her into Dunidaen," he said. "I visit her as frequently as I can, and it's fortunate she is here, in Rorin's State."

He sounded so determined about that, so decided. Yet if there was one warlord who might have the strength and cleverness to convince his people to accept a wyvern, it was Darmanin. But he wouldn't risk that. "You want to be High Warlord," she murmured.

"I want to see my father destroyed, and I want him to see the son he hates taking his place." Arya flinched at the venom in Darmanin's voice, but when he spoke again, all traces of anger were gone. "It isn't much farther to the meeting point. We should keep going."

"Keep watch from above." Arya pressed her hand against Elendryl's neck in farewell and stepped back so that he could take off.

Zaphirdryl waited until he was in the air before she took flight—and flew in the opposite direction. Arya hid a smirk, then hustled after Darmanin, who'd already started walking.

The forest turned quiet the further they hiked. Arya scanned their surroundings, uneasy. It might have been years, but she remembered how alive the forest had felt when she'd been on patrol with the Raiders. This was different. She'd only felt this kind of different once before. That patrol her shield had been on, right before everyone in SheerRock Fort was killed by a single pack of wraiths.

"Something isn't right," she murmured eventually.

Darmanin looked over at her, their gazes meeting. "You remember."

"All too well."

***

"This looks familiar," Arya noted when they scrambled to the top of a rocky cliff face a few hours later. It was the same place Ranier had brought them the night they'd left Heathrock to begin training for their Dreadwater run. "If Leanir shows up this time, I'll put an arrow through him."

"No, you won't."

She huffed a breath in acknowledgment. She wasn't even sure if she'd be capable of it even if she *did* want to. The Sky Lord bonds were so innate, so fundamental to her very being, that even the fact that Leanir had killed and hurt those she loved might not be enough to override them to do him harm. Besides, now she knew more of her magic, Leanir couldn't harm her either; as *cairdre* leader, she could control him through the bond between them.

"You can't control me, Arya Ravenstrike," Darmanin warned, as if picking up on her thoughts. "Sky Lord magical bonds or no."

"I wouldn't want to, Dar. I never have," she said quietly. "I think we share similar feelings about submitting to anyone."

He acknowledged that with a tight nod.

Ranier materialised in a blink. One moment the trees around the clearing were empty, the next he was stepping out of the shadows. On instinct, Arya reached for Elendryl's presence. He was close by and could be in the clearing in moments if needed.

All three studied each other. The Shadeweaver leader said nothing. He stood with eerie stillness, hands folded in front of him, shaven head bared to the icy afternoon, the scar on his face stark and vivid. The silence spread, drawing out.

Arya smirked and broke the tension. "I missed you too, Ranier."

His expression didn't change. "All business between us is over. What do you want?"

"You're the one who's been writing messages to *my* Sky Lord," she said sharply. "What do *you* want?"

Ranier shifted minutely, and Arya wondered if he were about to leave or attack. Whichever it was, Darmanin forestalled it. "Arya suspects the Nightstalker is planning invasion soon. We need to know what you know."

Ranier's glance shifted to Arya. "What do *you* know?"

"That the Icefolk er'fin was ambushed by a nest of wraiths on the Icelands-Falconcrest border a week ago," she said. "Your turn."

His gaze narrowed. "Did the er'fin survive?"

"And what do you care about that?" she said.

A beat passed. Two. Arya and Darmanin stayed silent. Ranier eventually spoke. "In the time since I sent a message to Darmanin, three of my scouts have not returned from routine patrols. That's not necessarily unusual given the environment, predators, and your Raiders. But all were scouting the same area. All were experienced scouts, and magic-wielders."

"They were scouting the area near the underground road?" Arya guessed.

Ranier inclined his head.

"Have your people actually *seen* anything? Wraiths, shadowhounds? Mauled bodies indicative of attack by those creatures?"

"No. Have your Raider patrols?"

"No." Ranier's information was thin, extremely so. But she knew the man well. He would never have reached out to Darmanin unless he thought something was going on. "Have you sent scouts into the tunnels?"

Ranier said nothing.

She stepped closer to him. "You're a scion of House Inkweaver. Nobleborn of Andahar. Don't tell me you don't know about the tunnels branching off from the underground road. Your House probably held maps of the entire network. Why haven't you sent scouts in to search them?"

"You seem to think I give a damn about what might be in those tunnels. I'm not risking my people, not for Dunidaen. The Nightstalker can have your country for all I care."

Another step towards him. "If that's true, why have you ever helped me? Why warn Darmanin now?"

He held her gaze. "Old oaths bind me. But be clear, Raider, I was hunted, those I love killed, by a mad usurper who killed a careless king. I have no interest in *any* of it. I seek only to survive now, and keep my people safe. If wraiths haunt these mountains, then they are in danger."

"Oaths to who?"

Silence. Such violence flicked in those dark eyes of his. What had Ranier seen, done, that placed that look there, that gave him such an aura of danger? Arya doubted it had always been there. "One day I'm going to have all your secrets, Inkweaver," she murmured.

His eyes glittered with violence. "No, you won't."

"Will you give us a map of the tunnels?"

"I don't have one."

Her gaze flickered to the edges of tattoo visible beneath his collar, at his wrists, and she wondered. "Dar, any more questions?"

He gave a little shake of his head.

She looked back at Ranier. "Map or no, we're going into the tunnels. If there is an invasion coming, expect another conversation with me. That's if you want your Shadeweavers in their unprotected camps to survive it, of course."

"And if there is an invasion, how do you plan to face it?" Ranier asked. "As a disgraced former Raider with a bounty on her head? Or as a Sky Lord of Andahar?"

She buried the flinch his words roused. "What does it matter to you?"

His dark eyes flashed. "One gets an audience with me. The other can expect all she likes but will suddenly find that I'm impossible to locate."

"We'll see about that."

"We will." Ranier's gaze shifted to Darmanin, and he nodded. "Darmanin. Until next time."

Before he could respond, the Shadeweaver leader had disappeared into the trees. Arya waited to be sure he was gone before reaching out for Elendryl and glancing at Darmanin. The wyverns would get them to the underground road much faster.

"Do you think he was lying, holding anything back?" she asked Darmanin while they waited.

"Absolutely." Darmanin looked thoughtful. "He doesn't feel any loyalty to us or to Dunidaen. He might have to Andahar once, but now … I get the sense he only helps us when he does because he feels like he has to. Those oaths he mentioned. Ranier has always held his honour above everything else. If not for that, I suspect he may never have helped us at all."

"That's problematic." Arya mused as Elendryl arrived, Zaphirdryl not far behind. "I have a feeling we might need all those secrets he's got locked up inside one day."

"Not if we leave Andahar to itself."

Arya looked away, wishing with every fibre of her being that was possible.

***

The wyverns brought them down outside the opening to the underground road as dusk approached. They landed a good distance apart and watched each other warily at all times. Arya wondered how much their mutual suspicion was mirroring the current distance between her and Darmanin, and how much was natural wyvern behaviour. Something else Ranier probably knew but would never tell them.

The thick layer of snow covering the road rose to Arya's ankles as she slogged towards the grand stone archway at the entrance. This time, her gaze went straight to the words etched above it, shining in the orange glow of sunset.

Unleash the storm

"Something wrong?" Darmanin asked as he came up beside her.

"No, let's get in there."

"Should we light a torch first?"

She tossed him a smile. "No need."

Arya raised her right hand and summoned a trickle of magic, just enough to form a ball of sparking blue light in her palm. It provided enough light that they could see the road immediately ahead, but not enough to reach the tunnel walls on either side. Hopefully it was dim enough that it wouldn't be a beacon advertising their presence to anyone, or any*thing*, else under the mountains.

She started walking, boots echoing on stone. A half moment later, Darmanin followed. "You *have* been learning with the Etherean."

She smirked, enjoying having shocked him. "The basics are easy enough. We can use our magic as an elemental force—which is what I'm doing now, only I'm controlling the amount I let out, so it doesn't explode and kill us both or bring down the roof on our heads. Beyond that ..." She sighed. "The elder has no knowledge of the more complex uses of Sky Lord magic, and he says I am too impatient and distracted to learn them even if he could teach me."

"Did he?"

She scowled. "That better not be amusement in your voice, Darmanin Crowtalon."

"I wouldn't dream of it."

She glanced over, caught the little smile on his face, and felt a cascade of relief in her chest. It had been so long since she'd seen that smile of his. She'd missed it more than she realised.

Moving fast, they arrived at the deliberate rockfall blocking up the underground road without incident. In silent accord, they searched every inch of its surface and found no signs of disturbance.

"So, he's not coming through here, at least not yet." Arya avoided Darmanin's pointed look. "The question is, how do we find these tunnels if we can't get through the blockage?"

Darmanin turned back the way they'd come. "I know one of them from my time with the Shadeweavers. I didn't realise what it was at the time—we used it as a place to store supplies."

"Let me guess, Ranier showed it to you?" she muttered. That was why Ranier had refused them a map. He knew Darmanin had enough information to get them started.

Night had fallen by the time they emerged from the underground road. Arya asked Elendryl to watch from the skies. *"Darmanin knows one of the tunnel entrances, but he can only find it on foot."*

"Watch," he agreed, then spread his mighty wings to leap into the sky.

After casting a suspicious look after him, Zaphirdryl followed suit.

They hiked for well over an hour before Darmanin stopped at the base of a rocky cliff and pushed aside the thick bush which grew at the base of it. A gaping hole only a few feet high was revealed.

Arya regarded it dubiously. *"Elendryl, will you stay close while we go in, keep an eye on our back?"* She didn't like them being separated, but there was no way he'd fit through this entrance.

In response, she received a pulse of worry and agreement combined.

Darmanin held back the branches while Arya scrambled through, using a moment of focus to bring her light back to life. A blue glow broke through the darkness.

"How long can you keep that up?" Darmanin asked.

"It doesn't take much power to feed it. The trickiest part is the focus required not to let too much energy out."

"Which would result in an explosion that would kill us both?" he clarified.

"Exactly. It would be much easier to just do that." She snorted. "I don't think Salyarin taught me this as a way to conjure a light source, I suspect he used it as an excuse to practice my control."

"We'd best go silently from here. *If* there are wraiths or shadowhounds or scouts in these tunnels, we don't want them hearing us approach."

"You'll get no argument from me," she murmured. "I'll keep the light dim."

The surface under their feet gradually changed from hard-packed soil to stone. Arya shot Darmanin a curious glance when they stepped out of the narrow space into a much wider and taller one. "I think we're back on the underground road," she whispered. "The tunnel must have brought us around behind the rockfall. A shortcut, perhaps?"

Darmanin nodded and they continued, soon turning a corner in the road to find another stone archway directly ahead. It was similar in size and grandeur to the one at the entrance to the underground road. When Arya walked through it, she emerged into an open space.

Behind her, Darmanin stopped. "Look at this stonework. It's been done by a master."

Arya raised a hand to run her fingers over the faded stone. It was cool to the touch and covered in a patchwork of long-gathered dust, moss, and the occasional spiderweb. Still, there were no gaps that she could discern between the blocks of stone.

On impulse, she allowed more of her magic to seep out, increasing the size of the light in her palm so that it illuminated the entire cavern. It took more effort than she'd expected, and when she could see it all, she stared in astonishment.

They stood at the entrance to an incredible atrium; an indoor space larger than any she'd seen before. The opposite side was so far away she could barely make it out. Skylights crisscrossing the roof opened up to the mountain air and showed glimpses of cloud-covered night sky. Empty buildings lined the amphitheatre, running up in circular tiers to an enormous height.

"Could you imagine what it must have looked like?" she said in awe, her boots echoing on the stone as she walked further inside, craning her head to see everything. "Back when the road was in use?"

"It would have been lit by Sky Lord magic, and every traveller would have been welcome to marvel at its grandeur," Darmanin said quietly.

"That was poetic, Dar." And utterly unlike him.

He shook his head, an uncertain look crossing his face. "You should dim the light, just in case."

She did so reluctantly. As Arya walked further inside, the floor under her changed from stone to tiles of sapphire-veined white marble. The colour was dulled under a layer of dust and lichen, but even so it was stunning. "No footprints other than ours." She pointed out quietly.

He nodded. He was distant, his thoughts clearly elsewhere. "This must have been a waypoint and a trading post for travellers. It's sad, seeing something like this so empty. It should be full of life."

Arya hummed in agreement, her attention caught by the sight of an enormous letter 'D' etched in the amphitheatre floor in gold tiling. Curious, she kneeled, running her free hand over the surface to clean it of debris. To the left of the 'D' was an 'I'.

Heart beginning to race, Arya cleaned the dust from all the golden letters stretching across the diameter of the amphitheatre.

"Stormrider," Darmanin read out.

Arya made no reply. The sight of her ancestor's name in such a setting sent a rush of emotion sweeping through her. She couldn't name what it was, but it shook her to her very core. "It's my House," she murmured, then swallowed down a stab of pain. Not just hers anymore. "House Stormrider, the ruling House of Andahar."

He kneeled beside her, reaching out to touch the gold. "Arya Stormrider. A fitting name for you."

"It's not my name," she said softly. "One of the happiest days of my life was when Rorin's mother made me a Ravenstrike."

"A person can be more than one thing." Darmanin's hand settled on her shoulder. It was the first time he'd touched her since that night in Gateport and she froze, fighting the urge to lean into it. If he knew the truth, he'd never touch her again.

"I suppose that's true." She managed, then stood, and his hand dropped away.

"My guess is that this waypoint marks the official border between Andahar and Dunidaen," Darmanin mused. "The lettering is bold and proud. A welcome and a challenge both."

Arya tried a wry smile. "At least we know the nazal haven't technically invaded yet."

He stood. "It's late. Shall we get a few hours rest in one of those empty buildings we saw?"

Arya didn't want to stop moving yet, but realised the sense of it. The further they went into the tunnels, the more likely they'd come across danger.

Better to be well rested when that happened.

***

Just as they reached the opposite side of the atrium, the cloud cover in the sky above cleared away, and shafts of silvery moonlight illuminated the cavern through the skylights. Arya instinctively let her magic die and once their eyes adjusted, they could see thousands of sparkling, multi-coloured gems lining the walls, set alight by the silvery moon. They stopped and stared, drinking in its beauty.

Eventually, Darmanin gave himself a shake and started up one of the paths. Arya followed reluctantly. In the homes and shops they glanced into as they passed, there was evidence that people had once lived there. A pair of rotted shoes sat idly by a step; a long-dead plant drooped over a windowsill. An empty quietness hovered over everything. It was as if the town were sleeping, just waiting to be re-awakened.

"This will do." Darmanin stopped outside a home halfway up the atrium wall.

They dropped their packs to the floor and busied themselves, drinking from their water flagons and munching on bread and cheese. Arya settled back against the wall, legs stretched out, blanket over her legs. Despite her poor sleep recently, she felt too wired to rest. "I wish we had time to explore. Don't you think this place is amazing?"

"It is," he admitted. The dim glow of the moonlight gave his grey eyes an eerie cast as he watched her. She couldn't read the expression in them. He'd always been reserved, but now she wasn't sure there were any chinks in his armour.

"Andahar has always been this distant dream. I've never really seen it as a real place, or felt as if I would ever go there," she said. "Don't you think it's such a shame that this place no longer lives?"

"There's no purpose for it anymore. The borders have been closed for decades."

"I know, but…" She hesitated. "It's had a detrimental effect on all of us, hasn't it? Countries need trade to thrive. I know it's impacted the Etherean. And I doubt there would be so much tension between the warlords if they had stronger alliances with the Icefolk, Khadini, and Andahar. All this distrust and isolation stifles the growth of all our kingdoms."

He gave her a look. "An Andahari invasion could certainly have the unifying effect among the warlords that you're seeking."

"If you let it," she said pointedly.

"You think I would ruin Dunidaen in my attempt to get revenge on my father?" he asked.

"I don't know. You've always hated him so much, and for good reason," she said. "I know there's not much *I* wouldn't do to avenge Thiara Ravenstrike's death."

"I am warlord of Crowtalon, Arya, and my priority is whatever is best for my State. And when I become High Warlord, I will act in the best interests of Dunidaen."

"And what of Andahar?"

"Andahar is not my life or my home. You've always agreed with me on that."

"Yes, but I lost my life and home."

"That's not true," he said firmly. "You belong with your friends, your family. You're the one that told *me* that, remember? At our first Winterfest at Heathrock?"

Arya had no good answer to that. It felt both true and untrue at the same time. She took a bite of bread and chewed it.

After a moment's silence, Darmanin asked. "What was it like living with the Icefolk and Etherean?"

Glad of the easy question, Arya answered, "I like the Icefolk. Death is always close in the Icelands, and so they live the more for it, I think. They welcomed me without asking for anything in return. Er'fin At'eir has become a good friend." She huffed a laugh. "But their winters are far too cold for me to stay. The Etherean … I don't know. They have a beautiful home, and they too are friendly. But when I'm there I feel like I am constantly being judged and considered unworthy. Or that I'm letting them down somehow."

He absorbed that, then asked, gaze downward on the bread in his hand. "Have you been happy?"

She responded without thought. "I'm not sure how I'll ever be happy again, not after what happened." Not with the terrible burden of what she'd had to do weighing down every single breath she took, not to mention the constant underlying terror of the Nightstalker finding out about it.

Darmanin's mouth tightened but he said nothing further. He was angry with her; it had lined every single interaction since her return. But was he upset for the same reasons Essa was? Arya shook her head. It didn't matter why, she deserved it.

With Essa, Arya had confidence that eventually they'd find their way back to the friendship they'd had. She knew Essa, had faith in her. The problem with Darmanin … he wasn't the boy or young man she'd known. He was harder. More dangerous in some ways. Their relationship had fundamentally shifted. She didn't know what she wanted from him anymore. Or what he wanted from her.

"Why did you ask me to marry you?" she asked softly. It was a question that had drifted into her mind often over the past years, and one she'd never been able to come up with a good answer for.

He shifted slightly, and his grey eyes glimmered. "I was a foolish boy."

Arya had to chuckle at that. "You were never a foolish boy, Dar."

"I was then," he said sharply.

"Are *you* happy, Darmanin?" She threw his question back at him.

He took a moment to respond, thinking. "Much like you, Arya, there have been few times in my life when I've been truly happy."

She nodded, staring down into her lap as a small smile crossed her face. "Winterfest at Heathrock."

Silence, then: "Yes, Winterfest at Heathrock."

And when she looked up, the iron mask he wore had softened. "I'll take first watch, Dar. Get some rest."

Chapter 9

It was still early morning when they started moving again. Below, the amphitheatre was bathed in golden sunlight; the skies over the Diamondfang uncharacteristically clear. Arya's footsteps slowed as she trailed Darmanin, eyes once again drinking it in.

A closer search of the amphitheatre wall revealed two narrower tunnel entrances apart from the main road at either end. Both were signposted, so must have been official side-roads through the under-mountain.

Darmanin paused at the second one. "It's not big enough for a carriage, or even large horses. Probably a shortcut between two sections of the main highway for smaller groups travelling on foot." He glanced around. "Let's take it. It looks like it's heading deeper west into the mountain."

"You don't want to follow the main road?"

"If the Nightstalker is marching an army through here, he'll use the main road as much as he can. I wouldn't want to walk right into them or have them see your light and know we're here."

She let out a breath, a smile flickering unbidden over her face. "Thanks, Dar."

"For what?"

"You don't believe an invasion is imminent, yet you're treating this scouting mission as if an army *is* coming." She held his gaze. "My thanks for taking me seriously."

"I've always trusted your instincts, Arya. Always will."

In those words, the simple sincerity with which he said them, Arya saw the boy she'd known. The one that had once fought at her side against wraiths and shadowhounds, as much a child as she'd been—though both would have furiously denied it—the one that had grown up with her and Rorin and Essa, loyal and true.

He was still there, inside the man Darmanin had become.

Her smile widened in relief, but all she said was: "As I do yours. Let's take this tunnel."

Once they'd gone into it far enough for the light from the amphitheatre to fade entirely, the tunnel was small enough to trigger Arya's terror of confined spaces. Her light helped, and the fact she could stand upright, so she gritted her teeth and tried to ignore the tightening of anxiety in the pit of her stomach.

Time was hard to parse in endless darkness and unchanging surroundings. She thought they'd been walking maybe a half hour—she'd been distracting herself by trying to figure out how they'd kept this side road lit when it was in use—when something she'd been noticing in the back of her mind finally registered. She stopped and cut off her magic, extinguishing the light glowing around her hand.

"Arya?" Darmanin murmured.

"Give me a moment." Closing her eyes, she took a deep breath and concentrated. When she did, she could more clearly scent the faint tang on the cool air of the tunnel that had caused her to freeze. "I can smell something, just barely," she breathed. "It's familiar, but I can't place it."

He went silent. Arya couldn't see anything in the dark, but assumed Darmanin was concentrating too; his sense of smell had always been keener than hers, something to do with his ability to shapeshift into a shadowhound, she assumed.

Then his presence at her side turned rigid. "I recognise it. Shadowhounds," he murmured.

Arya's heart sank. "Shit."

"Quiet." He leaned down to whisper in her ear, his breath warm on her skin. "Shadowhounds have excellent hearing."

She turned her head, gave him a quick grin, and murmured, "You would know."

She felt his smile curve against her cheek. "Shall we get closer? See what we're dealing with."

"You're a man after my own heart, Crowtalon. Let's go."

They moved slowly now, careful of where and how they placed their feet to minimise noise, just as Ranier had once taught them. Without light, they traced their fingers along the smooth stone wall to ensure they didn't get turned around. Arya kept her breathing light, soundless.

Her heart thudded when she heard a distant growl ahead. The closer they moved, the louder the sounds of growling and barking grew. After several minutes, a glimmer of light appeared. Arya dropped to the ground, shimmying forwards—achingly slow so as not to make a sound—until she reached the tunnel's end, where a set of wide steps led down to the surface of what had to be the main road.

Darmanin crawled up beside her, and they lay pressed together in the darkness. At the base of the steps was a circular area with high roof—it looked like another waypoint, though only a fraction of the size of the amphitheatre they'd left—with the main highway feeding in from each end. The tunnel they were in emerged halfway between those two points.

And the reason they could see all this ... multiple torches lit the cavernous space, and Arya's stomach knotted at what they illuminated. It looked like a Raider camp; tents set out in strict squares and soldiers standing sentry at each end where the highway entered the cavern. To Arya's trained eye, it looked as if they'd been encamped there for a while; the neat piles of supplies and refuse had a permanent look about them.

But these weren't Dunidae soldiers. They wore uniforms of all black with a snarling grey shadowhound emblazoned over their chests. The barking and snarling came from makeshift pens on the far side of the space, directly opposite the tunnel entrance, where shadowhounds were penned. Arya counted maybe fifty of the creatures.

What if a nazal was here too?

With habit born of constant fear, she checked that her cazaix blade was at her waist, that Darmanin wore his. Reached inside herself to check the threads that bound her to him were muted. Didn't relax until she'd confirmed all three things. Even then, faint panic beat at her. She couldn't put herself in a position where the nazal from Gateport might be able to break into her mind.

Arya's gaze swept the camp again. She saw no sign of a nazal, but that didn't mean anything. If it was the nazal she'd faced that horrific night, it could be controlling the minds of any of the human soldiers below.

"You were right," Darmanin said, barely audible.

She gave a minute shake of her head, leaned over to murmur into his ear, wary of shadowhounds' hearing. "That's not an invading army. Judging from the number of tents, I'd guess a hundred soldiers at most."

"A scouting force?"

Her gaze narrowed. "Maybe. Who's controlling the shadowhounds, do you think, and what are they using them for?"

A tiny shrug. "Do you know whether magic is required, or can they be trained to obey human orders?"

She shook her head. She had no idea. "This doesn't make sense. Ranier suspected there were already wraiths or shadowhounds in the Wraith Forest, attacking Shadeweavers. Yet the rockfall is unbroken, and this camp has been here a while, the shadowhounds penned up."

"It could have been a much larger camp to start with. What if they've been slipping into Dunidaen in small groups, and this is just a staging post? The Nightstalker knows about all the tunnels, official *and* unofficial, remember?"

She muttered an expletive. "Then what are they doing in Dunidaen? Creeping about taking out the occasional Shadeweaver for fun?"

"Preparing," Darmanin said quietly. "Scouting the layout of the foothills and the Wraith Forest, mapping them, identifying the clearest path to march an army. There are miles upon miles of isolated territory for them to operate within. If it were me, I'd be caching supplies of food and weapons, setting up small camps that could be used for supply lines during an invasion."

"Raven's balls." That made a terrible amount of sense. "That's why Ranier hasn't seen any proof of their presence. They're deliberately hiding so nobody figures out what they're up to and quietly taking out any Shadeweaver that stumbles upon them."

Darmanin turned to her, a frown on his face. "Why didn't the Nightstalker use these tunnels before?"

"What do you mean?"

"Nine years ago, when he sent his wraiths and shadowhounds into the Wraith Forest looking for us … he made a hole in the rockfall blocking up the underground road. If he knew about the other tunnels, why didn't he just use those?"

"An excellent question, but one we should ask *after* we've gotten back to Heathrock to warn everyone."

They'd begun inching backwards when movement came from their right, a tall, rangy man coming along the road from the Dunidaen end. He wasn't wearing the same black uniform as the soldiers, instead he wore a motley attire not unlike Shadeweavers. Two shadowhounds trailed him, and they were agitated, snarling and tossing their heads. They had the frantic energy of hounds who'd scented prey but were being restrained from chasing it.

The sentries addressed the new arrival, seeming to grow animated at whatever he told them. The shadowhounds circled their handler restlessly, snarling. Orders were shouted by the sentries, and a couple of soldiers headed for the shadowhound pens.

"This isn't good," Arya murmured.

"Think they might have been patrolling and picked up our scent back at the amphitheatre?" Darmanin asked.

"Be still, just in case…"

One of the loose shadowhounds stopped suddenly and sniffed the air. Then he began snarling viciously. The handler's head came up, looking almost straight at them. He snapped an order. The moment the words left his mouth the two shadowhounds leaped into a run straight at the tunnel entrance. The sound of frenzied barking from the penned shadowhounds grew deafening.

Arya reached out a hand to stop Darmanin as he drew his sword. "If we're seen by the soldiers, they'll know Dunidaen is warned. It might provoke the

Nightstalker to invade sooner, if not immediately, which would be disastrous. Dunidaen isn't prepared."

"We can't outrun shadowhounds, Arya!"

But all she could think of was the possibility of a nazal nearby, of needing to avoid it at all costs. "Let's try. The handlers don't know *what* the hounds have scented, and if they never find it, they won't know we were here." Arya burst into a sprint, hoping he would follow. After another check to ensure her bonds were muted, she drew upon enough magic to create another ball of light, making sure she didn't fall over her own feet in the dark. Darmanin's heavier footsteps pounded behind her.

The cacophony of barking behind them echoed eerily as the two shadowhounds entered the tunnel, growing steadily louder. Arya's heart sank. Her hopes of outrunning them, not high to begin with, were fading. Even so she pushed harder. They burst out into the amphitheatre at a sprint. Behind them, the note of the barking changed pitch.

The shadowhounds had found their prey.

In tacit agreement, she and Darmanin slid to a halt, spinning to see the two shadowhounds emerging from the tunnel after them. Arya did a quick calculation and decided there was no way they'd make it to the other side of the amphitheatre before the creatures were on them. And their pen-mates wouldn't be far behind; they'd have been loosed by now.

"Is a nazal with them?" Darmanin seemed to have come to the same conclusion. His gaze was focused on the oncoming enemy, sword ready, feet lightly placed and ready to move.

She forced down her terror at the thought. No time for fear if she was to survive. "I don't know. Let's hope not."

"Surely we can take on a single nazal?" He risked a quick glance at her, seemingly surprised at her lack of confidence. "You've been learning your magic."

"And what magic have *you* learned since the last time we faced one?" she countered. "Maybe if all five of us were here, we could take one nazal, *if* we were very lucky." Even then ... her confidence faltered. She couldn't risk it.

He huffed a breath of irritation. "We've never required magic to succeed. There's no need to start relying on it now."

"Here they come."

The two monstrous grey shapes raced across the marble floor. Darmanin leaped forward with his cazaix sword flashing. He swept the head off the first creature to reach him. The second leaped, snapping at his neck. He dropped, twisted, and rammed a knife into the creature's throat before rising back to his feet in one graceful movement to return to the ready position.

Arya watched, stunned.

He'd always been a promising fighter, but this Darmanin fought with the skill of an Icefolk warrior. It wasn't going to be enough though. The rest of the shadowhounds were streaming out of the tunnel now. Darmanin turned, dark ichor dripping from his blade, spattering his face and tunic, and lifted an eyebrow. "Planning to help, or continue spectating?"

At his look, her fear receded entirely. She grinned, stepped up to his side and swung her sword. "I was enjoying the show."

His grey eyes darkened, and she winked at him. This time *she* was the one to leap forward and engage the first shadowhounds to reach them. Her cazaix blade slashed, killing two of the creatures leaping for her. But they were quickly surrounded, so many claws and fangs it was hard to get enough space to fight well. She ducked under the next attack, kicked out with a booted foot to send one shadowhound flying, decapitated a second, then spun to face Darmanin. "Get clear!"

In a single movement she sheathed her sword and brought her hands up, summoning all the magic that constantly wanted to explode out of her. She fed it, then brought her hands apart with a roar and sent pulsing electric magic tearing through the shadowhounds around her. It ripped them apart, ichor and gore exploding in an ever-widening circle.

As Arya slowly brought her hands back together, the energy drain was noticeable, like she'd run a full day through the mountains. Her shoulders sagged, legs trembling under her.

But the shadowhounds were all dead.

"Just the basics, huh?" Darmanin spoke into the silence, eyes wide as he took in the carnage strewn across the amphitheatre floor.

"It looks impressive, but it's a very blunt use of our magic." She looked at him, still flushed with the adrenaline from the fight. His eyes glowed with the same feeling. "Nice swordsmanship, by the way."

"Thank you." He sheathed his cazaix blade. "What next?"

"Running was worth a try." Arya looked around, figuring out their next move. "But those soldiers are going to appear any minute and find their shadowhounds all dead. With the element of surprise gone, who knows what the Nightstalker will do."

"I trust your assessment. What do you recommend?"

She glanced up at him, surprised.

"You were a brilliant general for Ravenstrike, Arya. Your mistakes don't change that," he said.

Her heart sank. He was so wrong, and he didn't even know it. Arya wasn't that person anymore. She'd ruined that ability with her recklessness and anger. She faked a casual shrug, and demurred. "I'm not the only clever strategist standing here. What do *you* recommend?"

If he was surprised by her words, he didn't show it. And he didn't even have to think about his answer. "What if we collapse the roof further along the underground road, trapping the scouting force between two falls and stopping them from retreating into Andahar? Then they can't report back our presence, at least not until they're able to dig their way through."

"That's assuming there aren't other tunnels they could use to get around a cave-in." She let out a breath. "But it's worth a try. My magic is strong enough to bring down the roof."

"We can't go back through the shortcut. That means following the main road—we'll need to get *through* the camp somehow and bring down the roof on the other side."

"I'll figure that part out," she said quickly, glancing over her shoulder. They didn't have long. "You'll have to get back to Heathrock as quick as you can."

"*I* have to get back?" His voice turned dangerously quiet.

"I'm going into Andahar. All we found is a scouting force, Dar. Worrying, yes, but not the proof Rorin needs. If you carry back news of what we found, Rorin can use the Raiders to wipe out any creatures already in the Wraith Forest or the foothills and destroy any supply or weapons' caches they've set up. Zaphirdryl and Alletryl can cover miles of ground from the air to help find them. But to mobilise the Dunidae army in the current political environment we need more proof of invasion—timing, numbers, all of it. Those answers will be in Andahar."

"You are a war commander, Arya. *You* are needed to muster the Dunidae army."

"You're forgetting about the bounty on my head." She stepped closer to him. "Dar, *you're* the one that can muster the Dunidae."

His mouth tightened. "And when will we see you again this time, Arya? In another four years? Longer?"

The sounded of running feet sounded faintly, a man's voice calling an order that sounded like 'move faster.' Arya glanced at the tunnel entrance the shadowhounds had emerged from. The soldiers were almost on them. "I will bring back news of whatever I find. My word on it, Dar."

His gaze searched hers, as if seeking some sign of whether he could trust her. In the end he nodded, "Then I will do everything I can to help Dunidae prepare. My word on it."

He looked so earnest. So sincere. A face that was too fierce, too hard, to be truly handsome, but one that held so much when you knew what to look for. Arya shook herself, stepped away. "Be safe, Dar."

"And you, Arya Ravenstrike."

He turned and was gone.

***

Arya ran, following the underground road away from Dunidaen and not looking back. It wound multiple times under the mountain before reaching the next waypoint, and she understood quickly why a shortcut had been chiselled from the rock. The sharp tang of dog excrement on the air warned her first. Then she finally rounded a corner to the orange glow from the torchlit waypoint they'd spied upon earlier.

Momentum carried her a few steps, but then fear closed over her like a vice. Without thinking, she backed up and pressed herself against the shadows of the wall, heart pounding, sweat slicking her skin. If a nazal was with this scouting force, surely it would have showed itself by now. Or it would be among the soldiers following the shadowhounds into the amphitheatre.

But what if it wasn't?

Shit. Shit. Shit. Arya *knew* she had to move. Knew she had a limited amount of time until at least some of the pursuing soldiers returned to their camp and saw her here. But she was trapped in place by her fear. She couldn't risk it, couldn't risk the nazal breaking into her mind and learning—

Five soldiers emerged from the waypoint at a steady lope, swords drawn, presumably having been dispatched in support of their comrades. Before Arya could figure out what to do, the third one along spotted her pressed against the wall.

Shit.

The soldier's shout of alarm was out of his mouth before Arya could launch herself off the wall and drive her sword into his chest. After that it was four on one, and her panic vanished in the desperate clash of blades. They were making too much noise, which meant more soldiers would be coming, ruining the element of surprise she'd been hoping for.

Deciding on the fly, she killed the man closest to her in a frantic flurry of blows, then ducked under the next blade swinging at her neck, spun away, and sprinted towards their camp. They gave chase, bellowing to alert their fellow soldiers.

Arya kept moving in a flat-out sprint, breath sawing in her chest, exhaustion tugging at her limbs. She had to get through to the other side. Once she did that, she'd be okay.

And then one of her pursuers tackled her from behind. They hit the ground, rolling. Arya drove a knee into his groin, shoved him off her, and scrambled to her feet and reached for her fallen sword. More soldiers were swarming, though there didn't seem to be many more left in the camp. She killed two more before she could get free again and then she was running desperately. On reaching the other side, she ran several metres further along the dark road, then spun back and drew her hands together.

She drew a deep breath in, calling roughly, bluntly, on the well of power inside her. Soldiers were close behind, swords drawn, shouting. She gritted her teeth, pulling on more and more power, dredging up every scrap she had left.

And then she let her magic out.

Blue-sparking energy exploded towards the ceiling, crashing into it with a deafening roar. A cracking sound cut through the tunnel. Shards of rock began raining down. The shouts of challenge turned to shouts of fear and the soldiers began scrambling backwards in a panic.

A breath later, the whole thing came down. Falling rock and sediment crashed to the floor, forcing Arya backwards, coughing, dust filling her lungs. Exhausted and dazed, she stared at the enormous pile of rubble now filling the tunnel. Her chest heaved as she gulped in air, and her hands shook with exertion.

Distantly, one of the muted threads inside her shivered with awareness. The Nightstalker.

With instinct born of terror she frantically focused on muting it, swallowing it, stifling it until she could feel it no more. Then she sagged against the nearest wall. A wave of worry swept through her mind from Elendryl. *"Okay?"*

"I'm all right," she soothed, then let him see in her mind what she'd done. Satisfaction filled him. *"Now?"* he asked.

Arya took a deep, steadying breath, then dragged herself off the wall. Everything ached, her legs swayed, but she couldn't stay here. *"Now we go to Andahar."*

Chapter 10

Arya arrived at an impressive stone archway denoting the exit from the underground road four days later. It was night and darkness shrouded what was beyond the archway, but she could hear the melodic patter of heavy rain. There were no signs of soldiers or a camp nearby, so she decided to shelter inside the tunnel until dawn, when she could get a better idea of what lay beyond. Her body was exhausted, and as soon as she found a niche in the wall hidden from casual sight of anyone traversing the road, she curled up and fell asleep.

Elendryl's voice in her head woke her some hours later. *"Coming."*

"Where are you?"

He sent an image of foothills stretching out from the snowy peaks of the Diamondfang, then showed her a distant image of the exterior of the stone archway she'd reached the previous night.

"Don't come down here," she warned. *"You can't afford anyone in Andahar seeing you. And we don't know if their army has watchtowers or guard posts along the border."*

A snort told her what he thought of that, but he followed it up with a reluctant. *"Hide."*

"The Nightstalker and his nazal can't know I'm in Andahar, and if anyone sees a wyvern flying around, he'll know fast. Will you stay close and hidden in the foothills in case I need you?"

Frustration seethed from him. Elendryl was becoming less and less comfortable with her insistence on hiding him—or at least, that hiding him meant he couldn't accompany her. For the past four years, they'd rarely needed to be separated. *"Not long!"* he instructed.

Arya stood and stretched, then stilled.

Unlike the entry from Dunidaen, this archway was marble, with veins of gold running through the ivory surface that picked up the morning sunlight and sent it scattering in all directions. Several stories high, it was a magnificent feat of architecture. Exquisitely rendered wyverns were carved into each side of the archway, their wings spreading out to either side, both greeting and challenging anyone entering Andahar. Beautiful scrollwork decorated the top of the arch; on this one the words *Unleash the Storm* were etched out in thousands of tiny sapphires. Arya recognised the hand of an Inkweaver artist in the wyvern carvings and wished Essa were here to see this with her. Her friend would have been fascinated.

"Unleash the storm," she murmured, testing it out on her tongue. The words shivered through her with a tease of power. "Arya Stormrider."

"*Ours,*" Elendryl sent with a burst of warmth and pride.

"*We can't claim it.*" Arya said, ignoring the disappointment that stirred deep down. "*It's not safe.*"

Sharp disagreement from her wyvern, who then left her thoughts with a huff.

Shaking herself out of her reverie, she took one last admiring look at the archway, then stepped through and into Andahar proper. There she stopped again, trained gaze scanning her surrounds for any potential danger.

The area was deserted.

The road continued, weathered and potholed from years of disuse. Behind her, and to the north and south, the foothills and peaks of the Diamondfang reared majestically. Low foothills rose to either side of the road as far as she could see, limiting her vision of what lay beyond. "*Elendryl, any signs of danger?*"

A swift dissent, then a quick flash of the landscape from his eyes. He was flying high so as not to be seen, but she couldn't see any trace of encampments, or even guards, posted in the hills lining the road. "*Thank you.*"

Within a half hour, the incline to either side of the road began to recede, and then the road curved, and as she rounded it, the plains of Andahar lay spread out before her.

All she could see was rolling emerald plains dotted with lakes, rivers, and streams that glittered in the sunlight. The road wound through the plains until it reached a village in the distance—buildings huddled around the edge of a lake, tendrils of smoke curling into the blue sky above. Arya hadn't expected to be so affected by the sight. It seemed almost as if everything was brighter, somehow. The anxious knot that had been curled in her chest for days loosened, her breath coming easier, a little more energy in her step.

A hint of curiosity came from Elendryl. She shared an image of what she was seeing. "*If the Nightstalker is planning an invasion soon, he hasn't moved his army to the border yet.*" There was no sign of a soldier encampment anywhere. Relief shimmered through her. That meant Dunidaen had time.

"*Good.*"

"*It's coming, though.*" Deep in her bones, she knew it. "*I have to keep going, Elendryl, find out what I can of his plans.*" She hesitated. "*Much more distance and we won't be able to communicate directly.*" They'd tested this over the past years. While no matter how far apart they were, their sense of each other never vanished, their ability to communicate coherently faded with distance.

"*Fine.*"

He wasn't happy, and she wasn't either. Elendryl made her feel safe, always. She didn't fancy a long trek into the unknown without him watching her back. "*While I'm gone, will you scout the border along the foothills to see whether he is gathering his army somewhere else?*"

He sent a more cheerful assent; happy to have something to do.

"*Farewell, my friend. I will be as quick as I can.*"

"*Mine.*" He sent back with the equivalent of a mental hug.

Taking a deep breath, Arya set off down the road.

She reckoned she could make that village by nightfall.

***

It turned out the village wasn't on the main road, which curled away to the south before reaching it. A signpost stood where a wide dirt track diverged in the direction of the village. A start of surprise went through Arya at recognising the writing carved into the wood. So, the Andahari spoke—or at least wrote—in Dunidae. She huffed a laugh at herself. Perhaps it was the other way around.

In any case, the sign pointed to a place called Wain's Anchor, which she assumed was the village. Shrugging, she turned off to follow the track. Though she was wary of testing whether her Dunidae coin would work, she was keen for a bed with a roof and a hot meal after days under the mountains. Not to mention the supplies in her pack were already running low. If her money drew too much attention, Elendryl would have her away from Andahar and over the Diamondfang before anyone could come looking for her.

The dirt road followed the southern banks of a swift-flowing river, and the late afternoon air was alive with the croaking of frogs and rustling of the breeze through thick reeds lining the shore. Gleeful shouts from behind made Arya turn. A small boat, its sails billowing, raced along the river. Three children—fourteen or fifteen at a guess—manned the boat with casual skill. She watched them until the boat disappeared out of sight around a bend, heart heavy.

Arya reached the town as the sun settled low on the horizon. Its fading orange glow illuminated a myriad of patchwork roofs. An inn stood on the main road through the town, as she'd hoped, the creaking sign out front naming it The River Rose. Warm light and chatter spilled from its open windows and patrons crowded the large room beyond the open doors.

Before going inside, Arya suppressed her magic as deep as she could, ensuring it wouldn't make her eyes glow. Other than that, her travel-worn state and messy hair would hopefully do enough to mask anything that revealed her as a magic-wielder. Once satisfied, Arya entered and weaved her way through to an empty stool at the bar, where she sat gratefully, dropping her pack to the ground.

Unsurprisingly for a small town, the barman instantly recognised her as a stranger, but when he came over, he wore a welcoming smile. He was rotund, middle-aged, with an unruly thatch of greying brown hair and twinkling blue eyes that matched his smile. "Welcome to Wain's Anchor and The River Rose, visitor. Our home and hearth are yours."

Arya cleared her throat, taken aback not so much by what must be a formal greeting, but the sincerity with which it was said. "Thank you."

"What can I get you? A cold ale to start, I think—you look as if you've been walking a ways."

She matched his friendly smile. "A cold ale would be wonderful. I'd also like a room for the night if you have one?"

"Ale coming right up," he promised. "And I'll have my wife bring you a room key. Would you like something to eat? Our cook is famous for his fish stew, and we've got a batch simmering on the cookfire. There's also some cold mutton and freshly baked bread with herb butter. Or a beef pie."

"The stew sounds great," Arya said, curious about how this cook's famous stew compared to Peemla's, one of Arya's favourite meals.

"Excellent choice. Won't be long." He winked and bustled off.

It was stuffy in the crowded inn, and she was already hot from walking all day, so she shrugged off her jacket and pushed up the sleeves of her shirt. The barman returned with a frothing pint of ale, the condensation on the glass telling her it was as cold as she'd been hoping for. The man's gaze lowered as he made sure the mug didn't spill when he handed it to her, but when Arya took it from him, he seemed to freeze, eyes widening before flicking up to her face, startlement written in their depths.

"Something wrong?" she asked.

He shook off the odd expression, replacing it with an easy smile. "Curious, is all. I've not seen you here before, and I have a pretty good memory for faces." He stuck out a hand. "I'm Vanil."

"Arya." She approved of his firm but not challenging grip. "And you're right. I'm just passing through."

"If you need anything while you're in town, just ask my wife or me. We'd be happy to help."

"I appreciate that," she said, touched by his friendliness. "But if your fish stew is as good as you say, I'll be one contented traveller." Anxiety knotted her stomach as she braced herself to show her Dunidae coin. "How much for the ale and the food?"

Vanil waved a hand. "We look after our guests in the Riverlands. This is your first night in Wain's Anchor, and so your drinks and meal are on the house."

"I appreciate that, Vanil. Thank you," Arya said in gratitude.

He left to tend the busy bar, and Arya savoured the cool, bitter taste of her ale. She was barely a third of the way through when a woman appeared to place a trencher of thick stew in front of Arya.

"I'm Dina, Vanil's wife," she said with the same welcoming air as her husband. No wonder this inn was so popular. "I hope you like the stew. If you need anything else, please don't hesitate to ask."

Arya ate hungrily, devouring every bite and then wiping up the remnants with crusty bread. It was *almost* as good as Peemla's. Vanil wordlessly placed another pint at her arm when he noticed she'd finished her first glass, but otherwise left her in peace to eat. A group of musicians arrived to scattered cheers from the inn's patrons and set themselves up in a corner. Their merry tunes permeated the crowded bar. A few customers were moved to dance.

The music made Arya think of Chiarn. Despite his fear, he'd eventually have to leave the citadel to find his wyvern. It wasn't something he could ignore forever. But thinking of him only made her frustrated and anxious, so she turned her attention to the minstrels, trying to let the music relax her.

It had been so long since she'd experienced a moment of simple normality like this. Her time with the Etherean had been all about learning her magic and ignoring or avoiding the elder's increasingly pointed comments about her future, and with the Icefolk she'd joined their warrior training and regular hunts with a single-minded focus that had allowed her to forget about all her grief and guilt and fear.

Arya sat on her ale for hours into the night, listening to the chatter around her. None spoke of war. It was all crops and seasons and village gossip. Eventually, after Vanil's refills began making her head fuzzy, she waved to Dina and asked to be shown to her room. A burst of raucous laughter rang out as Dina led her upstairs and down a narrow hall to a room at the end.

"I hope this will do," Dina said, a note of anxiety in her voice. "It's the best room we have. There are fresh sheets on the bed, and my lads have warm water waiting for you in the bathing room—second door to your left."

Arya was taken aback. These were strangers, yet they were treating her like an honoured guest. But then Tomin and his family hadn't been all that different in Taskari, she recalled. Perhaps it was the way of Andahari folk. She thanked Dina, then dropped her pack on a chair and headed straight for the bathing room. It was small, with only two barrels, but steam curled from one of them. Sighing in delight, Arya undressed and climbed in, revelling in the warm water.

Finally, skin pruning, she clambered out, realising there were no towels at the same time as the door opened and Dina appeared with a stack of them. "I'm so sorry, I forgot to make sure there were fresh towels for—"

The woman stopped when her gaze fell on Arya, eyes widening. Arya had never been bothered by nakedness; any modesty that had once existed had vanished after becoming a soldier at fifteen, but something in Dina's look made her reach for one of the towels and begin vigorously drying herself. "Thanks so much. I really appreciate it, Dina."

"Sleep well, Arya. We'll make sure to have a hearty breakfast ready for you in the morning."

Dina left with a wave and warm smile as if nothing had happened and Arya shook her head. Weariness and ale combined were making her see things. As soon as she was dry, she headed back to her room and collapsed on the bed, into blissful sleep.

***

Bright rays of sunshine streaming through the window awoke Arya the next morning, and she rose with a start. It was later than she liked. She'd wanted to get on the road early, aiming to reach a bigger town—hopefully one with a barracks—where she could listen to the soldiers' gossip and hopefully learn what she needed. But she couldn't deny it felt good to have had a full, restful night's sleep. She hadn't had one of those in three years.

Downstairs, Vanil was busy polishing the bar top and Dina swept the floors, the two working in companionable silence. A group of men, dock workers, Arya guessed from their look, enjoyed breakfast at a table by the door, but otherwise the inn was empty. When Vanil saw Arya appear, he waved, but his wife spoke first. "Take a seat, Arya, and I'll get you some breakfast."

Arya headed for a stool at the bar, stomach growling in anticipation, but one of the farmers called out to her. "Morning, visitor. Our home and hearth are yours. Would you like to sit with us? Breakfast doesn't taste half as good when you eat it alone."

"I can promise they won't bite." Vanil told her with a chuckle. "But I'd advise you to protect your bacon ... they're not above thievery."

"We'd never!" the man protested, before turning back to Arya. "If it helps, I'll swear an oath not to steal your bacon."

Arya chuckled and went over. "Appreciate you all including me. My name's Arya."

"I'm Garvelin." The man leaned over to pull out the empty chair near him. He was burly, with fair skin and a thick sandy beard. "My business runs out of Wain's Anchor. These are my sons, Ventin and Dokarin." He pointed to two younger men who were his mirror images. "And this crusty sailor is a river trader, and my cousin."

"Rengalin." The trader offered his hand; he seemed more reserved than Garvelin, pale brown eyes studying her as they shook hands. He looked about Garvelin's age, with the same sandy blonde hair, and she could see a faint family resemblance in their features.

"Here you go, Arya. Fresh guava juice." Vanil placed a tall glass of pink liquid before her, then dropped into the remaining empty seat at the table.

Arya eyed the drink. What exactly was a guava? Shrugging, she lifted the glass and took a sip. Sweet tartness flooded her tongue.

"Vanil and I have been friends for years." Garvelin started talking again. "I make sure my boys offload his produce from the barges first so it's fresh, and in return we get a free breakfast now and then."

"Father likes to escape mother's cooking as often as possible." Ventin and his brother shared a smirk.

"Where are you heading, Arya?" Rengalin asked.

"I don't have a particular destination in mind," she said. "But I'm heading west."

Ventin frowned. "Not as far as Darkclaw Deep?"

"You don't want to be going to the Nightstalker's stronghold, surely," Garvelin added.

Arya took another sip of juice to give herself a moment to think. She'd never heard of Darkclaw Deep, but if it was the Nightstalker's stronghold, it might be the best place to go if her goal was to understand his invasion plans better. "I know of it, of course, but I've never been there." She gave a casual shrug, then asked carefully, trying to learn more. "It's as dangerous as they say, then?"

"More so. The Nightstalker is often away, but it's full of his soldiers. Even look at one of them the wrong way, and you'll find yourself in the cells there before you can blink," Rengalin answered, a dark look clouding his face.

Arya smiled to lighten the atmosphere. "I'll make sure not to look sideways at any of the soldiers, then. And don't worry, I won't linger. Just passing through."

Garvelin, Vanil, and Rengalin shared a look that Arya couldn't interpret. Instinct prickled at the base of her neck; something was going on here that she was missing. Or maybe she'd said something wrong in her ignorance.

"I can take you some of the way if you like," Rengalin said. "I'm sailing this morning for Murton, which is just east of Darkclaw Deep and the trading post there."

Arya hesitated. "I'm not sure I'd have enough money for passage that far, though I am grateful for your offer."

"Rengalin won't charge you," Garvelin said. "He owes me a debt, and he can repay it by giving you passage to Murton."

"I wasn't going to charge her anyway." Rengalin smiled a little. "But if I get to discharge my debt then all the better."

Arya's unease deepened. This was more than just warm hospitality. "I don't understand. Why would you give me free passage?"

Rengalin shrugged. "We take care of first-time visitors here in the Riverlands. Besides, I'm going to Murton anyway. Having you on board isn't going to cost me any extra."

"Dokarin and I could go too, father," Ventin said. "We could pick up the supplies we need to fix the storehouse roof. You know the merchants in Murton have the Horselord wood we'll need."

"I don't want you boys going so close to Darkclaw Deep." Garvelin's mouth tightened. "Our distance from the capital is your greatest protection from the conscription laws."

Arya's eyebrows shot upwards. "*Forced* conscription?" As soon as the words were out, she regretted them, especially at the reaction they caused.

"Where are you from that you haven't heard of the Nightstalker's conscription laws?" Ventin asked incredulously. "All boys and girls over sixteen are liable to be taken."

"And all so he can subdue his own people and invade a country that has done nothing to us," Garvelin spat.

"Hush friend, you know he has spies everywhere," Rengalin warned, eyes glancing around the tavern. "In the Riverlands more so than anywhere."

Fortunately, the mention of spies distracted them from Arya's misstep, and a cloud of fear descended over the table. Awkward silence fell until Dina bustled over with a plate of crispy bacon, sausages, and whipped eggs. The talk resumed, centring around Garvelin's business. Rengalin promised to place an order for the wood he wanted in Murton and Ventin began writing out the dimensions he needed.

Eventually, the men rose.

"I plan to leave in an hour, Arya," Rengalin said. "If you decide to accept my offer, mine is the green boat at the docks."

"Goodbye, Arya," Garvelin said, lingering as if reluctant to leave. "We are honoured to have met you. May the waters you travel always be calm."

"Thank you," she said, hoping there wasn't a formal response required. "I am glad to have met you."

"Bye, Arya." Ventin tipped his hat before following his father out. Dokarin joined him, giving Arya a jaunty wave in farewell.

Arya was left alone at the breakfast table, tossing up whether she should accept Rengalin's offer. A tremor of bone-deep fear shivered through her at the idea of going so close to the Nightstalker. If he caught her ... a surge of terror twisted her stomach so sharply she couldn't swallow her next bite. She fought it. Logically, he had no way of knowing where she was, as long as she didn't use magic near him or his nazal. And Rengalin had implied he might not even be there. As her hands began trembling, she moved them under the table, curling them into fists.

Protecting Rorin, her home and family in Dunidaen, that was just as important to her as keeping her secret hidden. She had to stop letting her fear trap her into inaction.

The seat of the Nightstalker was where she'd have the greatest chance of getting the information she needed. Trading posts were full of merchants and travellers who loved to talk. And there were guaranteed to be soldiers stationed there. If she found their favourite drinking holes, listening in on their chatter should tell her what she needed to know. Not to mention the anonymity of a larger city. It would be far quicker and safer than hiking from village to village until she picked up enough information to take home and risking someone reporting her presence.

If Rengalin meant her harm, she had enough magic and fighting skill to defend herself. And despite how oddly Vanil, Garvelin, and Rengalin had behaved toward her, she'd sensed no malicious intent in them. She would go to Darkclaw Deep with Rengalin.

Decision made, Arya uncurled her hands, took a deep breath, and continued eating, trying not to think about how close to the Nightstalker she was going to get.

And what she was risking by doing it.

Chapter 11

Arya travelled west with Rengalin for eight days. She spent most of her time sitting at the prow, watching the Riverlands flow past. Smaller craft shot by constantly, careening at a reckless pace. Larger barges trundled along, heavily laden with trading goods or passengers. Towns lined both sides of the river at regular intervals, and each had extensive docks to house the constant boat traffic. She kept a wary eye on Rengalin, but apart from sleeping on the boat each night rather than taking a room at an inn at the towns they docked near—which she thought odd—he did or said nothing untoward.

The riverfolk were Tomin's people and travelling through his home made Arya think of the Andahari community on Taskari. None of the missives the Icefolk queen received from Khadini had mentioned trouble, so she assumed Kulan hadn't begun his rebellion against the emperor yet. But each time her thoughts drifted to Kulan she instantly stopped herself and focused on something else; often getting up and walking around the deck or helping the crew to distract herself. Sometimes it worked. Too often it didn't.

A thick fog descended on the seventh day out, and for the first time Arya had to shrug her jacket on. As they were casting off, a young woman came running up to the dock, leaning down to murmur something in Rengalin's ear. A troubled look crossed his face, but he said nothing, and didn't so much as glance in Arya's direction. The fog cleared by mid-morning and the hazy outline of mountains was visible on the western horizon.

"The Horn," Rengalin said. He sounded cheerful, despite whatever news he'd been given that morning. Arya hadn't failed to notice his gaze scanning the banks far more often than usual though. "We'll be in Murton by tomorrow. Then you'll have only a couple of days' hike to Darkclaw."

"The Horn?" she asked without thinking.

Rengalin gave her an odd look. "The horn-shaped mountain range that bisects the middle of Andahar. Darkclaw Deep sits on its eastern face, poised over the Horn River, the only passage through the mountains."

"Right." She nodded briskly, like she'd already known that, but he was still looking at her oddly, so she gambled on a guess. "I've heard that the Nightstalker charges expensive tolls to anyone passing through Darkclaw into the Horn."

Rengalin glowered, and her shoulders unclenched. "It's robbery, what he charges, and all just to fund his army, too. War with the marshfolk is never-ending; he'll never subdue them entirely, but he keeps trying anyway."

Arya didn't let on her interest, but it was piqued, nonetheless. The Nightstalker was already involved in some kind of war? Could that be why he'd held off so long invading Dunidaen? She wished she could think of some innocuous way to ask Rengalin more about it.

The outline of the Horn grew clearer as they sailed. The mountains didn't reach anywhere near as high as the Diamondfang, but they were imposing enough, dark and brooding. Just before reaching Murton, the river widened into a picturesque lake, with the big town spread out along its southern shoreline. Open plains surrounded the lake in all other directions.

While his crew tied up at one of the jetties, Rengalin turned to her with a smile. "I must be off to hire workers to help me and the lads unload. I suppose it's time for us to part ways. I hope you have enjoyed the trip, Arya."

"I did, and I am very grateful to you for bringing me this far."

"There's plenty of daylight left, so I recommend you get straight on the road to Darkclaw. No point lingering in town." He smiled, but there was something of a warning in his eyes. "If you ever need to get back east, look me up. I'd be happy to take you with me. Good luck, Arya. May the waters you travel always be calm."

"And you, Rengalin." She smiled, but wondered at his words. Was he being helpful, or did he not want her lingering in Murton for some reason?

He tipped his hat, then strode off, calling out to the huddle of men and women gathered outside one of the warehouses waiting for work. Arya hefted her pack and walked along the pier, merging into the busy path running along the banks. A short walk brought her to the main street heading into the town. Rengalin's parting words aside, she'd already decided to keep going. She was wary of trying her foreign coin in a place so close to the Nightstalker's seat. Besides, it was nagging at her that she'd been in Andahar almost two weeks with nothing to show for it.

She couldn't fail the people she loved again.

Fear surged so strongly in Arya at that thought that it dispelled any notion of staying in Murton. It took her some time to navigate the packed streets, but eventually she found the western exit and passed through the gates onto a road bound west. A signpost confirmed it led to Darkclaw Deep.

Not far out of the town, a troop of twenty black-clad soldiers galloped past, heading towards Murton. She instinctively lowered her head, focusing her gaze on the ground. A peek from the corner of her eye showed other travellers on the road doing the same. Fear shivered through her and she instinctively reached for Elendryl. They were too far away now for direct communication, but she could feel him nestled there in the back of her mind. If something went wrong with either of them, the other would sense it. Arya allowed that to reassure her.

"Excuse me?" A voice called out behind Arya.

She turned, breaking abruptly from her thoughts. The soldiers were well into the distance, and she caught a flash of blonde hair as a man dodged around a group of farmers behind her. He was tall and broad-shouldered, and she put him no older than his early thirties. He didn't wear any visible weapons, but even so, her hand drifted towards the hilt of her sword. "Something wrong?" she asked, remembering how friendly everyone seemed to be in the Riverlands and trying to keep the edge of suspicion from her voice.

"You're Arya?" he asked, not out of breath despite his quick pace.

"Who's asking?" she said warily.

"My name is Niallin. I'm a friend of Rengalin's. My home and hearth are yours." He bowed his head. "Rengalin mentioned you were heading west and asked if I would accompany you since I'm heading that way."

Raven's balls, these people! She scowled. "Why would he do that?"

"He said you planned to cross the Horn, but that you'd never been through Darkclaw fortress before. I've been back and forth multiple times so I can show you the way."

Arya lifted an eyebrow. She felt no threat, but this was getting ridiculous. The riverfolk might be friendly and helpful by nature, but that's not what this was. "And how do I know that you're really Rengalin's friend?"

He paused; she got the impression he was sizing her up. "You *don't* know. But as you can see, I am unarmed, and I give you my word that I mean you no harm." He grinned. "Rengalin thinks I'm doing him a favour, but between you and me, I go a bit spare on the road without company. I'm a talker, as you'll find out."

Arya snorted. She wasn't buying an inch of his story. If nothing else, Niallin's appearance confirmed that her suspicions about her overly friendly reception in Wain's Anchor were right. She waited until the group of farmers passed, shooting them curious looks, before demanding, "What is going on?"

"What do you mean?"

She crossed her arms. "Why all the help for a stranger none of you know anything about? Nobody is that helpful. Or trusting."

Niallin shrugged. "Arya, I'm going in the same direction as you are, and I'm offering company since you haven't travelled this road before. It's up to you whether you accept it. If not, we'll part ways now, and I'll travel on ahead of you, so you can be confident I'm not following you."

If he did that, she'd never know why Rengalin had asked him to help. And her instincts were quiet, so whatever the two men were about, she was confident enough that they didn't mean her harm. At least not yet. And if she travelled with Niallin, it would ensure she didn't get delayed or lost on her journey.

So, she capitulated. "I prefer company too, as it happens. Shall we?"

"Great." He fell into step beside her. "I tell you what, the timing of our departure was fortunate, Arya. I suppose you saw that unit of Nightblades heading for Murton?"

Nightblades. She guessed that was what the Nightstalker's soldiers were called. "I did."

"That's the third lot to arrive since yesterday. Rumour is, they're looking for someone."

A ripple of instinctive fear went down her spine, even though it would be impossible for the Nightstalker to know she was in Andahar, let alone Murton. "Who?"

"Could be anyone. Most likely a conscript who's escaped. That's my guess, anyway." He gave a mock shudder. "Not a good time to be in Murton though." He smiled then, shaking off any unease, and turned the smile on her. "Not to pry, but can I ask what takes you to Darkclaw? I've got family in Navaria, on the border of Horselord territory, so I'm heading there to visit."

Horselord. Marshfolk. Riverfolk. Arya's curiosity wanted to know what all these terms actually meant, but she didn't dare ask. "I've never been beyond the Horn, so I'm exploring," she said, mostly truthfully. "Are you a river trader like Rengalin?"

"Something like that. We've known each other since childhood."

Niallin *did* prove to be a talker, and he kept their conversation going with ease. Arya was glad of it, despite her suspicions. She always felt better when others were around. Too much time alone with her thoughts always left her feeling flat and drained.

They camped overnight at an area that seemed to be designated for travellers to do so; with a latrine pit dug a distance away, and fresh water available at a bubbling stream the road had been following a while. There seemed to be two distinct groupings of people making use of the space, though, leaving a clear space between them, which she found odd. But the presence of other travellers left Arya feeling safe enough to get a few hours restless sleep.

Niallin started talking again the moment they rose the next morning. "More arwein moving around than usual," he commented, gaze on those that had made camp on the opposite side of the clearing.

Raven's balls. More bloody words she didn't understand. She couldn't tell the difference between those he called arwein and the travellers she and Niallin had camped near. "Why do you think that is?" she asked, hoping his answer might give her more context.

He shrugged as they started walking. "Avoiding the Nightblade conscription parties would be my guess." He eyed her. "That wouldn't be what you're doing, is it?"

Good. That topic gave her an in. "Would I tell you if I was?" She lifted an eyebrow. "I got the impression Rengalin was worried that the introduction of conscription meant the Nightstalker might intend to invade Dunidaen, though I haven't seen any signs of his army in the east."

"We *are* worried. It is bad enough our king keeps us embroiled in a constant civil war with the marshfolk. Four decades and he hasn't been able to subdue them, yet he keeps sending soldiers there to be killed. And now to think he wants to use more of us as fodder in a war with another country who hasn't done anything to us." He shook his head sadly.

"Who's we?"

He smiled. "Rengalin and I."

She huffed a breath. She'd never met such a master of polite and friendly evasiveness. "And what is it exactly that makes you worried he's planning an invasion now?"

"I was just making idle conversation, Arya."

"No, you weren't," she said sharply.

"You're overthinking it." He gave an easy smile. "But I apologise if it felt like I was pushing. Like I said, I'm a talker. It can get irritating. I've been told this many times. Rengalin says its why I remain unmarried."

He was good, but she still didn't buy it. And she was growing increasingly irritated that he seemed to expect her to. As if he thought she was a fool. Still, she dropped it for now. She'd made some progress, and they still had plenty of travel time left for her to keep working on him.

***

Arya's first sight of Darkclaw Deep came three days into their journey. For most of the morning they'd been heading up a low valley wall, and now the road crested it before winding down into a forested plain sprawled at the foothills of the Horn.

Darkclaw sat high above the plain, majestic and grim and imposing. It was a tiered stone castle of many levels split across opposite mountainsides. Suspended mid-way up was a stone bridge that joined the two sections of the castle. Below the bridge, in the gap between the mountains, ran a white-watered river, deep and swift, flowing down into a lake in the foothills north of the keep. The fortress looked as ancient as time. She slowed to stare up at it, open-mouthed.

"First time you've seen Darkclaw?" Niallin asked.

"It's impressive."

"Intimidating is a better word. And it was designed to be that way." His tone was carefully neutral. "The southern side of the fortress houses the trading post, toll booth, and a small city. The northern side is the seat of the Nightstalker."

"And this road will take us there?" She tried to hide the shiver of dread she felt. Maybe this was a terrible idea. The information she sought could probably be found if she went back to Murton instead of getting so close to the Nightstalker. Risking him capturing her.

"Yes. If we stay on this road, it leads through the forest you see ahead, then up to Darkclaw and through the trading post before continuing west through the Horn and out the other side into Horselord territory, or the Marshlands if you head south. The Nightstalker is away in the Marshlands at the moment, so you picked a good time to travel through."

She turned with an arched eyebrow. "How do you know that?"

"Heard some Nightblades talking in Murton. It pays to pick up information like that if you want to stay safe travelling." He gave her a slightly pointed look. "As I assume an experienced traveller like yourself already knows."

"My preferred method is to steer clear of Nightblades," she said dryly.

"Right you are." He hefted his pack, and they started walking again.

Arya tried probing for more as they set off once again. "Who held Darkclaw Deep before the Nightstalker? In Dunidaen, we know he came to power after a coup, but little more than that."

"House Stormrider, the true rulers of Andahar. They didn't spend much time there, though."

"Why?" she asked curiously.

He threw her an expressionless glance. "There are many nicer places in Andahar to live. They had their seat in..." He trailed off, an odd expression crossing his face, as if he couldn't quite grasp what he'd meant to say.

"Were they good rulers?"

He shrugged. "I was born after the last Stormrider king died, so I can't tell you from my experience. No ruler is ever perfect, but my father said they ruled with a firm and fair hand, and their Sky Lord *caidre* ensured Andahar prospered. Many people long for their return."

"If that's so, why hasn't anyone challenged the Nightstalker?"

"He's too powerful." Niallin shrugged. "The Sky Lords are long gone, and nobody else has the strength or magic to face the Nightstalker and win. The marshfolk are only able to resist his subjugation because they have vicious fighters and the advantage of hostile territory that even Xaphistryl can't overcome. But they're not strong enough to face him outside of the Marshlands. The Nightstalker has built a powerful army, led by dark creatures he created with his twisted magic. They are almost as dangerous as he is, and his army is battle tested from his ongoing war with the marshfolk."

Arya looked away. Niallin's words echoed what she'd always thought so profoundly that she didn't want to risk him seeing it on her face. What would her chances truly be against such a powerful Sky Lord? Especially when he had entrenched his rule so deeply.

What she *could* do was try to stop his influence spreading beyond Andahar. Niallin had skilfully avoided all her attempts to learn about the status of the Nightstalker's army or his invasion plans, so either he didn't know or was unwilling to tell her. But time in Darkclaw should tell her what she needed to know. She could be home by Winterfest if she moved quickly enough.

Niallin broke the silence. "You're thinking hard."

They were within the forest now, the trees blocking their sight of the mountains and fortress ahead. "I'm just thinking about the next part of my journey."

"And?"

She snorted. "You decide to be honest with me about your real intentions, Niallin, and maybe I'll think about telling you mine."

"Arya, I—"

"Save it." She lifted a hand to cut him off. "I'm not an idiot. I know there's more behind you and Rengalin helping me, and to be honest, it's really pissing me off that you think I'm stupid enough to believe otherwise."

His eyebrows shot upward in surprise. "I'm sorry that you..."

Niallin trailed off as his attention was caught by a large group ahead, heading towards them. They'd just turned a corner into a long section of straight road, forest clinging to the edges.

Arya counted about thirty in the group, almost all young women and men; a couple of them children, the oldest around Arya's age. They walked in neat rows, surrounded by eight Nightblades. All carried whips, with swords sheathed at their hips. A shudder went through her as memories of the Khadini pit mine roused.

"Something wrong?" she asked. Her companion's face had gone tight with anger, and his hands were curled into white-knuckled fists. "Who are the prisoners?"

"Conscripts being taken to the barracks north of Murton; that's where basic training takes place." He gritted out the words. "They've been removed from their homes in the west to join the Nightstalker's army. Once they've finished training, they'll be sent to the staging grounds in the east before being used as fodder against the Dunidae."

What?

"So, he *is* planning an invasion?" she asked sharply. "When?"

"Your guess is as good as mine." Niallin hadn't torn his gaze from the oncoming group. "He's been gathering recruits for months. There are thousands gathered near Murton. And it's the wrong side of the Horn for them to be gathering for an offensive in the Marshlands."

"You didn't mention that before. Why?"

He finally turned to her. "Why are you so interested?"

Arya swore and studied the oncoming group. They'd come close enough that she could see the ragged state the conscripts were in. A soldier swung his whip at a boy lagging behind, and it cracked as it licked across the boy's shoulders. He fell to the ground with a cry of pain and burst into tears, his sobs heartrending. He looked no more than ten or eleven years old.

Just a small child. A *boy*. No different from—

Arya's breathing started coming faster as white-hot fury stirred.

The Nightblade grabbed the boy's ear to yank him back to his feet. The boy stumbled, fell again, and the soldier lifted his whip with a shout of anger. One of the older conscripts, a young woman Arya's age, leaped to the boy's defence. The soldier pivoted and the whip came down across her back instead. She stumbled with the force of the blow, blood a bright red line soaking through the rent in her shirt. Her face whitened but she didn't make a sound. Banked fury shone in her eyes.

Ayra's temper surged, her magic flaring with it, but she fought it back. She couldn't use her magic. Not even a drop of it.

Still. Her fingers curled at her sides. Niallin had said the Nightstalker was away.

"Arya," Niallin said with warning, presumably seeing something in her expression. "You can't help them. You'll only get them *and* yourself killed."

The woman straightened, tried again to put herself between the boy and the soldiers. The whip cracked, the sharp retort sparking Arya's temper into flame, and the woman fell. The other conscripts watched helplessly, some sobbing in fear. The boy stared wide-eyed between the soldiers and the woman, frozen. Tears streaked his face.

Arya's step quickened ever so slightly.

Niallin matched it, murmuring. "I know it's hard to watch, but there's nothing you can do. There's nothing *anyone* can do. We must keep walking and ignore it. Don't look at them. Don't say anything to them."

Arya knew he was right.

But she couldn't stand by and watch. She'd *never* been able to stand by and watch. And she never would.

Niallin shouted a warning as Arya broke into a run, covering the ground towards the group in quick strides, teeth bared. The Nightblades' attention was on the conscripts, the woman defying them, and so they were slow to notice her approach.

A snarl ripped from Arya's mouth as the soldier lifted his whip once more to bring it down on the woman's back. She drew her sword with a clear ring. The blue cazaix gleamed as it flashed down and sliced into the soldier's neck, taking his head clean off his shoulders. Blood sprayed wide, splattering Arya's face and tunic.

Everyone froze. Soldiers and conscripts alike.

Arya didn't. It was one against eight and she needed every advantage possible. Lunging, she went at the Nightblade nearest the sobbing boy and drove her blade through his heart before withdrawing it with another warm spray of blood and spinning around to face the others.

One of the soldiers shouted an order and four of them converged on Arya while the remaining two began herding the conscripts into a tighter group they could watch more easily. Arya dodged the first lunge, stepped through to counter the second man's strike, swept his blade aside and ran him through the heart. Continuing the movement without pause, she spun back to the first and slashed across the back of his neck, dropping him without a sound.

Four more to go. The two guarding the conscripts had given up on that and come to help their comrades contain Arya. She faced them, heart pounding, blood racing, mouth curled in a silent snarl. Fury consumed her, and the urge to destroy them all burned in her chest.

They rushed at her as one.

She parried the first and second thrusts, ducked under the third, and came up slashing. Her sword sliced down, opening up an arm, then she backed away. "Come on," she taunted, swinging her blade so that droplets of blood flew through the air. "You can take on a child, surely you're brave enough to face a woman?"

They came at her, warier this time. They were competent swordsman, good even, but they had nothing on the Icefolk warriors Arya had trained with for three summers. She sent one blade spinning away, gutting its owner, then blocked two thrusts in quick succession and killed the sixth. Pushing her advantage, not giving them time to reset or gain their balance, she flew at the final two. Blunt, powerful blows designed to smash through their defences.

Once they were dead, she stood catching her breath and surveying the area for any further threats. The Nightblades' bodies lay scattered on the road. The surrounding forest was quiet and empty. For now, nobody else was coming in either direction.

Assured there was no further immediate threat, Arya turned to the conscripts. Niallin had arrived and moved them to the edge of the road, where he was studying the bleeding wounds on the woman's back. They all stared at Arya as she approached. A mix of fear and wonderment filled their gazes. Splattered with blood and gore, she must look a sight.

"Is she okay?" Arya asked, lowering her sword, still dripping blood.

"She'll be alright if we can get her to a healer and have the cuts cleaned and bandaged." Niallin faced her, mouth in a tight line. "That was a stupid thing to do."

"I don't care if it was stupid. I wasn't going to stand by and do nothing."

His mouth tightened further, genuine anger kindling in his mild blue gaze. "The Nightblade conscription parties always have a unit of mounted soldiers trailing them in case any of the conscripts escape. They'll be here any moment and there's no way we can hide all those bodies, or the blood everywhere, in time. They'll kill us all."

Shit.

Arya looked down the road. She couldn't see anything through the thick forest, but if Niallin was right, they'd soon be in trouble. Panic tried to rise but the immediacy of the threat allowed her to ignore it. "Have you got somewhere safe you can take them?"

He hesitated. "I have friends who can help."

"Then go, get off the road and make your way through the forest to these 'friends'. I'll hold the soldiers off so you can get clear."

"They'll kill you."

The sound of hoofbeats broke the silence. Arya rounded on Niallin. "That's not for you to worry about. Keep those children safe," she said. "Niallin, GO!"

Arya hadn't lost any of the command edge to her voice, and he moved without further protest, ushering the conscripts off the road. The young woman who'd been whipped held back. Up close, she was tall and thin with blonde hair and dirt-streaked skin. "What's your name?"

"Arya. Will you be okay to run?"

Determination filled her expression. "I'll be fine. Thank you, Arya. I'm Esdee."

"Look after them." Arya glanced over her shoulder. Then in a quick movement, unbuckled her sword belt and passed the woman her cazaix blade. "And keep this safe for me."

"I swear that I will." Esdee took the sword, offered her a quick smile, then disappeared into the trees.

Niallin reappeared then. "They're moving. Show me your forearms."

She stared. "What? Those riders will be here any—"

"Do it, please. Show me your forearms."

At the determined look in his eyes, she huffed out a breath and rolled up the sleeves of her tunic. His eyes went instantly to the zig-zag-shaped scar on her right forearm, and when he saw it, his face burned with a sudden intensity.

"Niallin, go! I won't be able to hold them long. If they see you, they'll catch all of you."

He tore his eyes from her arm and began backing away. "Stay alive, Arya. For all our sakes, stay alive!"

Then he was gone.

Moments later a unit of mounted soldiers appeared. Arya faced them, hands in the air, demonstrating that she wasn't an immediate threat. Their shocked cries as they saw the bodies filled her ears. In the moments it took for them to process the situation, she considered her options.

There were too many for her to defeat. She could put up a good fight, kill many before they took her, but that way she was likely to end up badly hurt or dead. Better to keep herself as healthy as possible so she could escape when there was a better opportunity. So she stayed where she was, kept her hands in the air.

The riders surrounded her moments later. One of them barked a command and two Nightblades dismounted to bind her hands. They weren't gentle. "Who are you?" one demanded.

"My name is Arya."

"Why did you kill the soldiers?"

She shrugged. "I was just minding my business, travelling to Darkclaw, but they pulled me up. Then they called me a bad word."

"Where are the conscripts?"

Arya pointed back towards Murton. "They ran that way. The fighting scared them, so they were in a bit of a panic. You'll probably catch them quickly."

He looked at her like he thought she was an idiot. "They ran straight down the road, did they?"

Arya licked her lips, pasted a flicker of nervousness on her face. "Yep, making a racket about it too." But as she spoke, she allowed her eyes to flicker off to her right, into the trees on the opposite side of the road to where Niallin had fled.

He stepped away. "Four of you, into the trees north of the road. That's where they went. Two more head straight down the road, just in case. You don't find anything, you start a broader search. I want them all recovered and back in Darkclaw by nightfall."

Arya lowered her head as if defeated, but inside she only felt fear. It wouldn't take long for the soldiers to realise they hadn't run north, and she hoped Niallin got them far enough to the south before that happened. They were on foot though, and it seemed unlikely.

"The commander will want to question her." The leader snapped a few orders, and something hard smashed into the back of her head.

Chapter 12

Arya had awoken in a dark cell to find Elendryl gone, a void in the back of her mind where his presence was always coiled. It was only after repeated frantic attempts that she realised she couldn't access her magic at all.

More than a handful of days had passed since then, but how many? It was difficult to tell. Food had been brought at irregular intervals—a bowl of slop and a mug of water each time. Faint orange light filtered through a barred opening set high in the thick wooden cell door, not even strong enough to reach the ground. The walls and floor were stone, slick with icy damp.

Arya crouched in the corner, pressed against the wall, fighting regular surges of panic. Her hands shook, heart thudding too hard. The space was so small. So dark. She couldn't quite catch her breath. She'd expected an interrogation, removal from the cell, a chance to fight her way out. But none of that had happened. Instead, she'd been left in the damp cell to rot.

And the longer she spent in here, the more dangerous her predicament grew. If the Nightstalker or one of his nazal became aware of her presence, he'd destroy her in the blink of an eye. Worse, he'd find out about—

She was a fool. A stupid, idiotic fool. She'd put everything at risk again. She pressed her face into her hands as guilt rose up, twining with the panic to take a stranglehold over her senses.

But how could she not have acted?

Her head ached. A trickle of cold damp seeped through the back of her shirt. For the hundredth time, she scanned her surroundings for escape options. The main obstacle was the door; once she was through that, she had a chance of fighting her way out. *If* there weren't too many guards stationed beyond. And then … well, she assumed she was inside Darkclaw Deep, but didn't know where in the fortress her cell was or where the exits were.

The bark of Desomer's laughter echoed in the back of her mind. She wondered what her old mentor was doing right now. Probably relaxing by a fire with his cigars and a good ale. Arya took another breath, and another. The panic receded, calmed by her planning. But it simmered under the surface, ready to surge back and claim her. It was too dark in here, too small, too—

She cut herself off. Took another deep breath.

Surely, they'd come for her eventually. Then she could act.

***

More time passed. Her best guess was two days, making it at least five she'd been in the cell. The sudden sound of heavy boots thumping towards her cell made her start. Usually only one guard brought her food, but she counted at least three. Wondering if this might be an opportunity, she struggled to her feet when the door swung open and two Nightblades entered, one placing his sword at her throat. Another waited outside.

Without speaking, the soldiers closed manacles around her wrists, then pulled her from the cell, gripping her upper arms in a bruising hold. They stared straight ahead, fixed expressions in place. No emotion flickered in their eyes. Arya flexed her wrists, testing the strength of the bindings, but they were secure. The metal chafed painfully against her cold skin.

Arya tripped multiple times as they forced her up a set of narrow stone steps too quickly. At the top, her ears popped, and an echo of her magic shivered through her. She reached for it desperately, but it dissipated before she could take hold. The harder she tried, the less success she had. Realisation flashed. The constant ache in her head, the lack of Elendryl's presence.

The manacles.

Her cell.

Cazaix. Or something that worked like cazaix. It must be in the walls of the cell. And the manacles weren't as effective because there was less of the material. But it was enough to stop her *using* her magic.

But maybe that was for the best. The one thing she had to avoid at all costs was to reveal herself to the Nightstalker or his nazal by using magic. Even to escape. And Darmanin had been right. She didn't need magic to get herself out of here. With that in mind, she studied her surroundings as they walked, mapping the route, looking for guards, doors that looked like they could be exits. Storing it all for later.

But the soldiers dragged her through empty, lamp-lit stone corridors. Grim realisation seeped through her. Her cell wasn't at the trading post, or the barracks near it. She'd been taken to cells on the Nightstalker's half of Darkclaw Deep. With that came a deep, rising, fear.

What had she done?

They finally approached a double arched doorway. More soldiers stood guard here, but they appeared to be expecting her arrival and one stepped aside to open the doors. They wore the same fixed expressions as the Night-blades escorting her. If her thoughts weren't so frozen with growing panic, she might have wondered at that.

Beyond was a dark, cavernous great hall. Arched windows let in grey daylight, and torches lined the side walls, but their combined light wasn't enough to fill the space, and the centre of it was shrouded in dim shadow. Arya's guards withdrew. She didn't realise they were leaving entirely until she heard the echoing clang of the doors closing behind her.

Dread crept up her spine, shivers of ice that triggered a barely contained panic.

A door slammed somewhere in the dimness ahead. Footsteps echoed. She swallowed. Her neck prickled, her gaze uselessly trying to penetrate the shadows. Sweat beaded on her temples. Her mouth turned dry.

Moments later a tall man appeared out of the shadows.

The Nightstalker.

He looked exactly the same as he had that first time she'd laid eyes on him at SheerRock Fort nine years ago, and then again in Gateport four years earlier. Raven hair swept back from his face, highlighting spare, ascetic features and pale skin. Simple clothes tailored to show his lean frame to best effect. But like before, the simplicity of his appearance was designed for only one thing.

To reflect and enhance his sheer power.

It was palpable, filling the surrounding air with every gesture, every movement. Sublime, practised, instinctual magic. It found her fear and heightened it, turning it to dread, to certainty that she wouldn't live through the day. Not trusting herself to speak and betray that fear, Arya merely watched him. Escaping was likely impossible.

So, her focus narrowed to one thing, keeping her secret from him.

"Finally," he remarked. "I have the Stormrider heir in my hands. I admit it took longer than I'd expected. Your father was much easier prey."

Arya shrugged, summoning every scrap of courage she had to feign nonchalance. "You're really going for the whole villain aesthetic here, huh? Very dramatic. I approve."

His smile stretched wider, a terrifying sight. "My Nightblades have been searching for you since you first stepped foot in Andahar, but it was awfully polite of you to simply come walking in the front door."

Shock rippled through her. Which of the friendly riverfolk she'd met had betrayed her? But how had *they* known who she was? She couldn't see how it was possible. She felt sick with how wrong her assumptions had been.

"I can see the questions spilling over your face. Does it really matter how I found out? You still ended up in my dungeons."

Arya straightened her shoulders, trying for more bravado. Maybe she was lost, but she wouldn't give him the satisfaction of letting him see her despair. "They'd be *my* dungeons, actually. You stole this place from my family."

"I see you got the full serve of Stormrider arrogance." His face curled in distaste, as if he'd eaten something sour. "You think I'm a monster."

She swallowed, forced her voice to come out steady. "I'd say forcing children to fight in your army is monstrous behaviour."

"Your ignorance is appalling. You think your grandfather did such a good job? The marshfolk *started* this war, and it wasn't under my watch." He laughed, again with that hint of madness. "Oh, I'm sure your riverfolk rebel friends have filled your ears with what a wonderful king your grandfather was, but of course they would say that. They were his favourites."

Arya's heart pounded, despite her best efforts at calm. She knew she was trapped, that this man before her could squash her like a bug. But if she could keep him talking, distracted, maybe an opportunity would arise she could take advantage of. It was a slim hope, but she had to try. "What do *you* say, then?"

"I say the marshfolk hated him, and by extension his Sky Lords. And they weren't the only ones. You say I'm a monster, but our enemies won't rest until we're all wiped out. Every single one of us."

"But that's what you've doing too, no? Killing every Sky Lord you find. Or at least, *trying* to. Haven't had much luck with it recently, have you?"

"Talk big all you like, but you were stupid enough to place yourself in my hands, and now I'm going to kill you. You don't truly think otherwise?"

"No," she said, straightening her shoulders and looking him in the eye. "You have to kill me. I'm a threat to you."

Lucius Nightstalker threw back his head and laughed, the sound echoing through the hall with a maddened edge. "You are no threat to me, but you *are* a loose end. I'll offer you a deal. Tell me who your Sky Lord *caidre* are, and where they are, and I'll kill you painlessly."

"That's never going to happen."

He watched her for a moment, something flashing over his face that made her more afraid than she'd ever felt in her life. "Then tell me about your child."

Arya's breathing stopped. Chill silence fell over the hall.

No. He couldn't...

Her breathing lurched back to life, too fast now. Panic, the desperate need to protect, was the only reason she was able to speak, to say, "What are you talking about?"

The Nightstalker regarded her in a way that sent horror tricking down her spine. "An interesting thing one of my spies told me. Convenient that she is a midwife. She says you carry stretch marks, signs of carrying a child."

Arya's hopes burned to ashes. Dina. The innkeeper's wife in Wain's Anchor. That look on her face when she saw Arya getting out of the bath naked. The panic of a trapped animal descended over Arya. She could no longer think straight, *see* straight.

The Nightstalker continued. "I have no intention of letting another Stormrider heir live. Tell me where the child is, tell me who your Sky Lords are, and I'll kill you quickly."

"There is no child." But he could see it written all over her face. Surely, he could. Because the thing she'd been hiding for three years, terrified of anyone learning ... her son. The child she'd given birth to months after fleeing Gateport. And then abandoned, all in an effort to keep him safe, hidden, away from her and the danger that followed her everywhere. Every decision she'd made since had been about protecting him.

And now the Nightstalker knew.

Despair surged through Arya like an overfilling cup, and she didn't know how to fight it. Had never had to before.

Lucius smiled. "That was the answer I wanted. Killing painlessly is much less fun."

Arya braced herself. "Do your worst, Nightstalker. You're not getting anything from me."

"Oh, but I will," he said, and the simple confidence in those words ate into Arya's soul.

Two Nightblades stepped out from the shadows along the wall at an unseen gesture from their king, circling behind her. She braced herself as one stepped up behind her, a key clicking into the lock of her manacles before they loosened, and the soldier yanked them off her wrists.

She let out a breath of relief, shaking off the tension in her wrists, then shifting to attack, to—

The bond linking her to the Nightstalker flared to life and he instantly had hold of her magic in a strangling grip. She tried to suck in a breath, failed, and a moment later screamed in pain, taken completely unaware as the soldier's fist drove into her right kidney. Agony stole her wind, making it that much harder to fight as the Nightstalker's magic suffocated hers.

"Tell me," he demanded with both voice and magic, *compelling* her. "Where is the child?"

Arya whispered one word. "No."

A fist slammed into her other side, and she sagged, groaning in pain. A booted foot swept hers out from under her and she hit the ground hard. She scrambled to her feet, ducking aside as one of the Nightblades lunged at her, then getting close enough to drive an elbow into his side. He grunted, staggering away, but the second soldier grabbed her around the waist. She fought him bitterly as he wrestled her to the ground and held her there.

"Tell me," the Nightstalker ordered. The pull of compulsion grew stronger, fiercer. "Tell me, now."

"No." *Never.* She'd never give up her son. She threw her head back, trying to headbutt the soldier holding her down. He grunted and shifted backwards, giving her the opportunity to shove him off, try to get to her feet, but the second Nightblade had recovered, and his boot slammed into her abdomen. She heard bone crack, then felt shards of stabbing pain. She whimpered, body curling in on itself as she crumpled to the floor.

Arya could hear herself gasping as the echo of '*no*' beat through her thoughts. The thread connecting her to the Nightstalker was fiery agony. He demanded and demanded and demanded and she couldn't *think* couldn't—

The onslaught stopped, and the Nightstalker kneeled by her head, one hand gripping her hair and viciously yanking her head toward him. "The pain won't end until you tell me where your heir and your *cairdre* are. I want *all* of it, do you understand?"

"I'll die first," she rasped, meeting his stare with as much strength as she could summon.

He laughed again. "I'm not going to *let* you die first. I *will* get the truth out of you. First the child, then your Sky Lords. It's inevitable. The sooner you realise that, the better for both of us."

He let her head drop back against the stone floor, hard. Her vision blurred, something cracking in the left ear she'd landed on. She tried to get up, force herself to her knees, but dizziness swamped her and she slumped back to the ground. She tried again. Failed. Neither Nightblade tried to stop her.

The Nightstalker watched her efforts in apparent amusement. Then, the fourth time she tried, his boot slammed into her stomach, and she convulsed, gasping desperately for air. The kick was quickly followed up by another, this one to her face, breaking her nose. Hot blood trickled down her check, and she could no longer differentiate between the sources of pain in her body.

He was breaking her down, undermining the strength she needed to fight his magical compulsion. And it was working. Arya's world narrowed to those silver eyes piercing hers, demanding to know where her child was, using the combined onslaught of magic and pain to weaken her.

"Boy or girl?" he hissed in her ear.

The magical summons was so strong it felt like it was tearing her apart from the inside, and she could feel herself giving in. There was simply no way to indefinitely resist the Sky Lord bond.

She couldn't give up her son. Not ever.

But he was going to win through. She had to give him something.

A boot to her ribs, another strong demand through the bond. "Where is the child?"

"No," she whispered. But she was slipping, her resistance fading, and he knew it.

"Just give it up." The voice was almost crooning now. "You can't keep it from me. Tell me and all this pain ends."

She screamed as he pulled even harder on the bond, his compulsion reaching into what felt like every bone and muscle in her body.

"Leanir," she whispered. "Leanir Mindbreaker. One of my Sky Lords. He's a Shadeweaver."

Sick nausea roiled through her. She'd given up her Sky Lord. Tears of shame streaked her cheeks.

But the beating stopped. The thread fell quiet.

Arya lay curled on the floor, whimpering. The Nightstalker took hold of her hair in a bruising grip again, those silver eyes seeking hers. "As you've just learned, you can't fight the bond forever. I rule you and you *will* eventually tell me everything." The words were matter of fact as he let go, stood up. "Now, your child. Where is it?"

But he'd made a mistake in letting go of the compulsion, even momentarily. Before he could re-establish it, Arya lifted her head and brought it slamming down on the stone floor.

Blinding pain.

Then darkness.

Chapter 13

Feverish dreaming, interspersed with memories that she'd kept buried for years and now came flooding out. Her son, the fierce cries he'd made when he was born, his little snuffling sounds of contentment when Tomin had handed him to her to nestle against her chest. The look of delighted awe on Kulan's face—all the doubt and worry he'd felt when she'd first arrived at Taskari and told him she was pregnant gone, vanished, never to be seen again.

And the last time she'd seen him, barely a week old, gurgling happily as Kulan tickled his tummy before placing him down for a nap, Yarmina hovering protectively with an extra blanket. A Stormrider heir and a defenceless baby. Keeping her son safe from the Nightstalker had immediately become Arya's first and only priority. So, she'd kissed his forehead, then flown away from the small camp deep in the Khadini jungle and never gone back. As confident as she was that Kulan would love and protect his son, she'd felt his loss every single minute, hour, and day since.

Arya woke into horror.

She lay face down in her cell. Warm blood slicked her face from a line of fire on her left cheek, a gash above her right eye, and a busted lip, not to mention a swollen and bleeding nose. Her right eye was swelling too, limiting her vision to a narrow slit. By the stabs of agony in her chest every time she shifted, several ribs were probably broken. One or more of her fingers was broken too, something she realised when she tried to brace herself on her left hand to change position and it exploded in agony. The fogginess of her thoughts and blurriness in her good eye implied at least a minor concussion, if not worse.

Giving up on movement, Arya stayed where she was. Her breathing came in wheezing gasps, and part of her thought she should be worried about that, but the rest of her was too concussed to care.

The Nightstalker would be back for her. She'd only bought herself time. His compulsion would force her to give him everything eventually. It hurt too much to move, so she lay there, wheezing, waiting for the Nightblades to come for her. Or to die. Because that was going to happen sooner rather than later without treatment of her injuries.

And that was the best she could hope for. Death before he could wring those names out of her. But if she was alive when they came...

Arya could never, *would* never, give up her son's location. And not Dar-manin, or Essa. A sick twist of guilt already filled her at her betrayal of Leanir, sapping any will she had left. She needed to do whatever it took to prevent another audience with the Nightstalker.

And she remembered that her cell was lined with cazaix, but not beyond.

***

The Nightstalker was clearly impatient, because they came back for her remarkably soon.

The door screeched open, two Nightblades entered. Unable to do it under her own steam, Arya let one of them drag her to her feet. Agony tore through her so powerfully she cried out. She gritted her teeth through it, picturing her son, her need to do whatever it took to keep the Nightstalker from him, letting that give her strength. The second Nightblade reached for her wrists, manacles ready, but before he could get them on, Arya launched herself at him.

It was a stumbling, grasping effort, and she almost sent them both tumbling to the ground. And the pain was more intense than anything she'd ever felt. But she thought about her son, and she forced her broken body to run, one step, two steps, three steps...

...and then she was outside the cell. The third Nightblade ordered her to stop, his sword swinging. She swayed to avoid it and fell, hitting the wall and sliding down it. She cried out at the pain, her broken ribs twisting inside her chest, dizziness flooding her.

But she had access to her magic now, and she let it loose, attempting no control of it, simply allowing it to explode through the narrow space outside her cell. The three Nightblades died before they knew what was happening, blood and gore raining down. And her magic was gone again. Her use of it had been blunt, desperate, scraping every bit of it she had.

She had to move. The Nightstalker would have sensed her use of magic.

She gritted her teeth and began dragging herself towards the stairs. Standing upright was impossible, so she moved hunched over, good arm wrapped around her middle, injured arm hanging uselessly at her side. Her vision blurred so much that she kept tripping and falling.

Halfway up the stairs she fell and didn't have the strength to rise to her feet again.

A fevered daze had taken over her, so when the roar of an angry wyvern tore through what felt like the entire world, she thought she might be hallucinating.

But then it came again. The second roar shook the steps under her, reverberating through every agonising spot in her body. It was full of indignant fury. Arya's good eye snapped open.

Xaphistryl.

Something had roused the Nightstalker's wyvern.

She had to move, somehow get out. If she couldn't walk, then she'd crawl. Sobbing with the pain of it, she started dragging herself up one step after the other. She had no idea what she was going to do once she reached the top, but she had to try.

Shaking, wheezing, sobbing in pain, she got to the top step, pulling herself up and dropping flat to the floor of the corridor beyond. Her breath was hard to catch, and she felt hot and cold all at once, vision spinning and spinning.

Running feet approached. She moved her head in that direction dreading the appearance of guards who would take her back to her cell. Dizziness swamped her even at that little movement, and her stomach threatened to empty its contents. She'd have to fight them somehow, get to—

"She's here!" A familiar voice called out. Then faster running, boots sliding to a halt, and, "Arya?"

Surely it couldn't be…

Arya sucked in a breath, hope and relief squeezing her chest so tightly it was hard to whisper the word. "Dar?"

He kneeled before her. "Oh, Arya, what has he done to you?"

The broken note in his voice made all her despair come rushing back. A sob racked her, making her ribs flare in agony. "Dar … it … I can't…"

"Shush," he murmured, lifting her gently into his arms. "I've got you."

He smelled of home and Darmanin and leather, and she buried her head in the warmth of his chest, ignoring the wash of agony and vertigo that swept through her at being lifted. Tears streaked through the dried blood on her face. She wanted to go home so badly she couldn't bear it.

"Is she all right?" another voice murmured. She thought it sounded familiar, but trying to place it only made her vertigo worse. Nausea surged. "We might have a chance now, finding her so fast."

"Be still," Darmanin murmured in her ear, trembling relief in his voice. "You could worsen your injuries. Raven's balls, Arya, if you hadn't dragged yourself up here, we'd never have known where to—"

Another voice broke in. "Our window is closing. Let's go."

That voice was even more familiar. When she opened her good eye, a face came into blurry focus. A jagged scar, dark eyes, shaved head. "Ranier…" she rasped. "How…?"

"I've got her," Darmanin's voice rumbled. "We're right behind you."

Alarm bells started ringing then. No doubt the Nightstalker raising the alert after sensing her use of magic. Nightblades would be descending on her cell in moments. She squeezed her eyes shut, trying to remember the route she'd memorised when they took her to the Nightstalker. "Don't go left," she managed to get the words out. "…run straight …into them. Go … right … the way you came."

Ranier nodded. "Good, we can get to where we need to be that way."

The Shadeweaver leader led them at a run. Two other men—all four of her rescuers wearing Nightblade uniforms—holding torches fell in behind them as they headed up a flight of stairs. Arya whimpered with every step Darmanin took, even though he tried to jostle her as little as possible. They paused at the top to wait for a pair of patrolling soldiers to march past. They had their swords drawn and looked alert. She stifled a groan as her magic began trickling back.

And in that same moment Elendryl was there at the back of her mind. The relief was more intense than anything she'd felt in her life. He was there, and he was close, and he was...

"*What are you doing?*" she sent, panicked.

His matching relief at the restoration of their connection thrummed with tension. "*Concentrating.*"

He sent her an image, looking over his shoulder; a massive, winged shape blotting out all the stars in the night sky, chasing him, chasing him and ... Zaphirdryl was there too, just below Elendryl, both of them skimming dark treetops, desperately trying to stay ahead of the massive wyvern hunting them.

"They're drawing Xaphistryl off," Darmanin murmured as they started moving again, following Ranier's sure strides. "I know you're worried. Just let us concentrate on getting out of here for now."

"*Be safe, please.*" She sent to her wyvern, then left him to focus.

It was raining heavily outside, forcing them to slow on slippery cobblestones. It took all Arya's self-control not to cry out with every jolt and alert the guards to their presence. Once across a rain-swept courtyard, they flattened themselves against the stone wall, then edged along to a side gate. Incongruously, it stood open and unguarded, despite the alarm bells pealing through the fortress.

"Ranier, can one of your men take Arya?" Darmanin asked. "I'd prefer to take lead in case anything awaits us out there."

"No," Arya whispered, her uninjured fingers curling into the leather of his tunic. "Please don't let go."

His grey eyes sought hers, and he stared solemnly at her before promising, "I'll never let go."

"I can handle anything that comes up." Ranier swept a gaze between them. "Let's go."

Ranier slipped through the gate, Darmanin and their companions following, and Arya found herself outside the fortress walls. The main highway wound down to their left, and up to their right, but otherwise forest surrounded them.

Shouts echoed behind them. Arya looked back to see guards already converging on the gate, realising it was open and unguarded. They were hidden for the moment by the darkness, but surely they'd start searching in this—

"Into the trees. Now!" Ranier set off at a run.

Another wyvern scream sounded, but it was distant. Arya scrabbled for Elendryl and was reassured by his steady presence in her mind. "*Okay?*" she asked.

"*Flying. Escaping,*" he said, a mix of exhilaration and terror in his response.

"Is Zaphirdryl okay?" she asked Darmanin, Elendryl's fear echoing through her. She couldn't imagine the terror of being hunted by Xaphistryl. And she couldn't help Elendryl, couldn't...

"They're both fine," he said. "Now stop talking, you're badly hurt."

"I know," she whispered, eyes closing as her head fell back against his chest. "Everything hurts."

None of them spoke as they concentrated on keeping their breath and their footing on the slippery ground. The two men with Ranier had dropped their torches back at the fortress gate, and now they ran through the dark and rain. Most of the going was uphill, but Darmanin seemed to carry Arya's weight with ease.

Soon, though, the movement became too much. Unbearable pain lit up all her nerve endings, and her breathing grew shallower, until she was gasping, panicked she couldn't get enough air. Without thought she

and blue-eyed, a rugged wariness to him. The other was small and dark haired and looked out of his depth but determined. Ranier looked at Darmanin. "Well?"

He closed his eyes for a moment. "The wyverns have broken free of Xaphistryl and found a place to hide and rest."

Arya tried reaching for Elendryl too, but apart from a faint sense that he was okay, she couldn't do more. At least he was okay. But she had to get to her son. And Leanir, he—

"Arya, this is Fisk and Mervin," Ranier's voice sent her thoughts scattering, and she blinked, trying to focus on what he was saying. "They can be trusted."

"Where...?" she tried but couldn't get any more out.

"South through the Horn to a safe place," Ranier said. "We're going to get you onto a stretcher that Mervin made, and he and Fisk are going to carry you between them. It's going to hurt, but we need to move as fast as we can. All right?"

That was good. She had to get clear, get free, so she could get a warning to her son's protectors. To Leanir. "I'll deal with it," she promised.

He nodded as he stood. "Of course you will. You haven't changed since the moment we met, Arya Ravenstrike."

Chapter 14

Ranier finally called a second halt at dusk when they reached a small clearing ringed by enormous trees. It was the only level ground anywhere around. To the north the trees sloped up to the top of a ridge, while to the south they sloped down to a cleft between two mountainsides.

By then, Arya's entire body was rigid with pain and her breathing had worsened. Even lying still, she felt like she wasn't able to get enough air into her lungs. It didn't help that she had to keep convincing Elendryl to remain where he'd hidden himself and not risk flight. He could tell how badly she was hurt, and he wanted to be near her with an instinct that almost overwhelmed them both.

Mervin and Fisk laid her stretcher down before setting up camp. Darmanin gave her a little smile before disappearing to scout the area. Ranier came to clean and re-bandage Arya's wounds. She winced. "Why ... did you come for me?"

"I have my reasons."

She swore, tried to suck in enough breath for talking. "Who are ... these people? Why are *they* helping ... me? And ... how do you still know people here after all this time?" She coughed, eyes watering with the effort.

He gave her a quelling look. "If you don't stop talking, you're going to run out of air. Your single working lung is struggling enough already."

She gritted her teeth. "I will ... keep ... asking. Until ... you ... tell me something."

"You're lucky, as it turns out. My contacts in the Andahari rebel movement are limited and dated, and they may not have acted on my request alone. If Niallin had not already met you—"

"Niallin?" Arya's head came up, and she groaned at the wash of vertigo it caused.

"He's one of their leaders."

She swallowed. "I knew ... there was something odd about Niallin."

"Your instincts are rarely wrong, yet your recklessness continues to put you in danger." Ranier said, mouth in a tight line. "Somebody back in Wain's Anchor saw the scar on your arm. If it had been *anyone* but a rebel sympathiser, you would have been in trouble much earlier and without anyone to help you. As it was, word passed through the network from there, and they mobilised resources to watch over you."

A chill shuddered through her. There *had* been a spy in Wain's Anchor. The friendly innkeeper and his wife.

"Rengalin!" Arya said in understanding, the puzzle pieces suddenly coming together and distracting her from the pain. And then Niallin after Murton. "But what's so special ... about my scar?"

"Only one family in Andahar has ever possessed that scar."

"I got this scar in a prison camp in Khadini. Thousands have it."

Impatience flashed across his face. "Do they? Or is yours different because you fought when they gave it to you and the brand slipped? You *have* noticed it looks exactly like a lightning bolt."

If she'd felt strong enough, she'd have lifted her arm to look at it. But she wasn't. She'd already talked too much and she felt feverish, nauseous, out of breath.

"All Stormrider heirs bore the lightning scar on their bodies, yet none were ever born with it. Some accident in childhood, usually, but all had it by adulthood. *Only* the heirs." He met her eyes. "Before their wyverns were ever born, before they came into their Sky Lord magic, they had the mark. That way all knew who would take the throne after the reigning king or queen died."

A new voice spoke into the silence that followed Ranier's words. "It's true then, you are the Stormrider heir?"

Fisk and Mervin had been listening. She thought it was Mervin that had spoken; he was the taller, blonde one.

She looked at them, glanced away. "Yes."

"You saved my sons," Fisk said gravely. "I owe you a debt I can never repay."

"Fisk's not one of our fighters." Mervin shoved him affectionately on the arm. "He's arwein, a farmer, and his land is west of the Horn. He has two sons, and both are of conscription age. He's been trying to hide them from the conscription units, but it was only a matter of time."

"The conscripts ... on the road?" Arya wheezed, realisation dawning.

"They were taken two weeks ago." Fisk nodded. "I was heartbroken, and their mother is inconsolable. We did not have the strength to stop them from being taken. If we'd tried, the Nightblades would have razed our entire village."

"He came to me for help, and we were travelling through the Horn, planning to contact my associates in Murton and see if they could help. We ran into Niallin just after your friend ..." Mervin shot Ranier a dubious glance. "...arrived, only to find the boys rescued and recovering at the safe house. To make a long story short, Fisk insisted on being part of your rescue party."

"Are all the conscripts safe?"

"They're already being moved to a safer long-term location," Fisk assured her. "It will be a while before my wife and I can see our boys again, but at least we know they're okay."

"Ranier, wait." Arya rasped as he stood to leave. "I have to..."

"Rest, Arya," Ranier instructed, and his hand pressed against her forehead. "If you keep trying to talk, you will kill yourself. That's not an exaggeration."

"Thank you," she whispered. "For coming for me."

"There's a healer where we're going. Survive the journey and make sure my efforts are not for nothing." A frown crossed Ranier's face when he placed a hand on her forehead. "Your fever is worsening."

She swallowed. "Hurts." She tried to say more, but her voice came out as an incoherent rasping. Blackness dotted her already blurry vision and Ranier's frown deepened. "Rest. I'll be back with some food and water."

"*Okay?*" she sent to Elendryl.

"*Okay*," he replied immediately. "*Come?*"

"*Hide.*"

He didn't like it, but acceded. Arya managed a few mouthfuls of the broth Fisk made over a small fire. Then Darmanin doused the flames and took first watch while Fisk, Ranier and Mervin curled up near Arya to sleep. Despite the pain, she let Elendryl's presence calm her, and drifted off to a feverish doze.

She awoke abruptly sometime later.

The old scar on her forearm throbbed faintly, and magic brushed across her senses. Gasping in pain, she slowly rolled onto her side, searching the darkness until she spotted Darmanin staring out into the dark night. A mist hovered over the ground and a light rain pattered on the leaves above. Her movement caught his attention, and he came over. "I was just about to wake Mervin for his turn at watch," he murmured. "Is there something wrong?"

Before she could reply, an ear-splitting screech rent the night air. Arya's heart stopped, then began racing. Her eyes scanned the surrounding darkness, but saw nothing. The screech came again, tearing into her eardrums. Ranier and Mervin awoke and rolled quietly out of their blankets.

"Arya, stop moving." Ranier took her good arm and helped settle her back down on the stretcher.

An uncontrollable shiver racked her frame. "A nazal hunts us. It's near, I can feel it."

"I know," he said quietly. Fear reflected in the eyes of the other two men, but neither moved. Darmanin drew his sword, grim determination settling over his features. "If we move now, it will hear us, and we can't outrun it. Our best strategy is to remain still and quiet and hope it moves on."

At Ranier's soft order, Mervin and Fisk removed all traces of a camp, then spread out around the clearing, hunkering in the shadows of the largest tree trunks. Ranier remained beside Arya in a ready crouch, body thrumming in a way that told her he was ready to explode into movement at any second. Darmanin settled on her other side, fingers curled around the hilt of his blade.

The thread that joined her to the Nightstalker shivered faintly, as if he were trying to liven it, but he didn't have a good enough grip to do so. A moment later, Arya *felt* the nazal searching for her as a prickling sensation all over her skin. Icy fingers crawled at her mind, searching for her, for a way in. Dread shuddered through her.

It was the nazal who'd controlled Nain. The one who could breach her mind.

Slowly, she reached for her cazaix blade, sliding it far enough out of its sheath that she could press her palm against the cool metal. It burned her skin, but tonight that was a comforting sensation. Ranier glanced down, saw what she was doing, and nodded silent approval. Darmanin, too, saw what she was doing and placed his bare palm against his sword.

The high-pitched screech echoed again, closer now. It sounded annoyed, like it knew she was close but couldn't quite pin down where. A flock of disturbed birds flew out of the trees nearby, squawking loudly and causing her to jump. Arya bit down on her lip as agony flared in her side, and she tasted blood trickling into her mouth. Her gaze focused in that direction, where there was a break in the trees higher up the slope above them. The shadows there flickered.

Slowly, very slowly, she moved her good hand, pointing. Ranier nodded imperceptibly. Fighting down terror, Arya hoped the others would hold still. If they broke and ran, the nazal would be on them in seconds. Her heart thudded and sweat slicked her skin. She'd never felt so vulnerable, so sick and in pain, in her life. She wanted to reach for Darmanin, his steadiness and strength, but didn't dare. It would reveal them both.

"Danger!" Elendryl sounded panicked.

"Stay," Arya commanded, hating the weakness in her mental voice. *"We must be still and quiet."*

"Sick." Worry now combined with the fear.

"Please, Elendryl. If you are not safe, I cannot ... please stay safe."

Reluctant agreement.

The flickering shadow resolved into a dark figure, the mist rising to the fetlocks of the horse it rode. The nazal was hooded and cloaked. It sat there for a long moment, as if tasting the night air for their scent.

Her entire body was rigid. This creature had murdered Thiara Ravenstrike and her husband. They'd given Arya *everything*; position, prestige, and the Ravenstrike name. More than that, they'd loved her. They'd given Arya, a Nameless, a home and a family.

And this monster had torn all of that away.

The fist of her uninjured hand clenched, nails drawing blood from her palms. She lay there, gasping silently, memories flooding her mind and heart, a rush of images she couldn't stop. Tears streamed silently down her face.

Something inside her broke and for the first time in four years, when she no longer had the strength to hold it back, Arya grieved for Thiara Ravenstrike and Matte Eaglesoar. And then she cried for the son she'd had to leave behind.

And then the muted threads to her Sky Lord *cairdre* flared to painful life.

The Nightstalker. He—or more likely his nazal—was close enough to liven the thread between them. Arya choked as the Nightstalker pulled hard. The impulse to reveal herself, to make herself known to the monster so close, was overwhelming.

Ranier shifted, clearly sensing something was wrong. But Arya could do no more than writhe, fighting with everything she had against the compulsion—but she was weakened, ill, in pain. He was going to have her again.

As if to punctuate the point, a wyvern screamed in the night. Xaphistryl.

And then Ranier was above her, hands gripping her wrists with brutal intensity, voice hissing in her ear. "You have to break the thread," he told her. "You are the Stormrider heir. Supremacy is yours. *Take it.*"

"How?" she begged, back arching as she fought down the scream that wanted to escape her. The Nightstalker wanted her to move, to go to the nazal, to submit, and she couldn't, she couldn't...

Ranier's hands on her wrists tightened further and agony flared. The pain held her in the clearing, provided a point of focus as he spoke again. "Find

Elendryl. Use his strength. Stop fighting the Nightstalker's compulsion, stop hiding from it, then grab it and rip it from you."

"I can't ... if I let him ... I'll..."

"If you die here, then all is lost. He will rule unassailed with no chance of another Stormrider to challenge him."

"No," she whispered, so close to letting go, *wanting* to let go. She was so tired, in so much pain. And she *wasn't* the only heir anymore, but before those words came out, some final shred of sanity stopped her from speaking them.

Ranier was relentless, hurling the words in her ear. "Isolate the thread. Stop fighting it. Then tear it from your magic."

"*Elendryl?*"

Her wyvern was there. He wanted to fly to confront Xaphistryl, but she held him off, told him she needed his help instead. The nazal's scream echoed with another cry from Xaphistryl. Even though Arya's eyes were half closed, she knew the nazal had turned in their direction.

He was trying to flush them out. Dimly she realised Darmanin had gone rigid on her other side, halfway to his feet.

"Ranier." She wheezed, arching again as the Nightstalker pulled harder, more determinedly. He was so strong, so powerful. "I can't. I'm too weak, sick."

Ranier whisper-bellowed the words in her ear. "I am Ranier of House Inkweaver and I hold the knowledge of the Sky Lords in my blood and body. So, listen to me, Arya Stormrider, daughter of Torin Stormrider! Summon your will. Claim your House. Isolate the thread and tear it from you."

The compulsion tightened, agonising, overwhelming. So much so that it was easy in the end to stop fighting it.

I am Arya Stormrider. And I ride Elendryl.

She followed Ranier's instructions without any further hesitation. The moment she stopped resisting the Nightstalker, she drew on Elendryl's presence inside her, found the thread binding her to the Nightstalker, grabbed hold of it and *wrenched.*

He fought it.

The nazal lifted its head and screamed.

Xaphistryl echoed the scream and sent the world around them shaking.

Somehow Fisk and Mervin remained still and silent. Darmanin's grey eyes focused intently on her, silently urging her on.

Arya dug in. With every inch of determination she possessed, she held on to the end of the thread and she yanked at it. Taken by surprise, the Nightstalker scrambled to stop her, throwing his strength into the fight, but Elendryl bolstered Arya, the two completely merged.

Ranier's hand closed over her mouth right before she tore the bond free and screamed aloud with the agonising tearing of the thread parting from her magic. And then she sagged, utterly drained.

The Nightstalker was gone.

Chapter 15

Elendryl's presence in Arya's mind brightened, his mind tentatively wrapping around hers, offering comfort and strength. Everything had gone silent.

"Well done, Arya Stormrider." A hint of disbelief and awe coloured Ranier's voice as he sat back, releasing her wrists. "But we're not out of the woods yet. He and his monsters can no longer track you through the bond, but they can still hunt us, and they're too close, especially with the speed they're moving."

Darmanin nodded grimly. "We need to draw them off."

"Yes."

There was a moment's pause, then Darmanin said, "I'll take Zaphirdryl and lead Xaphistryl and the Nightstalker away from you. That should give you enough time to get clear of the Horn."

"No," Ranier snapped. "You're his heir, even if he doesn't know it yet. He wants you almost as badly as he wants her. You're going to leave now on Zaphirdryl, fly back to Dunidaen. It's far too risky for you to remain here. I'll lead the nazal away while Fisk and Mervin get Arya to safety."

A thick silence fell over the clearing.

"Ranier, if you think for a second I'm going to abandon—"

"Dar!" Arya managed to say it strongly enough they both turned to her. "You have to go." She swallowed, her guilt rising up to choke her. He mistook it for dizziness and leaned down to hear her better. Her eyes closed in shame as she whispered, "Dar, I gave up Leanir. I didn't want to, but ... you have to go back to Dunidaen and warn him. Please."

"What was that?" Ranier asked.

A moment's hesitation, then Darmanin's hand settled on her shoulder. "Nothing. I'll go back to Dunidaen. Zaphirdryl is on her way." He said nothing else, no recriminations, no judgement. Her eyes slid closed in relief.

"Good. Mervin, Fisk, get the stretcher, you'll need to move now."

Mervin looked troubled. "I think we should just keep moving, fast as we can. Deliberately getting the nazal's attention is a death sentence."

"That's my problem, not yours."

"Ranier..." Arya sucked in a breath, tried to talk. "You can't."

"I can do as I wish, Stormrider. I am no Sky Lord of yours."

"But I need..." she couldn't get the words out as her breathing caught, stilled, and she had to work to get another breath in. She needed his knowledge. She needed him to survive if she had any chance of ever defeating the Nightstalker.

"I'll see you at the meeting location." And then he was gone, moving into the trees, disappearing into darkness. Mervin and Fisk looked at each other, then moved to get their packs and the stretcher. A shadow swept over the trees, circled, then came down to land.

Darmanin looked at her. "You'd best mute the bond again while we're still so close to him, just in case."

She blinked, confused, until she realised that the thread that joined her to Darmanin was pulsing and alive, and that she was still entwined around it, drawing on his strength and comfort. He must be exhausted. It was incredibly hard to deliberately unwind herself and then mute the bond, almost impossible. And the moment she did she felt cold and sick and alone.

"Stay safe Arya, I'll see you soon."

"Don't let him catch you, *or see you*, Dar." A shudder of remembered horror rippled through her. He'd destroy Darmanin, just like he'd come too close to destroying her.

"I won't," he promised.

Her eyes tracked him as he strode away, scrambling onto Zaphirdryl's back before she swooped back into the sky. Moments later Fisk and Mervin were there, gently helping her into the stretcher.

And then they were moving.

***

When Arya woke next, she was racked with the chills of a deepening fever. Fisk and Mervin were still moving, carrying the stretcher. She turned her head, thinking to ask one of them for some water, but slid back to unconsciousness before she could get the words out.

She continued to slip in and out of consciousness during the day, not waking fully until Mervin checked her wounds that night. She alternated between too hot and too cold, and breathing was a continued struggle. Any time she moved her head, vertigo made the world spin around her and gorge rise. And her magic felt odd. Flickering out every time she tried to touch it.

She coughed. "You worried?"

"I suspect something has become infected, perhaps an internal wound we can't see." His glanced flicked up to her.

"Sounds dire."

"We've got a couple more days' travel. You'll last that long." He flashed a grin.

If Arya wasn't so sick, she'd have chuckled at the rebel's good humour. Fisk appeared with a steaming bowl. "This is my speciality stew. Let's see if we can get a few bites into you."

A gust of air swept over the clearing and then Elendryl was there, landing beside her, sending both Mervin and Fisk scrambling backwards. The wyvern's head snaked towards her. "*Hurt.*"

"Yes, hurt," she admitted.

Elendryl's nose pressed against her head with a gentleness that almost made her cry, then he settled to the ground, one golden wing covering her and instantly making her warm.

The effort it took to swallow a few mouthfuls of stew sent Arya spiralling back into fevered unconsciousness.

When she woke to lucidity again, it was halfway through the following day, and they were on the pebbled shore of a fast-flowing river. Elendryl was only a short flight away, but grounded in thick forest and hiding during daylight hours. Mervin was wading out of the water, dragging something behind him.

A raft.

"Another rafting trip?" she asked Fisk weakly, memories of running the Dreadwater flooding her.

He gave her a nod. "A nice smooth one, I promise. A straight run down to the coast with one of the riverfolk at the helm. Mervin will keep you steady, don't worry."

"You're not riverfolk?" she mumbled.

His mouth shaped a reply, but consciousness was receding, and she fell into another doze.

For a day and a half straight, they sailed along the swift-flowing waterway through the Horn and out to the southern coast of Andahar. Being able to lie still made Arya's pain more manageable and allowed her to stay awake longer. But consciousness meant lying in a constant miasma of weakness, fever, and nausea.

On the morning of the second day, Elendryl gently entered her thoughts. *"Friend."*

"What do you mean?" He felt closer than he had been, and a spike of fear went through her. *"Are you safe?"*

"Friend. Coming."

"Who? What friend? You're supposed to be staying hidden."

He responded, but she wasn't able to hold onto his reply, her magic still weak. She wasn't even sure she'd understood him properly. Elendryl's concern for her pulsed constantly in the back of her mind, but she no longer had the mental focus to shape clear communication with him.

Mervin's concern had palpably deepened with every hour that passed, despite his attempts to hide it. By midday, they'd left the mountains. As the sun reached the midpoint of the sky and began sliding towards the horizon, they were moving through the rolling hills and plains of the Riverlands before the river carried them into a village that nestled in a curve of flat land where the river flowed out to the ocean.

Mervin brought the raft bumping gently to the shore just north of the village. As both he and Fisk were manoeuvring Arya's stretcher onto a wide grassy bank, a cry echoed through the skies. Arya looked up to see two wyverns circling. She blinked, wondering if vertigo was making her see double.

"Elendryl!" she rasped, heedlessly pushing herself up on her uninjured hand, and ignoring the pain and dizziness that resulted.

Her golden Valheran landed with a gust of air that blew her tangled hair into even more of a tangle. His long head snaked out towards her, and she pressed a palm to his scales.

"Hurt." He snorted, worried.

"I will heal," she promised. But she could only manage the strength to sit up for a few seconds before collapsing back to the stretcher.

When she did, she could see the second wyvern had landed a short distance off. He was younger than Elendryl, smaller, with stunning copper scales and scarlet underwings. Like ripples of flame. Dismounting from his back was a familiar face, shock filling it as he got a look at her. "Arya, what happened? Asandryl said Elendryl was panicked about you, but we're still working on communication, and he wasn't particularly clear on why." He trailed off as Mervin stepped in front of him, one hand on his knife.

"Name yourself!" he snapped.

"Chiarn." He lifted his hands in the air. "Fair warning. I'm quite terrified of men holding knives on me. Asandryl is getting ready to eat you if you take another step towards me. Our bond is quite new, so I don't know how well I'd do at holding him back."

A threatening snarl rumbled from the copper wyvern, as if to punctuate Chiarn's point. His mouth opened, revealing fangs as sharp as Elendryl's. Mervin took several steps backward.

"Arya needs a healer," Fisk interrupted, wary gaze on the two wyverns. "Mervin, where do we take her?"

Mervin lowered the knife, tore *his* gaze away from Elendryl and Asandryl. "Larin's hut. I'll show you the way."

But the villagers had seen the descent of wyverns from the sky and were gathering outside the village, some carrying weapons, others pitchforks or clubs. On seeing Mervin with them, however, most weapons were lowered.

"You there, Larin?" Mervin called ahead. "We've got someone that needs your help and fast."

A tall, spare man emerged from the pack and strode towards them. "Mervin, who are these people and why are there two wyverns on our doorstep? Tell me they're not with the Nightstalker."

"They're not, I swear it." Mervin said, gripping Larin's shoulder and pointing to the stretcher. "I'll explain everything later, but right now Arya needs your help. She has a fever which won't shake loose, her breathing grows worse, and I'm afraid she might have an infection and a punctured lung. There's a concussion too."

Larin stepped up to the stretcher, a studied gaze running over Arya. "What happened to her?"

"She was badly beaten in the Nightstalker's custody."

"Badly indeed, from the looks of it," he murmured. "Follow me, but do it gently please."

At some sign from Larin, the villagers backed away, most returning to wherever they'd come from, but slowly, and not without many backward glances. Fisk and Mervin carried her stretcher into a spacious home. Arya lost track of Chiarn.

Her groggy senses registered a fire crackling in the hearth of the main room, and the scent of a myriad of herbs and spices. But Larin led them straight through into another room, where, as gently as they could, Mervin and Fisk transferred Arya onto a soft bed. They were then promptly ushered out of the house.

Larin went over her injuries in a practised way that made her think of Tomin at Taskari. They had the same colouring too, blonde hair, blue eyes, fair skin. Riverfolk. Eventually, he stood back. "You're going to need more help than I can give you," he murmured. "I'll be back in a moment."

His footsteps creaked, the door opened and closed. Arya sank into a doze, before the creaking of the floorboards roused her. Larin was back with a tray of items, one of which was a steaming mug. "Drink all of this," he instructed her. "It will help with the pain."

He placed a hand under her head, waiting patiently until Arya had swallowed every mouthful of the sweet tea, before taking the mug and gently placing her head back on the pillows. A warm lassitude swept through her, and finally, *finally,* the stabbing pain in her body faded to a dull throb. The relief was indescribable.

Someone else entered the room then. Roughly Arya's height, but far too skinny and with a shock of silver-white hair and pale blue eyes. Arya's eyes widened, and for a moment she was sure her fever was making her hallucinate. But her vision seemed clear, the tea taking the edges of fever and pain away.

"*Tiya?*"

"Hello, Arya." The healer smiled, then placed a hand on her forehead. "Rest now, I'll take care of you."

A moment later, she was asleep.

***

When Arya woke again, she felt vastly better. The pain and fever were gone, and she could breathe again. Instead of nauseous exhaustion, she felt the heavy weariness of a body recovering after illness. There was a splint on her left wrist and fresh bandaging covered the more serious cuts on her body.

When she explored moving her head, she found she could do so without pain, but the dizziness was still there...

...and Tiya sat in a chair by the bed.

"I wouldn't try moving too much yet," Tiya said. "You had six broken ribs and a broken wrist. Add to that a collapsed lung and infection from several wounds. There was severe bruising across multiple areas of your body, including a nasty spot near your left kidney, which caused some damage. I mended the breaks, healed the infection in your blood, and eased the bruising. Still, everything will hurt for a while, and you'll be pissing blood for a few days. You're likely to have a scar on your right eyebrow."

"What about the concussion?"

"It wasn't that. A blow to the left side of your head hit hard enough to damage your inner ear. I did what I could for that, but it's going to be slow in healing, which means the vertigo is going to take a while to fade completely."

"It sounds like I'll live though," Arya croaked.

She smiled slightly. "You'll definitely live."

Arya took a deep breath, relaxing when she could do it with ease. She'd never take for granted the ease of breathing normally again. But with returning health came urgency. The Nightstalker knew about her son. She couldn't stay here, she had to warn his father. "How soon can I get up?"

"Not for another full day at least, unless you want permanent injury." Tiya's voice was sharp. "I'm not exaggerating, Arya. Don't even think about it."

"I can't stay here." Desperation coloured her voice.

"You can for another few days, or you can risk permanent disability or death."

Arya tried to fight the desperate need to be away. The Nightstalker hadn't got her son's location out of her. He was no doubt looking, but wouldn't even know where to start. And he might go after Leanir first—a greater threat than a child. Even so, Kulan had to be warned as soon as possible. Her worried thoughts went straight to another question. "Is Ranier here yet?"

Tiya shook her head. "No, I'm sorry."

Arya swore. On foot and alone he should have been much faster. Had something happened to him? Guilt surged, and to distract herself from it, she asked, "All right, then answer me this. What in raven's balls are you doing here, Tiya?"

She let out a melodic laugh, one Arya remembered well despite the years since she'd seen her ex-lover. "You know better than anyone what it's like for magic-wielders in Dunidaen. I had no choice but to leave. Andahar was easier to get to than Khadini from Heathrock."

Tiya made it sound so simple, so matter of fact. "You disappeared without a word. I went looking for you. I was worried."

"When I left, you were far away in SparrowWing fighting fires and not coming back anytime soon." Tiya arched an eyebrow. "And there was a nazal in Heathrock. It wasn't like I could wait for you."

Arya's gaze narrowed. "You know about the nazal?"

She huffed a breath, as if that were a foolish question. "I had no idea who *you* were though. Not until a day ago when you showed up with a golden wyvern, and another Sky Lord. Here's me thinking you were a simple Nameless Raider."

"And here *I* was thinking you were a simple tavern owner." Arya could see it now. Having spent so much time with the Etherean in the past three years, it was impossible not to recognise their blood in Tiya. "You're Etherean."

"Not entirely," she said shortly. "And I don't want to discuss it. Now, your friends are eager to speak with you and assure themselves you're okay. I'll let one of them in, but only for a short time. You need to eat, drink at least two full glasses of water, and then get more sleep."

She was up and opening the door before Arya could respond. She *really* didn't want to talk about it, then.

Chiarn was the one to come through the door after Tiya left.

"Well." He propped at the door, gaze raking her. "You certainly look much better than you did when you arrived." He pushed off the wall and entered. "That Etherean magic is something, isn't it? And I thought Tiya was just a highly competent inn owner who took pride in refusing my charming advances."

She didn't respond to that, instead studying him, spotting the shadows under his eyes, the slight trembling of his hands. The way he kept looking over his shoulder every time there was a noise outside. "You finally left the citadel to find your wyvern."

His shoulders slumped. "You were right, I didn't have a choice in the end."

"He's beautiful," she ventured.

"His name is Asandryl. He hatched in the far north of the Horn. Fortunate, because it kept him from being noticed." He waved a hand. They'd *all* been lucky in that regard. She wondered if it was luck, or something else. "And before you ask, one of Cerilla's warriors flew me down into the foothills. I hiked from there into the Riverlands, avoiding towns and people. Asandryl met me halfway, so I didn't have to travel too far."

"Do you regret it?" she asked.

Bitterness flashed over his face. "Not for a second. But you already knew that too. I can't even imagine not having him in my life anymore, and it's only been a week."

Not wanting to push, she changed the subject. "How did you end up here?"

He hefted a sigh. "Your wyvern found mine as we were on our way back to the Etherean citadel. He insisted you needed help, and apparently Asandryl wasn't able to say no. I fell off at least ten times on the way here. It made Asandryl furious with me for embarrassing him, but he caught me every time."

"You have to stop resenting your connection with Asandryl and be open to it if you want to avoid falling off. I've never come close to falling from Elendryl's back."

His jaw clenched. "Are you well enough to leave? Being here is problematic."

"Problematic how?"

"Your companions told them all who you are, who *we* are. Our presence here gives them false hope. *And* puts them in danger."

She closed her eyes, head sinking back to the pillow, despair creeping back over her. "Whether or not we claim our heritage, people will get hurt and die. It won't end while the Nightstalker is alive."

"It's not our fault that the Nightstalker oppresses his people. It's not our responsibility to get ourselves killed trying to save them, either." He crossed his arms over his chest. "Having Asandryl doesn't mean I have an obligation to become a Sky Lord."

"No, Chiarn, it doesn't," she said. She was tired.

Tiya appeared then with a tray, shooing Chiarn out. She insisted Arya eat the entire bowl of soup she'd brought, as well as all the water in the tall glass. Once that was done, the healer left the room, and Arya settled back against the pillows.

But she couldn't sleep for worry and guilt and shame, all of it tangling up inside her. She'd betrayed her Sky Lord. The Nightstalker knew she had an heir.

She had to leave.

Chapter 16

Arya woke from a nightmare at a firm knock. For a moment she wasn't sure where she was. She blinked, dispelling images of the Nightstalker's face leering at her, revelling in how his knowledge of her child terrified her.

The knock came again.

Arya abruptly remembered *how* the Nightstalker had learned of her son. A spy in Wain's Anchor. And if he had a spy there, then there was one, or more, here too. Panic started her heart racing, and she pushed herself up against the pillows. As soon as the dizziness passed from moving, she called out. "Come in."

Niallin entered, a relieved smile spreading across his face. "It's good to see you alive, Arya."

Was he a spy? Surely not. Or he wouldn't have gotten the conscripts away to safety. Some of her fear faded, but her heart continued to race, and she fought to keep her voice even. "I would say I'm surprised to see you," she said. "But I heard you were instrumental in my rescue, so thank you."

"One doesn't ignore requests from Sky Lord House nobles, even if they have been presumed dead for decades." Niallin made a face. "And it's not like Ranier Inkweaver had to do much to prove his identity. I'd heard stories of Inkweaver tattoos, but to see them in person." He trailed off. "They're astonishing."

She saw something in his face. "He's not back yet?"

"I'm afraid not."

"We have to assume he's dead." Tiya entered then, followed by Chiarn. "Or captured. And if he's captured, he'll eventually lead them to us here."

Niallin stood aside so they could gather around her bed. "Even if he's not captured, it won't be long before one of the nazal tracks you here," he said. "The Nightstalker has an incredibly comprehensive spy network, and he will be devoting all his resources to finding you. We have to move."

Arya swallowed, gaze darting between them. "The entire village, or just us?"

"The nazal will raze this village to the ground when it arrives whether you're here or not," Tiya said.

Chiarn paled, freckles standing out starkly against his white skin. "Surely if we leave now, the nazal never has to know Arya and I were here?"

Arya shook her head, and regretted it immediately as her vision blurred. "No, they're right. Niallin, it was the innkeeper's wife in Wain's Anchor who betrayed my presence to him."

Niallin's jaw tightened, genuine shock in his eyes. "*Dina?*" He let out a heavy breath. "I am sorry, Arya. We did not know."

Tiya sent a pointed glance at Niallin. "The Nightstalker's spies will surely report that your rebels have contacted the Stormrider heir and one of her *caidre*. That is a threat the Nightstalker will not allow to develop further, not when he must worry about the marshfolk too. He will raze the country to wipe you out if he has to."

And he will do the same to Dunidaen. Arya kept that thought to herself. She didn't know what to say. She'd brought this upon them. She wanted to suggest some way to help, a plan, but couldn't trust herself to give advice that wouldn't hurt them even more. Chiarn sat heavily, head in his hands, which were shaking.

"It cannot be helped. We knew the consequences when we agreed to help Ranier Inkweaver," Niallin said. There was a feverish light in his eyes. "It is enough for us that you live, that there is a chance of..."

His voice trailed off, but she knew what he didn't say. She quailed at it. At his obvious hope. Chiarn lifted his head, looked at her in misery, as if to say, "*I told you so.*"

Before she could respond, Niallin frowned and cleared his throat. "Even so, don't mistake our gladness at finding you alive for unquestioning loyalty. It is clear your heart lies in Dunidaen, not here with us."

And she couldn't even stay to help them escape, because she had to leave—not just to put herself out of the Nightstalker's reach, but also to make sure her son was okay. That his protectors knew that the Nightstalker and his nazal would now be searching everywhere for him. "You could flee into Dunidaen?" she offered. There, she *could* help them.

Niallin hesitated. "We would have to cross the Diamondfang in winter, which is almost as dangerous as staying here while the nazal track us. And none of us wish to leave our home."

Tiya interjected. "Arya, you cannot travel yet, let alone hike over the Diamondfang. I used your body's reserves to heal you, and they were already at dangerously low levels. If you push on those healing muscles and bones too soon, you will risk worse than reinjury. Not to mention you won't be steady on your feet until your ear heals."

Arya swore. "Can I fly on Elendryl?"

"For a short distance, maybe, but you certainly couldn't fly the time it would take to get back to Ravenstrike State. You would know even better than I how much strength and balance it takes to remain balanced on a wyvern's back while flying."

"She cannot stay either!" Niallin said sharply. "We must assume word is already on its way to Darkclaw that Arya is here."

Shit. Shit. Shit. Arya lifted a hand to her throbbing temples. "I have to risk it, Tiya. The Nightstalker cannot find me here."

"Where?" Chiarn asked. He sounded hopeless, like he knew death was coming for him and he might be better off just waiting here and accepting it. She couldn't abandon him, so he'd have to come with her. Somehow, she'd figure out how to keep him from learning her secret.

"It's best they don't know." Arya gestured to Tiya and Niallin. "For all our sakes."

Silence fell. Tiya studied her, before loosing a breath. "Fine. But if you fly more than a handful of hours, you risk death, Arya. Let me be clear on that." She paused, letting those words sink in, then continued briskly. "I'll pack some healing unguents and the ingredients for the pain-relieving tea. Chiarn, you'll need to come so I can show you how to mix them properly."

She left, Chiarn trailing after her, leaving Arya alone with Niallin.

"He has spies everywhere, not just in Andahar," Niallin warned. "So, wherever you're going, be very careful."

"I will."

He hesitated, then, "And once you've recovered, you intend to go back to Dunidaen to help them defend against the Nightstalker's invasion?"

"Yes."

"And after? If you succeed and push him back?"

She took a breath. "I honestly don't know what I *can* do."

"Then our paths diverge here." Niallin turned for the door, but paused before leaving. "I hope to see you again one day, Arya Ravenstrike."

"You helped save my life," she said. "I won't forget it. My promise of protection in Dunidaen has no strings attached." She hesitated, then, "Is there a way I can find you, if I need to?"

***

Tiya hadn't been wrong. While Arya had felt close to normal lying in bed on soft pillows, as soon as she pushed back the covers and stood up, the energy drain was fast, and she had to move slowly to keep her balance. Even dressing left her breathing hard, legs trembling. And walking from the hut to where Elendryl waited outside felt like a miles' long hike. Asandryl crouched nearby, tail waving impatiently, Chiarn seated on his back, looking uncomfortable.

Around them, the village was a bustle of activity. Already some of the villagers were moving along the road leading east, heavy packs on their shoulders. She had to stop, catch her breath and let the spinning in her head fade, before she could try climbing onto Elendryl's back. It scared her, how weak she felt.

"*Protect,*" Elendryl promised as she slumped atop him, gasping and sweaty, hands trembling. Would her legs be strong enough to keep her astride him when he flew?

"You'll have to," she muttered. "I'm not good for anything right now."

"*Where?*" he asked.

She sent him a mental image of their destination, unwilling to speak it aloud. He sent an assent back.

Tiya appeared then, passing up a pack to Arya. "Take it easy," she repeated. "If you push too hard—"

"I get it. Thank you Tiya, for saving my life."

The bright smile Arya remembered flashed out again. "You're welcome, Arya."

"What will you do now?"

"I'll go with Niallin's people. They could use a healer, and while Andahar is not my home, I feel better having a purpose." Her expression clouded. "I don't think I could ever go back to running an inn."

"I know there's no time now, but I'd love to hear the story one day, of how a half-Etherean came to be running an inn in Heathrock, and then ended up with the Andahari rebels," Arya murmured. "I missed you, Tiya."

"And I you. If we meet again, I might even think about telling you that story." Tiya winked.

Chiarn called out. "Asandryl is getting tetchy."

Arya nodded. "Let's go." Her gaze shifted back to Tiya. "I *will* see you again."

Elendryl was as gentle as possible, but Arya barely held on as he took two lurching strides before leaping into the sky. Despite her poor physical state, relief loosened her shoulders as they climbed high and angled southeast.

Soon she'd be able to make sure her son was okay.

***

By the time the two wyverns circled above Taskari, Arya was dizzy with exhaustion. Maintaining her seat, no matter how smoothly Elendryl flew, had taken too much strength she didn't have.

"All right?" he sent anxiously as they approached the jetties on the northern side of the peninsula.

"Just get me down," she gritted out.

He gave his wings one last mighty beat before folding them back against his sides and gliding in towards the sturdiest-looking jetty. Vertigo swamped Arya as his taloned feet touched down with perfect grace, his weight sending the light structure rocking violently. Asandryl landed on the jetty across from them, and amidst her daze Arya heard shouts of astonishment from those crewing fishing boats nearby.

She tried to climb down from Elendryl's back, but her legs gave out, and instead she collapsed into a heap. Elendryl gave a mewling sound, his scaled nose nudging her with concern.

"I'm all right," she sent groggily, closing her eyes against the spinning. *"Walking might be an issue, though."*

Chiarn jumped the gap between jetties and wrapped a wiry arm around her waist, helping her get to her feet. Interestingly, Elendryl didn't react badly to his sudden approach either, as he hadn't with Rorin. She filed that away for further consideration when she was able to string two thoughts together.

By the time she was standing, swaying alarmingly, several Taskari residents had gathered where the jetties terminated, staring and pointing, but presumably not willing to come any closer to the two wyverns who growled warningly in their direction. But then a familiar young man—maybe eighteen years old—pushed out of the group, tall and long-legged with messy brown hair. He shouted a greeting as he ran towards them. Elendryl roared, head snaking forward, teeth bared.

The young man halted abruptly, put his hands up, his eyes wide but not afraid. "Arya, it's me, Kader."

"Friend, Elendryl." She steadied herself, then said. "Hello Kader. You've grown tall."

Kulan's brother's face creased in concern and when Elendryl reluctantly backed off, he hurried over to help Chiarn take her weight. "Ayra, you're black and blue. How are you even standing?"

"With help," she muttered. "I'm okay. The flight here was a little too much, that's all."

"Rafal, Tanifa, fetch a stretcher," Kader called out. "Muham, let Healer Tomin know Arya is coming and needs help."

"Just get me some … voseni, and I'll be fine," Arya protested.

Kader looked at her and snorted. "Let's start with getting you off this jetty." He looked over at Chiarn, offered his free hand. "Kader."

Chiarn shook it. "Chiarn. Thanks for your help."

Rafal and Tanifa appeared with a stretcher as they reached the end of the pier, and despite Arya's great embarrassment she gratefully slumped onto it.

"Good to see you again, friend Arya," Tanifa said cheerfully, picking up her end of the stretcher as if it weighed nothing.

"Good to see both of you." Arya managed a smile. She'd met both rebel warriors in the Khadini mine camp she'd been imprisoned in with Kulan. They'd escaped with her, then helped her and Rorin steal their cazaix before escaping Khadini.

"Seems you have a story to tell us." Rafal nodded his head towards the two wyverns.

"Later," she promised.

It was a swift journey up through the warren of streets and caves to Tomin's healing cavern, Rafal, Tanifa, and Kader chatting the whole way, Chiarn trailing with a bemused look on his face, Arya sliding her eyes closed until her vertigo settled.

Tomin waited for her, surprise and consternation in his expression. "Arya, this is a surprise. What happened this time? A bit more than an infected cut, it seems."

"I'm just tired. Very tired. And dizzy." Her words began slurring despite her best efforts.

Tomin's blue eyes flicked from Arya to Chiarn, then widened in surprise. Whatever he'd been about to ask died on his lips.

"Chiarn," he introduced himself.

"Chiarn. And you are?" he said faintly.

"A minstrel." Chiarn snapped, arms crossing over his chest as he sent a challenging glare Tomin's way. "Arya was badly beaten recently. An Etherean healer fixed her up, but it drained her reserves and she wasn't quite up for the flight here. Exhaustion's the problem …. I think."

"I'll be the judge of that," Tomin said, turning businesslike. "Carry her through, and then I need you to tell me as much as you know of her injuries."

Arya was laid on the cot in one of Tomin's healing rooms. She listened to the murmur of voices outside until the healer appeared, closing the curtain for privacy. Exhaustion was dragging her down into sleep she desperately needed, but she forced her eyes to stay open until Tomin leaned over her to begin his examination.

"Is he okay?" she whispered.

"He's well and thriving." Tomin murmured, laying a hand on her arm. "And you are safe here. Rest, Arya, and let me take care of you."

Relief cascaded through her, and she dropped into a dreamless sleep.

***

When Arya woke, she had no idea how much time had passed, but she felt immensely better. Her energy had returned, and it no longer felt like too much effort to move. The spinning sensation when she turned her head had lessened in intensity too.

"She wakes!" Chiarn's musical voice announced.

Arya rubbed at her eyes. "How long did I sleep?"

"Two days."

Her eyes widened in shock, but Chiarn continued before she could say anything. "Every time you looked close to waking, Tomin put you back to sleep with another dose of one of his concoctions. He insisted that you needed sleep more than anything because it would allow your Andahari magic to heal you faster." A mixture of fear and anger crossed his face. "Why did you tell him who you are?"

"I knew the very first time I met her." Tomin breezed into the room. "Although arriving two days ago on wyverns also gave the game away. Chiarn, some privacy while I do an examination, please?"

Chiarn left and Tomin took the seat by Arya's bed. "How are you feeling?"

"Much better than I was." She lowered her voice. "He's still all right?"

"He is." Tomin's face creased in concern. "Do you have a reason for worry? Is that why you really came here?"

She gave a faint nod. "We need to talk, but not now, not so soon after I've arrived. It needs to look like I only came here for healing. Understand?"

"I understand, Arya. Do not worry."

She let out a breath of relief, then gave him a look and returned her voice to normal volume. "You did *not* know I was a Sky Lord the first time you met me."

"Oh, but I did." His blue eyes twinkled.

"But..." Arya hadn't revealed herself to him until arriving pregnant and needing his help. But then she remembered what Ranier had said about her scar. "It was my scar, wasn't it? You saw it when you were cleaning out the infected cut. I thought it was strange how insistent you were about bandaging my arm even when the wound looked well healed."

"If any other Andahari here had seen that scar, they would have known you instantly," Tomin said. "It's lucky that you had the infected cut, or I would have had to invent some other excuse for you to cover your arm."

She frowned. "Why didn't you say anything back then?"

"The first time we met, I didn't know if *you* knew. It seemed like you didn't. And if that was the case, it was far safer for you if I said nothing," he said.

She changed the subject. "Am I alright?"

"In short, yes. The sleep helped immensely, and your broken ribs are knitting nicely, as far as I can tell. It will still be some time before your energy levels return to normal. And you're going to have to rebuild your running and fighting stamina—and go slowly until your inner ear heals fully and you can balance properly again."

"Does Kulan know I'm here?" she asked, then cursed herself for the question. She and Chiarn had arrived on wyverns in full view of Taskari. Of course, Kulan would know.

Tomin smiled. "He's been in to see you once or twice, but you were asleep. Chiarn is staying with his family." He hesitated, the question written in his eyes.

Arya smiled. "Chiarn is a Flamewielder, I believe, though a very reluctant one."

Tomin's eyes widened in stunned awe. "When I first saw that scar on your arm, I knew there would be four others, and I had my suspicions about Essa. But to see him in the flesh. And then your wyverns…"

"Don't let your hope run away with you, Tomin. I am in no position to be what you or your people want. And Chiarn wants nothing to do with any of it."

"I am not so foolish as to have false hope," he said. "But I am troubled that your identity will now be known at Taskari."

"I'm told it's highly likely that the Nightstalker has spies in the Andahari community here. If he does learn I've been here, it will be dangerous for you all. That's why I'm only here briefly for your healing assistance," she said, speaking just loud enough that if anyone were eavesdropping, they'd hear.

Tomin nodded. "Do not fear for us. There are limited ways of getting messages out of Taskari, and Kulan and I will ensure nothing leaks out." A sad smile flicked over his face. "Over the years here, the identities of those who spy have not escaped me. Until now, there has been nothing of note to report, and so I let the messages go through."

"I am so sorry to have brought this to your door."

"It is the Nightstalker who puts us in danger. You did not choose this, for yourself or for us."

Stricken, wishing she could believe that too, Arya fought tears welling in her eyes. "Thank you, Tomin."

"Yes, well." He cleared his throat and pushed his chair back. "I think you're well enough to be released from this room. I recommend you stay with me while you're here so I can keep an eye on your recovery." He spoke cheerfully, but his eyes were serious. He was doing as she'd asked.

"I won't intrude for long," she promised.

***

Arya woke the next morning to the tantalising scent of voseni wafting through the air. She carefully pushed back the covers and managed standing with much reduced vertigo, and pleased with that, walked slowly down the short hallway to Tomin's dining area without feeling like she was going to lose her balance.

Chiarn sat at the table drinking from a steaming mug, while Tomin's nephew Atarin hovered over a steaming pot on the cookfire. The first merely nodded at her arrival, but the second offered a cheerful wave.

"Hello, Atarin. I take it you're my assigned babysitter for the day," she grumbled without rancour as she lowered herself into a seat, glaring at Chiarn when he looked ready to reach over and catch her if she stumbled.

"That's right, I'm under strict instructions," Atarin grinned. "You're to eat everything in that bowl on the table, and only then are you allowed to have a mug of voseni. Once you're done, Chiarn is to escort you to my uncle so he can check on you."

"You weren't wrong about this voseni stuff," Chiarn noted as Arya obediently began spooning up mouthfuls of warm porridge and honey. Her stomach was in knots—guilt and shame over what she'd done to Leanir, fear for her son, fear of what the Nightstalker might do next to find her, and who else he'd hurt in the process—and she had no appetite. "They really need to make it in Dunidaen."

"They really do," she agreed distantly. "But the beans only grow in the jungles here. We'd have to import them."

"Something wrong?" Chiarn asked.

Arya realised her knee was jiggling where she sat, a betrayal of her emotions. She had to figure out a way to talk to Tomin and Kulan discreetly, but importantly she had to seem like everything was fine. She forcibly stopped her leg moving and offered a faint smile. "Just waiting for my voseni fix."

The food made Arya feel sleepy again, but when Atarin handed her a mug of steaming voseni, she sipped it greedily, feeling her energy come surging back. Atarin winked at her as he collected the empty bowls and carried them over to the sink.

Soon after, Chiarn escorted Arya to Tomin's healing centre. They moved slowly, Arya enjoying the brisk sea breeze whipping through the tunnel and the sound of seabirds on the air. Chiarn was maudlin, the glow of his voseni fading quickly.

"Everything okay?" she asked, because she was frustrated by how slowly she had to move and needed a distraction.

"No," he said. "The Nightstalker's going to find us here, eventually, isn't he? We'll have to leave soon. Only to go somewhere else he'll inevitably find us. Hunted like prey for the rest of our lives until he finally catches up with us and kills us."

"You've really been thinking about this," she said dryly.

"What else is there to think about? Not all of us are brave hero warriors who laugh in the face of mortal danger. Some of us know we're going to die and are quite terrified of it."

"Raven's balls, Chiarn, if only you knew." She stopped, shoulders sagging, grief and guilt and terror rising to choke off her breath. "I've never been more afraid in my life."

There was a long silence, then, "I didn't know. You always seem so strong."

"I'm not," she said sharply. "Not even close."

She lurched back into movement, and he followed, changing the subject. "I've been staying with Kulan and his family. They're very hospitable. If you hadn't told me, I wouldn't have guessed they're related to Emperor uq-Danresan. I played at a reception the emperor attended when he was in Gateport for the High Warlord vote, and what I remember most was a severe and bored looking man. His servants seemed terrified of him." He gave her a tentative smile. "I can take you to see them after Tomin checks you over. I know you're close friends."

"Maybe." she said.

Her tone didn't invite more questions, and silence fell. Arya was weary by the time they got to Tomin's healing offices, but was pleased that she'd managed to get there without her dizziness worsening. The murmur of voices came from inside, and she and Chiarn entered to see both Kulan and his mother Yarmina chatting with Raysa, Tomin's apprentice.

"Arya!" Kulan saw her first, his handsome face widening into a warm smile of welcome.

Pleasure swept through her, and she returned his warm hug fiercely. "Hello, Kulan. I'm sorry for the unexpected visit."

"Are you kidding?" He pulled back, green eyes dancing. "It's always a delight to see you, no matter the circumstances."

Yarmina smiled a more reserved but no less warm welcome. "We came in the hopes of running into you, Arya. I'm so glad to see you better. Kader told us you looked awful when you arrived."

"It's good to see both of you," Arya said, meaning it. "I have to—"

A child's laughter drifted from one of the smaller caverns Tomin used for consultations. Her eyes shot to Kulan's, and he took a step towards her. "Arya."

Before he could finish, Tomin stepped into the main room, the little boy in his arms giggling as he poked at Tomin's face with one of the healer's instruments. The child's beaming face brightened further at the sight of Kulan. "Papi, papi, papi!"

Kulan scooped the boy into his arms, swinging him in the air until he dissolved into chuckles of delight. Arya stared, unable to move, far too aware of Chiarn's puzzled gaze as he looked at her face, not to mention Raysa's presence.

"Arya?" Yarmina's hand fell on her shoulder.

"Are you feeling dizzy again?" Chiarn stepped closer, as if to help her stay upright.

"I'm okay." She cleared her throat at the shake in her voice and gave Chiarn a firm nod. "I'm good. Just a little moment, but it passed."

Tomin spoke briskly. "Chiarn, thanks for bringing Arya. Raysa is off to get some supplies we need. She offered to show you around—you told me you were keen to explore the markets?"

He brightened. "I'd love that. Thank you, Raysa."

Once they were gone, Tomin drew the curtain across the entryway, so no passersby could see inside.

Yarmina's gaze searched Arya's. "Tomin said you needed to speak with us. I wasn't sure whether to bring Kirin, but I thought … well, I thought you would want to see him. There's nobody else here."

Arya was still staring, gaze fixated on the little boy. Kulan brought him over. "Kirin, I want you to meet someone. This is my friend, Arya."

A pair of deep blue eyes scrutinised her for a moment, then the toddler beamed at her, exposing a missing front tooth. "Ayah."

He looked like Anjurin.

The thought slammed into her, almost sending her rocking back on her heels. His colouring was different from Rorin's son, the opposite in fact, but something about his face … she was delirious. Arya shoved aside her fanciful thoughts and managed a smile. "Hello, Kirin."

"Do you want to hold him?" Kulan asked gently.

Yarmina's hand, still on her shoulder, squeezed gently. "Take him, Arya. He's your son."

Arya bit her lip, wavering. Kulan handed the boy over and she took him with trembling hands. As soon as he was settled against her side, his tiny fingers reached up to play with her blonde hair.

"Pretty," Kirin announced, giving it a good tug.

"You think so?" Arya asked him, rocking slightly. Her son was warm and soft against her, his dark curls a match to his father's, his skin light brown like all Khadini. When he looked at her though, he had her Andahari blue eyes. The deep blue of the riverfolk. She thought he might have her slightly crooked nose, too. When their gazes met, Kirin beamed, a smile full of character and charm.

Arya swallowed, overcome. She couldn't have named the emotion rushing through her if she tried. Growing bored, Kirin squirmed in Arya's hold, and a moment later he held out his hands to Yarmina. The older woman took him with a smile, and Arya relinquished her son, reaching out to run a hand over his soft curls. "Thank you for taking such good care of him."

"He is my son," Kulan said. "I will always love and protect him."

Arya swallowed. "The Nightstalker knows about him."

A horrible silence descended on the room. Tomin went to the curtain across the entrance, looked out to make sure the corridor beyond was empty, and then stayed there, keeping watch.

"He doesn't know how old he is, whether he's a boy or a girl, but he knows I had a child." Arya rushed the words out before her courage deserted her. "You'll have to take him away, into the jungle, the camp we made where he was born. He'll be safer there."

"Arya, take a breath." Yarmina said quietly. "I am a mother too, and I understand your panic. But that is not the right course of action. If Kulan and I disappear with his son right after your arrival, it will raise eyebrows. It will be noticeable. The best and safest thing we can do is nothing."

"Kati is right," Kulan said gently.

Arya raised a trembling hand to her forehead to rub at her throbbing temples. "He'll be looking for Kirin everywhere. Kulan, are you sure nobody knows that we were lovers?"

"Kader knows, but would never breathe a word. Otherwise, it is only the people in this room. I swear it." Kulan held her gaze. "All here continue to believe Kirin is my son born of a lover who died in childbirth."

"If there is even the *slightest* sign of danger, you—"

"My son is more important to me than *anything*," Kulan said fiercely. "If anyone or anything comes for him, I will run and take him to safety, I swear it to you."

"I'm so sorry for all this. It's all my fault. I've put you all in so much danger."

"It is my son's fault as much as yours," Yarmina said tartly. "And not one person in this room regrets Kirin's existence."

Kulan reached for Arya's hand, squeezing gently, his green eyes warm and safe on hers. "Friends always, Arya."

She squeezed back, allowing herself to take the comfort he was offering. "Always. Kirin is lucky to have you both."

"Someone comes," Tomin spoke quietly from the door.

"It was so good to see you, Arya," Kulan said cheerfully. "Now, we're holding up poor Tomin, and this one needs his nap."

"It was good to see you too," she said, looking at Kirin as he gurgled happily in his grandmother's arms, playing with her necklace.

"Arya, come on back and I'll check you over," Tomin spoke. "My next patient will be here soon."

Yarmina hefted the boy. "Kirin, say goodbye to Arya."

"Bye, Ayah!" he waved happily.

"Bye, Kirin," she murmured, and she couldn't tear her eyes away until they'd vanished through the curtain.

She had to leave him *again*. It was harder than she could ever have imagined. He was safer this way, but she was still abandoning her child. He would grow up without his mother, just like Arya had. He would always be in danger, always hiding, just like Arya.

Unless she did something about it.

All her guilt and shame coalesced into something hard and knotted inside her. There was one way to make it so that Kirin didn't have to grow up without her. To make sure he would be safe and able to live a normal life. A way to protect Leanir. To make up for her mistakes, to avenge Thiara Ravenstrike's death.

Destroy the Nightstalker and take his place.

As Tomin checked her over, tactfully leaving her to her thoughts, Arya turned that realisation over and over in her mind. Kept thinking on it as she left his healing rooms and headed back to his quarters, stopping halfway to rest. There, she stared out over turquoise ocean, enjoying the breeze on her skin.

She didn't know how she'd do it. Doubted that she could.

But what other choice did she have now?

Chapter 17

Over the following three days, Arya slept more than she was awake. Each time she woke, she felt stronger and less dizzy when she moved. But with recovery and proper sleep came the nightmares. She started waking abruptly from them in the pre-dawn, the darkness of her room closing over her like a suffocating blanket, the images burned starkly clear in her mind's eye; the sadistic glee on the Nightstalker's face as he beat her.

But each night before the nightmares she had a different dream. This one reminded her of when she'd started dreaming of Elendryl. The dreamscapes had the same vibrant colours, the same crispness of detail, the same *knowing* that it wasn't just a dream. After the first, she wondered if it was Salyarin trying to reach out to her, but the distance was surely too far. She tried calling out his name anyway, but only received silence in response.

And just like in the dreams she'd once had about Elendryl, she was dragged from each one into the nightmares, until they finally released her into the waking world, gasping and afraid, and already wavering in her new resolve.

On the sixth morning this happened, Arya woke, heart pounding, sitting up to swing her legs over the side of the narrow bed. The quick movement made her head spin, and she closed her eyes to breathe until her head and heartbeat steadied. Even then, her hands still trembled, and she curled them into fists. After several moments, she uncurled her fingers, but the trembling was still there. Fear lurched in her stomach. "Dammit."

Would this weakness ever heal? She felt bone-deep terror that it wouldn't. How could she keep anyone safe, especially Kirin, like this?

Outside, a cool breeze whipped off the ocean and drifted through the walkways of Taskari, and Arya could taste the salt on her tongue. She walked slowly up the winding pathways and tested herself on the ladder leading to the cliff top. The climb tired her more than it should have, and fear returned.

It was still dark, but a line of orange light on the horizon promised the dawn. Arya could hear the soft lapping of waves against the shore far below, and the musical trilling of the birds in the jungle as they woke for the day. Elendryl and Asandryl slept nearby, a wary distance between them. Surprisingly, Chiarn was there too, standing at the cliff edge, staring northwest towards the Andahari coast.

Arya slowly walked over to join him. "I didn't think musicians woke before midday."

He shrugged. Didn't look at her.

"Do you want me to leave you alone?"

He took a breath, then gave himself a little shake, as if shrugging off some deep thought. "No. In fact, there's something I'd like to show you. Are you all right to keep standing for a while longer?"

"I'm fine. What are we waiting for?"

"You'll see."

They waited in companionable silence, Arya breathing deeply of the sweet morning air and allowing its peace to dispel the vestiges of the nightmare from her mind. Her taut shoulders slowly uncoiled. Her trembling hands settled.

And then, in a matter of moments, the sun crested the eastern horizon. Stunning pink and orange light lit up the ocean and spread across the sky. Arya watched in wonder as the rising sun brought bright colour to her surroundings; the green of the grass carpeting the clifftop, the golden yellow of the sand below, the azure blue of the water. And far, far in the distance, the hazy outline of what had to be the Riverlands in Andahar.

Chiarn said, "I don't think I've ever seen anything so beautiful. Even at the Etherean citadel. It's beautiful there, but cold, stark. This feels like new beginnings. Hope. Wonder."

"And there's the famous minstrel I know," she murmured, still transfixed.

"I'm going to write a ballad about it." His voice was animated in a way it hadn't been for months, years even, if she thought about it. "I'll call it *Sunrise over Andahar*, and every time I play it, I'll remember what it was like to stand here and watch it unfold."

No more was said, both watching as the sun broke away from the horizon and rose slowly into the sky.

When it seemed right to speak again, Arya cleared her throat. "Earlier, I woke from a nightmare, it's why I couldn't sleep. But I've been having other dreams too, and they feel ... did you dream it too? Is that why you were out here so early?"

Chiarn's jaw tensed. He hated admitting it when they shared dreams. She supposed he feared that every time he did, it locked him into a future and a destiny he didn't want.

She sighed. "I get it Chiarn, I truly do. But you were right the other day. The Nightstalker *is* going to continue hunting us. There is no way to stop that. Unless..." She hesitated. Saying it out loud felt like a risk, like making it *real.*

"Unless what?" he demanded.

She took a breath, reminded herself there was no choice anymore. Not if she wanted to keep Kirin safe. Leanir too. "Unless he is destroyed."

Chiarn made a dismissive gesture. "You say that as if it's possible."

She closed her eyes. How was she going to convince him if she couldn't even convince herself? "Look—"

He cut her off. "Yes, I had the dream. You're going there, aren't you?"

She simply nodded. It was a risk, going back to Andahar, one that filled her with fear. But the dreams would continue until she went there, and maybe this place, whatever it was, would help her in a fight against the Nightstalker.

He barked a laugh. "So, either I go with you to find some place that probably doesn't even exist, or fly back to the Etherean citadel alone while Xaphistryl is no doubt still searching the skies for us? I'll come, but after you're done and we're back at the citadel, I'm out. My greatest odds of staying alive are hiding, and that's what I plan to keep doing."

"Fine." She wasn't going to change his mind, not yet at least. "We leave this morning. Let's say our goodbyes and meet back here."

***

Tomin was rising for the day when Arya arrived at his home. He poured her a mug of steaming voseni. She took the cup. "It's time for me to leave."

"I'd prefer you spend another few days resting," he said. "You risk becoming ill again if you push too hard."

"I have to go." Part of her was afraid if she didn't leave now, her resolve already wavering, she might never summon the courage to do it.

He accepted that with a nod, but held her gaze. "Arya, the way you were beaten—that doesn't just leave physical wounds to recover from. It will take time."

She stopped herself looking away with an effort of will. "I'll be fine. Thank you so much for taking care of me again." She smiled sadly, then drained the voseni, relishing its taste and texture. "Keep well, Tomin. And don't forget our agreement. If there is trouble here, you bring your people to Ravenstrike. I have no power there any longer, but my brother rules as warlord, and he will help you."

"And the next time you get yourself hurt, know that you're welcome here."

She chuckled. "I'll keep that in mind."

Kulan was coming through the front as Arya turned to leave, and his face creased in relief when he caught sight of her. "Chiarn came to collect his things and said you were leaving."

"I think it's best. I know you've both discussed making sure any spies here are unable to get word out of our presence, but it's still safer for you if I don't linger too long." *And for Kirin.* The words went unspoken, but he heard them all the same.

"I wish I didn't have to agree." He hugged her. "But please don't forget you have friends and a safe place here, Arya, whenever you need us."

She returned the hug, more fiercely than she'd initially intended. "I'm glad that we're friends, Kulan."

"So am I. And one day you'll be back here. I know it in my bones."

"I hope you're right. Goodbye, Kulan."

She forced herself not to look back as she walked out, not to think of how Kirin's hair, his smile, was exactly like Kulan's. That she was walking out on Kirin *again*. Instead, she focused on the fact her son would be safe and happy here with a father and grandmother who loved him and would protect him with their lives.

Until Arya could make things safe for him.

***

On their first day of flying, Arya and Chiarn crossed the ocean between Khadini and Andahar, landing after sunset to make camp not far inland from the Riverlands coast. They sat before a small fire while Elendryl and Asandryl hunted under the cover of darkness. Around them, night insects buzzed continuously, occasionally interrupted by the growl of a toad or the hoot of an owl.

"This side trip is going to delay you, not to mention the longer we're in Andahari airspace the more danger we're in." Chiarn spoke, false casualness in his voice. "Don't you have to get back to Dunidaen to warn them? You don't look the picture of health after a day's flight either."

"Ah, still enthused by the detour, I see," Arya observed dryly. The truth was, she was exhausted, the world still spinning even now resting by the fire. She had to hope a night's rest was all she needed. "This feels like something I must do. I suspect you feel the same but are refusing to admit it to yourself."

He sighed in capitulation. "The dreams felt so rich, so real. Do you think the others shared them?"

"Probably." Even though she'd torn free of the thread connecting her with the Nightstalker, Arya had been wary of un-muting her bonds with the others in their *caidre,* especially Leanir, in case it put him in more danger. Damn Ranier for disappearing on her. He'd have been able to tell her whether it was safe.

Silence fell. Another owl hooted mournfully in the distance.

"This was what I loved most about being a minstrel," Chiarn said. "Nights like this when I was on the road between towns, the open sky above me. Sitting by my fire and counting the stars until I fell asleep."

"It sounds nice," Arya agreed. "Unless you were travelling through Ravenstrike or Falconcrest in the winter, I imagine?"

He laughed. "Touché."

"I miss my old life too, Chiarn."

He must have heard the note of bitter grief she'd been unable to hide, because he changed the subject. "How long to get where we're going, do you think?"

"I know as much as you do." Since waking, the place Arya had dreamed of had remained as a little pulsing light in her magic. At least, that's how best she could describe it to herself. It was like a faint compulsion—but not a nefarious one. A tugging from somewhere that wanted her, or that she wanted to be. Ugh, this magic was ridiculous.

The wyverns seemed confident they could find the place, but neither had a grasp of the distance to travel to get there. She sighed, giving in to the exhaustion tugging at her and curling up under her blanket. "Get some sleep, Chiarn. The wyverns will watch over us."

"*Safe.*" Elendryl assured her.

***

Despite the hard ground, Arya woke feeling surprisingly well the next morning, the exhaustion of the previous days' flight gone. And over the next few days, as they made sure to always take off and land under the cover of darkness and fly high enough that nobody below would be able to see them, she didn't worsen in any way. Chiarn, too, seemed lighter in spirit.

It was the morning of their fourth day of travel—on a steady northwest heading—when Elendryl informed Arya he thought they were getting close to their destination. Not long after midday, the two wyverns reached a rugged coastline. Arya gazed around with interest as they dropped below cloud cover and turned north, skimming along the tops of the cliffs. The ocean this far northwest was a deep azure, white-capped waves crashing powerfully against the rocks.

Elendryl and Asandryl dropped below the clifftops, great wings skimming the tops of the waves, challenging each other as to how low they could get. As they followed the curve of the cliffs, a wide gorge opened ahead of them. At the mouth of the gorge, two massive waterfalls cascaded down into the ocean.

The wyverns flew unhesitatingly towards the waterfalls, engulfing their riders in a fog of mist and spray. When they emerged from the mist, they were flying over a narrow stretch of water with high cliffs looming on either side. The water below churned angrily. But it wasn't long before the gorge opened into a tranquil azure bay. Arya gasped and straightened, staring. Above the water of the bay, high on a grassy hillside rising from the water, sat a wondrous marble palace.

Exactly what she'd seen in her dreams.

Four gold-veined marble towers soared into the sky at each corner of the outer walls, with a fifth tower, the tallest of them all, rising from the heart of the palace. The midday sun glittered off the gold and ivory, transforming an already graceful structure into something out of a minstrel's tale.

"*Take me there,*" she urged Elendryl.

Her wyvern crossed the bay and soared over the walls of the palace to land at the top of the central tower. A strong breeze whipped around them, ruffling her bound hair. Elendryl stretched out his wings in bliss.

Moments later Asandryl landed, and Chiarn dismounted, eyes wide with wonder. "I've never seen anything like it," he breathed.

Neither had Arya.

She could see for miles around; ocean to the west, rolling hills to the north and south, and un-tilled farmland to the east. Arya walked into the centre of the platform, boots echoing on the smooth marble surface. "The others should be here." The words spilled out of her without thought. "They need to see this, to feel this."

This had been her grandfather's seat. She just knew.

"Why is it empty?" Confusion filled Chiarn's voice. "This is far more beautiful and luxurious, not to mention dripping with grandeur, than you described Darkclaw Deep. Why didn't the Nightstalker move in here the moment he took the throne?"

"I don't know."

He snorted. "I assume you have the same answer to why we dreamed of this place. I'm going to look around a little."

She nodded, a bit distracted. "Me too."

Arya turned to Elendryl. Catching her regard, he came up behind her, resting his head gently on her right shoulder. She reached up to press a palm against his scales, and they communed.

"Ours?" he asked.

Her answer to him was long in coming, but when it did, her voice was firm and sure.

"Ours," she agreed.

***

Arya spent hours walking through long-empty hallways and rooms, boots echoing on unused marble staircases. Unlike the homes and shops on the underground road beneath the Diamondfang, everything here had been cleaned away. No half-eaten meals or opened closets, no untidy beds. It had been stripped bare of everything that had once made it a home.

As the sun lowered in the sky, Arya returned to the top of the central tower to watch the sunset. Something had shifted in her in the long hours she'd walked these empty halls. The Nightstalker's beating, how easily he'd dominated her, it had decimated whatever remnants of her confidence were left after Thiara Ravenstrike's death. She was physically weaker than she'd ever been. Her nightmares ever since had eaten away at her resolve to face him, to destroy him, the only way to keep Kirin safe. To be able to have him in her life.

But being here, it made her realise that things *weren't* entirely hopeless, even if they felt that way. In the weakest moment of her life, both physically and mentally, she'd torn the Nightstalker from her magic. In that one small way, she'd bested him.

That was something she could hold onto.

She was going to do this. Take everything that was hers by birthright and use it to destroy the Nightstalker.

So, fight it was. One step at a time. Even if fear and weakness dogged her with every breath. Even if her confidence was in tatters. She would fight.

A nudge from Elendryl warned her of Chiarn's arrival, and she turned to see him standing a short distance off, watching her. The orange glow of the setting sun set his copper hair aflame. "Something on your mind?" she asked.

"I have to know, Arya. Why did we come here? Why did you even come to Andahar in the first place? Are you going to exploit these people's hope, their belief that somehow we're going to save them?"

"I came to Andahar originally to scout the Nightstalker's army, to learn whether he planned to invade, and if so, how soon and with what numbers."

He folded his arms over his chest, giving her a pointed look. "And now?"

Arya walked to where the Stormrider name was spelled out in sapphire gems in the centre of the floor. "The power to do what is needed to make things right," she murmured.

"What?"

Chiarn could never know about Kirin, her true motivation for finally deciding to face the Nightstalker, not until their enemy was dead, anyway. So, she looked at him, and told him something that was also true. "It's what I've always wanted. The power to make things right. And now I'm going to take it."

His shoulders slumped, arms falling to his sides, and he let out a long breath, looking tired and beaten. She recognised the look intimately; she'd worn it more than once.

"What is it you want, Chiarn, if there was no Nightstalker and you had the freedom to choose anything?" Arya had asked Essa this question once and now she wanted to know Chiarn's answer.

Because she had to win him to her side.

There was no choice. The best chance of killing Lucius Nightstalker was with a powerful *caidre* at her back, so she had to do whatever it took to make that happen. Kirin's life was at stake.

"I want to be what I *was*! A popular minstrel. I want to travel wherever I like, whenever I like. I want a life where I'm not being hunted. Where I'm free, Arya. That's what I want." The words burst out of him, angry and raw.

"I can give that to you."

"What?" he asked, looking exasperated.

Arya faced him. "If you do this with me, if you accept what we are, and help me kill the nazal and bring down the Nightstalker, then I promise you that life."

He stared at her, as if he thought she might be joking, then laughed. "I'll die helping you kill a nazal or trying to take down the Nightstalker. What kind of promise is that?"

"You'll die if you don't," she said bluntly. "You know that already. It's why you're here now, why you eventually went to find Asandryl. The best chance you have of survival is to join with me. Do that, and you'll also have the life you want when it's all over."

"Even if we managed to somehow win, I'll be a Sky Lord of Andahar, and trapped in that life," he said.

"If we win, Chiarn, I will set you free. I swear that to you now. My word on it."

Surprise crossed Chiarn's handsome face, then a brief flash of hope that quickly died. "We won't survive it."

"The odds are low," she admitted, hiding her doubt and fear deep where he'd never see it. "But I've won against low odds before."

He swallowed, then slowly shook his head. "You can't save me, Arya. Only hiding will do that."

"Think about it, that's all I ask," she said. "Your freedom in return for your alliance. My word on it, Chiarn Flamewielder."

He opened his mouth as if to dispute her naming of him, but then thought better of it. "I'll think on it, but don't hope for a different answer."

"Thank you. Now, I need a favour."

He eyed her warily. "What is it?"

"Don't worry, you'll be going back to the citadel, and not alone, I promise. We're just going to make one more little detour first."

***

The two Valheran hugged the southern coastline of Andahar as they flew east. Nauseas fear curdled in Arya's stomach as they approached the mountains of the Horn, but they kept to the coast and stayed well clear of Darkclaw Deep. Then the lake and river-filled landscape of the Riverlands was below them and they had to risk flying lower as they approached their destination so that Elendryl could identify the landmarks Arya had been told to look for.

Eventually, he shifted into a dive, and Asandryl followed suit. They dropped towards a grassy valley floor full of movement. It appeared to be a long distance from any towns or villages. People ran about, loading supplies onto carts and wagons, while others worked to dismantle what looked to have been a long-term camp.

As soon as the wyverns were spotted, shouts echoed, and everyone stopped what they were doing to stare. Arya deliberately brought them down a distance away so that she had time to close her eyes and let the vertigo of her rapid descent settle. When she opened them again, her vision was clear and Niallin's tall figure was striding toward them.

"Arya. Chiarn," he greeted them, astonishment filling his voice.

She glanced around, taking in the loaded carts and packed tents. "It looks like we just caught you."

"We have word the nazal have learned of this camp and are on their way with a troop of Nightblades. It's a shame. This was one of our most secure bases."

"Where will you go?"

A grim look settled on his face, even though his voice when he spoke was confident. "To the next safe place."

"And how many next safe places do you have?"

His mouth tightened, and he didn't reply.

Arya glanced over at Chiarn, who gave her a resigned nod. "Take them over the Diamondfang, Niallin."

"We are not yours to command," he said steadily.

"Yes, you are."

"Arya, I—"

She raised a hand to stop him. "I am going back to Dunidaen to help them stop this invasion. In the meantime, you and your people will be safe in the Etherean citadel. And I'm going to need all of you to stay safe and uncaptured. Because I'm going to come back to Andahar, and when I do, I'll need an army behind me, Niallin."

Niallin glanced between the two of them, looking as if he were too afraid to hope.

"I mean it," she said firmly. "I will come back for Andahar, but I need to help stop the invasion first. If he takes Dunidaen, that gives him more territory, more resources. We cannot afford to let that happen if we want to defeat him."

Niallin hesitated only a moment longer before placing his palm over his heart and bowing slightly. "We will march for the Diamondfang today."

Arya ran her eyes over those assembled. "Chiarn will wait for you in the foothills to escort you. His fire magic can keep your people warm, and Asandryl will keep any predators away. The Etherean healers at the citadel will be able to treat any injuries from the hike when you arrive."

Niallin straightened, his eyes shining. "I hope to see you soon, Lord Arya Stormrider. May the waters you travel always be calm."

For the first time ever, Arya did not protest the use of her true name. It settled over her shoulders, feeling new, and not quite fitting yet. Like a new pair of boots.

But it also felt right.

Chapter 18

Arya and Elendryl swooped through the cavernous entry to the Etherean citadel with a gust of icy mountain air. She climbed down slowly, his body leaning into her in case she lost her balance. She didn't feel quite as good as when she'd left Andahar that morning, but attributed it to the altitude.

"*Go.*" She pressed a palm to his side. "*I'll be well.*"

Leaving him to hunt before seeking his stable, Arya made straight for the elder's quarters. Weariness tugged at her bones—it seemed weariness *always* tugged at her these days—but she pushed through. The dizziness was harder to manage, the altitude exacerbating her vertigo, but she gritted her teeth and pushed on.

The guards outside Salyarin's quarters let her straight through, which told her she and Elendryl had been spotted approaching the citadel. The elder waited in his reception room, hands clasped at his front, sky-blue wings folded behind him. As usual, his expression gave nothing away. Arya stopped before him and took a moment to catch her breath. "Elder, thank you for seeing me so quickly."

"I was eager to learn how your visit to Dunidaen went."

"It went as well as could be expected," Arya said. "But that's not why I'm here, and I won't be staying. I came to let you know that a large group of Andahari rebels are on their way here, under Chiarn's protection. I ask that you give them safe haven when they arrive."

Salyarin cleared his throat, a small expression of the surprise flaring in his eyes. "And why would Andahari rebels be coming here?"

"Because the Nightstalker is hunting them, and I told them I would protect them if they came here."

He lifted an eyebrow. "And they listened to you, because?"

She held his gaze. "Because I told them I'm going to do everything I can to destroy the Nightstalker. And I know I can't do that without accepting my heritage and becoming a Sky Lord."

He blinked, but his expression didn't change. After a moment, he waved her over to where comfortable chairs surrounded a small table beside magnificent floor-to-ceiling windows. Sunlight glittered off the peaks and the riot of colour of Etherean out taking advantage of the weather.

Salyarin poured them both a cup of tea from a steaming pot on the table, then sat back in his chair. "Tell me what brought about this sudden change of heart?"

The tea was not quite sweet enough, but pleasantly warm, so she took another sip. It gave her time to arrange her thoughts, bring to mind her rehearsed answer, the same one she'd given Chiarn. "It's the only way to protect my home and the people that I love."

"Ah, I see." He seemed calm, as if she'd come to tell him she preferred fish stew to beef. It made her itch, but she fought shifting uncomfortably in her chair. Salyarin always managed to make her feel like a wayward child. "And you've just come to that realisation now?"

Her jaw tightened. "I've said I'll do it. You don't need to question my resolve."

He sighed. "There are fading bruises on your face, not to mention the healing gash above your right eye. Did the warlords react that poorly to your presence in Dunidaen, or do your injuries have more to do with why Andahari rebels are on their way here?"

"They were the result of an encounter with the Nightstalker," Arya said bluntly.

That got a reaction. Finally. Salyarin turned ashen. "You went to Andahar?"

"Yes. It's a long story, but I was captured and taken to Darkclaw Deep, where the Nightstalker found me."

Salyarin placed his cup down, his hands trembling so much the fine pottery clattered against the surface. "How are you still alive?"

"I escaped before he could kill me. The rebels helped. I wouldn't have gotten out without them." She had to take a breath, push away those memories before they overwhelmed her. "But I was in bad shape for a while."

Salyarin shifted on his backless chair, wings rustling in agitation.

Arya took pity on him. "Despite what happened, my travel to Andahar brought me critical intelligence on the Nightstalker's invasion plans—critical because the Dunidae warlords are divided and at each other's throats. Unifying their armies is going to be challenging."

As fast as that, Salyarin's frustration was back. "Why bother with Dunidaen? If you've made the decision to destroy the Nightstalker, then why not *do* it."

Arya settled back in her chair and eyed him with a narrow gaze. "You're serious?"

"Dunidaen wouldn't be in danger if you killed the Nightstalker."

She tried to swallow the frustrated temper that made her want to snap a reply. Salyarin *was* serious, he wasn't trying to rile her. But it revealed how little he understood military strategy. Arya did, and she'd been thinking about this ever since that moment in Tomin's healing room, when she'd first allowed herself to face the idea of going after the Nightstalker.

"Elder, I tell you categorically that I cannot face him in a direct fight and win. If I want any chance at all, I need three things. First, an army, and allies. Second, I need time, to get stronger, for my *cairdre* to get stronger. And third, most critically of all, I need knowledge that you can't give me. Because I probably won't ever win a stand-up fight against the Nightstalker. Which means I need some other way to get at him, something creative, that he hasn't thought of. I need the Inkweaver archives, and so I need an Inkweaver."

Arya paused, let that sink in, then continued. "I can't stop the Nightstalker coming for Dunidaen, but I *can* help them wipe out his army, and by doing so, blunt his strength. An allied Dunidae army at my back would be a serious help in a fight against the Nightstalker."

Realisation cleared Salyarin's expression. "You want to win the warlords to your side, so they march at your back."

"Yes. Then the Khadini. I'm going to bring the entire world against Lucious Nightstalker and his nazal." Arya spoke confidently, hiding her incredible doubts about how achievable that was going to be. One step at a time.

He let out a long breath. She thought it might be relief. Then he smiled and leaned forward. "I have a gift for you, Lord Arya Stormrider, heir to the ruling House of Andahar. Will you accept it?"

She spoke as formally as he had. "I would be honoured, Elder Salyarin."

Salyarin stood, then propelled himself across the room with a single beat of his beautiful wings. He disappeared through a door—presumably his private quarters. When he returned a few moments later, he carried a rolled piece of Etherean silk which he placed in Arya's hands before taking his seat.

She stood, allowing the silk to unroll. It was a deep cobalt in colour, but the ink used to make it shimmered in the light, revealing a myriad of differing shades and hues of blue. Silver thread traced the edges of the cloak in a complex, beautiful pattern, not unlike Inkweaver art. And as the cape unfolded entirely, Arya gasped at the large image at its centre.

A silver lightning bolt, firmly gripped in the talons of a raven, wings spread wide and proud.

"The lightning is the sigil of House Stormrider," Salyarin said quietly. "But I have heard you all these years, Arya. I understand that in your heart, you are not only Stormrider, you are Ravenstrike. So, I modified the sigil in the hopes you would be willing to wear it one day."

"It's beautiful," Arya whispered. She had not expected such a gracious and thoughtful gift. "I am truly honoured. Thank you, Elder Salyarin."

She put the cloak on. Its collar buttoned comfortably around her neck, then fell across her shoulders and down her back in shimmering waves, stopping just short of the tops of her boots. The fabric was so light she barely felt its weight.

She only wished she felt worthy of it. For all her confident words to Salyarin, she still didn't truly believe she could pull any of it off.

"This, also, is yours." Salyarin held out his palm. Nestled within it was a gleaming ring, forged from twisting strands of silver and dotted with small glittering sapphires. "This was your grandfather's ring, and it was given to him by his father before him, and by the queen before that. Only the heir to House Stormrider may wear it."

"How do you have this?" she asked in wonder.

"I've held on to it for many years."

Arya slipped the ring onto her right index finger. It fit perfectly. "You knew my father?" she asked him.

The elder smiled. "Not well, but yes. His name was Torin."

Arya sat, her eyes still on the ring. Her father had never been a consideration in her life, neither of her parents had. To Arya, family was Ravenstrike. Seeing something that had belonged to her real father though, it shook her. "Will you tell me about him?"

Salyarin leaned forward to refill both their cups of tea, then sat back with his, eyes distant as he searched his memories. "You look very much like him, the same blonde hair and blue eyes. Torin spent a lot of time here when he was young, when my mother ruled the Etherean. He loved the mountains. It seemed the higher he could get, the happier he was. He couldn't wait for the day he would become a Sky Lord and fly through the skies like we do."

"How did he die?"

"That I don't know." Sadness flashed over his face. "After the Nightstalker murdered his father, Torin fled Andahar with a friend. They made it here safely, and my mother kept his presence here a secret. But they both knew that one day he would be found, and so he left rather than place us in danger. I believe he planned to hike into Dunidaen. Part of him must have feared he wouldn't live long, because he left that ring with my mother."

"Do you know who my mother was?"

"No. We despaired after my mother dreamed of his death, because she assumed that was the end of the Stormrider line. Torin didn't have any siblings, uncles, or aunts."

Arya frowned. "So how did you learn that I existed?"

"The simple answer to your question is that I dreamed of you." Salyarin shrugged. "Dream-walking is a power held only by the rulers of the Etherean and their heir."

Curiosity made her tear her gaze from the ring. "Was the friend who came here with my father killed too?"

"Torin fled Andahar with Ranier Inkweaver."

Silence filled the room.

She'd known. She'd *known* Ranier was from House Inkweaver. Known he was Andahari.

But this...

Salyarin gave her a gentle smile. "They grew up together. Best friends from the time they were knee high."

"So Ranier survived when my father did not." And how did that fit with Ranier knowing Darmanin's mother, the Nightstalker's own daughter?

"I cannot tell you any more than that. I have not seen or spoken to Ranier since he left with Torin to hike into Dunidaen."

It all clicked into place for Arya. *This* was why Ranier looked out for her, despite his lack of caring for Dunidaen or its welfare, despite his violent and merciless nature.

She was the daughter of his best friend.

"Do you have any idea where Ranier might go in Andahar if he was hiding?" she asked, explaining how the Shadeweaver leader had vanished after drawing the nazal off.

"None, I'm afraid." Salyarin look grim. "I never got to know Ranier like I did Torin. He was always secretive, withdrawn. It was an unlikely friendship, and not only because Ranier wasn't his family's heir, so not in Torin's social sphere."

Curiosity niggled at Arya. "Who is *your* heir, Elder? You mentioned your dream-walking ability earlier. Would he or she be able to dream-walk me if needed?"

His expression closed over. "She is lost to us."

"I'm sorry." Arya apologised. "The death of a child. I can't imagine. I shouldn't have brought it up."

"She is not dead." Salyarin spoke so quietly Arya barely heard him. "But lost all the same. Now, we will welcome these rebels when they arrive, as you have asked. But they cannot stay long. If the Nightstalker hunts them, he will eventually learn they are here, and I will not place my people in that kind of danger."

Arya winced inwardly. More lives she was placing in danger. Without thinking, she reached up to unbutton the cloak and take it off before folding it neatly. She didn't want to offend the elder, but she couldn't wear it. She didn't deserve to.

"I understand, and I will be in touch."

Chapter 19

I t was Winterfest eve when Arya arrived back at Heathrock.

The castle was lit up, carriages filled the entry yard, and there was a double guard of Raiders on the walls. It seemed Rorin was upholding his mother's tradition of holding a formal Winterfest eve reception in honour of his vicelords.

As tempting as the thought was, Arya decided not to ruin the proceedings by having a wyvern land atop the walls, and instead dismounted a half mile out from the front gates. Her head felt much better for being away from the thin air of the citadel, but the underlying weariness she'd felt since her beating was still there, warning her not to push too hard.

She wore a woven Etherean tunic and breeches in deeper blue, matched with grey leather boots and silver laces. Her cazaix sword swung at her hip, in a new cobalt-dyed leather sheath, another gift she'd found waiting in her room at the citadel. She lifted her right hand, studying the platinum ring that glimmered on her index finger.

Perhaps Winterfest eve was the perfect time to have arrived.

As she walked, she took a deep breath, bringing to life the bond that joined her to Leanir. She'd made the decision to try reaching out to him on the flight down, judging the risk small if she only kept the thread alive for a short time. Her fear for him, and the associated guilt, grew with every day that passed since she'd told the Nightstalker his name. If he was with the Shadeweavers in the Wraith Forest, she'd be able to sense his presence, and go and find him.

But when the thread shimmered to life, it was dull with distance. He was alive and well, but far away. As quickly as she determined that, she muted the thread. She would just have to hope Darmanin had managed to warn him. The lights of Heathrock came into sight through the trees, and Arya reluctantly unfolded the cloak Salyarin had given her, buttoning it over her shoulders. It made her itch with discomfort, but it would be necessary for what she was about to do.

A light snow began falling as Arya approached the main gates, but even in the dark and weather the alert Raiders recognised her this time and waved her through without protest. The captain in charge of the shield on duty wasn't a woman Arya recognised though, and she watched Arya warily as she crossed the main entry yard.

Straightening her shoulders, Arya strode through the open doors and across the dim entry foyer, making straight for the opened double doors to the great hall, where light spilled across the stone floor. There, she came to a halt at the top of the hall. She nodded her head to the flustered-looking servant whose job it was to introduce the guests. "Lord Arya Stormrider of Andahar."

People were already glancing her way, noticing the new arrival and how different she looked. When the servant called out her name in a voice designed to project through the large space, a shocked silence quickly swept through those gathered.

Arya stood tall, one hand loosely on the hilt of her sword, cloak shimmering in the light, letting the stares and the whispers wash over her. Movement came from her left—Rorin, weaving toward her, a blinding smile on his face. Arya's gaze shifted from him to study the room, noting the finely dressed vicelords and their spouses, Peemla with Vicelord Lerin, lifting her hand in a delighted wave, and then ... Darmanin stood by the windows, glass of wine in one hand, a little bubble of distance around him.

Arya met his gaze, smiled, and bowed her head, placing her hand on her heart.

He smiled back, tipped his glass toward her.

And then Rorin was there, reaching out to touch her arm, clearly realising a warlord shouldn't hug a foreign dignitary even though he obviously desperately wanted to.

"Lord Stormrider. Welcome to Heathrock." The announcer translated his signing, loud enough for all to hear.

While he did that, Rorin signed discreetly. *"I'm going to have to tell them who you are."*

"I know," she murmured. "We'll do this together."

Technically, they should have choreographed it, sought Essa's advice as to what to say to allay any concerns, but they were here now, and her brother stood at her side. As soon as the servant finished translating, Arya took a breath and spoke for the whole room.

"Thank you, Warlord Ravenstrike." She bowed her head politely. "I am honoured to be in your home again."

Rorin continued seamlessly, *"Vicelords, family, guests, you'll remember my adopted sister, Arya Ravenstrike. Arya came to House Ravenstrike as a Name-less, yet we've recently learned that she is descended from the ruling House of Andahar—abandoned as a baby after her father was killed by the Nightstalker's hunters."*

Arya let those words settle before continuing, "And though I stand before you tonight having claimed my place as a Sky Lord and heir to the Andahari throne, it does not make me any less a Ravenstrike," she said, her words reverberating through the hall. "This place was my beloved home for many years. I have not and will *never* forget it."

The reaction to that was muted, but she noticed not a few faces nodding along in agreement.

"Lord Stormrider will always be welcome in Ravenstrike State," Rorin fin-ished. *"And I ask that you all treat her as a close ally."*

They walked into the room together and slowly the chatter and clinking of glasses resumed. Arya smiled at those who looked directly at her, and pretended to ignore the fact that all the whispering was about her.

"You do like an entrance," Rorin signed. *"You're well?"*

"Getting that way," she assured him. "I can't see Essa and Taze in here. Are they okay?"

"Both fine. Essa has been in SparrowWing and hoped to make it back in time for this, but bad weather held her up. Taze is in Anduil as Arken's representative with the Lances. We won't see him until the State Council in Gateport."

Reassured, Arya took a breath. "Right, shall we split up? I'll greet as many vicelords as I can with my charm and wit, while you go around assuring them that although I'm a magic-wielder, I'm not a monster who's going to eat them?"

He chuckled. *"In the absence of Essa's advice, I think that's as good a plan as any."*

***

Much later, Arya meandered through the great hall of Heathrock, a half-finished glass of spiced wine in one hand. It was growing late, guests having long since trailed up to their rooms or climbed into carriages if they lived close enough. Exhaustion thrummed under her skin, warning her to get some rest before illness claimed her again. But she needed to find Darmanin first. Find out whether he'd managed to get a warning to Leanir.

Rorin appeared at her side, close enough their shoulders pressed together. *"Dramatic entrance notwithstanding, it warms my heart to have you back here again for Winterfest."*

"I'm sorry I didn't have a chance to warn you beforehand. I didn't time it deliberately, but when I arrived and saw the occasion, I figured it was as good a time as any to announce myself to Dunidaen."

"I sense the reason you wanted to do that is a longer story for another time, so I'll leave it for now, but you should know I didn't have to do as much reassuring as you thought I would," he said. *"The vicelords couldn't stop talking about the Sky Lords rising again. I think they're as excited as they are wary about what it all means."* He gave her a look. *"News will leak south to Gateport. People here know you, and that's eased the reaction they might otherwise have had to you being a magic-wielder. That won't be the case everywhere else."*

"I know," she said, turning to him curiously. "But I'm honestly surprised that there hasn't been a stronger reaction here too."

He shrugged. "*Things are different in Ravenstrike. Not how I want them, not yet, but Essa and I have been working hard. Branding magic-wielders is now outlawed here, as is refusing housing or employment to a magic-wielder. Unless they break the law, magic-wielders are, under law at least, to be treated the same as any other citizen.*"

Surprise flashed through Arya. "How have your people taken that?"

"*Better than I'd expected. There has been some outrage. Many still ignore the new laws. But there's also been a lot of relief. Especially from people with loved ones who are magic-wielders.*" He paused. "*And Arken has ensured the Raiders police the new laws actively.*"

"Oh Rorin." She turned to him with a smile. "I don't even know what to say." *Better than she would have done* might have been it. "You didn't need me at all."

His expression turned uncharacteristically serious. "*Arya, I want you to know something. When I saw you tonight, with the presence you now have about you, it's clear that you're not just a Ravenstrike anymore. And I'm glad of it. I know you made some mistakes, but you truly weren't to blame for my parents' deaths.*"

"Rorin, I—"

"*Let me finish,*" he hushed her. "*You were never meant to be anyone's general. But I want you to know that you will always be my sister, and that Anji will always know you as his aunt, his family. You are Ravenstrike as much as you are Stormrider.*"

Tears pricked Arya's eyes and for once she didn't fight them off. "I never had family until the day we met, Rorin. You were the first person in the world I truly loved, and you will always be my little brother."

"*We've been worried about you, ever since Dar came back from Andahar. He said you were in a bad way, he said—*"

"I was, and I still have a little way to go, but I'm going to be fully well again. I promise you."

"*I don't ever want to lose you.*" He swallowed. "*Please, Arya. Never again.*"

"I'll do my best if you promise me the same."

He grinned and hugged her tightly. "*Do you remember our first Winterfest when all of us were together?*"

"I came back from a patrol to find Taze and Dar spiking Peemla's punch while you and Essa distracted her. Instead of chiding you, I let you get away with the prank." Arya smiled at the memory. "Speaking of, where *is* Dar? I saw him when I arrived but didn't manage to catch him in the crowd after. Too many people to talk to."

"*He left to go for a walk some time ago.*"

She raised an eyebrow. "It's snowing outside."

Rorin shrugged. "*You know Dar. Even after all this time, he still struggles to let us in. And Winterfest eve is the anniversary of his mother's death.*"

Arya frowned. "I might go and make sure he is okay."

"*If anyone can help, it will be you.*" Rorin squeezed her arm. "*Will you have breakfast with Peemla and Anji and me? Peemla missed you too and I know she'd love some time with you.*"

"I'd like that," Arya said. "You seem truly happy with her. More settled than you used to be."

"*She's my safe place. She and Anji both.*" He paused, seemingly trying to find the right words. "*When you have that, it changes you. Or at least, it did for me.*"

"How did you know?" Arya asked, curious now. "We grew up together, all of us, Peemla too in many ways. How did you know you were in love with her? That it was different to what you felt for the rest of us."

A boyish grin broke out across his face. "*It was the day Dar and I came back from fostering in Hawkesdale. I'd gone from fourteen to seventeen in those years, and I walked in here that day, saw Peemla, and my chest, it went tight, but in a good way, and the room settled around me, and I felt … warm and happy. Just looking at her.*"

"Do you think it could be slower than that? Like, something that creeps up on you without you realising?"

Rorin cocked his head. "*Are you asking for romantic advice, because if you are, you just need to give me a moment to jump up and down with glee, and then I promise to be a good younger brother and be serious about whatever you ask.*"

Arya snorted. "No, I'm not, thank you anyway."

"*Asking for a friend, huh?*" He laughed silently. "*I can tell you that it was dif-ferent for Peemla, not so sudden. She was smarter than me, knew how problematic it was, for a chamberlain to fall for a warlord's heir.*"

"That shouldn't matter," Arya mumbled. "I'm sorry I made it matter."

"*Things are never black and white, sister mine, and I have long forgiven you that. Now go on and check on our erstwhile foster brother.*"

Arya hugged him again. "See you at breakfast tomorrow. We do need to talk—I came back with what you asked me for, and I've made a decision we need to talk through."

His face turned serious. "*Can it wait a day? Tomorrow is Winterfest, and the first time we'll have you here for family lunch in years.*"

She hesitated, but in the end, agreed. "It can wait a day, but no more."

"*I hear you.*"

***

Arya headed out into the night. Her steps felt lighter after her conversation with Rorin. Guessing Darmanin would have avoided the main gates, Arya instead made her way through the kitchen gardens and out to the side gate set in the wall along the frozen lake.

A voice called down from above. "Looking fancy tonight, General."

She looked up. "Charlin! Still here, I see. Not too old to heft that axe of yours yet?"

He snorted. "No need for insults. It hasn't been that long."

"You good? What about Wattin—how long's that beard gotten?"

"Far below regulation length, General." The man himself leaned over the wall. "Good to see you."

"I'm not your general anymore."

"No, you went and got yourself a shiny title." Charlin's disdainful sniff showed what he thought of that.

She chuckled. "Pass my greetings to the others, if you will."

Charlin scowled. "Come find us in the mess for an ale and do it yourself. If you're not too good for us anymore, that is."

"Yeah, yeah, I'll come find you."

Still chuckling, Arya pushed through the gate, gaze going to the clear boot prints in the snow that led along the narrow path beneath the wall. She followed the prints, her own boots sinking deep into the crisp snow. The air was biting cold, causing her breath to frost, but there was no breeze. It was a perfectly calm night, with flakes of snow drifting through the air and catching in her hair.

She loved this place with a fierceness that still stole her breath away.

She'd reached the end of the wall when her searching gaze caught on a tall, lonely figure standing out on the ice, face lifted towards the sky. Darmanin had strapped on a pair of skates to traverse the frozen surface, but he wasn't moving. In moments like these, it was hard to credit the elder's claims that he was a danger to her. Tonight, his entire being exuded only loneliness and sadness.

Arya made her way through the trees to the small boat shed that sat on the lake's edge. Inside, she found her old pair of skates and strapped them on. It wasn't long before she was skating out towards Darmanin. Vertigo initially made her head swim at the quick movements, and she had to slow, let her head and body catch up.

He turned as she approached, sensing her presence. "Arya. It's good to see you looking so much better."

"Leanir?" she asked.

Darmanin gave a little shake of his head. "I'm sorry, I haven't been able to track him down. My Shadeweaver contacts are old, and I've let them lapse since becoming warlord. Either they don't work anymore or he's ignoring me. Can you sense where he is?"

"He's not close." Arya swallowed bitter disappointment. "Do you hate me, for what I did? Is that why you've been avoiding me all night?"

"I know you never would have given him up willingly, and I know you would have fought the Nightstalker with every bit of strength you had. There is no blame to be apportioned."

There was. Arya had chosen her son over Leanir. But she couldn't tell Darmanin about Kirin. So, she bit her lip and looked away, unable to bear the shame she felt. "I'll find him. Make sure he's safe."

"I'll keep trying too." Darmanin sighed. "Aren't we a pair of grey clouds tonight?"

She looked at him, holding out her hands and forcing a grin. "Come on. Let's see if you can keep up with me."

He reached out after only a brief hesitation, taking her hands and allowing her to guide him around the lake. They skated loose circles on the ice, breaking apart and coming back together as if orchestrating the steps of a dance. The night was quiet as they skated, not talking, just moving together.

Then, Arya tried to perform a quick turn that sent a wave of dizziness flooding her senses. She lost her balance, falling to land painfully on the ice. Darmanin skated up. For a moment he was silent, then his grey eyes gleamed and he burst out into laughter. Caught by the beauty of his laugh, she joined in, and for a long moment they laughed together.

"Hey, I have still-healing bones," she said with a mock-scowl.

"Here." Darmanin bent and offered her his hand, still smiling.

She gripped the offered hand, but as soon as he'd committed himself to lifting her, she tugged backwards. He overbalanced and fell. She laughed again, whooping loudly in triumph. He lifted himself onto his elbows, but after shooting her a glare of reproach, his face softened into another smile.

She moved on instinct then, pushing him back down to the ice, throwing a leg over his waist to straddle him, and pinning his wrists above his head. "I want you to join my *cairdre*, Darmanin." She held his gaze as she spoke the words, and reached for the bond between them, opening up so there was nothing hidden. "I want you with me, at my side. I know you're going to say no, and I know why. But I need you to know that I want you."

He stared up at her for a long moment, remaining still in her hold. When he did eventually speak, his words were whisper soft. "You've truly decided, then?"

"I am Arya Stormrider," she said. "And I've accepted that. I'm going to fight and defeat the Nightstalker. At least, I'm going to give it my best."

Pain rippled across his face. Grief too. "Then I've lost you."

"No." She shook her head faintly, reached to him through her magic, sending a shiver of reassurance through the thread between them. "That's impossible."

They were so close, his grey eyes silver in the moonlight, bare inches from hers, his chest rising and falling in a steady rhythm she could feel *and* sense through the Sky Lord bond. Her next words tumbled out without thought. "You wanted to marry me."

She still remembered the way he'd looked at her that night—it had seared itself on her brain, as vivid now as it had been then. Even now the memory of it made her chest ache with a fierceness that had nothing to do with her healing ribs.

Did he still love her?

Always brave, he didn't flinch from her gaze. "And you said no."

"We grew up together. I couldn't see you as anything other than my foster brother, someone for me to protect and help."

"And now?"

Now Darmanin was a powerful warlord in his own right, a man grown, and what had been making her so uneasy since she'd come home was that the dynamic between them had forever changed. Darmanin was no longer a sibling to be responsible for, but someone who could stand with her. He'd come for her, in Andahar, and what she'd felt on seeing him, how she'd been able to surrender completely, *knowing* he'd keep her safe and get her out.

Arya took a breath, forced herself to have the courage to say, "Now I'd very much like to kiss you."

He went still under her, but she couldn't read the expression on his face. Time froze for an eternity. Then that little smile of his flashed out, "I dare you, Arya Stormrider."

And Arya had *never* backed down from a dare.

Her mouth pressed against his, fierce, demanding, her hands letting go of his wrists so his arms could move, one of his hands sliding into her hair, the other wrapping around her back and pulling her flush against him. His hips twisted, sending them rolling, and Arya wasn't sure whether the dizziness that swept her was from the movement or his mouth tracing down her neck, hands sliding up over ... not to be bested, she wrapped her legs around his waist, sent them tumbling again, ice and snow soaking into their clothes, laughter rumbling between kisses.

Eventually Arya pulled away, pressing her head against his neck when the vertigo became too much. He lay there in silence while she recovered, one hand gently massaging her neck through her hair. "You okay?"

Any other partner would have made a joke about his or her touch causing Arya's reaction, and in the past, that had been the exact kind of partner Arya preferred to bed. But one that saw her weakness, yet didn't make her feel lesser for it—that made the breath rush from her chest, made her suddenly understand what Rorin had been talking about earlier. "It's getting better, but the healers say it will take time to resolve completely," she mumbled against his skin.

"Makes sense." Darmanin sat up slowly, bringing her with him. "I'm in awe that you made it through that beating at all."

Head settling, Arya sat back so she could look at him. "I wouldn't have, if you hadn't come for me."

"We will always come for each other, Arya." He reached for her hand, looking down as he toyed with her fingers. "Dares aside, things *have* changed. You're Arya Stormrider now, and I'm warlord of Crowtalon."

His words rang with finality. Arya swallowed, then nodded and stood up, reaching down to help him up too. He was still close enough that his presence pulled at her, made her want to be closer, to kiss him again. She ignored the urge. "We will continue to be friends and allies though?"

"Always. And I'll keep trying to get into contact with Leanir, I promise." Darmanin looked away. "I might skate another few laps before turning in. I'll see you tomorrow?"

It was a dismissal, albeit a gentle one. "Of course. Sleep well, Dar."

He skated off without another word, smooth, graceful movements, and she watched him until he was out of sight. She turned back for the castle, cold fingers unbuttoning her cloak and stripping it from her shoulders before folding it up and tucking it in her belt.

Suddenly the night was cold.

***

Family lunch the following day was almost exactly as Arya remembered it, even though they keenly felt Essa and Taze's absence. Anjurin's shrieks of laughter and the sight of his face covered in gravy added a new and wonderful element to the day, though it also made Arya ache with a fierce desire to see Kirin here too, playing with his cousin. And she couldn't help the sadness that drifted over her to think of Thiara and Matte missing all of it.

She'd messed so many things up.

Yet the presence of her family was a balm to Arya's aching soul. They sat lazily together before the fire that afternoon, full and content, a fire crackling in the grate, snow falling outside. Anjurin slept in his father's lap, Peemla curled up beside the two. Arya's chair faced them, her feet stretched towards the fire. Darmanin sat in a chair opposite, their eyes meeting frequently, unguarded after plenty spiced wine and good food.

Rorin let Arya know he'd convened a strategy meeting the following day. *"I'd planned it before you arrived, but it's even better now you've returned with information from Andahar."*

Arya hesitated. "It's not good, Rorin."

"Whatever it is, we'll deal with it."

"I'll make sure all our guests are well taken care of," Peemla said.

"Or you could join us." Rorin signed carefully so as not to wake the sleeping boy in his lap.

Peemla shook her head, then glanced at Arya. "He always asks, so does Essa, and I know I'm welcome, but I've no interest in strategy and politics. It's enough that they respect my opinion enough to invite me."

"Not to mention running a household like this is an incredibly important part of being a successful warlord," Arya said pointedly. "Always they overlook it, but I've noticed. If your guests aren't looked after properly, it impacts on Rorin."

"If you two weren't married, I'd have offered you Crowtalon State's entire fortune to come be my chamberlain, Peemla," Darmanin agreed.

Peemla's cheeks pinked, and Rorin gave her an affectionate glance.

The door opened to reveal Essa, cheeks flushed from riding. "I'm so sorry I didn't make it in time for lunch, the roads were…" She trailed off at the sight of Arya sitting with the family.

"Essa, you're back!" Arya leaped up, winced at the immediate rush of dizziness, and had to balance herself against the arm of the chair.

Concern flooded Essa's face. "Arya, are you alright? We've been so worried."

"I am getting better every day." Arya let go of the chair as the dizziness faded. "Especially now you're here too."

"She announced herself as Lord Arya Stormrider of Andahar to all our guests last night," Rorin said wryly.

Essa's gaze grew wide. "Clearly you have a lot to catch me up on." Then she spun to Rorin, eyes growing even wider. "How did your vicelords react?"

"How about I fix you a plate of leftovers and a glass of wine and you can sit down and eat while Arya and Rorin tell you all about it?" Peemla offered.

"How about I do that instead?" Darmanin rose before Peemla could. "You're not our servant."

Arya's gaze trailed Darmanin as he left, but then Essa dropped onto the couch on Rorin's other side and looked at Arya eagerly. "Tell me everything."

"The Andahar stuff can wait until tomorrow," Arya demurred. "But you have to let Rorin tell you about what Vicelord Lerin was saying to Vicelord Tempes when he didn't realise Rorin could hear, and the *look* on his face when he realised."

In minutes they were all in stitches of laughter.

Chapter 20

The following morning, once everyone was gathered in his office—Rorin, Arya, Essa, Arken, and Darmanin—the Ravenstrike warlord didn't bother with pleasantries. *"Arya, would you begin by updating us on what you learned in Andahar?"*

Arya launched into her tale, giving them a full report of everything she'd seen and learned. The silence was thick when she'd finished. By the looks on the faces around the table, they were trying to figure out exactly where to start with addressing what she'd told them.

Essa was the first to break the silence, her tone crisp and clear. "To confirm, you're officially Arya Stormrider now, Sky Lord of Andahar? And you claim the Andahari throne as yours by right."

"I do." The words were still hard to say, reluctantly given over, but it wasn't a decision Arya was going to walk back from.

Her clever gaze narrowed. "And what does that mean, practically speaking?"

"It means I'm going to take back my throne by killing the Nightstalker, but I can't do it by facing him directly, at least not yet. If he takes Dunidaen and all your resources, defeating him grows even more impossible. So, I figure a good start would be helping you contain him here, keep those resources from him, *and* bloody his nose by wiping out a substantial portion of his forces."

Nods around the table. Only Essa sensed there was more, and sent a pointed look Arya's way, but she simply smiled. Best to wait until *all* the warlords were more kindly disposed towards her before asking their army to march at her back into Andahar.

Rorin glanced at Arken, who asked, "Arya, are you able to provide any further details on the makeup of this force of conscripts the Nightstalker has gathered, including confirmed numbers?"

"I can't give you an exact figure, but Niallin estimated thousands gathered at the staging camp. And not just conscripts. Trained soldiers too."

Arken absorbed that. "The key piece of information we're missing is *when* he intends to invade."

"In a worst-case scenario where the Nightstalker invades soon, it still couldn't happen before spring. It will take that long to dig through the existing rockfall in the underground road, not to mention the new one Arya created," Darmanin said.

"We can move more Raiders into the forts well before spring," Rorin said.

Arken shook his head. "There isn't room for a substantial number of new arrivals without significant costs to morale, supplies, and fighting capacity, Warlord."

"And if the Nightstalker comes in spring, you'll need an army arrayed along the north-western border to push back against the invaders. Your three forts alone can blunt the edge of their attack, but they won't hold an army tens of thousands strong," Arya added.

"We can't withdraw Raiders from our borders to form defensive lines here—it will leave us vulnerable to Falconcrest in the east," Essa warned.

"I don't think we have a choice." Rorin frowned. *"An invading army is a more dangerous threat than Falconcrest."*

"Is it?" Essa asked. "Both want to take your State from you."

Rorin let out an exasperated sigh. *"What do you suggest then?"*

Darmanin sat forward. "I can have four thousand Lances on your eastern border in three weeks. They'll hold against Falconcrest for you. It will leave my army stretched thin, but I judge the risk worth it."

Arken cleared this throat, then ventured, "I think what Arya was getting at is that what we need is a unified Dunidae army waiting here come spring to push back the invasion. Ravenstrike can't do it alone, even if we have your help on the eastern border, Warlord Crowtalon."

Arya sent a grateful look at the man who'd once been her rival and then her second. "Yes, that's exactly what Arya was getting at."

Essa looked torn between amusement and frustration. "It's fortunate the State Council is happening soon, then. A wonderful opportunity to mend fences between the warlords, unify our armies, and do all that with enough time to march everyone's forces north to Ravenstrike by spring."

"It will never happen," Darmanin said. "I don't say this to be difficult. My father simply isn't going to listen to what we have to say."

This was the opportunity Arya had been looking for. Winning the warlords as allies was going to take time, and the earlier she started the better. Just as importantly, if Leanir wasn't in the Wraith Forest, then he must still be operating with the Shadeweavers in Gateport. She needed to go there as quickly as possible. "I will attend the State Council in my capacity as Sky Lord and Stormrider heir," she said. "And inform them that my allies and I are convinced of an upcoming invasion. I will tell them everything I have seen with my own eyes, and offer to assist."

Rorin looked sceptical. "*Your allies?*"

"The Etherean will ally with me, and the Icefolk already have," she said.

Essa gave Arya a look. "Mathas Crowtalon will not care two figs for what foreign leaders are telling him—especially you, whom he despises—and neither are any of the other warlords. If they even listen to you at all when they realise you're a magic-wielder."

"*That's a good point. Can you even risk coming to Gateport?*" Rorin asked. "*It could be dangerous for you. There's a bounty on your head.*"

"I will be travelling to Gateport formally as a foreign dignitary." Arya shrugged. "If Mathas still tries to arrest me ... well, I'll be riding a great big bloody wyvern, so I dare him and his Defenders to try."

Her interests and Darmanin's were suddenly firmly aligned, she realised. Getting rid of Mathas Crowtalon would be critical to eventually winning the Dunidae as allies. He'd never do it.

"Official dignitary or not, your presence will have to be a secret until you appear at a State Council session," Essa warned. "Otherwise, word *will* leak to the Nightstalker that you're in Gateport. Not to mention Mathas will have time to prepare to counter whatever you have to say."

"Understood," Arya said. "I'll travel in secret until you, Rorin, and Dar can get me in to address a Council session."

Rorin nodded slowly. *"Very well. Then we go to Gateport for the Council."*

Darmanin rose. "I will ride out today. That way I can speak to Helden SparrowWing on my way through to Anduil."

Darmanin's departure broke up the meeting. Rorin, Arken, and Peemla left to begin preparations for their departure to Gateport. Arya presumed Essa had to do the same, but the woman approached her as she left Rorin's office.

"How do you feel about sharing a cup of tea with me by the fire in the library?"

"Are you sure?" Arya hesitated. She hadn't forgotten that Essa had asked for space, and she wasn't sure whether her friend was still angry with her.

"I'm sure," Essa said firmly. "Come on, it has been a long time since we talked like we used to."

Once they were curled up on a cushioned sofa by the fire, Arya started with, "Can I ask how you feel about my decision to claim Andahar's throne?"

"I'm a little surprised," Essa admitted. "You've been so determined to ignore your heritage."

She wanted to tell Essa so badly. Reveal everything. Maybe that would ease some of the burden she carried like a dead weight. But she couldn't. She had to put Kirin's safety above all else. Even if she hated hiding things from those she loved. "I didn't feel I had a choice anymore."

"That doesn't sound like the confident Arya that I knew." Essa spoke gently, letting Arya know she was there if Arya felt like talking.

"Now that I've faced him, Ess..." A shudder of remembered horror went through her. "The Nightstalker is so powerful, and so are the nazal that hunt us. How can I even begin to tackle that?"

"It's an incredible challenge, to be sure," Essa said. "But what did you always tell me was the best way to tackle seemingly impossible challenges?"

Arya smiled. "By breaking them down into small steps and taking them one at a time."

"Are you sure this is what you want, though?" Essa looked troubled.

"I don't have a choice."

Essa searched her face for a moment, then nodded. "Then the first step is stop this invasion and deplete the Nightstalker's strength in the process. You were right about that. Then, once that's done, we can identify the next step, and move on to that one."

"We?" Arya asked carefully.

Essa was quiet for a moment, her gaze on the steaming tea in her hand. Eventually she looked up to meet Arya's gaze. "I will stand at your side for what comes next."

Though quietly spoken, those words had all the weight of a promise, and Arya tried not to let herself hope too much. Stunned, she asked, "What about Rorin?"

"He is part of our family, and I enjoy being his chief advisor, but you already know what I truly want. That isn't ever going to happen until the Nightstalker is gone."

"What about the risk to your life? If you openly declare yourself as part of my *cairdre*, you and Alletryl will be in incredible danger. The nazal won't have to look for you anymore. They'll come straight for you."

"They might." Essa shrugged. "But I also wonder ... that's two of us together now, Arya. We're not an easy foe to face. If we're standing together, they can't pick us off."

That was true, but she knew Essa was putting a positive spin on things. Even together the nazal was an adversary they couldn't easily defend against. And Arya was hobbled by her fear, her shattered confidence, her need to protect Kirin.

"I'm so sorry, Essa. I've betrayed Dar by accepting all this, and Chiarn already hates what we are. I feel like I'm alone in a place *I* don't even want to be in and dragging you all in after me."

"You're not alone." Essa touched her hand.

Arya hesitated. "I know you've been angry with me, and—"

"I was." Essa said. "But you gave me the space I asked for, and I've been thinking a lot, especially since Alletryl came into my life. This isn't a spur of the moment decision. I am a Sky Lord. Next time a monster threatens someone I love, I want to fight back. I don't want to feel this guilt anymore." She looked up. "And if there's anyone I trust to help me with that, it's you, Arya Stormrider."

"I missed you." Arya managed a smile, but it quickly died, her voice choking. "I missed you a lot while I was away."

"I missed you too." Essa squeezed her hand.

Arya almost ... but she didn't. Instead, she let go of Essa's hand and moved away, sinking into the cushions of the couch. "You'll never guess who I ran into while I was in Andahar?"

Essa listened intently, the fire crackling, a servant bringing them fresh tea, as Arya talked about Tiya helping her recovery, and seemed even more interested when she spoke of what Chiarn had been up to, and how he'd found his wyvern. "I asked him to join us, promised him freedom if he did, but he said no."

"You'll keep trying though."

"I most certainly will."

"What about Leanir? Have you heard anything from him?" Essa asked.

Arya froze. The guilt curled inside her again, hot and nauseating. "Ess, I..."

But she couldn't get the words out, her shame choking them off. Essa sat silently, waiting. Arya swallowed. "I need to find him. That's part of the reason I was so insistent on going to Gateport."

Essa could have pushed. Could have demanded to know why. Instead, she reached out to touch Arya's arm. "Then I'll look for him when we get there. Don't worry Arya, we'll find him."

Arya shook her head. "He threatened to kill the next person I send looking for him."

Essa smiled her bright smile. "A good thing you're not *sending* me, then. Besides, he's already had his chance to let me die—and he risked his life jumping off a cliff to save me instead."

"All right, thanks, Essa," Arya said slowly. Her stomach would remain tight with anxiety until she laid eyes on Leanir and saw he was well, but having the first steps of a plan outlined, it made her feel like breathing was a touch easier.

***

Arya woke early the next morning after little sleep and headed straight to the drill yard. When she passed the kitchens for a sneaky piece of toast to tide her over until breakfast, both Rorin and Peemla were already there, huddled over cups of tea.

She gave her brother a suspicious look. "You're never out of bed this early."

He shrugged. "*We had some planning to start—it's only a few days until we leave for Gateport. Are you headed out to the drill yards? I'll come with you. It's been a while since I've gotten practice in.*"

Arya pierced Peemla with a suspicious look. The woman simply smiled. "Enjoy drill. I'll make sure the cooks have your favourite breakfast ready when you're done." Her gaze narrowed. "And don't push it—you're still healing, remember."

"Yes, boss." Arya flashed her an echo of her old grin.

Rorin was smiling a little smile as they walked in companionable silence, but shook his head every time she asked him why. A sharp nudge to his ribs didn't help either. He simply shrugged, blue eyes laughing at her.

When they arrived, several shields were already at drill, but Arya's gaze went straight to where Laskin's familiar figure waited at the edge of the yard. Lined up neatly behind him was his shield; Kait, Etan, Allicen, Charlin, Wattin, all of her original shield-mates from their Icecliff days.

Only, for the first time since she'd known them, they weren't wearing their red Raider uniforms. Instead, they wore a thick quilted tunic and breeches in a deep cobalt. The lowered cowl around their necks was a silvery grey, and the lightning bolt—cradled by a striking raven like on the back of her cloak—over their hearts was the same colour. At her appearance, they all saluted sharply. Rorin moved off to the side, failing at holding back a grin.

Arya frowned at Laskin. "What's this?"

"You've taken on the title of Lord Arya Stormrider, heir to the throne of Andahar," he said. "So, you'll need soldiers, an army, of your own. Especially if you want to impress the other warlords enough that they'll listen to you in Gateport."

"But you're Raiders, sworn to Ravenstrike."

At her side, Rorin snorted. She ignored him.

Laskin's jaw tightened, and his eyes were suspiciously damp. "Oh, lass, we've always been yours. Always."

When she looked helplessly at him, Rorin began signing. "*Laskin and his shield came to me and requested to be released from my service. I gave them my permission. You* do *need soldiers.*"

Arya rubbed at damp eyes. She didn't deserve this. She wasn't worthy of it. They shifted uncomfortably when her silence lingered, and she knew she had to say something. The old Arya would have accepted their loyalty without question. This Arya was undone by it. She cleared her throat. "Laskin, are you sure that this is what you want? All of you?" She lifted her gaze to meet each of their gazes in turn. "You must know that openly joining me—it will be incredibly dangerous. Far more so than swearing allegiance to a Dunidae warlord."

"I'm more sure of this than I've ever been about anything," he promised.

"These uniforms are nicer," Charlin offered.

"*Much* nicer," Kait added emphatically. "The red really washed out my complexion."

"Figure sticking with you means an adventure or two in my future," Etan said. "I've always wanted a good adventure. It's why I signed up to the Raiders."

"Never worked with or for a better captain," Wattin remarked, astonishing them all by speaking a full sentence out loud.

"Me, I'm signing on because I heard that Andahar is much warmer than this ice box. I'm sick of the cold, frankly," Allicen said.

A chuckle escaped Arya, despite herself. Maybe this was what she need-ed. Those she trusted more than anything at her back. If she was going to defeat the Nightstalker, she couldn't let her fear and guilt drown her. She was going to have to figure out a way to rise above it, not just once, but repeatedly. For Kirin's sake. For Rorin's and Essa's and Darmanin's. Chiarn and Leanir too. Not to mention her new shield.

So, she let out a breath, a genuine smile spreading across her face. "Thank you. All of you. Now get to drill. If you're to be my army, I want a damn sharp one."

"Aye!" Laskin saluted.

Rorin was beaming when she turned to him. *"Do you like the uniform? Peemla and her staff worked on them all night so they'd be ready this morning."*

"You weren't up early. You were up all night?" A lump rose in her throat. Rorin shrugged.

She stepped forward and hugged him. "Thank you."

"You're welcome. Now off you go and drill with your new tiny army," he said. *"Peemla and I are going to bed."*

Chapter 21

The Ravenstrike household and its accompanying battalion reached Gateport three weeks after Winterfest. The gloomy, rainy weather they found on arrival—in combination with the fact she'd be separated from Elendryl, hiding with Alletryl east of the city for the duration of their stay—quickly broke the bubble of comfort Arya had found in those brief few days in Heathrock.

Now, eight days later, as she stood at the window of her room in Rorin's residence watching rain sheet down the glass, she felt even worse. Since stepping foot back in the city, her thoughts had been filled with the terrible memories of what had happened to Rorin's parents. The previous night, she'd woken screaming from a nightmare reliving her beating at the hands of the Nightstalker, bathed in sweat and having to fight the desperate urge to fly to Taskari to make sure her son was all right.

It didn't help that Essa was yet to find Leanir, and while Arya's bond with him indicated he was much closer now, she didn't know where. Her connection with him was too unfamiliar, too untested, for her to get any more than that he was alive and *probably* near Gateport if not in the city itself.

What if the Nightstalker had him? As if on cue, she felt the trembling beginning in her hands. Frustration and fear lapped at her in equal measure. She needed *something* to happen. While Rorin had been in the capital a week, neither Falconcrest nor SparrowWing had arrived. Meanwhile, the Nightstalker was continuing to develop his invasion plans, and the time they had before spring arrived was ticking away. She couldn't fail at this too.

"*Bored,*" Elendryl pushed into her thoughts.

"*Yes, I know.*" She tried to be patient, but didn't quite succeed. The two wyverns were growing increasingly restless at the lack of interaction with their riders.

"*Come soon?*" he demanded, then added a hopeful, "*Leave soon?*"

"*I hope so,*" she said, letting him feel how badly she wanted to be gone too.

He grumbled, but resettled quietly at the back of her mind.

A bell sounded downstairs, rescuing Arya from her heavy thoughts. Darmanin and Gelfrey Hawkesdale were dining with Rorin tonight. It would be her first audience with the Hawkesdale warlord after her ignominious escape from Gateport three years earlier.

It had been Essa's suggestion. "We'll have a much greater chance of convincing Mathas to unite the armies and march them north if we have some warlords already on our side when Arya addresses the Council."

"*And what if Hawkesdale immediately goes marching off to collect the bounty on Arya's head?*" Rorin protested.

"We have to risk that. Winning Hawkesdale's support for an alliance against invasion is crucial. If it goes well with him, we should speak to SparrowWing too."

"I agree with Ess." Arya had said decidedly, desperate to be doing *something.*

So Rorin had invited him to dinner.

Despite her worries about how it might go with Hawkesdale, Arya hadn't seen Darmanin since Winterfest, and it was seeing him that she most looked forward to.

She gave herself a critical once-over in the mirror before heading downstairs. Her golden hair was neatly tied back in a bun, and she wore her Etherean outfit of high collared tunic over fitting breeches in a deep blue. Her cazaix blade hung at her side, but she hadn't been able to bring herself to put the Stormrider cloak on. She took a deep breath, reassuring herself that she looked nothing like the reckless Raider general who had lost her mind and murdered the High Warlord's chief advisor in the middle of the Council chamber.

When she reached the reception room, Rorin and Darmanin were grinning at each other over some joke, both holding glasses of wine. Peemla sat near the fire, Anji curled in her lap, fast asleep. All three looked up at Arya's appearance.

The smile was still on Darmanin's face as he looked at her, and she swore it brightened further. So rarely bestowed, his smile had always arrested her, and it did so now. "Hello, Dar."

"Arya." He held her gaze. "Rorin was just telling me about the sad demise of the shirt he originally intended to wear tonight."

Rorin sighed. "*I was trying to steam it. Peemla walked in just as I'd managed to burn a hole right through the arm.*"

Arya's mouth quirked and she forced herself to break Darmanin's gaze. "You couldn't manage to save it, Peemla?"

"It was hopeless." Peemla shook her head. "The shirt had been murdered right before my eyes."

Another smile lurked at Darmanin's mouth. "Surely not murdered. Perhaps dismembered?"

Everyone laughed. When the doorbell rang again, Rorin placed his glass on the mantelpiece over the fire and took a breath. "*Everyone ready?*" But it was Arya he looked at with a pointed glance.

"I promise to be on my best behaviour. No losing my temper." She spoke with an innocent smile that had him rolling his eyes.

While they waited, Arya looked at Darmanin. "Leanir?"

His mirth faded. "I'm sorry. Nothing. If he's in Gateport, he's ignoring my attempts to reach out. Essa's too."

Could the nazal have found him already? But no, Arya had been regularly checking her connection to the Shadeweaver assassin. He was alive. And it was just as likely he *was* ignoring them. Leanir certainly held no love or trust for her. But that didn't necessarily mean he hadn't been captured. She swallowed, mouth dry with anxiety.

A moment later a servant showed Warlord Gelfrey Hawkesdale in, accompanied by a young woman with black hair and the warlord's brown eyes.

"*Warlord Hawkesdale.*" Rorin bowed his head politely, Peemla translating. "*You are welcome in our home.*"

"Warlord Ravenstrike." Gelfrey returned the gesture. "May I formally introduce you to my daughter, Lady Illia Hawkesdale? You will recall her from when you fostered with me?"

Arya wondered at why Hawkesdale had brought his daughter, instead of his chief advisor or general. Or one of his three sons. Dinners like this were commonplace leading up to a State Council, and they were without exception political affairs—opportunities to hash out deals, make alliances, design plans. She filed the question away for consideration with Essa later.

"*Of course I remember. Lady Illia, you are very welcome,*" Rorin signed, and then straightened his shoulders, his bearing becoming more formal. "*Warlord, you remember my sister, Arya?*"

Arya stepped forward, and Gelfrey's eyes widened in surprise and shock. "Arya Ravenstrike, is that really you?"

"It is." Ayra had decided not to bow or make any other deferential gesture toward the Dunidae warlords, but she made sure her voice was warm and sincere. "You may not feel the same way, but it is a pleasure to see you again, Warlord Hawkesdale. And I am pleased to meet you, Lady Illia."

Hawkesdale shook his head. It was hard to tell what the irascible man was thinking, but Arya took the fact he wasn't storming out as a positive sign. "I never thought to see you again. And yet you're not the same young general that once stood before me. I've heard rumours, too, which I took to be nothing more than silly fancy. Now I'm not so sure."

"I'm not sure what rumours you've heard," she said evenly. "But I am a Sky Lord of Andahar. More, I am the rightful heir to its throne. Arya Stormrider is my true name."

There was a beat of silence, then his eyes flashed, and he bellowed, "*You're* the one the Nightstalker has wanted all this time?"

Anjurin sat up on his mother's lap, letting out a surprised gurgle at the shouted question, blue eyes wide. Hawkesdale glanced at the little boy, somewhat sheepishly. "My apologies little lad, Lady Ravenstrike. That was not polite."

Arya smiled. "Maybe not, but I suspect I would have reacted similarly in your position, Warlord. And the answer to your question is, yes, I am."

His eyes narrowed. "And how long have you known that?"

"For years. Since just after the Nightstalker's first incursion over our borders."

Rorin signed, "*I understand this is shocking news, Warlord, but would you truly advocate for handing over innocents to the Nightstalker? Especially one who was instrumental in saving us from that incursion?*"

"Innocent?" Hawkesdale barked. "She murdered the High Warlord's advisor in full view of half the Council."

"Nain was behind the murder of my warlord and her husband," Arya said coolly. "I was angry and grief-stricken. The attack was not unprovoked, but I admit that it was foolish."

His gaze narrowed. "You have evidence for that claim?"

"None that will convince you."

"And if you *are* one of these Sky Lords, then you are a magic-wielder?"

"I am."

Hawkesdale was still processing this, his daughter looking like she was hiding a smile at his side, when Essa chose to enter the room. She'd presumably heard the first part of the conversation, because her first words were, "Hello, Warlord Hawkesdale, I'm sorry I'm late. If we're discussing magic-wielders present, then you should know I am one too."

"Chief Advisor," Hawkesdale said, his ruddy cheeks turning redder. "What have you got to do with all of this?"

Essa took a breath, visibly gathered herself, and then said. "I am Lord Essa Inkweaver, a member of Arya's Sky Lord *cairdre*."

"I remember the stories my mother told me well enough to know there should be five in a *cairdre*." Gelfrey looked around the room as if they might be hiding in a closet. "Where are the rest of you?"

"For now, it is just Essa and I, Warlord," Arya said.

Hawkesdale sat abruptly. "Get me some wine, Ravenstrike. A large glass. One of your best, if you don't mind. Actually, bring the whole bottle."

"*Yes, sir.*"

Illia joined her father on the sofa, but she didn't seem overly upset by the evening's revelations. While Rorin crossed the room to ask a hovering servant for wine, Darmanin moved away from the fire towards Illia. He bowed before her, and she offered her hand. He kissed it politely. She smiled back. "Lord Crowtalon," she said.

"It's good to see you again, Lady Illia."

Arya stared. Was Darmanin courting the Hawkesdale daughter? Is *that* why her father had brought her? The mouthful of wine she'd just swallowed stuck in her throat. With an effort, she shifted her gaze to where Anjurin had fallen asleep in his mother's lap. Putting down her glass of wine, Arya went to Peemla. "Can I take the little one to bed? It will give you a chance to help Rorin and Essa explain things to Hawkesdale without me here to upset him."

By the time Arya had settled Anji—he'd woken and demanded her blue light ball dancing above his bed before he'd go to sleep—dinner was being served and the party had moved to the formal dining room.

"I brought Illia tonight for a reason," Gelfrey announced just as Arya walked in. "I plan to nominate her as heir to Hawkesdale, and I'd like your support at the confirmation hearing, Ravenstrike, You too, Crowtalon."

A surprised silence settled over the room. While Illia was Hawkesdale's oldest child, he had three sons. Custom would be for Hawkesdale's eldest son to be his heir. Thiara Ravenstrike had been the first ever female warlord, and that had only happened because her only male relative when her father died was a child. Even then she'd barely been confirmed.

"*You have it.*" Rorin looked utterly delighted, and even though Essa shot him a sharp look at making such a decision without consulting his advisers, or, more importantly, extracting a concession in return, she didn't look truly displeased. "*Without reservation.*"

Hawkesdale seemed taken aback. "I see. Thank you."

"Lady Illia has my full support also," Darmanin said. "Without reservation."

That *did* astonish Arya. Both young men could have leveraged valuable political capital in exchange for supporting Illia, and she'd expected Darmanin to ruthlessly go after everything he could. *She* would have.

"I feel confident SparrowWing will support your choice, even if unconventional," Darmanin continued. "I wouldn't be concerned about the vote, Warlord."

"Thank you, both of you." Illia spoke, clearly surprised, but also shining with delight. "I am incredibly grateful for your support."

"As am I." Hawkesdale said, then heaved a sigh. "You could have asked a lot of me, both of you, and I would have given it. So, I am grateful enough to entertain further discussion of Sky Lords existing again, as disturbing as I find it."

Arya said, "I find it equally disturbing, Warlord. Unfortunately, it doesn't make it any less real."

He fixed her with a look. "Despite your big talk, someone already sits the throne you say is yours, and he won't be handing it over anytime soon."

"That is also true," Arya said stiffly.

Hawkesdale's eyes narrowed. "You were a very good general, great even, but you were brash and overconfident, and you badly underestimated your rival in Mathas Crowtalon, as did Thiara Ravenstrike."

"You agree then that Mathas Crowtalon's chief advisor was behind the deaths of my warlord and her husband?"

Hawkesdale sat back, considering her. "Rorin has explained your account; that Nain was controlled by a monster sent by the Nightstalker. But even if I accept that as true, you won't ever convince me that Mathas *knew* a monster controlled his chief advisor or ordered him to kill Thiara and Matte. He hates magic-wielders with a passion, he would never have allowed one so close to him."

"I agree," Arya said. "But his chief advisor's actions certainly made it a guarantee that Mathas would be voted in as High Warlord, no?"

"You're saying the Nightstalker wanted Mathas Crowtalon as High Warlord?"

Illia spoke as Arya was forming a reply. "Father, don't forget that if Arya is right, Nain also almost killed Warlord SparrowWing's heir and stole a lot of money from the warlord not long before that State Council—and Crowtalon was locked in a dispute with SparrowWing over trading rights at the time. Whatever its intentions, the nazal certainly seemed to want things to go in Crowtalon's favour."

Arya gave her an approving and grateful look. The young woman had clearly paid attention to the undercurrent of politics at the previous State Council.

"All very fascinating." Hawkesdale speared a piece of meat and pointed it at Arya. "But that's not what I was talking about. I speak of your behaviour after Thiara's murder. Rather than containing the situation and acting rationally, you chose to attack the man you believed responsible in public and without warning."

Arya swallowed down her guilt. She'd been bitterly regretting the same thing over and over for the past three years.

"*Warlord, I think you are being too harsh. Arya was as upset about my mother's death as I was,*" Rorin intervened. "*Without being there, having seen what we saw…*"

"No," Arya said quietly. "The warlord is right. I acknowledge the mistakes I've made, and I can only assure you I've learned from them."

"That remains to be seen." Hawkesdale returned to his meal. "Good fare this, Ravenstrike. I need to send my cook along to have a chat with yours, I think."

Arya and Essa shared a look. The warlord was reserving his judgement for now.

Well, that was better than condemnation, fear, or a flat-out refusal.

It was enough for Arya to work with.

Chapter 22

It wasn't long past dawn when Arya walked the mostly empty Gateport streets to the Raider barracks after another sleepless night, making sure she had her hood drawn over her face. The rain had finally stopped, but a thick fog hugged the ground. Rorin had given Arya's shield accommodation in the Raider barracks—uniformed as Raiders for now—and she waved at the guards on the gate as she entered and made her way to Laskin's room. He answered on the first knock, dressed and with his sparring sword already in hand. "Morning. How did dinner go?"

They fell into step, heading for the training yard. "Hawkesdale wasn't thrilled to find out who I was, but he didn't storm out in a huff either."

Laskin scratched his beard. "That's a best-case scenario, I'd say."

"I agree." A damp wind gusted over them as they exited the building. "Ready to be trounced this morning?"

"Big words from someone who's had their ass kicked all week so far."

It was true. Arya was working hard to regain her strength and stamina, but it was proving difficult. Quick movements still set off her vertigo, so she was reduced to sparring at a slower speed. And it got worse when she grew tired. They quickly settled into the pattern of previous mornings; Laskin probing her defences, gradually forcing her into quicker actions, testing where her limits were. Soon, sweat dripped down her forehead despite the chill air, and it felt good.

At the sound of a challenge at the front gates, Arya's head whipped around, lightning fast. Dizziness swamped her senses, and the wily veteran took advantage. He dashed in and banged the flat of his blade hard against her ribs before she could react.

"Raven's balls!" she swore, pressing her hand against her eyes until the dizziness faded.

"You're doing okay. Better than yesterday," Laskin said.

She rubbed her bruised side. "I'm improving too damn slowly, Laskin. If the nazal or even a *soldier* attacked me now—"

"They'd have to get through all of us to get to you," Laskin said pointedly. "Same again tomorrow morning?"

Arya saw that it was Darmanin coming through the gates, one of the Raiders on guard pointing him over to her. "Thanks, Laskin. I appreciate it."

He lowered his blade, bowed politely toward Darmanin, and left.

Darmanin lifted an eyebrow. "You were just beating up on poor Laskin, weren't you?"

She scowled. "I wish. Right now, he's beating *me* up."

He said nothing, just waited.

Arya huffed out a breath. "Time is running out for me to find and warn Leanir, all the warlords aren't here yet while an invasion looms, and I can't even win a sparring match. I feel like I need to *do* something, but I'm trapped into waiting instead."

"Makes sense," he said easily. "I have an idea if you're willing to try? You'll need to unmute the thread between us."

"I'm game." She did as he asked.

Darmanin unsheathed his cazaix blade and shifted in a fighting stance. A moment later, for the first time ever, she felt him reach for her along the *cairdre* thread that bound them. She reached back without hesitation and energy thrummed along the link. All the weariness from her sparring with Laskin faded and her head felt clearer than it had in a long time.

"Let's see if you can beat me now." Darmanin challenged. Without giving her a moment to prepare, he leaped at her with all the grace of a lunging shadowhound. His cazaix blade arrowed straight for her throat. Reacting with pure instinct, Arya dragged her wooden blade upwards and into his, deflecting it at the last second. His blade came so close she felt the whisper of air against the skin of her throat.

He disengaged and came at her again, lightning fast. For a few minutes, Arya was on the back foot, hard pressed to hold him back. Gradually, though, she adjusted to his speed and rhythm. And she *could* keep up. Her muscles felt as strong as they'd used to, her focus sharp, his magic and energy feeding hers where it was low.

They circled their corner of the training yard, blades a blur of movement. As hard as she tried, Arya couldn't get through Darmanin's defences, nor he through hers. Attack, parry, counter. Darmanin was taller and stronger, but she was a hair quicker. Sweat slicked Arya's skin, and her breath came faster. Time passed, and still neither of them gained the upper hand. Arya's breathing grew more and more laboured. Sweat poured down the inside of her tunic. The burn of weariness spread through her muscles, but she refused to give up.

There was no way she was going to let Darmanin defeat her.

Time to try something unexpected. Darmanin came at her with a high sweep at her head. She brought her blade up to halt his blow inches away from her ear. As their blades touched, she drew her belt knife with her left hand and stabbed for his throat. He threw himself backwards, moving into a flip to avoid her knife. She dropped the knife and followed his movement with her sword. As he landed gracefully back on his feet, Arya was already swinging at his neck. He bought his blade up just in time and they clashed together with a loud clang, gridlocked.

Arya strained against him, feeling his superior strength taking effect. Thinking quickly, she drew her second knife with her left hand and pressed it into his ribs just as she felt a sharp jab against her right ribcage.

"I think they call that a draw," he murmured. They were so close she could see his chest rise and fall with the quickness of his breathing, feel his warmth pressed against her.

She lifted her eyebrows. "Your experiment worked well. Sure you won't join my *cairdre*?"

His gaze narrowed. "Never."

"We'll see about that." Arya shifted even closer, smiling until his eyes darkened, until the pull between them grew so strong *she* could barely resist it, then stepped away. She lowered her sword, only now feeling the sweat pouring off her skin and the ache in her muscles. The wooden blade was badly nicked from Darmanin's cazaix.

He sent a little shiver along the thread between them, then slowly withdrew the strength he'd been sending her. "Feeling okay if I do that?"

Arya steadied herself; the exhaustion was back, but it felt like normal weariness after a fight, not illness. And the anxiety that had taken up permanent residence in her chest had seeped away with exertion, leaving her feeling lighter than she had in weeks. "I think so. How did you learn to do it?"

"I didn't. It happened instinctively when I was carrying you away from Darkclaw, remember? You were reaching for me, needing help, and I just gave it, I think. I wondered how it would work if we tried it deliberately."

"It makes sense. *Cairdres* are supposed to be able to strengthen each other, share magic and energy. Salyarin has spoken of it, he just didn't know the mechanics of how it works."

"I'm glad I could help." He sheathed his blade, that remote look returning to his expression. Arya sensed she'd stepped too close to what he still wanted to deny.

He was meant to be in her *cairdre*. She suspected he was meant to be even more than that. But she couldn't force him to see or accept that.

Another challenge from the gate guards rang out. A mounted Raider cantered in, sharing a quick word with the guards, who pointed them in Arya and Darmanin's direction. He spurred his horse into a reckless gallop across the yard, sending drilling Raiders scattering.

Arya started running, heedless of the oncoming horse. The Raider leaped from his saddle to greet her, taking two long strides before they collided, wrapping arms around each other and holding on wordlessly.

"Taze Nameless." She murmured into his shoulder when she had control of herself. "It is so very good to see you."

"Arya." His hold tightened, then he let go, stepping back to take her in. "You're okay."

"I'm okay."

Taze nodded, holding her gaze a moment longer before grinning a greeting at Darmanin. "Dar told me about you officially declaring yourself as a Sky Lord. It's about time."

"Lord Stormrider!"

Arya turned at Laskin's voice, reading the grim look on his face as he strode towards them. "What is it?"

"A few of the Raiders were out drinking last night. Heard talk of some nasty killings in the harbourside district. Witnesses reported odd hissing and shrieking sounds. They're laughing it off, blaming it on drunkards being too deep in their cups."

"A nazal." Arya breathed as horror rippled through her.

"You don't know that," Taze said.

Laskin hesitated. "The story Wattin heard, it was several men killed, inside an inn, late at night. The dead men were armed, but didn't appear to have had time to draw their weapons. And they were tortured, like whoever did it was looking for information."

"Which inn?" Darmanin asked quietly.

"The Seawind."

Darmanin turned to Arya, grim understanding in his grey eyes. "The Seawind is a Shadeweaver tavern."

Dread crept through her chest. "Laskin, Taze, will you leave us? Taze, I know Rorin can't wait to see you. I'll meet you at the townhouse later."

Laskin saluted and left. Taze looked uncertainly between her and Darmanin, but eventually nodded. "If I can help—"

"It's okay, Taze," Darmanin murmured.

As soon as he was gone, Arya looked at Darmanin. "A nazal is hunting Leanir."

"If he's not in the city, then he's okay for now."

"Who knows where else a nazal is hunting him, the Nightstalker has five of them!" Arya shook her head. She'd been reluctant to play her final card so far. She'd already done enough to Leanir, destroying *any* remaining potential for developing trust between them was the last thing she wanted. But if it meant his life... "Will you lend me your strength?"

She reached for their bond, and he let her in without hesitation. After taking a steadying breath, she enlivened her bond with Leanir and gave it a firm pull. Once. Twice. Three times. She filled each tug with overwhelming compulsion and demand.

And then she let go.

"What now?" Darmanin asked in clipped tones. His darkened expression told her he sensed what she'd done and didn't like it.

"Now we wait for him to come to us."

"And if he doesn't?"

"Then I keep doing that until he does."

"Aren't you risking the nazal finding either of you through using magic?"

"The nazal will find him eventually unless he's warned. And now that I've torn the Nightstalker from my magic, well, this will be a good test of whether that has rendered him incapable of tracking us that way." Arya spoke confidently, unwilling to admit to doubt in front of Darmanin.

She just hoped she was right.

***

That night at family dinner, Arya was quiet, barely able to eat. Her knee jiggled and she had to constantly stop it before someone noticed. Darmanin threw her terse looks across the table. Eventually Rorin put his cutlery down and demanded to know what was wrong.

"We think there might be a nazal here hunting Shadeweavers," Darmanin said.

Arya explained what she'd done. "I just hope Leanir comes to us before they find him."

Rorin frowned. "*Why are they looking for Leanir?*"

"I..." Again, she couldn't get the words out, the shame of what she'd done taking a stranglehold on her voice.

"It's just as likely they're looking for Arya or me, or all three of us," Darmanin intervened. Arya sent him a grateful look.

Essa sat up straight. "Arya, we need to do more than just warn Leanir and wait for something to happen. I think the three of us should spend some time outside the city so you can teach us to use our magic."

"That's a great idea," Arya said, relieved at the idea of *doing* something until the warlords arrived. But then hesitation descended, sparked by fear. "I don't know if we should risk it."

"You can both do as you like, but I'm not coming," Darmanin said flatly.

Essa put down her cup with a clatter. "Raven's balls, Darmanin, what are you going to do if a nazal attacks you? You plan to fight the thing off with only your sword?"

Taze coughed to swallow a laugh, then shared a delighted look with Rorin.

"I'm not a Sky Lord. I'm warlord of Crowtalon," Darmanin said stiffly.

"Don't give me that." Essa was relentless. "You're smart enough to know the Nightstalker will eventually learn your identity, and he isn't going to leave you alone just because you refuse to be a Sky Lord. What if you get married and have children? What if one of them is a potential Sky Lord? You think he'll leave your heirs alone?"

A beat of silence fell. For her part, Arya was in awe of her friend's unrelenting bluntness in the face of Darmanin's incredibly intimidating stubbornness. Darmanin's hand, where it sat on the table, curled into a white-knuckled fist.

"*Don't you need to be careful about using your magic in case the nazal tracks you?*" Rorin asked, defusing the tension.

Arya shook her head. "Not as much anymore, I think."

"You *think*?" Darmanin levelled a cold gaze on her.

She shrugged, unable to mount a convincing argument, once again mired in her fear and doubt.

"I say the risk is low. I can't see *how* the Nightstalker could sense or track any of us when he's no longer connected to you, Arya." Essa said determinedly. "And if you want to destroy him, we're going to have to start taking risks."

Taze spoke into the tense silence that fell. "Dar, learning to protect yourself and your family is not the same as agreeing to be a Sky Lord or giving up being Crowtalon warlord."

Darmanin's mouth tightened. "Fine. I'll come." He stood. "I have business tomorrow. I'll be here the morning after for a dawn departure."

Essa winced as the door slammed behind him. "Dawn? Really?"

"*You look pensive.*" Rorin signed towards Taze.

"I was just thinking." Taze put his mug down. "I understand why someone on the outside—like Elder Salyarin—might worry that Darmanin is a threat to you, Arya."

Rorin snorted. "*What rubbish. I have to get going too—Essa, you're coming with me to the Council chamber today, yes?*"

"I'm right behind you."

Taze trailed out with them, leaving Arya alone at the table staring thoughtfully after them. His words reverberated through her mind, and a little green shoot of hope tried to wriggle out from under her guilt and fear.

Her oldest friend had just given her an idea. Not a fully formed one yet, but maybe something.

An idea the old Arya would have been proud of.

Chapter 23

Arya arrived for breakfast at the Ravenstrike townhouse the following morning to find Essa uncharacteristically awake, dressed and vibrating with energy. She was dressed oddly though, in ratty, nondescript clothing that was totally unlike her.

"I thought you'd have slept extra today to account for tomorrow morning's dawn departure," Arya said, staring at the bouncing woman who'd met her inside the front door.

"This got pushed under the door overnight." Essa passed her a note. "It's Shadeweaver code. A meeting time and location."

Relief cascaded through Arya so powerfully her vertigo swirled, and she had to brace herself against the wall, the note crumpling in her hand. "When?"

"We have to go now." Essa made for the door.

Arya stepped in front of her. "How about I go alone? Warlord Ravenstrike's chief advisor cannot afford to be seen meeting with a Shadeweaver."

"We discussed this, Arya. I'm not just Rorin's chief advisor anymore," Essa said. "Besides, we'll keep our hoods down and nobody will see us."

"And what if the nazal chooses this particular location to attack while we're there?"

Essa folded her arms over her chest. "Then you'll have backup instead of facing it alone."

"All right," Arya conceded, drawing her hood back up over her face. "We both go. All discreet like."

***

Arya lurched from guilt to fear to dread as she followed Essa through the rainy streets, boots sinking into mud. Her feelings about Leanir were … complicated. The first time she'd met him, it was after he'd slit the throat of one of her Raider comrades on patrol. Years later, he'd come after Rorin and Darmanin, before escaping and critically injuring the general she loved and respected, costing him his job and position.

But then Leanir had run the Dreadwater Gate with them. He'd saved Essa's life, and risked his own to do it. And they'd formed an alliance of sorts shortly afterwards, when the nazal had hunted them in the streets of Gateport.

And now she'd imposed her will on him via their bond, and he wouldn't have reacted well to that. This could be an ambush. In fact, there was a greater than good chance it *was* an ambush. She'd probably deserve it if it was, she thought.

Essa seemed to be thinking along similar lines. "It's a lovely morning to be murdered by a Shadeweaver assassin, don't you think?"

Arya shot Essa a look as her boot sank into a puddle of something that smelled like rat's piss mixed with roadkill. A few moments later, the Inkweaver turned and pushed through the doors of an inn. Inside was louder with chatter than it should be for this hour of the morning. There were so many shadowy corners and hooded patrons crowded around tables that Arya immediately figured there was no way she'd be able to pick out Leanir, even if he was here.

Essa made straight for the bar, and climbed onto the stool in the brightest section. Arya felt eyes crawling along her back as she followed. She briefly unmuted her bond to Leanir, then felt a thrill of relief. He was close.

"Right, so we're making ourselves bait." Arya swung up beside Essa. Her fingers started tapping in agitation against the wood. She made herself stop. "Nice."

At a quiet word from Essa, the barman—who had the shiftiest eyes Arya had ever seen—wandered off. Several moments later, he reappeared with two tin cups he plonked in front of them. Arya lifted hers to sniff the contents, and quickly spotted the folded note pressed to the bottom of the cup. She unfolded it, then snorted and passed it to Essa. "Is that supposed to be a drawing?"

"Up the stairs, second door on the left."

"Right." Arya drained her cup in one gulp, almost spat the bitter-tasting contents all over the bar, then stood and made for the stairs.

Where an ambush probably awaited them.

All was quiet in the dim corridor at the top though, and Arya—ready to draw her blade, Essa a step behind—crept down to the second door on the left. It was ajar, and she pushed it open.

Nothing moved, and she had to squint before she spotted the man waiting for them in the back corner of the room. He slouched against the wall, arms crossed over his chest, looking no different from the last time Arya had seen him four years earlier. Dark eyes. Hooded gaze. Watchful and predatory air.

"Arya Ravenstrike," he greeted her, a condescending note to his voice. "How good to see you again." His eyes flicked to Essa. "Chief Advisor." He inclined his head in a mocking imitation of politeness. "What the hell do you want?"

Leanir's smug expression never failed to set off Arya's temper, but today she swept that aside. "No time for the usual witty pleasantries, Leanir. You need to leave this inn immediately and stay away from *any* location associated with the Shadeweavers."

A snort. "Why?"

"Because the Nightstalker knows your name, that you're a Shadeweaver, and that you're one of my *cairdre*."

Arya ignored Essa's indrawn gasp at her side, gaze firm on Leanir.

His lip curled and his voice was murderously chilly as he hissed, "How does he know that?"

"Doesn't matter. What matters is that there's a nazal in this city, hunting you."

His eyes glittered, rage, she thought. "You gave me up."

"I—"

He exploded away from the wall in a single step, rage in his eyes. Before Arya could move, he had a knife at her throat. "You *gave* me to him?"

Arya thought about denying it, but she didn't want to keep this secret anymore. Besides, he'd already seen the truth in her expression. She held his gaze and made no attempt to defend herself. "He captured me. I had no choice, Leanir. I'm sorry."

Essa muttered a curse word, and Arya felt a tug of apprehension. Essa *never* cursed. Then again, the woman didn't like being lied to either.

"But you *did* have a choice," Leanir snarled. "You could have given up Essa or Darmanin or the minstrel, but you chose me. You *willingly* gave him my name. You could have stayed away from him instead of allowing yourself to be caught."

"Yes," she said simply.

"I should kill you now."

"But you won't. You can't."

His fingers were white-knuckled on the blade at her throat. "Don't be so sure."

Arya took a step toward him, pushing the knife into her skin, feeling the sting of its bite. At her side, Essa shifted closer but said nothing. "I'm very interested in the fact that despite me *forcing* you to meet, Essa and I got a polite note at the bar, and a clear path to this very nice room where you were waiting for us. You wanted to talk to me. You've figured out a nazal was behind the recent deaths too, haven't you? You want my help."

Leanir held her gaze. There was so much violence in his dark eyes, but it wasn't unleashed. Leanir had impressive self-control. She supposed it was why he was such a good assassin. "Even if I did, I sure as hell don't want it anymore."

"You have my protection. I owe you that."

Contempt flashed on his face then and he stepped away from her, lowering the knife. Warm blood trickled down her neck. "You can't even protect yourself, let alone me."

"Then you have you flee, somewhere far from any Shadeweaver haunt. He knows you're a Shadeweaver." He opened his mouth, and she cut him off. "Not the Wraith Forest. An army is about to march through it with another nazal at its head."

Leanir snarled, low and deep. "So, the dreams I've been having about an army marching under the mountains *are* true?"

"You're still able to eavesdrop on the nazal?" Arya asked sharply.

"The one that can talk mind-to-mind like me is here in the city. I can listen in on its conversations with the others." Leanir paced, anger and bitterness vibrating from him. "Do you have any idea of the position you've put me in? *I have nowhere to run, Raider.*"

Into the tense silence, a familiar sensation whispered over Arya's senses, and as she processed that, she realised that she could no longer hear the murmur of voices drifting up from the main room of the inn below. She dashed for the window, pressing herself into the wall before edging forward just far enough to see out. The rainy mist from earlier had thickened to the point that the buildings further down the street had faded from view. Even as she watched, the oppressive grey fog enveloped more and more of the street, creeping slowly toward the inn.

"What are you doing?" Leanir asked.

Terror rippled down Arya's spine as her gaze caught on the cloaked figure stopping at the inn's entrance, glancing both ways, before pushing open the door. "A nazal is here."

A moment later the screams started.

Leanir didn't hesitate. He made it to the window in two strides, slid up the window frame and swung out. There, he paused only a second. "I might not be able to kill you, Raider, but I *can* make your life a misery."

"Leanir, wait!" Arya called, but he was already dropping to the ground, disappearing into the mist.

"What do we do?" Essa's knives were in her hands, fear in her green eyes. But she was in ready stance, clearly prepared to fight.

The screams were louder now, chairs crashing below. It wouldn't take long for the nazal to kill its way up to the second floor. Leanir had said the nazal in the city was the one who'd killed Nain, who'd easily gotten into her head that night. All Arya could think was that if it got close to her, if it got inside her mind, it would see Kirin. Where he was.

Arya motioned to the window, panicked. "We must go. Hurry."

"What about all the people down there? We can't just leave them."

"We can't face it, Ess, we're not ready. If we go down there, we die."

"Arya, that's not you." Essa stared at her in shock. "We can't turn our back on them."

To keep Kirin safe, she had to.

"We don't have a choice." The words came out harshly, fuelled by her own self-loathing. "Essa, go! Before it gets up here."

Essa hesitated, but eventually gave in, sheathing her knives and running for the window. Arya followed her out, and as soon as they reached the ground, they ran, not slowing, until they reached the Ravenstrike townhouse.

As soon as they were through the gates, Arya excused herself, walked around to the garden behind the townhouse, and emptied her stomach into the bushes. Then she stayed there, in the rain and wet, until her stomach stopped heaving.

***

More rain drizzled from the sky as Arya, Essa, and Darmanin rode out of the city the next morning. Essa had been withdrawn since the nazal encounter, and Darmanin didn't want to be there, so tense silence hung over the group. While relieved Leanir had been warned and had presumably gone into hiding, Arya couldn't escape the guilt she felt over what she'd done to him. How she'd left an inn full of people to die because she'd been afraid. Essa's words rang through her head over and over *"That's not you."*

Finding her thoughts unbearable, Arya finally broke the silence and started telling the other two what she'd learned about their magic from Salyarin.

"Who *used* to train Sky Lords?" Essa asked. Some of her distance faded as her intellectual curiosity stirred.

"Their families. Each Sky Lord House possessed generations of learning and knowledge on their Houses' particular ability." Arya sent Essa an apologetic look. "I got bored when Salyarin explained further. But your father knows a lot more."

"How else does the magic manifest in us? Apart from the blunt use of energy you've described."

"Once we've learned how to access our magic, which I gather is largely an instinctive process, we're faster, stronger, and more agile than normal humans. Our eyesight and hearing are sharper, we have no fear of heights and as you can see, we look different."

Essa dissolved into thoughtful silence, and Arya was surprised when Darmanin was the one to break the quiet. "What's your particular ability, Arya?"

Arya shrugged. "I've no idea. Salyarin tells me it will manifest once I've learned some patience and control."

"We need the generational knowledge of our Houses," Essa said in frustration. "Mine in particular. Could you imagine what we might be capable of if we could study the Inkweaver archives?"

"I agree. The archives will be critical to defeating the Nightstalker. But one step at a time, remember?" Arya reminded her friend.

"Right." Essa took a breath. "We're far enough from the city. There's a clearing up ahead. Alletryl's waiting."

Elendryl was there too, and Darmanin stood aside while Arya and Essa spent several moments with their wyverns. Elendryl's scales were smooth under her hands, and his nearness soothed all the edges of her tiredness and anxiety. She'd missed him terribly. Eventually, the two creatures settled at opposite ends of the clearing to watch. She sensed a hint of amused anticipation from Elendryl and levelled a glare in his direction. He yawned in response.

Arya turned to Essa. "Are you sure about this?"

Enlivening the threads between them *should* be safe, but there was no way to be certain, especially with a nazal so close.

"Yes," she said determinedly.

Feeling a ripple of relief, Arya carefully unmuted her bond to Essa, dormant for four years. The restoration flooded her with magic and *rightness*. It glowed between them, bright and strong, before settling to the little thrum of awareness she'd shared on and off with Darmanin since he'd rescued her from Darkclaw.

"I felt that too," Darmanin said curiously, one hand unconsciously pressed against his chest. "It feels…"

"Right." Essa answered. "Like I can breathe properly again."

"The cazaix you wear will give you mild discomfort when you use your magic," Arya warned. "But unless it cuts your skin, it won't do more than that. You'll adjust quickly."

Essa rubbed her hands together. "Let's get started."

***

Several hours passed in which Arya did her best to show Essa and Darmanin how to access and use the magical energy in their blood. Essa was a fast learner, eager to try everything. Darmanin was the opposite, but he did as Arya asked.

Eventually Essa called time. The trees and ground around them were gouged from magical blasts. Her face was pale with weariness. "I think that's all I can manage for one day."

Arya nodded and Essa headed for Alletryl, settling against his side while one of his wings came down to cradle her. The Inkweaver's eyes slid closed, and a little smile crossed her face.

"You didn't bring Zaphirdryl to Gateport?" Arya asked Darmanin.

"It's safer for her to remain hidden in the Diamondfang."

"For her or for you?" she asked.

His mouth tightened, and he didn't answer, instead changing the subject. "Want to practice some more? Practicing in calm and quiet is one thing.

Using it in the distraction of a fight is a whole other story. How about we introduce weapons?"

Arya huffed an amused breath. "You couldn't care less about learning more of your magic. You just want to beat me in a sparring match."

He shrugged, that note of challenge returning to his eyes. "See who breaks first?"

"It won't be me, Crowtalon."

Initially they both struggled to summon and use their magic while sparring. Joining their strength and energy was instinctive, something the bond between them allowed without thought. But consciously deploying her magic in an offensive blast while concentrating on not getting stabbed by a superior fighter—that was somewhat more difficult.

Essa watched, occasionally offering encouragement or enthusiastic clapping. Arya was the first to successfully send sparking blue energy along her blade as she lunged at his chest, but a minute later Darmanin had the ground near her feet exploding in spatters of mud.

"Missed!" she taunted, dancing away from his blow.

The longer they sparred, the better Arya got at keeping a part of her consciousness focused on accessing and controlling her magic, while the rest engaged in the fight. She was never able to hold it for long, but she could isolate her magic more frequently, until they were both breathing hard, exchanging rapid-fire blows and destroying the clearing around them with poorly aimed magical blows.

Eventually Darmanin stepped back, raising his sword. "Arya, I think being able to use magic like this makes us capable of facing a nazal and defeating it."

"You're wrong," she said flatly. "At least, not without hours more practice."

"You don't know that. Essa was right the other day. If you want to kill the Nightstalker, you'll have to take risks. And defeating him will be substantially easier if you kill his nazal."

"Facing a nazal now would be a foolish risk."

He shrugged, sheathed his blade. "Water?"

"Thanks." Arya caught the flask he tossed her way and gulped down the contents before tossing it back. She'd pushed herself too hard in sparring with Darmanin—but it had been so much *fun*. And it had been so long since she'd had simple fun.

Darmanin drank, then lowered the flask. "I'm glad to see you getting better, Arya. I never doubted you would, but I could see *you* doubting it."

"You seem to be helping me out a lot these days, Crowtalon," she murmured, sending a shiver of gratitude along the thread between them.

Sudden movement as Essa heaved herself to her feet had Arya starting, tearing her gaze from Darmanin's. "I was dozing there for a moment," Essa exclaimed. "We're not going to be late for dinner at Hawkesdale's, are we?"

"Not if we ride fast." Darmanin turned, heading for his horse.

Essa still seemed worried. "I don't want to make things difficult for you with courting Illia, Dar."

Arya sent a sharp look Darmanin's way.

He didn't look at her as he responded to Essa. "I haven't decided to do that yet."

"Yes, well, we still shouldn't be late."

Despite the sting of the mention of Illia, Arya couldn't help but laugh at her friend's bossiness as she scrambled into the saddle. "Lead on, Ess."

They were approaching the city when Essa looked over at Arya. "You're mulling something. Out with it."

"Today has made something clear. I've taught you what I can, but I think it's time for you to go to the Etherean and let Salyarin teach you more about your magic. He has books you could read, ones I never had the patience for. Maybe you could learn something about the Inkweaver archives, a way to access them without your father. And Chiarn will be arriving there soon with the Andahari rebels."

"What about the two of us addressing the Council?"

"I will miss having you at my side, but I honestly don't think your presence will make a difference to whether or not the warlords listen to me."

"All right," she said. Already her expression was alight at the thought of learning. "I'll go to the Etherean."

***

The mood was sombre as they returned from Hawkesdale's residence late that night for a cup of mulled wine by the fire in Rorin's study, Darmanin joining them.

Rorin let out a sigh as he sank into a chair. He'd looked tired and worried ever since Arya and Essa had passed on what Leanir had told them, that he'd dream-walked a nazal leading an army under the mountains. "*I don't know how I'm going to fare without you, Ess.*"

His shoulders slumped, and Arya saw how much weight he was carrying. He was ultimately responsible for Ravenstrike State, and right now he must feel like it was being besieged from multiple angles. Peemla reached over to take his hand, and he managed a smile for her.

"I'll go north with Essa." Darmanin spoke into the grim silence, pushing out the words like they were the last thing he wanted to say.

They all swung to him in surprise.

"Once Arya's news is delivered to the Council, the focus will be—*has* to be—on uniting Dunidaen's defences, not creating more instability by holding a High Warlord vote." His jaw was tense. "That will have to wait until after the Nightstalker's army has been pushed back."

Arya let out a breath. "You're right, but I know what it means to you. Thank you, Dar."

Essa reached out to touch Darmanin's hand in support. "But that doesn't mean you have to leave Gateport."

Darmanin shook his head. "My father is far more likely to listen to you if I'm not here—my very presence puts him on the defensive. I'll appoint Andrian to speak for me at Council and go north to help Arken prepare Ravenstrike's defences. If nothing else, Zaphirdryl and I can help scout the Diamondfang. I'll also be able to liaise with the Shadeweaver scouts, see what they know."

"*Dar, thank you,*" Rorin said. "*That's a massive weight off my shoulders.*"

He nodded. "Give me tomorrow to sort Crowtalon's affairs and ensure Andrian is across everything he needs to be. Essa, we can leave the day after."

A sharp knock came at the door, and one of the servants brought a message to Peemla, who opened it and leaned close to her husband so he could read the words too. Once done, Rorin looked up at the rest of them. "*Falconcrest arrived in Gateport yesterday. This message is from Mathas. The Council formally opens a week from today.*"

Taze looked unimpressed. "That's almost a fortnight late."

Essa stood immediately. "Before I leave, I'll put together a pitch to get Arya on the agenda as soon after the Council opens as possible, *without* actually telling anyone who she is."

She was gone before any of them could say anything, the door swinging shut behind her. Arya sat back in her chair in relief. *Finally,* the Council was starting. She didn't have to hide out in Gateport while a nazal stalked the streets for much longer.

Darmanin rose too. "Good luck, all. I hope to see you in Heathrock soon, bringing news of the Dunidae army marching behind you."

"Be safe, Dar." Arya told him, wishing he wasn't leaving, even though it was what they needed. "And stay clear of the nazal when you scout."

"I know, Arya. I'll be careful."

Arya couldn't help the worry filling her. She *hated* that she was trapped in Gateport instead of on the front lines, where she belonged. But maybe it was better to leave things in Darmanin's hands. She didn't want to make another terrible mistake.

"It's going to be okay." Taze tried to rally Arya and Rorin, who looked as concerned as Arya felt.

"I can see it's going to be a long day of preparation tomorrow," Peemla said. "I'll make sure you have what you need. I have faith in you all."

Arya managed a smile of thanks, but it faded quickly. She remembered sitting at this table four years ago, feeling alive with confidence and anticipation—sure that Thiara was about to beat Crowtalon in the vote and that soon she'd be ruling Dunidaen, and they could seek her help with the

Nightstalker. Confident beyond a doubt that together, they could handle anything.

Now she felt the opposite.

Chapter 24

Arya waited outside the State Council chamber. It was too warm in the hallway, the burning fireplaces along the exterior corridor overcompensating for the cool, rainy day outside. She adjusted her cloak for the hundredth time, made sure the hood covered her features so that none passing would recognise her.

Remember Arya reminded herself. *No overt displays of magic. No terrifying the warlords and their generals. You must win them to your side.*

At which point her temper piped up to point out they'd cancelled her appearance twice already, that it had been almost three weeks since the Council opened, and today they'd kept her waiting over an hour so far.

No magic she repeated. *No matter how petty and rude they are. Calm and poised.*

You need them.

Her palms sweated. It had been four years since Arya had attended a formal State Council. And the last time she'd been in the room beyond, she'd been maddened with fury and grief and run her sword through Mathas Crowtalon's chief advisor. A man controlled by the nazal who was back in Gateport, killing Shadeweavers. She swallowed, glanced around, as if it might even now be stalking the halls of the Council chamber, hunting her.

It didn't know she was here. Neither did the Nightstalker. She was safe.

That didn't work to calm her, so she distracted herself by thinking of Darmanin and Essa. A bird from them had arrived two days earlier, announcing their safe arrival in Heathrock. Chiarn must be close to arriving at the citadel with the Andahari rebels too.

Abruptly, the doors in front of her swung open.

A Defender motioned Arya in wordlessly, giving her shapeless cloak and hooded features a suspicious glance.

Fighting the dread and nausea in the pit of her stomach, Arya forced herself to walk inside, gaze scanning the interior from habit. She clocked the Defenders standing guard either side of the door, others arrayed around the walls. Then she turned her attention to the table in the centre. Every warlord and their general and chief advisor were present, chatting among themselves. High Warlord Mathas Crowtalon sat at the head of the table, Warlord Rian Eaglesoar to his right, and Andrian to the left. Rorin sat on Andrian's other side, with Hawkesdale opposite him. SparrowWing was next to Hawkesdale, and Falconcrest beside Rorin.

Arya's gaze settled on the High Warlord. He looked older than the last time she'd seen him. There was the odd streak of grey in his well-groomed hair, and new lines around his eyes. But his control over the room was easy to discern.

The chatter died as they realised Arya had paused inside the doors, waiting for them to close behind her. As soon as they did, she shrugged off the cloak, made sure her head was up, and walked confidently towards the table. Her cobalt Stormrider cloak flowed around her legs as she walked, and she wished she felt more comfortable in it. As it was, it made her feel an imposter.

Mathas Crowtalon was the only one at the table who did not look shocked at Arya's appearance, at the magic gleaming in her eyes, at the finery she wore. Even Hawkesdale seemed uneasy, though he'd known this was coming. The shocked silence deepened until she came to a halt. Falconcrest glanced towards the Defender guards, SparrowWing watched her carefully, and Andrian gave her a little smile. Everyone else glanced surreptitiously at Mathas as they waited for him to take the lead on how they should respond.

"Arya Nameless," Mathas said flatly. "Daring of you to walk straight in here. Ravenstrike didn't tell us he was bringing a wanted criminal to address us today."

Immediately her patience was tested. Not just at the smug look, the contempt in his voice, but at the look he sent Rorin's way, as if promising punishment later. She wanted to leap at him, wrap her hands around his throat and destroy him. The urge was close to overwhelming, and Arya shifted forward before getting a hold of herself. She'd lost control like that before, and it had destroyed everything. She wouldn't make the same mistake again.

Taking a deep breath, she spoke politely. "High Warlord, Warlords. Thank you for allowing me to address you today. I understand there is a bounty on my head, but if you give me a moment, I will demonstrate that I'm only here to help."

"Warlord Ravenstrike claims you have some urgent news for us, information that affects the safety of Dunidaen," Mathas Crowtalon said, voice dripping with condescending disbelief. "Which is the only reason I'm not immediately having you arrested and sent to Andahar. You're on a short leash, don't test my patience."

Bullshit. Crowtalon was intrigued by her presence, and confident enough in his ability to handle her that he was willing to let things play out. Her hands curled into fists at her sides, but she forced herself to unclench them. *Calm and polite.*

"Thank you, High Warlord. I would first like to take this opportunity to formally apologise for attacking your chief advisor and causing fear among the guests gathered here on the night of the last High Warlord vote." Arya's voice rang with sincerity, an emotion she didn't have to fake. She wished so many things could have gone differently that night.

Rorin shot Arya a look of muted approval, and she took enough strength from that to push back the grief that wanted to rise at the memories.

Mathas huffed an impatient breath. "Why should we believe you? I remember you, Nameless. You were arrogant and stupid, with no noble blood or relevant experience to validate your rank as general. The biggest mistake Thiara Ravenstrike ever made was placing her trust in you."

"You can believe me or not, High Warlord. An apology was owed, and I wanted to give it."

His mouth tightened. "Why are you here?"

"I am here to formally introduce myself to Dunidaen's leadership, so that you take my news with the spirit with which I bring it; a sincere desire to help."

"Introduce yourself?" Warlord Falconcrest smirked. "We know who you are."

"You know that I'm a Sky Lord potential, yes. That's what is written on my bounty, anyway. There's more, though, that the Nightstalker *didn't* tell you when he was busy demanding that you do things on his behalf." Arya met each warlord's gaze in turn, lingering finally on Mathas. "I am Arya Stormrider, rightful heir to the throne of Andahar. *That's* why he wants me so badly. Because he's sitting on *my* throne."

Someone's breath hissed out. Another shifted so hard in their chair it screeched on the floor. Around the table the men wore expressions with varying degrees of surprise, fear, shock, and distaste. Even so, she suspected the reactions were less about the title she'd claimed than her confirmation that the Nightstalker was right, that she *was* a Sky Lord.

"Magic-wielder!" Falconcrest spat before Arya could respond. "How *dare* you—"

"Settle down, Nashdar," Mathas said, his gaze on Arya. "Her claims are as ridiculous as what she is wearing. Don't pay them credence by growing so angry."

"I'm aware of your attitudes towards magic." Arya worked hard to keep her voice firm but calm. "But I pose no threat to you. I am here to help. Only if we work together can we hold back the might of the Nightstalker."

"*High Warlord, please,*" Rorin spoke before Mathas could, Taze translating for him. "*Arya speaks the truth. Her news affects the whole of Dunidaen, and it is vital that the Council hears it.*"

"She's here now, we should at least listen to what she has to say," Gelfrey Hawkesdale added his support to Rorin, reluctant though it was.

Mathas nodded at Hawkesdale's words and waved a dismissive hand. "Go on, then."

"The Nightstalker intends to invade Dunidaen," Arya said. "He has mustered a large army of soldiers, wraiths, and shadowhounds. They are entering the Diamondfang as we speak and could break through into Ravenstrike by the start of spring."

"How do you know this?" Hawkesdale barked.

"I've been into Andahar. The Nightstalker has been conscripting soldiers for months, thousands of them. His army is led by a nazal, a monster with nearly as much magical power as he possesses, and it's using the underground road, in addition to other tunnels under the mountains."

"Have *you* seen evidence of this invasion, Warlord Ravenstrike?" SparrowWing asked.

"I have not, but I trust Arya's word. And Darmanin has been into the road under the Diamondfang; he saw the scouting force of Andahari soldiers himself. My Raiders have since sought out and destroyed multiple small encampments with cached food and weapons supplies left by that scouting force."

"Shadeweaver supplies, no doubt," Falconcrest snapped, "Or did you actually see foreign soldiers at these encampments?"

"My Raiders saw signs of—"

"Bah! Ravenstrike is hardly a credible witness, nor is Crowtalon." Warlord Eaglesoar spoke for the first time, causing Arya to sigh inwardly. She'd hoped Rorin's uncle would support them.

"Indeed," Mathas agreed dryly. "The both of them are so busy closing their borders to my Defenders, I can't see how they've had the time to notice an invasion from the northwest."

"The Defender battalion is on your border now, waiting for entry approval which you've so far refused to give," Falconcrest said to Rorin. "Let them in, and they can help with this supposed invasion."

"Perhaps now might be a good time to talk about that policy, High Warlord," Hawkesdale barked. "I don't need your Defenders poking their noses in where they don't belong."

"Then perhaps you should speak with Warlord Crowtalon. If he hadn't murdered Nashdar's Aggressors without cause, I wouldn't have had to implement such a policy," Mathas snapped, sending a dark look at Andrian as he spoke. "I am High Warlord. My word is law." Hawkesdale's flush deepened at being spoken to in such a way, but Mathas held his gaze. "Is that clear?"

"Crystal." Gelfrey gritted out.

A cold smile spread over Mathas' face as he swung his gaze from Hawkesdale to SparrowWing. "I am issuing a new command. Each of you will allow a battalion of Defenders into your States. If your armies prevent them from entering, I will strip you of your position as warlord, appropriate your holdings, and hand your State over to someone else."

Hawkesdale went purple, and SparrowWing shared a glance of shock with Rorin. But none of them protested. Andrian shifted in his chair, darted a glance at this father, but didn't seem to know what to say. Arya had a sudden wish that Thiara Ravenstrike were still alive; there was no way she would tolerate this. Worse, the warlords' attention was now firmly on their own infighting, not on her news.

She tried to cut in as politely as she could. "Warlords, High Warlord, there is more to discuss. You are facing an invasion, and I think we need to work together to—"

Mathas waved a dismissive hand, cutting her off. "You've said what you came to say, and you have no right to participate in a State Council discussion. Be glad I am not having you arrested. Yet. Handing you over to the Nightstalker *will* be on the table for our discussions. I doubt he will be so keen on invasion if we give him what he's been wanting all this time."

She didn't look away, mouth curling in a silent snarl. She had to win them. Kirin's safety depended on it. It was all that held her back from losing her temper.

"Ravenstrike, I assume she's staying with you?"

Rorin gave a terse nod.

"She doesn't leave your residence unless I give permission, is that clear? If she does, I'll arrest the both of you."

Rorin's shoulders turned rigid. It wasn't often he grew genuinely angry, but Arya saw it in him now, and it saved her from her own. She shifted forward just enough that she could press her palm against his back.

"Ravenstrike, am I clear?" Mathas snapped.

Rorin signed a single word. "*Yes.*"

Mathas's gaze shifted to Arya. "Leave," he said, holding her gaze, enjoying the stymied temper no doubt reflected in her eyes.

Arya saw the Defenders take a step away from the walls and relented. She spun on her heel and strode out, brushing past the guards, and trying to fight back despair.

That had *not* gone well.

***

"I should have demanded they listen to me." Arya stormed, pacing up and down Rorin's study. Her head clipped a hanging lantern, sending it swinging wildly from side to side. She swore fluently and raised a hand to rub at the spot.

Andrian grinned, but was wise enough not to comment.

"*He wouldn't have allowed it,*" Rorin said wearily. "*And if you'd pushed, he'd have set his Defenders on you, and killing their solders in front of them would end any prospect of an alliance.*"

Her brother had been in the Council for the remainder of the afternoon and had come directly from there with Taze and Andrian to meet with Arya and figure out what to do next. Peemla had come and gone, making sure they had food and giving Rorin a chance to hug his son goodnight before putting him to sleep.

Arya slumped into a chair, despair clawing at her. "I don't know what else I can do. I hold an empty title. Without an army or formal recognition, I have little real power. And Mathas could decide to carry out his threat and have me arrested at any time."

And the longer she stayed here, the greater chance the nazal would find her. Especially now news of her presence in Gateport would spread.

"You *and* Rorin," Andrian said grimly.

"*They'd have to go through the Raiders to do that.*" Rorin was still angry, his shoulders tight, signing more terse than usual.

"Thereby giving Mathas an excuse to strip you of your title and hand Ravenstrike over to someone else?" Taze said. "Things aren't completely hopeless, though. It's not Mathas you must convince, Arya, but the other warlords. A High Warlord *can* be outvoted in Council decisions."

Andrian flashed a winning smile. "Arya, you *are* the strategic genius among us. You can come up with something, I know you can."

She avoided his gaze, eyes dropping to the floor. She liked Andrian well enough, but she wished Darmanin was here. Wished it more than was probably sensible. "The bitter truth is, I burned all my bridges here the night I killed Nain," she admitted. "Even those warlords who liked me before see me as violent and potentially unstable." It was going to take time to win their trust and alliance. Time that was rapidly running out.

Silence fell, the sound of crackling flames in the hearth provided a calm counterpoint to all their frustration. Then, one of Arya's Sky Lord bonds flared to life in her chest. It was pain and shock and nothing else, a livewire of desperate reaching.

Darmanin.

Before she could suck a breath in, reach for him, the pulse faded, and the thread went dull. Another thread flared to life then. Leanir? Pain stabbed through her head as a flash of images were dumped into it. Elendryl roused, growling, seeing the same images.

Darkness. A fight. A flash of reddened eyes.

And then the images were gone too, Leanir's thread fading with them.

"Arya!" Taze's voice shouted, but it was distant.

Arya had slumped forward, head in her hands, a swell of terror closing over her chest. She reached for Darmanin and Leanir, but both had gone dull, and she couldn't get a response out of either. Essa and Chiarn, too, were too distant for her to reach with any kind of coherent message. The only thing she knew was that all four still lived, though Darmanin's thread seemed weaker. It felt limp, bleached of any vibrancy.

He was hurt. Badly.

Panic closed over her throat. *"Elendryl!"*

He read the intensity of her mental call. "*I come!*"

Rorin grabbed her arm to get her attention. "*Arya!*"

She lurched to her feet, the room spinning. "I have to go north. Elendryl is already on his way."

"*WHAT HAS HAPPENED!*" he signed fiercely.

"Darmanin is hurt, badly, I think. Somehow Leanir was with him, maybe," she mumbled, thoughts spilling out everywhere. "Why would Leanir go north when I warned him a nazal was there? But he sent me images. I think Darmanin was ambushed, in the tunnels. A nazal was there. Now I can't reach either of them, and my bond with Dar is..." She shook her head, swallowed. "I have to go."

"Arya, no," Taze said. "You need to be here to speak to the warlords. Besides, if Dar is as badly hurt as your fear, by the time you got there..."

His words trailed off, but everyone understood his intended meaning. Rorin looked between Taze and Arya, seemingly torn by which approach he should support.

"It's critical that the Dunidae armies unite," Taze pushed. "I would do anything for Dar, but he would want you to stay here too."

"*Essa is there,*" Rorin said shakily. "*She could help him, if anyone can. And Taze is right I think.*"

Arya shook her head. "Darmanin is a part of my *cairdre*. I won't leave him to die."

Andrian looked at Arya, pleading. "If you can help my brother, then, please, I ask you to do whatever you can."

"What about the warlords?" Taze asked again.

"I don't care about the warlords!" she snapped.

A brief silence fell.

The part of her that was desperate to protect Kirin warred with the part of her that wouldn't, *couldn't* leave Darmanin to die.

She had to go. She'd come back for the warlords. She could still win them.

Rorin took a deep breath. "*If you're leaving, Taze and I will have to follow with Peemla and Anji. Otherwise, the Defenders will come to arrest me as soon as Mathas learns you're gone. I will speak to the warlords individually first, do my best to convince them.*" He reached out to hug her tightly. "*Good luck.*"

She clung to him. "I'm sorry to put you in this situation, but—"

"*You have to go. I understand.*"

Arya ran from the room and took the stairs two at a time, stopping only to grab a voluminous cloak. She slipped out through the back garden, hood fully down over her face. Once clear of the residence, she moved into a run, racing through the city streets, heading for the western wall—the closest—and the gated exit there. She slowed only so as not to catch the attention of the Defenders guarding the gate.

Once on the road beyond the city, Arya ran again.

Soon, a bright shape descended from the sky. Arya swung herself onto Elendryl's back before he'd even landed properly, and then they were leaping back into the air.

***

When Elendryl began to tire, Arya used her magic, bolstering his strength with her own. The further they went, the deeper she reached into her well of strength. They flew through the night, the next day and into the night beyond.

It was dawn on the third day when they circled out of the sky above Heathrock. When Elendryl jolted to the ground, Arya half-climbed, half-slid to the cobblestones. Beside her, Elendryl sank down, just as exhausted. She spotted Raiders approaching, heard someone yelling at her as if from a distance. Blackness swam in her vision, and her eyelids flickered closed.

Gloved fingers touched her cheek. "Can you hear me?" Arken's face came into view overhead, creased with concern.

"Yes," Arya's voice came out as a rasp. "Just help me up. I'll be all right in a moment."

"Easy, Arya." Essa's voice was there then. Her hand rested comfortingly on the back of Arya's neck until she was able to take a few deep breaths and stagger to her feet. She reached for Elendryl. He sent a tired reassurance that he was fine.

"Are you alright? Is Warlord Ravenstrike all right?" Arken looked worried. "What happened?"

"I'm fine, and so is the warlord," Arya said, gaze shifting between Arken and Essa. "Dar?"

The general's face turned grim as he realised why she'd come. "We found him yesterday—it looks like the Shadeweavers dropped him at the gates. One of the Heathrock city healers is treating him, but it's not looking good."

Arya looked at Essa. "Show me where he is."

"Of course."

Arya took in none of her surroundings as she forced her legs to follow Essa into the castle. "What happened?"

Essa's mouth was tight. "I don't know all of it, but Dar came to me a week ago and said Leanir had contacted him to tell him he planned to go after the nazal. He wanted Dar's help. Something about taking the offensive rather than being hunted. Dar thought if he and Leanir killed the nazal, the invading army would lose its leader, and it would delay the invasion."

Arya swore, a sliver of temper rising to the surface. "What utter fools."

"I told him it was a bad idea, but he ignored me. They left and didn't return on schedule." Essa blinked tears from her eyes, and for the first time Arya saw how tired and drawn she looked. "Shadeweavers dropped Dar off, but I don't know where Leanir is, if he survived."

"He's alive," Arya said. "That's how I knew what had happened; he sent me images. But I don't know if he's hurt or where he is."

Essa stopped when they came to one of the castle's guest rooms. "He's just in there."

Arya took a deep breath and stepped inside. The room smelled fresh and clean. A fire crackled in the grate. Darmanin lay on the bed. His eyes were closed as if in sleep, but his breathing was shallow, his skin deathly pale. A livid purple bruise surrounded his left eye, and matching bruising decorated his right cheek and jaw. A seeping cut ran from his left eyebrow to his ear.

Arya pulled up a chair beside the bed, then reached out and took his hand. It was cool and dry in her grip, and she willed warmth back into it. "Oh, Dar," she whispered, then looked at Essa. "Is he...?"

Essa hadn't sat down, instead hovering near the door. Her pain and fear were obvious to someone who knew her well, even though she was pretending to be fine. "The Heathrock healer says that he has internal injuries; a broken rib that punctured one of his lungs, damaged kidneys and a lacerated liver. But she thinks there's something more wrong with him, something magic-related the nazal did, but we're at a loss. I don't know how to help him, though I've tried over and over."

"I can't..." Arya's voice caught, and she took a breath. "Surely there's something we can do. What about the Etherean?"

"If we move him to their healers, his internal injuries will kill him before we could get him there. I didn't dare leave him to fly to the citadel and ask Salyarin to send a healer here—it felt like me being close to Dar, the thread between us..." Essa shook her head, hands rising to her face. "It felt like if I went away, he would die. I couldn't risk it, I just couldn't. I'm so sorry, Arya."

"It's okay, you did the right thing." Arya felt determination crystallising in her. "I'll try to use my magic to stabilise him. Maybe as *cairdre* leader I can help in a way you can't. While I do that, you fly to the citadel, get one of the Etherean healers here as quick as you can."

Essa's shoulders straightened and she nodded, pulling open the door. "Alletryl will be fast. I promise you I'll have someone here by the end of the day."

"Fly safe, Ess."

Once the door closed behind her, Arya cradled Darmanin's hand in hers, then closed her eyes and calmed her breathing. Weariness floated at the edges of her mind, but she held it at bay. For a long time, she simply breathed in and out, relaxing her mind and body as Salyarin had taught her. Once she was calm, focus steady, she reached for her magic. With her magic came Elendryl's presence; he'd drunk a bucket of water and was resting comfortably.

From there, she directed her attention to her bond with Darmanin. She focused on that contact to the exclusion of all else, trying to bring life to the dulled thread between them. The skin-to-skin contact made that immeasurably easier.

What she sensed horrified her.

Darmanin's magical energy ebbed dangerously. Had the nazal *damaged* it somehow? Arya panicked, her surge of emotion causing the thread between them to wobble and almost snap. Instantly she forced calm and focus on herself and restored the connection, holding it between them with care.

She could do this. She *would* do this.

She'd brought their connection to life, but how to fix him? He'd done it for her, back at Darkclaw Deep, when she'd been terribly hurt. She thought back to those memories, hazy from pain and illness, to try and remember exactly what he'd done. She was still trying to figure it out when Darmanin's magical force ebbed again. On the bed, his breath rasped in his chest, and stopped.

No!

Arya dived after him, following the thread between them as it started to unravel, holding it together with the sheer force of her will and determination. A rush of images flooded her mind, and she was no longer in the cold room in Heathrock.

Darmanin as a tiny baby being rocked by his mother, a raven-haired woman with sad silver-grey eyes.

A tiny, raven-haired boy screeching with laughter as he ran around under the watchful eyes of his mother.

An older boy with silent tears streaming down his face as his father told him his mother was dead.

The two of them standing on the balcony on their first Winterfest eve with the Ravenstrike family.

An impassive youth sparring with Rorin in the Heathrock drill yard, mouth curled in a smile of amusement at a joke Rorin had made.

A competent young man striding through the halls of the State Council chamber, newly confirmed as heir to Crowtalon.

The rush of images stopped suddenly, and Arya opened her eyes with a start. She wasn't in Heathrock. Her surroundings were cast in an odd twilight, and the ground beneath her feet was rough but flat. Darmanin's tall form stood a short distance away, his back to her.

"Darmanin?" she called out, walking towards him.

Her voice echoed eerily in the strange place, and he didn't seem to hear her. She couldn't see anything else around them, and her feet made no sound as she walked. Moving was difficult, like walking through deep snow. She felt her energy drain with every step.

She spoke louder, stronger, "Dar, please?" Arya stopped, and with everything she had, she willed him to look at her. "Come on, Darmanin, I dare you."

Slowly, painfully slowly, he turned until he was facing her. She held her breath the entire time. When he was finally facing her, his eyes were blank, staring over her shoulder, his face expressionless. Gathering every bit of strength that she had—it seemed to be growing harder to move—Arya gritted her teeth, and lifted her arm, holding out her hand. "Take my hand."

For the longest moment, it looked as if he either couldn't or wouldn't move. He continued to stare over her shoulder. His outline faded, and instinct told her that was a bad sign.

"Darmanin, I'm here," she said, her voice firm. "We will always come for each other. That's what you said. All you have to do is take my hand. I will help you. One step at a time. Please."

He wavered, then took a tiny step forward. Strain echoed in his face. Arya used every bit of her strength of will to urge him to keep going. "I'm here, Dar," she said again. "I'm here, and I'm not going to leave you. Not ever. Come with me."

His tense stance relaxed, and he lifted his arm, his hand clasping hers in a sure grip. His distant gaze shifted, locked to hers, *alive...*

And then her eyes flew open.

Arya found herself back in the room in Heathrock. Sweat poured in rivulets down her face, and her heart raced like she'd been in a sprint. Exhaustion swept through her, and she slumped onto the bed, her body no longer able to hold her up. Darmanin's hand was still in hers, and she gripped it as she tried to catch her breath, stop herself from passing out. But she was too weak to move, could barely keep her eyes open.

"Arya?"

"We're here, Ess," she whispered. "We're both here."

Chapter 25

Arya woke to the warmth of sunlight on her face. Cracking her eyes open, she recognised her room at the Etherean citadel. A dull headache throbbed. There was a sluggishness in her limbs, and when she tried to focus, her vision blurred. Her first reaction was panic that the strength she'd painstakingly rebuilt was gone, the vertigo from her old injuries back. But then she remembered.

Darmanin.

Was he still alive? Had the Etherean managed to do anything for him? What if he had died while she was unconscious?

Elendryl made himself known. *"Worried."*

"I'm sorry to make you worry." She apologised.

"Sleeping long." He was unhappy about this.

"How long?"

Elendryl couldn't count, so all she got in response was an exaggerated sense of time passing.

"How is Zaphirdryl?"

He snorted, sent her an image of a black wyvern curled up on the opposite side of the stables from him, one eye cracked open and watching him carefully. *"Worried."*

So Darmanin wasn't dead then—if he was, Zaphirdryl wouldn't be just worried. She pushed off the too heavy blankets and swung her legs around until she was sitting on the edge of the bed. Her clothes were draped neatly over a nearby chair, and Arya dressed quickly, ignoring how the sudden movement made the room spin alarmingly.

Rubbing her eyes—it didn't help the grogginess *or* the spinning—she made her way to the open-aired corridor that led to the elder's quarters. Surely, he would know how Darmanin was doing. The marble roof arched above her, and the weather outside was clear and bright, showing a stunning view of the surrounding mountaintops. Arya barely noticed.

She'd almost reached the door to Salyarin's quarters when they opened, and the man himself appeared. The elder's normally serene face grew tight with anger when he spotted her, and his blue wings rustled at his sides. "What did you think you were doing?" he demanded.

Arya took an unconscious step back, his anger beating at her like a palpable force. Normally such a confrontation would spark her temper, but today she felt too weary and confused to respond. "Is Darmanin alright?"

"Is that really all you care about?"

Arya lifted a hand to her throbbing temple. "I just want to know if—"

"You were in Gateport, with a chance of swinging the warlords to your cause. You had a chance to ally Dunidaen against the Nightstalker, and you abandoned it."

"Darmanin was dying."

"Darmanin is still dying!" the elder snapped. "Your actions have done nothing to change that."

Cold fear clutched at her heart. "What do you mean? What happened?"

Salyarin took a deep breath, and Arya sensed he was trying to contain his fury; she'd done that enough times herself to recognise it in someone else. "I might have forgiven you ignoring your duty to come north, but what you did next was unconscionable. You invoked the most ancient and potent of all Sky Lord magic without even knowing what it was. Darmanin was on the verge of death, and you willingly followed him. Do you have any conception of the incredible risk you took? A thousand tiny things could have gone wrong, and you *both* would be dead now."

Arya swallowed. The aching in her temples was now a wince-inducing throb. She tried to recall what she'd done, what Salyarin was talking about. "I was just trying to save him."

"If you die, Andahar dies with you. There is no hope without you. Have I not drummed that into your head by now? Have you not listened to a word I've ever said to you?" The words were flung at her, icy cold for all their even tone, hitting like blows.

"I couldn't leave Darmanin to die," she protested. "He's a Sky Lord too."

"Rule your emotions, Arya!" Salyarin thundered at her. "Instead of letting them rule *you*. You told me that you accepted your heritage as the rightful heir to Andahar, but until you learn that speaking the words is not good enough, and that you must act like a queen before you can *be* one, Andahar is lost. And maybe you don't care about Andahar, but try thinking about us, or Dunidaen, or even Khadini and the Icelands. Without a credible threat to oppose him, the Nightstalker will end up destroying all of us."

She took those words, didn't protest them, and then asked, "What of Darmanin?"

"He is still unconscious," Salyarin snapped. "And the healers do not know if he will ever wake. You should also know that your Andahari rebels have arrived with Chiarn. More lives for you to toy with as you continue failing to understand the responsibility that sits on your shoulders."

Without waiting for any further response, the elder swept past her and spread his wings, leaping into the sky. Arya stared after him, speechless. Dizziness trembled through her, and she reached out to rest her hand against the wall for balance. Her fingers curled against the cool marble, but even that support wasn't enough, and she slowly slid to the ground, hot tears running down her cheeks.

An anguished sob escaped her, and then she couldn't stop the tears. She curled up in a ball, misery consuming her until she felt she would never stop crying. Soft fingers touched her brow, then an arm wrapped around her, helping her sit up. "Arya, it's me."

"Essa?" Arya opened her eyes to see her friend crouched beside her. She sniffed and pulled away, scrubbing the tears from her eyes in mortification. "I'm sorry."

"What for?" Essa smiled. "You're allowed to cry, you know. Honestly, I'm just relieved to see you up and awake. It's been a week."

"I slept for a *week*?"

"You were unconscious for a week." Essa said pointedly.

Arya swallowed. "Salyarin said Dar was still unconscious, that he might never wake up."

"But he's alive. He's still here with us." Essa squeezed her hand. "I don't know if what you did will save him, but I know without it, he would be dead."

Arya whispered, "How did we get here?"

"I flew you on Alletryl with Elendryl watching closely. The healers I brought to Heathrock had a stretcher to carry Darmanin."

"Oh. Thank you, Essa."

"Don't thank me yet." Essa winced. "The Etherean healers asked me what happened, so I told them what I knew. It made Salyarin angry."

"I'm such a fool," Arya whispered. "An arrogant and useless fool."

Essa studied her, green eyes dark with concern. "Where's that coming from? I've never known you to wallow in self-pity."

Arya cleared her throat and wiped furiously at her eyes. "I betrayed Leanir, Ess. The Nightstalker compelled me. I fought so hard, but I knew I would eventually lose, so I gave Leanir up. And that's why he felt he had to face the nazal, so he could be free. It's my fault Dar is so hurt. Every decision I make ends up in disaster."

"You know that's not true," Essa said quietly.

A comfortable peace settled around them. In that moment, Arya didn't want to keep everything hidden away inside. She couldn't bear to. The understanding and acceptance she saw on her friend's face made the words easier to whisper than she'd thought. "I have a son."

"Oh." Essa stared at Arya, eyes wide, as if that was the last thing she'd ever expected Arya to say. Which, to be fair, it probably was.

"In the days after Rorin and Dar were confirmed as heirs, we were so full of life and confidence. It seemed certain that Thiara would become High Warlord. I don't think I've ever been so happy. When Kulan arrived with the Khadini emperor, we were reckless." Arya paused, her eyes sliding closed as the words poured out. "After I fled, I found out that I was pregnant. I went to Taskari and had the child in secret, and then I left him with his father because I knew that if the Nightstalker found out there was another Stormrider heir … I left him, Essa. And now the Nightstalker knows. He knows, Ess, and I don't know how to keep him safe, to keep any of us safe. I've made such a mess of things."

Understanding spread over Essa's face. "That's why you gave up Leanir. To protect your son."

She nodded, unable to meet Essa's gaze.

Essa leaned into her side. "I'm so sorry, Arya."

Arya opened her eyes. "You're not…?"

"Upset?" Essa asked quietly, and finally their gazes met. "I have no right to be. No, Arya, I'm not upset. I ache for you, though."

"I'm going to fail, aren't I? I don't know how to get my confidence back, the clarity of thought I once had. Not when I have to weigh every single decision with the risks to my son, to you and Rorin and Dar."

"You're exhausted and worried sick about Dar." Essa squeezed her hand. "Go back to Heathrock and get some rest, then focus on defending Dunidaen. I'll stay here with Dar, until we know either way."

Arya straightened her shoulders. "Okay. Thank you."

"Thank *you*," Essa said. "For telling me about your son. I understand the danger he faces, and nobody will learn about him from me."

"I already knew that. It's why I told you." Arya hesitated. "Would you—"

"I should go." Essa pushed to her feet, voice turning brisk.

Stung, but quickly burying the feeling, as she'd done so often before, Arya nodded. "The elder told me that the Andahari are here. Have you seen them?"

"No, I've been with Dar almost every moment since we arrived."

"I'll speak with them before I leave. Chiarn too." Arya rubbed tiredly at her eyes. "I'll let them know you're here, and who you are."

"I'll make sure I go and speak to them." Essa started suddenly, as if she'd just remembered something. "Oh, I forgot to mention in all the worry over Darmanin. Arya, ever since I returned to Heathrock, I've been trying to contact my father, seek Shadeweaver help with scouting the tunnels, but I haven't been able to reach him."

Arya clutched at fading hope. "Is it possible he just didn't get your messages?"

Essa hesitated. "There are very few reasons that he wouldn't receive my messages, or wouldn't respond if he did get them. None of those reasons are good."

"Something happened to him in Andahar," Arya said heavily.

"It looks that way." Essa hesitated. "It's not your fault. He made his own choices to help you."

It didn't feel that way to Arya.

***

Chiarn was sitting alone by the window in his room, legs sprawled in front of him, mostly empty bottle of wine on the table nearby. His gaze was distant as he stared over the peaks. Arya paused in the threshold. She felt battered and bruised, both inside and out, and didn't have the capacity to hide that from him, so she didn't even try. "Hello, Chiarn."

He turned toward her, blurry gaze taking in her state. "Essa told me what happened. I'm sorry about Crowtalon."

"So am I."

"Come on in." He sloshed the wine bottle. "There's a little bit left to share."

She pulled up a chair beside his, dropped into it, and took a swig of the too-sweet wine. "Thanks for making sure the Andahari got here safely."

"No problem." He shrugged, then hesitated. "A question for you. What's next?"

"Next I fly to Heathrock and help Arken prepare the Raiders and some of Dar's Lances to defend against the army marching underneath us as we speak."

"You don't look like you could walk as far as the citadel entry, let alone lead a defence against an invasion."

"Gee, thanks for the vote of confidence," she muttered. The truth was, she had very little hope of succeeding, and it was hard to hide that.

He chuckled and took the bottle back from her, took a long swig, before setting it down and standing up. He only wobbled a little bit as he went to the chest at the foot of his bed. "The elder gave me this."

He too, had been gifted a silken cape. It was a deep, shimmering scarlet, edged in silver like Arya's. Etched in the centre of the cape was an orange leaping flame, with the Stormrider lightning bisecting it.

"That would look good on you," she commented.

He was silent, staring at the cloth.

She picked up the wine, drained its contents. Let him get to wherever he was going in his own time.

"I've been thinking." He expelled a long breath, as if bracing himself, then in one quick movement he shrugged the cape over his shoulders. His blue gaze came up to meet hers. "And I accept your offer, Arya Stormrider. My freedom for standing at your side to fight the Nightstalker. My word on it."

She straightened in her chair, astonished. "What?"

In lieu of replying, he simply stepped forward and held out his hand. His face was pale, jaw clenched, but he held her gaze. When Arya stood and took his hand, there was an unexpected spark in her chest, a flare of life and magic.

The thread between her and Chiarn coming to life.

It felt different to her connection with Darmanin or Essa. Stranger, not as comfortable. But it was live and strong and rippling with flame magic.

"You *are* exhausted." Chiarn's eyes went wide with surprise.

"Why change your mind?" she asked.

He smiled, let go of her hand. "Maybe one day I'll tell you."

She chuckled, some of her despair falling away. "Come on, Lord Flamewielder." Arya put down the bottle. "We have some people to see."

***

Chiarn led her to an area of the citadel that had been set aside for the Andahari travellers. The walk was long enough that Arya had time to replay the words the elder had furiously thrown at her. One particular phrase stuck out—his reference to her using old Sky Lord magic to save Darmanin. He'd never mentioned anything like that when he was training her. Which meant he'd been holding back. He didn't trust her enough to teach her everything she knew.

"Arya, you with us?" Chiarn nudged her.

She shook herself from her musings as they stepped out of a hallway into an open courtyard busy with training warriors. As they caught sight of her, the activity came to a grinding halt. Niallin's familiar face pushed through the rows of sparring partners, delight and surprise on his face. "Lord Stormrider. You've come."

"Hello, Niallin. I'm glad to see that you made it safely through the mountains."

"Roughly four hundred made the journey, and all survived thanks to Lord Flamewielder's ability to keep us warm. I thank you for it."

"I wish I had better news to convey, but the Nightstalker's invasion is imminent, and I'm about to return to Dunidaen to begin preparations to fight back."

"We can fight, Lord Stormrider." A woman spoke. When Arya looked at her, she bowed her head. "I am Laria."

"I have little doubt that you can fight, but you're not an army," Arya replied. "With time and training and discipline I can make you a formidable force, but not in time to join this coming battle."

Niallin's mouth tightened. "We do not wish to sit here in safety while those we love in Andahar remain in danger."

"I understand, but I can do nothing about the Nightstalker until his invading army is defeated."

Mervin spoke up, shooting a look at Niallin. "We will do as you command, Lord Stormrider."

"I want you to stay here and grow stronger," Arya said. "I meant it when I said I will turn you into an army. I ask you to be patient."

Niallin conceded with a reluctant nod. "As you wish."

As a peace offering, Arya said, "You should know also that another of my Sky Lords is here in the citadel. Essa Inkweaver. She'll soon come to introduce herself."

"An Inkweaver." His eyes glowed. "We will look forward to that very much."

Arya motioned Niallin a few steps away from the others and lowered her voice. "I've a question for you. Ranier—do you know where he might have gone in Andahar if he escaped the nazal?"

"I'm sorry. I don't know the man at all." Niallin frowned. "Is there something I can help with?"

"I need knowledge, Niallin, about Sky Lords and their magic. How a *cairdre* grows to its full strength. I'm told House Inkweaver was the repository of all Sky Lord knowledge. Is that true?"

"It was, yes. Their tattoos often depict some of their most precious knowledge."

"Then I need Ranier if I'm ever going to defeat the Nightstalker. He's the only one who can teach me what I need to know."

Niallin shrugged. "Ranier, or another of his House that holds the same knowledge."

"There are others still living?" she asked eagerly. She hadn't thought of that.

"He had an older brother—Remien, House Inkweaver's heir. Unlike Ranier, he did not escape the Nightstalker's coup. Lucius let him live because he was not a Sky Lord potential, but he was locked away in Blackstone Prison." Niallin hesitated. "I don't wish to offer false hope. So long in there, he may not still be alive."

"I assume Blackstone is in Andahar?"

"Deep in a valley in the western foothills of the Horn. There are many stories about it, rumours mostly, but it's not a place you want to end up in. All of Andahar's most dangerous criminals are sent there." Fear flicked over Niallin's face. The stories must be bad.

"Thanks, Niallin." She laid a hand on his shoulder. "Do as I ask. Remain here and grow strong. The time will come for you to fight."

He bowed. "Stay safe, Lord Stormrider."

She turned and left, the elder's words about the Andahari rebels ringing in her mind again. "*More lives for you to toy with.*"

***

Rorin and his retinue arrived at Heathrock a mere two days after Arya returned from the citadel. She met them in the entry courtyard—a weary, travel-stained bunch. Laskin and her shield were with them, and she lifted a hand to greet them, their presence steadying her.

Rorin ran to her. "*Dar?*"

"Still unconscious," she said. "He's at the Etherean citadel, being watched over by their healers. But he was badly injured, and they're unsure whether he'll wake."

Rorin paled. Arya squeezed his arm in silent sympathy, unable to summon anything useful to say. Taze and Peemla came over with Anjurin and Rorin wrapped an arm around his wife and son, holding them close.

"Did you have any trouble leaving Gateport?" Arya asked.

"We left at night and sneaked through the gates in disguise. Commander Derin split up his battalion and sent them all trickling out through different gates," Taze answered. "But we can expect arrest warrants have been issued by now."

"We didn't have any luck with the warlords," Peemla answered Arya's next question before she could ask it. "Hawkesdale and SparrowWing heard Rorin out, but Falconcrest refused our dinner invitation, and Eaglesoar said he was busy and would have to reschedule."

Arya expelled a breath. "It's just us then."

"*Andrian's gone back to Anduil to see how many Lances he can spare us, but yes, it's just us.*" Rorin signed, then gave his son a kiss. "*An invading army from the west, and Defenders from the south.*"

Arya's shoulders sagged, though she tried to hide it from her brother.

What were they going to do?

Chapter 26

A week later, Arya was at drill with her shield—physical exertion was the only way to ease the constricting weight of fear and guilt that she carried constantly—when Taze appeared from the main castle. "We've got quite the arrival at the main gates. You'd better come."

"What kind of arrival?" Arya asked suspiciously.

Taze's reserved smile flashed. "Probably best if you see for yourself. Rorin and General Rosenthal are on their way."

Arya motioned for Laskin to join her, handed her sparring sword to Kait, and followed Taze to the castle entry, where they came upon a yard full of soldiers in brown and gold. Three men had dismounted and stood at the base of the main steps, speaking with Arken.

Rorin was coming down the steps as Arya arrived. "*Warlord SparrowWing, Amius, Andrian,*" he greeted them, Arya translating, her voice full of surprise.

"Warlord Ravenstrike." Helden SparrowWing spoke formally. His shoulders were tense, and he didn't seem entirely happy to be where he was. "Lord Stormrider. Greetings."

She blinked in surprise at his use of her title, but didn't say anything.

"Is Dar okay?" Andrian asked. He had deep shadows under his eyes and a slump to his shoulders.

"*He is with the Etherean healers. He's unconscious and badly hurt, but they're doing everything they can,*" Rorin explained.

He frowned in confusion. "The Etherean?"

Rorin glanced at Arya. "*I don't suppose Darmanin ever told Andrian his origins?*"

She gave a little shake of her head and answered for him. "They are powerful healers, Andrian."

"You can't be serious." Helden SparrowWing huffed. "Nobody's seen one of the winged people in decades. Not since the borders closed."

"That's going to be changing, Warlord," Arya said. "We promise to explain everything. But for now…" Her gaze switched back to Andrian. "Dar is in good hands, but he was badly hurt. His healers aren't sure he'll recover."

Grief flashed across Andrian's face, and he rubbed a hand over his eyes before summoning a faint smile. "Is there anything I can do?" he asked. "Can I go to him?"

"I truly think you would do more good here, and Dar would feel better knowing Crowtalon was in your hands," Rorin replied.

When Taze translated that, Andrian sagged a little more, but then he took a deep breath and visibly straightened his shoulders. Arya remembered how little he'd wanted to be heir to Crowtalon, how glad he'd been to hand the title to Darmanin. Andrian had never wanted to rule. "You're right."

Arya cleared her throat. "I don't mean to be rude, but do you have a reason in coming here, Warlords?"

Helden nodded. "I heard your words in the Council. We left Gateport the day after you left, Warlord Ravenstrike. Amius and I stopped in Melbin only long enough to collect fifteen battalions before marching directly for Heathrock. The remainder of my army is helping Crowtalon's Lances keep the High Warlord's Defenders out of my State."

"You brought three thousand Firemen?" Rorin asked, face brightening in hope.

Amius nodded, smiling. "They're about two days' march behind us. My father and I disagree as to the seriousness of the threat we face from Andahar, but we *both* agree that we owe you whatever help you need. We haven't forgotten how House Ravenstrike came to our aid five years ago, how you helped us save Seelan, and asked no price for it. We've come to return the favour."

"My son speaks well," Helden said gruffly. "My Firemen are at your disposal, Warlord Ravenstrike."

Rorin looked at Arya, eyes full, and she felt the same.

SparrowWing's unexpected offer of help felt like the first rays of sunlight piercing the clouds after weeks of rain.

Arya cleared her throat. "What about the High Warlord? You must know what you are risking by depleting your forces to help us."

"It is time for hard choices," Helden said heavily. "As my son implied, I struggle to believe this fantastical tale of Sky Lords and monsters planning an invasion of Dunidaen, but if we truly face the threat you claim, then I'm casting my lot in with you." Helden stretched his hand out to Rorin. "House SparrowWing will march at your side to face whatever comes, young Ravenstrike."

Rorin smiled as he shook the warlord's hand. "*Thank you, Warlord.*"

"House Crowtalon will join you also," Andrian said firmly. "I know Darmanin has already committed all the Lances we can afford to you and to our borders, but I want you to know that I will carry out his wishes faithfully."

Rorin took a deep breath. "*Time for a war council. Arken, have your commander organise quarters for the warlord's Firemen, then join us. Bring SparrowWing's general with you.*"

"Warlord!" Arken saluted crisply and strode away.

"Laskin?" Arya summoned him while Rorin called servants to escort their guests inside. "Find Chiarn, bring him to this meeting."

His eyes went wide. "You want *me* there?"

"You're my general, Laskin."

He scowled.

"You wanted in, you're in. Now go and do as I order."

Arya's gaze roved over the brown and gold of Warlord SparrowWing's personal shield, thought about the thousands' strong force of Firemen marching their way.

Thought about how it was going to be nowhere near enough.

Rorin's hand closed gently over her arm, jolting her from her thoughts. "*This situation isn't your fault, you know that, right?*"

She sighed and ran a hand through her hair. "I should have stayed in Gateport."

"The Nightstalker is behind what is coming, not you. Caring so deeply about your friends isn't a bad thing, Arya."

"I'm supposed to be a leader."

"You are *a leader. You have been since the day you put on your Raider cloak,"* he told her. *"Now, I have an invasion to deal with, and I need the finest strategic mind I've ever met to help me do that. Are you with me?"*

Arya nodded, pushing away her exhaustion and guilt and focusing only on the present. She might have made a mistake in rushing from Gateport, but there wasn't anything she could do about that now.

"I'm always with you, Rorin."

***

They trickled into Rorin's office and took seats around his table. With Rorin and Arya, Chiarn, Helden and Amius SparrowWing, Andrian, Laskin, Taze, Arken, and SparrowWing's General Willem, they sat elbow to elbow.

A large map of the north of Dunidaen covered the wall at one end of the table, and Arken took up a position there. Arya was pleased to see her old nemesis so calm and in control. Rorin needed a highly capable general more than anything, and that was what she and Desomer had trained Arken to be.

Peemla had worked her magic, and the table groaned under the weight of pastries, tea, and warm cider. The smells wafting off it were heavenly, which meant it took several moments before the meeting could start while those gathered filled plates and cups.

"Your hospitality speaks well of you, young Ravenstrike," Helden said approvingly.

"Thank you, Warlord." Rorin signed, Taze translating. *"If we're ready to start? Good. Let's get everyone up to speed as quicky as possible. General Rosen-thal, go ahead."*

Arken turned to the map. "According to intelligence from Lord Stormrid-er, there's a large force of Andahari soldiers, wraiths, and shadowhounds marching underneath the Diamondfang. We don't know exactly when they're going to break through." Arken pointed to three spots on the map. "Our three forts are at full fighting strength; that's two thousand Raiders in SheerRock and Windfall, and three and a half thousand in Icecliff."

"The numbers you spoke of at the Council are now several weeks old, Lord Stormrider," General Willem spoke. "Have you more recent scouting reports?"

"We do not," Arya said.

"I assume holding the invaders at the chokepoint of the underground road exit isn't feasible for some reason?" he asked.

"There are other, smaller, exits from the Diamondfang, some closer to Icecliff and Windfall forts," Arya said. "And the Nightstalker knows them well. We can expect the invading army to attack from multiple places at once, and they may even avoid the underground road exit altogether as that is the one place *we* know about."

"*We must hold the invading army at the forts,*" Rorin spoke the obvious. "*And either wipe them out entirely or do enough damage that we force them into a retreat back to Andahar.*"

Ideally the former, if Arya had her way. Destroy the entire force and that was a critical wound to the Nightstalker's strength of arms. It was also impossible with the numbers they had.

"We need to be realistic. Holding them at the forts is unlikely to happen with only seven thousand Raiders to face an army of fifty thousand," Warlord SparrowWing said bluntly. "What is the plan if they break through?"

Arken and Rorin shared a glance, and the warlord gestured for his general to respond. Arken looked at Arya, but she shifted her gaze away. She knew both he and Rorin had been waiting for Arya to come up with a clever tactical approach that would win them the fight, but she had no answer for them. Despair weighed on her.

Arken said, "I am recalling every spare Raider shield I have to start digging lines of defence here, here, and here." He pointed to spots along the edge of the Wraith Forest, where trees turned into farmland and plains. "If the forts break, we'll retreat with whatever Raiders remain to these positions, and then we'll bunker down and hold as long as we can."

A grim silence fell over the table. The area they would need to cover was too broad to put up a meaningful defence. The mobility of the Raider force would help with being able to quickly respond when sections of the line threatened to buckle, but her estimation was that it would happen too often for them to hold it long.

"Things do not look good," Andrian spoke what everyone was thinking.

"*Arya has faced worse odds before, and come out victorious,*" Rorin reminded him.

Arya winced, wishing he would stop saying things like that. His faith only made her feel worse.

Andrian nodded, sat up straighter. "If it comes to the worst, I'll bring every Lance shield we have here to support you. Father and his Defenders will take Crowtalon, but it will be a hollow victory for him."

Helden nodded slowly. "All right. Where do you want my Firemen?"

"With your agreement, I'd like them protecting our supply lines into the forts," Arken responded. "Maintaining a continued run of weapons, food, and water will be critical."

Helden and his general shared a glance. Willem nodded.

"We can do that," the warlord said. "But keep in mind that while my Firemen are all trained in weapons, our combat training is not as extensive as your armies. We prioritise training time for firefighting."

"And you can expect the invaders to come at your supply lines," Willem rumbled.

"*What we need are the Falconcrest Aggressors and Eaglesoar Knights,*" Rorin muttered.

"A moot point," Helden grumbled. "Since Falconcrest and Eaglesoar are probably too busy trying to decide who gets what when Mathas takes our States from us."

"Some Hawkesdale Longbows would be nice too." Amius grinned, then subsided at a glare from his father.

A knock came at the door. Taze called for them to enter, and a Raider appeared, saluting sharply. "What is it, Captain?" Taze asked.

"My shield just rode from Icecliff with urgent news from Commander Sapontis," she replied. "The last patrol to leave the fort was attacked two days ago. Only two made it back alive."

"Attacked by?" Arya asked sharply.

"A pack of shadowhounds."

A grim silence settled over the room.

"So it begins," SparrowWing said.

Rorin nodded slowly. "*I ride for Icecliff tomorrow.*"

Helden stood. "I will send Amius with you as my representative. General Rosenthal, if you will show us your proposed supply line routes, General Willem and I will start planning for their defence immediately."

"*I will be glad to have Amius. Feel free to use Heathrock as your base of operations in my absence. Peemla will see you well looked after.*" Rorin paused. "*I cannot tell you how glad I am for your help, Warlord SparrowWing.*"

Helden nodded slightly. "You reap what you sow, young Ravenstrike. Now, good luck to you."

"*And you.*"

"Laskin, Chiarn, and I will ride to Icecliff with you, Rorin." Arya said. The Flamewielder had been silent for the entire meeting. His face was tight, shadows lingering under his eyes. "You will have House Stormrider help, such as it is."

Andrian stood too. "I must return to the border to oversee the Lances. I'm sure my father will make his move soon, especially when he hears of SparrowWing coming north to aid you. I'll do my best to keep your borders secure while you are gone."

"*Thank you, Andrian.*"

Chairs scraped and a low hum of conversation erupted as everyone ambled out to see to their various responsibilities. Arya made her way to where Arken was gathering maps to plot his supply lines. He straightened at her approach. "If you wish to take command of the Raiders for the duration of the fight, then I would not stand in your way."

"You would really do that?" she asked curiously. "Step aside and hand me the Raider army."

His face tightened, but his words were sincere when he spoke. "I railed against you for many years. I was bitter and jealous when you first came here. But that changed. The reason I stand here today, the *only* reason that I am a good leader and general, is you. You trained me, you respected me, and you chose me as your successor, despite how I behaved towards you." He paused. "The Raiders were always yours, Arya, and I count myself as one of those Raiders."

Arya stared at him, unable to respond for a long moment. She'd never, *ever*, expected words like this from Arken Rosenthal. But she found some to gift him with in return. "I have no intention of taking the Raiders from you, General. I have always respected you, in no small part due to your willingness to follow my orders even when you disliked me so much. If I had any doubts at all, then your performance this morning would have removed them. I am glad my brother has you to rely upon."

Arken offered his hand. "Then we are friends, Lord Stormrider?"

She shook it firmly. "Friends, General Rosenthal."

His stance relaxed. "In that case, will you sit in with me while I discuss supply lines with Warlord SparrowWing and his general? I would very much appreciate your advice."

She grinned. "I'd love nothing more. It's been too long since I've had a good strategic discussion."

"As long as you promise not to pull out those blasted coloured stones Desomer used to use on us."

Arya laughed. And it loosened something inside her.

If a man who'd once been bitter and jealous, overconfident and disrespectful, could stand before her a strong and capable general and tell her it was because of her leadership? Then perhaps she wasn't a total failure.

But how could she find the parts of herself she needed to help Dunidaen corral the Nightstalker and deal a blow to the strength of his army? A blow strong enough to give her a fighting chance at defeating him on his own ground. Always, always, Kirin was at the back of her thoughts. The Nightstalker would never give up hunting him, would be devoting extensive resources to it. Even now he might be close to finding him.

Arya didn't have the luxury of time. Yet, she now feared every decision she made might be a mistake that would end up exposing him, or putting someone she loved in danger.

And that doubt was killing any chance they had of winning.

But how to defeat it?

Chapter 27

Arya strained her hearing, but couldn't make out any sound beyond the thick fog shrouding her shield. Despite being unable to see beyond a horse length in any direction, each of them scanned their surroundings constantly, gloved hands hovering near weapons. A light snow fell from above, dotting their cowls.

They were the first patrol to leave Icecliff since the last one had been attacked.

Rorin and Arya had arrived at a fort brimming with tension. Not only had a patrol been attacked, but it meant they'd had to stop sending them out, limiting their ability to scout. At least Commander Sapontis was still getting messages from SheerRock and Windfall, indicating all was well there for now.

Driven by the inability to keep *waiting*—it gave her too much time to stew in worry and fear for Darmanin or Kirin or even Leanir—Arya had volunteered to venture up the highway toward the pass to confirm whether the invading army *had* emerged from the tunnels under the Diamondfang, and if so, get a sense of how strong the force was.

Thick fog had closed over them as they'd climbed into the mountains, bringing with it a sharp drop in temperature. The falling snow served to further hamper visibility. *And* her sense of direction. Yet, despite the danger, the tension of a patrol was so familiar that Arya felt more relaxed than she had in years. She turned to Laskin, riding at her side. "How far do you think we are from the pass?"

Laskin kept his voice as low as hers. "A good distance still, but we're in danger of being turned around in this fog. Can you sense any danger ahead?"

"*Elendryl?*"

A ripple of frustration echoed through her bond with the wyvern. He couldn't see any better through the thick fog than she could. The low-lying cloud hugged a wide area. And he hated that he couldn't see her either.

"*No bad smells?*"

Another frustrated shiver. He could scent wraiths, but wasn't confident he would in this weather.

"Elendryl can't see any danger," Arya said. "But that doesn't mean there's nothing there. In this fog, we wouldn't see if the entire invading army was encamped on the other side of those trees."

"Maybe we should move onto the road," Laskin suggested. "It would be a smoother path and guarantee we wouldn't get lost."

They were—hopefully—riding through the thick forest at the top of the embankment on the northern side of the road leading up to the pass. Her intent was to stick close enough to the road to spot an army marching along it without showing themselves.

"No," she disagreed. "If the army has emerged from the tunnels, we'd ride right into the middle of them."

"At least then we'd be able to confirm they're out there," Laskin said sourly.

The eerie silence persisted. Arya rode with one gloved hand on her sword, body tensed and ready for action. Her magic lay ready. Elendryl soared somewhere overhead, his presence a glimmer of golden light inside her. Chiarn and Asandryl remained back at Icecliff, in the event it was attacked in Arya's absence.

"I don't know what you expect me to do if we come under attack," Chiarn had grumbled. "I don't even know how to hold a sword, let alone use it."

"You have something better than a sword," she'd pointed out. "You have fire. Plus, your wyvern has big teeth, remember?"

He hadn't responded, and she hadn't missed the trembling in his hands. "My advice, Chiarn? Ask one of the Lances to show you how to use a shield in a fight. It will allow you to deflect a blow while your free hand deploys flame. It might make you feel more protected."

Her thoughts came back to the present as her horse tossed its head, unnerved by something. The ghostly outline of trees passed by to their left and right.

"*Strange.*" Elendryl slid into her mind. With it came a sense of silence.

She abruptly realised he was right.

The forest was never this quiet.

Arya made a hand motion that indicated her shield should be ready. The gesture was repeated down the line, and all drew their swords.

It saved them.

The attack was sudden and fast. Wraiths swarmed them from above, and grey shadows leaped from within the fog, nightmarish figures with deadly fangs and claws. Shouts echoed as the Raiders reacted.

"Stay together!" Arya bellowed, bringing her mare around. "Stay together."

Her words were barely audible amidst the cacophony of snarling and hissing. Arya lifted her free hand, summoned her magic, and flung a bolt of pure blue energy at the thickest pack of wraiths. It caught and exploded through them like fire, and they erupted in a cacophony of ear-splitting shrieks as they died. Her attack bought Etan time to use his flint to ignite the Khadini oil-soaked brand under his saddle, and in quick succession he lit the brands of those closest to him. Wraiths caught aflame in screaming agony, but the fire had less of an effect on the shadowhounds.

And there were so many.

Arya couldn't even attempt to count the mass of hissing and snarling creatures. The thrust of the attack had come from their right, and Arya and her shield found themselves being pushed left.

Towards the steep embankment down to the road.

"They're trying to send us over the edge!" she screamed. "Turn and let the horses find their feet, or else they'll fall. GO!"

The Raiders did their best to follow her order, but it was difficult to do anything under the relentless assault of teeth and claws. Arya kicked her feet out of the stirrups and leaped upwards. She gripped the bough of a tree above her and swung herself forward before letting go and falling through a group of wraiths assaulting Charlin and Allicen. Her dagger stabbed two creatures through the eyes as she fell, and they followed as she dropped to the ground.

There, Arya found herself confronted by several wraiths. She raised her cazaix blade and swept it around her, sending magic sparking along its tip. The wraiths screeched and burned. Arya hauled herself back into the saddle, and spotted Wattin and Laskin pinned down. They were trying to fight while their horses bucked and danced around the attacking shadowhounds.

Wraiths draped them, trying to get at bare flesh. She urged her horse in their direction and killed two shadowhounds from behind, then propped as the others turned to face her. They were huge animals, almost reaching her saddle in height, and they had long, curved fangs. Her horse danced nervously. "Come on then," she taunted, swinging her blade.

They growled and charged her together. She dodged to the right, slashing her sword along the side of one as it leaped past. The shadowhound fell to the ground, whimpering, but the second landed and came at her again, too fast. A sharp claw raked down her right arm as she decapitated the leaping creature. Swearing in pain, she swung around and ducked another assault, gutting this one in a long gash across its stomach.

Sweat covered Arya's forehead, and her breath was coming faster. She had to move quickly to face the remaining two shadowhounds, but by the time she'd dealt with them, Wattin and Laskin were free.

"Go!" she shouted, seeing they were the only ones left.

The three of them made straight for the embankment. They burst out of the fog and trees simultaneously, and her mare's next stride took them out into thin air. The horse came down heavily on the steep embankment, finding her feet and scrambling down. Below them the road was clear. Above and behind, the fog still lingered.

"Arya!" Kait called out, pointing upwards.

She looked, gaze going along the wide highway that wound up above the fog layer in a zig-zag pattern towards the far distant pass. Pouring along it, maybe a half mile away, was a host of mounted riders and wraiths. To their left, shadowhounds streamed down the embankment after them.

"Raven's balls!" Arya muttered, then searched out Laskin's gaze and shouted. "I think we've got the information we need. Get gone. I'll give you some breathing room."

"Retreat!" Laskin roared. "RETREAT!"

As one, the shield wheeled their mounts into a gallop along the road toward Icecliff. Arya dismounted, sent her horse racing after them, then drew in a deep breath and summoned her magic. Standing tall and straight, flinging her hands wide apart, she sent an enormous burst of pure energy at the shadowhounds coming at her down the embankment.

It tore them to shreds.

Breath heaving, sweat slicking her skin, Arya remained standing in the middle of the road. The wraiths clustered in the trees above, hissing in thwarted anger, but unwilling to come out in the open.

She could call down Elendryl and escape at any moment, but worried for her shield. If the pursuing host caught up with them, they'd be overwhelmed. Her gaze studied the oncoming army as it briefly vanished from sight around a bend in the road and then reappeared, ever closer. One rider drew ahead of the pack, and a chill ran down Arya's side; even from this distance she recognised a nazal. It howled, and the sound carried all the way to her.

It knew who she was, and it hungered for her blood.

Arya hesitated; with every bone in her body, she wanted to confront and kill the nazal. The one with mind powers had been in Gateport, meaning this one leading the invading army was one of the other four, and it couldn't attack her that way. Hatred for it burned through her, and she almost ... but what if it overwhelmed her, captured her? And if she faced it and lost, it would take her straight to the Nightstalker, who would use his magic to learn of Kirin, where he was.

Snarling in frustrated anger, Arya turned away.

"Another day," she promised herself, then reached for her wyvern. *"Elendryl!"*

He was already there, dropping out of the sky. Arya scrambled onto his back in seconds. As soon as she was settled, Elendryl spread his magnificent golden wings, and they leaped into the air.

"Quickly," she urged.

He flew low over the galloping Raiders and then on ahead, making directly for Icecliff. As they flew, she reached for the threads binding her to her *cairdre* and sent a burst of magic through Chiarn's thread in a clear summons.

By the time she and Elendryl swept in over the battlements and landed in the entry courtyard, Chiarn was waiting, Rorin and Taze with him. "What is it?" Chiarn called up.

"Laskin and his shield are heading this way, they're being pursued. I need you to help me give them cover."

He froze. Fear flashed bright in his eyes.

"It's time, Chiarn. I will protect you."

Jaw tight, his eyes flicked closed as he communicated with Asandryl. Nearby, a wyvern's cry echoed through the icy air. Unlike his rider, Asandryl sounded thrilled at the idea of a fight. As they waited, Arya spoke to Rorin and Taze. "Put archers on the walls," she told them. "And sound the alarm. The army is approaching along the highway. Get lit brands ready, and the barrels of Khadini oil."

"How many?" Taze asked.

"Several battalions of Nightblades, plus a couple hundred shadowhounds, is my guess, but there will be more behind them," she said grimly. "Hurry, Taze."

Taze sprinted away, shouting orders to the Raiders on the walls. Seconds later, bells began tolling throughout the fort. Asandryl arrived with a rush of air from his copper wings. Once Chiarn was mounted, the two wyverns climbed into the sky, winging swiftly along the highway.

It wasn't long before they flew over the fleeing shield of Raiders. Their horses were slowing, beginning to flag. Behind them came the mounted soldiers and the running shadowhounds, closing the distance quickly. Without hesitation, Elendryl dropped down to the road between the Raiders and their pursuers. The wyvern reared spectacularly, his challenging cry thundering through the mountains. Asandryl's echoing scream vibrated through every muscle in Arya's body.

The nazal shrieked in response, a hair-raising sound. Chiarn paled. Arya nodded at him reassuringly and called out. "That's a nazal in the lead. I assume you're in agreement that we don't let it get close to us?"

He swallowed, jaw tense as he stared at the oncoming hoard. "Seems sensible."

"Perhaps a roadblock might be in order? Something to hold them up long enough for Laskin to get into the fort and Taze and Rorin to prepare the defences?"

"A roadblock?" His voice was distant, scared.

"Raven's balls, Chiarn, I'm not the one who wields fire," she snapped.

Her tone seemed to break his daze, and he finally looked at her, comprehension flooding his face. "Oh," he said, then brightened. "Oh!"

"Hurry up about it. Use my strength if you need it. I've still got a bit left." She sent a shiver through the thread between them, making sure he could reach into her reserves of magic.

The Flamewielder's eyes slid shut, his palms coming to rest together against his chest. His shoulders rose as he took a deep breath.

And then, with a great shout, Chiarn swept his arms out wide. A mighty wall of flame roared into existence, stretching across the road, and rising to a majestic height. Sweat beaded his forehead, but he sat straight on Asandryl's back, bolstered by both Arya and his wyvern.

Arya stared at the wall of flame. Her connection with Chiarn was clumsy, new, but her Sky Lord was powerful. What could they be capable of one day?

"Well done, Lord Flamewielder," she said. "Now might be a good time to leave."

Chapter 28

Arya awoke to Icecliff's alarm bell pealing.

She sat up and rubbed gritty eyes. A glance at the window showed it was still dark outside. It had been just before midnight when she'd gone to sleep.

Another day in an endless series of them. Sleep, fight, eat. Repeat.

Fighting grogginess, she belted on her sword, then strapped a dagger to each of her calves, the newly-healed scar on her arm tugging as she reached. On her way out, she slung a quiver of arrows over her shoulder and picked up her bow where it rested against the wall.

In the hall outside, Raiders ran past, responding to the alarm. Arya followed them out into the main courtyard. Taze was there with Commander Sapontis, who was directing Raiders to the walls. He looked as tired as she felt, and drying blood trickled from a cut over his eye.

"Another attack incoming?" Arya asked.

Sapontis nodded, sparing a quick smile of welcome for Arya. "They're massing on the north and south walls along both halves of the fort."

Arya turned, warned of Chiarn's approach by the bond between them. It had grown deeper and stronger after long days of fighting together. His tunic and breeches were scuffed and torn and splattered with dried blood and ichor stains. His half-grown beard was scruffy and purple shadows ringed his eyes. The right side of his neck was reddened from healing wraith scratches.

Newly grown respect flickered in Arya. Her musician Sky Lord had so far held to his word to fight with her, and his fire magic had proved crucial to their defence. She doubted they would have held out so long without him.

"Arya, Taze." He smiled a tired greeting, his battered shield hanging loosely from his left hand. "I suppose breakfast is out again?"

Taze managed a smile, and Arya didn't fail to notice the respect in his eyes too. "Morning, Chiarn."

"I'll take the north wall. Chiarn will take the south." Arya squeezed Taze's shoulder, sought and held his gaze. "We'll keep going as long as we have to."

The endless attacks wore down on them all. They rarely had more than a few hours' sleep at a time. Arya felt like she'd been fighting for years and could barely remember what it was like to not feel bone-deep weariness.

They'd held the Nightblade army at the forts for almost two months. Far beyond what anyone could have hoped or expected. But it was a losing battle. They all knew it.

And yet Arya's spirit was lighter than it had been in years. The simplicity of battle, moving from breath to breath with instinct born from days and years of practice. There was no time for worrying or overthinking, there was only the moment in front of her and the simple goal of pushing back each attack on the wall. Not to mention the heart and grit with which her brother's Raiders fought, even wounded.

How could she be anything but proud to stand with them?

At her words, a smile curled Taze's mouth. "Right you are."

"Good," she said. "Now, Chiarn, ten silver pieces says we fight them off by dawn."

He managed a smile too. "Twenty pieces."

"I never knew minstrels could afford to bet so high." Taze shook his head. "Let's get to it."

Arya ran up the stone steps to the battlements along the north wall of the fort, ignoring the weariness in her body. Equally weary Raiders lined the wall, their expressions grimly determined in the flickering light of the torches. "I've got twenty silver pieces that says we'll see them off by dawn," she called out briskly. "Win me the bet, and you'll each get a mug of warm mead with your breakfast."

A ragged cheer went up, and Raiders started challenging each other over which section of the wall would see the invaders off first. Arya stopped halfway along the battlement, staring outward.

It was dark beyond the walls, still in the deep early hours of the morning. Torches were lit among the army below—a typical precursor of a night attack. As usual, she looked instinctively for Laskin's steady presence at her side, felt the sharp slide of disappointment at realising he wasn't there. She'd sent him and her shield to Heathrock castle when the battle had started in earnest. Peemla was running Ravenstrike State in Rorin's absence, and given Taze had stayed with Rorin, Arya had wanted soldiers she trusted implicitly at Peemla and Anjurin's side.

Rorin appeared, fingers flickering. *"How's it going, sister dearest?"*

"I'm hungry, exhausted, and in dire need of a hot bath," she said. "And you?"

"About the same." He grinned. Unlike most others at the fort, his good-humoured energy seemed limitless, and Arya hadn't failed to note how it gave his solders heart. *"You good here? I want to join those on the bridge, I'm worried it's a weak spot if they direct the bulk of their attack there."*

"Go for it," she said, then raised her voice. "My Raiders here are battling for some mead with our breakfast!"

The soldiers on her section of the wall banged their sword hilts against the stone in response. Rorin grinned and waved at them as he ran off.

"Ready, Elendryl?"

Eagerness came in response. The two wyverns flew in every battle, swooping over the Nightblades whenever they broke into open ground, scales impervious to their arrows, tearing them apart with teeth and tail and talons, and doing real damage to the wraiths. So far, the nazal general had reserved its shadowhound host to use against the Firemen defending their supply lines. Messages from Warlord SparrowWing to Amius indicated they were taking heavy losses, and Arken had had to deploy Raiders from Heathrock to bolster them.

The attack came minutes later. Wraiths swarmed out of the sky first. Then, hundreds of Nightblades rushed the walls, placing ladders against the stone and starting to climb while the defenders were engaged with the wraiths.

Arya's world narrowed to the section of wall around her. She ducked, cut and parried, all the while keeping an eye on the integrity of the overall defence. Whenever a ladder was placed against the battlement, she used magic to disperse the wraiths, then joined a group of Raiders in fighting back the Nightblades trying to climb up.

She'd learned early on to use her magic sparingly, that it was often of most use at the end of a battle when the Raiders were exhausted, and their numbers reduced by death and injury. Even so, her constant use of it meant bursts that had once drained her strength now required less energy, just like a muscle being built with weight training. The same was true of Chiarn.

It wasn't enough, though. Arya was still dogged by weariness and flashes of vertigo when she pushed too hard. And she rarely had a chance to rest. Without her and Chiarn the fort would have fallen in the first weeks. She worried about a complete relapse if she kept pushing her body without respite.

A wraith hissed in her ear, jolting her back to reality, and she ducked and swung just in time. Another two wraiths dropped on her, and she managed to sweep her blade through their glowing red eyes. Exhaustion weighed heavily, and it was an effort to simply raise her sword. It felt like the thing had doubled its weight.

With a cracking sound, another ladder slammed against the top of the wall. Arya forced her tired legs to run over, calling for the nearby Raiders to join her. She stabbed her dagger into the eye of the first Nightblade to appear at the top of the ladder, then fell back as two more leaped over behind him. Raiders stepped forward to engage them and the fighting wavered on a knife's edge. Eventually, they beat the Nightblades back, and Arya helped them pull the ladder up over the wall.

Arya sheathed her dagger and leaned on her sword, gasping for air and feeling her muscles tremble with fatigue. Her vision swum alarmingly, warning her to rest before the vertigo returned with a vengeance.

"Arya!"

She looked up as Elendryl swooped towards them. Raiders scrambled out of his way as his taloned feet landed on stone, dwarfing them all with his wings spread. "*What is it?*" she asked.

He showed her an image of the south wall. Nightblades swarmed it, and while Chiarn fought bitterly, the defenders were close to being overwhelmed. Arya sagged with fatigue, but took a steadying breath and climbed the battlement to haul herself onto Elendryl's back. Before he took flight, she called out to the Raiders. "Remember, mead with breakfast. You've got this!"

"Aye!"

The ragged response was tinged with weariness, but determined. Elendryl launched into the sky. Asandryl was a copper glow against the pre-dawn as he fought above Chiarn on a section of the wall swarming with Nightblades, swooping down and tearing a soldier apart with each attack. But only a small band of Raiders remained to hold them back.

Elendryl landed amid the fight, snapping his head out to close his jaws around a Nightblade and tear him in two. Arya's Sky Lord looked haggard with exhaustion, but still fighting grimly. "Together?" she called to him.

He took a deep breath. "I've got one good burst left in me."

"Get inside our circle," Arya shouted to the Raiders.

They hurried to do her bidding.

Chiarn and Arya gathered themselves, then let go and spread both arms wide, releasing the sheer energy of their magic. It exploded in a circle outwards, killing every Nightblade atop the wall. Raiders hurried to grab the ladders and pull them up over the wall.

"I think it's over," Chiarn rasped, swaying on his feet.

Arya looked up and saw the blue light of dawn glimmering on the horizon. Below them, the walls were clear of ladders and Nightblades. The army had retreated into the forest. A ragged cheer went up along the walls as the Raiders realised they'd survived another attack.

She let out a breath. One day at a time.

***

Chiarn and Arya headed straight for the kitchens. Another thing they'd both learned was that food, and lots of it, was the best way to recover when they'd drained their magic. It was just the two of them as they scrounged a bowl of stew each. Arya let the captain in charge know that those on the wall that morning should have an allocation of mead with their breakfast.

They sat in silence and devoured the food ravenously. Having seen this many times now, one of the cooks appeared with a second large bowl for each of them, placing them down with a smile and taking away the empty bowls. Chiarn was halfway through his second bowl when he stopped, his gaze rising to meet Arya's. "How much longer do you think we'll last?"

"I don't know," she said honestly.

He put down his spoon and leaned back in his chair tiredly. "I want to sleep for a month."

"Chiarn..." Arya hesitated. "How hard you've been fighting? It's impressive."

"Surprising for a coward, right?"

"I didn't mean that."

He waved a hand. "You agreed to give me my life back after all this is done. It's not your fault that I was hunted by the nazal or that I was born to be a Sky Lord. I've blamed you—and everything else I could think of—for too long, and it wasn't right."

"I know how that feels."

"If I want my own life after this, then I need to earn it. I need to fight for it, just like you are," he said. "No matter how terrified I still am."

"That's what I call courage," she said quietly.

He toyed with his spoon. "There's more to it than that. I saw what you did for Darmanin; you almost killed yourself to save him. I would like to be worthy of that regard one day."

She wasn't sure how to respond to that.

He smiled and spooned up another mouthful. "I hope they bring us a third bowl. I know it's watery and we're running out of the tastier vegetables after the Nightblades destroyed two of our supply lines last week, but I'm starved."

Arya chuckled and returned to her own stew. Her thoughts lingered on his question, though. How much longer *could* they last? The answer wasn't long in coming. Without help, and with the steady attrition of soldiers while the Nightblades came at them in endless waves? Grit, determination, and training had gotten them this far. But it wouldn't be enough to win.

She thought they'd be lucky to hold another two weeks.

Chapter 29

One late afternoon two days later, having barely fought off another dawn attack, Arya headed back to the walls after a few hours of sleep. For the first time in weeks, the sky was clear of heavy snow clouds. She hoped that the break in the weather held. It would improve the spirits of the Raiders. *And* make things harder for the wraiths.

Shouts rang out from the north-eastern corner of the fort as she was halfway up the stairs to the battlements. Arya ran towards the Raiders calling the alarm, squinting where they pointed. Something approached from the sky to the west. A few seconds later, the afternoon sun glinted off the flying figure, and emerald sparks glittered in the air.

Alletryl.

Instinctively she reached for Essa across the bond, and received a burst of reassurance and happiness along the thread. And then ... Darmanin. His thread pulsed with life and proximity. The breath whooshed out of her, and she sagged against the stone. Relief cascaded so powerfully she couldn't even think.

"Shall we call for reinforcements, Lord Stormrider?" the Raider captain asked in concern.

"No, stand down." A smile stretched across Arya's face. "That's Lord Inkweaver with Warlord Crowtalon."

She spun and took the steps three at a time, at the same time bellowing for all she was worth. "RORIN! TAZE!"

The two men burst from the keep as she reached the bottom, Chiarn emerging from another exit a moment later. Her Sky Lord had clearly felt her excited agitation through their bond.

"*What is it?*" Rorin asked, signing frantically. "*Another attack already?*"

"Essa and Alletryl are flying in. Darmanin is with them. He's okay!"

Joy filled Rorin's face and they stood in the yard, waiting, squinting up at the sky. Alletryl let out a cry of welcome as she circled above, graceful and stunning. The wyvern came down in the fort's mounting yard with a gust of air, head lifted proudly, as if she knew the eyes of all the soldiers on the walls had turned to her. Arya's heart gave a thump. Her gaze went straight to Darmanin as he dismounted after Essa. The wyvern gave an annoyed shake, sending him stumbling the last distance. Arya tried not to laugh.

"*Essa!*" Rorin wisely remained a safe distance from the wyvern, signing so fast it was barely decipherable. "*Dar!*"

Darmanin's grey eyes caught Arya's, and he held her gaze until he came to a stop before them. A healed scar ran from his left eyebrow across to his ear, and he was thinner than he'd been, but looked otherwise well. "Arya, Rorin, Taze," he greeted them, then gave Chiarn a nod of acknowledgment too.

Taze grinned at Darmanin and Essa. "You have no idea how good it is to see you two."

Rorin beamed. "*I want to hug you both, but I'm afraid Alletryl might eat me if I make any sudden moves.*"

Arya turned to Essa. She wore a deep violet cape with black edging. A line of stylised writing bisected by the Stormrider lightning was etched in silver on the back, and she wore a matching violet tunic. With her dark hair and emerald eyes, she looked stunning. "Salyarin gave you a gift too, I see. It suits you."

"Thanks Arya." Essa smiled.

"Your situation is grave," Darmanin said. "The Nightstalker's army has encircled you. The number of soldiers and creatures vastly overwhelms your forces. I'm surprised you've held out this long."

Rorin let out a sigh. "*Without Arya and Chiarn, and Sparrow Wing's Firemen managing to keep some of our supply lines open, Icecliff would have fallen weeks ago.*"

"What about SheerRock and Windfall?" Essa asked.

"The nazal's army has focused the intensity of its effort here," Arya answered. "But the other two forts weather attacks too. Elendryl and Asandryl fly regular patrols over them—there have been some occasions when the situation was dire enough that Chiarn or I have had to fly there to help them hold the walls."

"Warlord!"

Commander Sapontis strode over, a message clutched in her gloved hand.

"*What is it, Commander?*" Rorin frowned.

"Lord Andrian sent a message marked urgent," he said. "The High Warlord is marching from Gateport, heading for the SparrowWing-Crowtalon border near Seelan with ten battalions of Eaglesoar Knights and a similar number of Defenders. Falconcrest has deployed battalions of Aggressors from Falconcrest, and they're moving in the same direction. Lord Andrian plans to negotiate with his father to hold them at bay when he arrives, but doesn't know how long he can stall. He doesn't think it will be long."

A grim silence fell at this news. Arya rubbed at her forehead. One thing after another. Would it never end?

Rorin broke the silence, Taze translating for him. "*We'll need to send a message to Heathrock; Helden SparrowWing should know what's happening.*"

"If you do that, he'll have to take his Firemen back to SparrowWing to defend his borders. Then we lose the protection on our supply lines," Arya said.

"*Then we need to figure out a solution to win here quickly.*" Rorin signed. "*Commander, please gather the fort commander and captains.*"

***

They talked for the entire day, the Raiders getting a chance to rest as the fair weather held, but nobody had any new ideas on how to continue holding the walls against greater numbers, let alone defeating the force entirely in time to march back into Dunidaen and defend Ravenstrike against Mathas Crowtalon.

Darmanin and Essa had brought at least one piece of good news with them.

"The Nightstalker has stopped marching fresh troops into Dunidaen. Etherean scouts have been keeping watch." Darmanin said. "He and his nazal general must be confident they can take us with the numbers he already has here."

Arya shifted in her chair. They were right to be confident.

"*The wyvern scouting flights estimate roughly ten thousand soldiers, wraiths, and shadowhounds remaining,*" Rorin echoed her thoughts. "*That's still a far superior force.*"

Taze agreed, "Not to mention the nazal has dark magic it hasn't used against us yet."

"Why?" Essa asked, gaze narrowed.

"A good question. Something is off." Arya couldn't shake her unease. "The nazal will take losses on that ten thousand in defeating the forts, and then it has to move into Ravenstrike and hold territory."

"If there were a unified Dunidae army waiting to greet them, we'd win," Taze said grimly.

Heavy silence fell. That wasn't going to happen.

Arya didn't miss the multiple discreet looks directed her way, everyone waiting for her to save them with a piece of genius tactical strategy that would turn their weaknesses into strengths and allow them to defeat a numerically superior force. She'd tried, racking her brains over and over, but it just wasn't there, the spark that had once been the source of her creative victories.

They eventually broke for a rest at dusk, and Arya went looking for Darmanin, eventually finding him up on the battlements. He seemed impervious to the cold breeze, standing draped in the shadows of falling dusk, staring down into the treetops below. He turned instantly at her approach though, and she went straight into his arms, wrapping hers around his waist and holding on tight.

"You shouldn't have done it," he murmured.

She pressed her face into his neck, kissed the warm skin there. "I had to."

"Thank you, Arya." The words were fervent, whisper soft, his arms around her the warmest thing she'd ever felt. This was what she'd wanted ever since learning he'd been hurt.

Neither of them said anything more and for a long time they stood there, sharing warmth and comfort and relief. The nearest Raiders were a good distance away, leaving them alone in a little pocket of darkness and quiet.

Then Arya forced herself to step away, tone turning sharp. "You and Leanir, what were you thinking?"

Darmanin's face tightened. "I've never seen him so determined, Arya. He'd come north to help evacuate Shadeweavers from the Wraith Forest, but he'd been dream-walking the nazal leading the invading force, despite how dangerous it was. He knew it was close. And he was right—if we killed it together, the invasion would lose its leader, and we would be free of one creature hunting us."

"So you decided to ignore my warnings about how we weren't strong enough to face one yet and listen to him instead?" She made a gesture, cutting off his answer. She already knew what it would be. "And Leanir? He abandoned you when you started losing the fight, I take it? You didn't consider that maybe he was luring you into a trap as revenge on me for betraying him to the Nightstalker?"

Darmanin's jaw tightened further. He didn't like being chastened any more than she did, but he had no ready defence. "I'm not exactly sure what happened. My memories are hazy," he admitted. "He's still alive?"

"Alive, but no longer in the area. He's more of a danger to us than a help, now." Arya sighed, glancing out into the darkness beyond the wall. "Why are you out here? Did something catch your attention?"

"No, I just came out here to think."

She flashed him a teasing smile. "It might be more comfortable to think inside, in front of a warm fire."

He didn't respond, and she recognised one of his pensive moods, so she fell silent, knowing he'd speak in his own time. And eventually he did. "I'll have to ride south and take command of the Lances against my father," he said eventually.

Arya had expected as much. "If anyone can hold off Mathas until we can get there, it will be you."

His mouth quirked. "And if anyone can end this invasion so you *can* ride south in time, it will be you."

She shook her head, turning away. There was that misguided confidence in her again.

"Something wrong?" he asked.

"No. Just tired and sore." She changed the subject. "Zaphirdryl must have been unhappy that you rode Alletryl earlier." Arya could only imagine the fit Elendryl would have if she dared ride another wyvern.

Darmanin winced. "She's not talking to me right now. But I couldn't ride her here. Everyone here would have known what I am."

"I understand."

"If word gets out that I'm a Sky Lord and magic-wielder, I won't have a chance in hell of holding off my father."

"I said I understand, Dar."

His grey eyes settled on hers. "You're angry with me."

"No," she said. "I know what you want, and it's not to be a Sky Lord. But you also know what *I* want."

They stared at each other, wills clashing, neither giving in. His intransigence reminded her of that half-formed idea she'd had back in Gateport, an idea that had continued simmering away, that she'd returned to during the quieter moments between attacks on the walls. Shaping it into an almost-plan.

Arya let out a breath. "Dar, there's something I've been working on. A backup plan, in case everything goes badly."

He studied her for a moment. "You mean the fact that unless we figure out how to avoid it, the Nightstalker is going to come for you, *us*, himself, and that's likely going to be before we're strong enough to survive the encounter."

She loved how he could read her thinking, understand it so quickly. "Exactly."

"Lay it on me," he murmured.

"You won't like it," she warned.

He huffed a breath of irritation. "Just spit it out, Arya."

Glancing around to make sure nobody could see them, let alone hear them, Arya stepped in close, lowering her voice, and explaining what she'd come up with.

Darmanin swore, low and fluent, but admiration laced the horror in his voice when she replied. "That's ridiculously risky. But if it was done right, he'll never see it coming. It could *only* be a last resort, Arya. Too much could go wrong for it to be a plan we could rely on."

"I know. Could you do it?"

His gaze held hers. "You know I could."

"Then we'll need to start putting little things in place now, just in case it's needed. Nobody knows anything about it and neither of us speaks of it again. Agreed?"

"Agreed." He ran a hand through his hair, expelled a breath. He didn't like it. But he was willing to go along with it anyway.

Arya took his hand, tangled their fingers together, then pressed their joined hands over her heart. "Before we part now, then, there are some things you should know."

His grey gaze held hers the entire time she spoke, never wavering.

Once she was done, he leaned down to press his forehead against hers, squeezing their joined hands. "I am yours, Arya Stormrider."

"I know," she whispered, tears welling in her eyes. She lifted her free hand to run through his hair. "It might be some time before—"

"I know."

After a long moment, Arya reluctantly stepped away, clearing her throat of all the emotion clogging it up. "I am glad you survived, Darmanin Crow-talon. Now go and hold off Mathas for us."

"And you stop doubting yourself." Darmanin said. "*You* are Arya Storm-rider. Nobody else."

And then he was gone, striding away along the walls, disappearing into the dark.

Chapter 30

Despite a sleepless night, Arya still hadn't come up with a plan. Neither had any of the other commanders at the fort. A dawn attack took up all her attention, once again barely fighting it off.

Bruised and exhausted, Arya sought food in the kitchens as the sun lifted towards midday. Fear was a closed fist around her heart, tightening with every hour that passed. If she didn't figure out a way to defeat this invasion, Dunidaen was done. The Nightstalker would march through only to find a divided country without a unified army to fight him. He probably already knew it, too, which was why he'd stopped sending fresh troops.

What if she couldn't do it?

The kitchens were empty aside from a shield of off-duty Raiders, and she sat apart from them, spooning up food without tasting it. She kept hoping for a flash of insight, some inspiration. That's how it had always happened for her. But her mind was blank, a fog of opaqueness she couldn't push through.

Salyarin's accusations, combined with every decision she made coloured by fear of the Nightstalker finding Kirin, were robbing her of the focus and confidence she desperately needed. They tortured her, because she didn't know how she could have acted differently and still been able to live with herself. Arya knew she would have done the same had it been Essa or Rorin lying close to death. And if that was true, then wasn't it inevitable she'd fail everyone and everything she loved again by making reckless decisions?

She couldn't trust herself to lead Rorin's army against this invasion. Or keep Kirin safe, hamstrung as she was by her need to protect him.

Desomer's barking laugh echoed through her mind, the same one he'd let out every time Arya had been particularly stubborn in a line of thinking that wasn't working. He'd always followed up the laugh with a blistering instruction to get her head out of her ass.

Arya sat up straight, eyes widening.

Maybe she was looking at it all wrong. She wasn't doing any better now than she had before making all those mistakes. In fact, things were worse, and growing even more dire.

"You *are Arya Stormrider.*" Darmanin's parting words echoed through her mind.

Desomer had always been right.

After a moment, she picked up her tray, dropping it in the kitchens before heading outside. As she walked, she reached for Essa and Chiarn.

***

Icecliff's main courtyard was awash with activity as Arya emerged in the middle of shift change. Chiarn and Essa were just arriving too.

"I'm heading up to speak with Salyarin," she told them. "I won't be long, but will you watch over things while I'm gone? You know how to reach me if there's an emergency."

"Do you mind if I come with you?" Essa asked. "I had to leave something behind when I left. It was too heavy to bring down with me given Alletryl was carrying Darmanin too, but I'd like to have it."

"I'll watch over things here," Chiarn assured her. "If there's another attack I'll reach out through the bond."

"We'll be back soon," she promised.

In moments, Elendryl and Alletryl were lifting into the sky together, wings spread, flashing bright gold and emerald in the morning sun.

***

Arya paused at the entrance to Salyarin's chambers, taking a moment to catch her breath from the long walk up. The last thing she wanted was to enter his presence gasping for air. It took longer than she'd liked. Her body had rebuilt a lot of its strength since her injuries, but it still wasn't quite ready for the thin air at this altitude.

The two guards on the door were not doing a great job of hiding their amusement at her breathless state, so she ended up snapping at them to let her through before she was quite ready. When she entered, Salyarin stood alone by the arched window in his reception room. The usually stunning view was limited by thick grey cloud today. "Arya. I'm surprised you've come. My scouts report that the fighting in your forts is bitter." *And losing,* his tone implied.

Arya squared her shoulders. "I would prefer that you address me by my title, Elder, as I do you."

Surprise flitted across his face, but he didn't argue. "Fair enough, Lord Stormrider."

"I've been thinking about what you said to me last time we spoke." Arya joined him at the window. Salyarin's watchful gaze followed her the entire way. "You had a valid point."

"I am glad you understand."

She swallowed. "You said that if I am to be the heir to Andahar's throne, its future queen, I can't just *say* the words."

"That was not my only point. Your actions were—"

Arya raised her hand to forestall him. "I am *Arya* Stormrider, Elder Salyarin. I am not you, or my grandfather, or any other member of the ancient ruling house you insist on comparing me to. If I am to be queen, I will be my *own* queen, nobody else's."

"Think about—"

"I *have* made mistakes, and I am sure that I will continue to do so." Arya swallowed, taking the fear that had tangled itself so fiercely around her heart and ripping it away. And each word she spoke next was in direct defiance of that fear. No longer would she allow herself to be ruled by it. "*I* was born the Stormrider heir. I didn't choose it, but I've accepted it." She held his gaze for a beat, feeling a tiny sliver of that old confidence coming back. "And as Arya Stormrider, I will no longer tolerate being chastised like a wayward child. I will hear and consider your advice, but I will make my own decisions, and I will not be judged or condescended to."

The moment shimmered and held. Arya couldn't quite work out the expression on Salyarin's face. "You say you've accepted it," he said eventually. "But you've only done that because it gives you a way to seek vengeance. If that is your only goal, then you don't deserve the title of Sky Lord or queen."

He was both right and wrong. She'd accepted the title because it was the only way she could see to protect Kirin, to give him a chance at a safe, happy life. But to truly do that, Arya saw, she had to *become* that queen. She had to take the risk that going on the offensive would keep her son safer than permanently hiding would. At that thought, the fear shimmered again, threatening to come back. She wrestled it down.

She would protect Kirin, *and* her family, her *cairdre*, by being her true self. It was the only way this would work. And if it failed, then at least she'd have done everything she could.

"In that we are agreed." Arya paused, steadying herself. "I will do my best to destroy the Nightstalker and take my rightful place on Andahar's throne. Not for vengeance, but because it is the only way to safeguard those I love. And not just them, but all of us—Dunidaen, Khadini, the Icefolk, your Etherean."

Something indefinable relaxed in Salyarin's shoulders. "Those are words I am glad to hear."

"You won't like these next ones quite so much," she warned. "I would and *will* do everything I can to protect those I love. That includes risking my life without hesitation. Maybe Andahar is lost without me, maybe you all are, but I cannot be a queen, I can't save anything, if I cannot be myself." Those words settled inside her, bringing sharp relief from the agony of indecision that had been tormenting her. She wasn't going to be perfect. She was going to make more mistakes, and maybe those mistakes would end badly. But if she was free to be who she was, then she bet on herself in any situation. Kirin would have a mother he could be proud of.

"I hear you." There was a stiffness to the elder's response, but his acceptance sounded genuine.

She couldn't help a chuckle. "You might be pleased to know that Essa and Chiarn have agreed to stand at my side as part of my Sky Lord *cairdre*."

"Chiarn has?" Salyarin's eyebrows shot skyward. "That's quite the development. How did you manage that?"

"A story for another time," Arya said. "As for the others, Darmanin will decide his own future, and I am yet to decide whether Leanir should be incorporated into my *cairdre*. You will have no contact with either of them, dream-walking included."

The elder nodded. "I would only ask that you remember my warnings regarding Darmanin."

"I will not forget."

"Very well, Lord Stormrider." Salyarin smiled now too, and the tension that had been hovering between them broke. "Is this the only reason you came?"

"No," she said. "Developments in Dunidaen mean we have only a short time to break the back of this invasion, or we're all going to be in a lot more trouble. The help of your Etherean warriors is needed."

"You have a plan?"

"Not yet. But give me time."

Salyarin nodded. "I will order Cirilla to place our fighting force at your disposal."

Arya paused, taken aback by the Elder's easy submission to her request.

"Why the surprise, Lord Stormrider?" He seemed to take pleasure in surprising her. "We have sworn to an alliance between us. My warriors will fly with your forces. I ask only that you consider Cirilla's advice. I acknowledge your greater tactical skill, but he knows our warriors and their abilities."

"I would not think of doing otherwise," she assured him. "Will you have Cirilla fly to meet me at Icecliff? If he stays high, he should be safe, and the wyverns will ensure he makes it safely over our walls once he gets close."

"I will, Lord Stormrider. I will also send some of our healers with the warriors—I'm sure you could use them."

"That would be a boon indeed." She bowed her head slightly. "Until we meet again, Elder Salyarin."

***

Essa waited in the entrance cavern when Arya emerged. She glanced curiously at the three bulky silk-wrapped packages her friend held. "Are those what you came here to get?"

"With the help of the Etherean healers, I made something for each of us while I was here with Dar," Essa said, handing one of them to Arya; it was heavier than she'd expected. "It was a training exercise for my magic, of sorts."

Arya unravelled the cloth curiously, gasping in surprise when she saw its contents. Lying on the silk was a beautifully worked piece of silver-white chain mail. The metal gleamed with unearthly magic. Placed neatly atop the armour was a pair of leather gloves with the same metal woven over them to protect the hands and wrists, and a pair of greaves.

"I drew them with my magic, brought them to life, and the Etherean healers then infused the metal with their healing magic," Essa explained. "The armour will protect you from a direct hit, and the magic in it will provide a boost to your body's energy."

Arya slipped off her cloak, then carefully pulled the chain mail over her head. It fitted to her chest and shoulders perfectly, and was surprisingly light. The mail fell halfway to her knees, with a split down the middle for freedom of movement. The gauntlets were light and flexible, no impediment to gripping her sword, as were the greaves when strapped to her wrists and calves.

Essa's green eyes were alight as she regarded Arya. "You look every inch a Sky Lord."

"We're not there yet, Ess. I still have to come up with a way to deal with this invasion," Arya said thoughtfully. Something had shifted inside her. That no longer felt like an impossible task. "You and I are going to go back and closet ourselves away in a room until we can come up with—"

A shadow crossed Arya's mind. She frowned, gaze going straight to what she could see of the mountain peaks through the cavern entrance. When those revealed no immediate danger, she reached out to Elendryl. *"Is something wrong?"*

He sent the image of Asandryl into her head. *"Fear."*

Chiarn.

"Arya, what is it?" Essa demanded. She'd lifted a hand to her chest, as if she could feel the tension too.

"Where is he?" Arya sent as Elendryl flew toward her.

"Heathrock," he sent after a short pause.

Arya focused, and opened her *cairdre* up to each other, connecting the threads between her, Chiarn, and Essa.

Essa sucked in a breath. "Fear from Chiarn, but it's muddled."

"Asandryl is at Heathrock." Fear pounded through Arya—Peemla and Anjurin were there. "Let's get down there as fast as we can."

The two wyverns exploded out of the clouds a moment later, touching down only long enough for their riders to scramble aboard before lifting off again.

And then they flew.

Chapter 31

E lendryl flew swiftly, Alletryl a dark green shadow behind him, urgency wrapping both wyverns and their riders. A member of their *caidre* was distressed.

Arya didn't bother warning anyone of their approach over Heathrock, instead bringing Elendryl straight down into the entry courtyard. The moment they were on the ground she knew something was wrong. The air was stiff with tension, and she couldn't spot a single Raider on the walls. Her newly gauntleted hand instinctively dropped to the hilt of her sword.

"Wait here, but be ready," she told Elendryl.

"I can't see Chiarn or Asandryl, but they feel close," Essa called out. "I keep trying to make sense of what he's feeling, but it's too chaotic."

They were going to have to practice that, Arya thought, but dismissed the thought as soon as it had come. No time for anything but focus now. "Something is off. Stay mounted and be ready to fly."

Arya headed with quick strides towards the castle entry. Footsteps from inside alerted her to someone's approach, and she drew her cazaix blade with a clear ring that echoed through the too-silent yard. Seconds later, Commander Derin's familiar figure appeared through the entry. He held a drawn sword, and every line in his body screamed tension and wariness. Three Raiders trailed him.

"What is going on?" she snapped, coming up the steps. "Why are there no guards on the walls?"

"Who are you?" The words were out of Derrin's mouth before he saw Elendryl. As soon as he did, he looked back at Arya in dawning comprehension. "Arya, is that you?"

"Of course it's me, Derrin," she snapped.

He shook his head. The Raiders behind him seemed equally taken aback, and Arya spoke with an echo of her old command voice, trying to break through their stupor. "Commander, what happened here?"

"There was an attack, not even an hour ago. The boy was taken." He spoke slowly, distantly, as if he couldn't quite believe what had happened.

Her mind first went to Kirin, and the world dropped out from under her, but then she realised where she was. Dread curled around her heart. "*Anji* was taken?"

Something in her expression seemed to give Derrin heart. He straightened his shoulders, his next words sounding more like a capable commander reporting on the situation. "Yes, by one of those nazal monsters you've talked about. Laskin's shield went after them—General Rosenthal has everyone else gathering in the barracks to weapon up and go after them. You'd best go in. Lady Ravenstrike is in the great hall."

"Shit." Arya spun to bellow over her shoulder. "Ess, with me!" Then she turned back to Derrin and the Raiders. "I don't care what's happened, get Raiders up on those walls now."

Essa came running. "What's going on?"

"Anji's been taken by a nazal."

Essa blanched, horror written over her face as she swayed on her feet.

"Steady," Arya murmured, sending reassurance through their bond. "We'll deal with this."

Essa swallowed, nodded. Arya headed inside, anxiety building up inside her like a dammed river. Her boots echoed loudly as she strode across the entry foyer and into the great hall, Essa a stricken shadow at her side.

Arya's gaze went straight to Peemla. Her face was gaunt with grief and fear, making Arya want to tear apart whoever was responsible for that look. Because she felt that same fear shudder through every inch of her. But it wasn't just fear rising in Arya, it was an icy, flooding rage. Stormrider kin was under threat and her magic was responding from sheer instinct. Raiders hovered protectively around their warlord's wife. Arken was there too, huddled with two shield captains.

And so was Chiarn. All of them flinched at the sight of Arya.

"Arya! Essa!" Chiarn was the first to react. "It worked then, you sensed my panic? I was trying so hard to send it through our bond, but I didn't know how and—"

"It worked," she said, deliberately making her voice brisk. The people in this room needed calm, not more shaken panic. "Tell me what happened."

"Just after you left this morning, Asandryl flew a patrol. She saw the nazal heading behind the lines and toward Heathrock. She came back to get me, and we got here just after the attack." His shoulders slumped. "I'm sorry I wasn't fast enough."

Essa went straight to Peemla, wrapping an arm around her shoulders. "Peemla, is it true Anji was taken?"

Peemla took a shuddering breath. "He was playing just outside the walls—you know how he loves climbing the trees. The nazal killed the entire shield protecting him and took my boy. The Raiders on the walls saw it happen, but couldn't get there quickly enough. Laskin roused his shield and went in pursuit."

Arya asked, "It didn't make any attempt to attack the castle walls?"

"It was a targeted attack." Arken's expression was drawn and tight. "The creature went directly for Anji and left."

Something about that didn't sit right with Arya, and she frowned. "Why didn't they kill him?"

Peemla cried out, and Essa drew her closer, flashing a chiding look at Arya.

Arya gentled her voice, allowing the part of her that knew all too well what Peemla was feeling to slip through. "I know this is upsetting, but it's an important question. Why did the nazal kidnap Anji instead of just killing him?"

"Has something changed in the battlefront?" Arken asked. "Could the Nightstalker have reason to think kidnapping the boy and ransoming him back in return for handing over the forts is a good approach?"

Arya frowned in thought. "We've held them off longer than he could have expected."

Realisation cleared Essa's expression. "If the nazal ransoms Anji in return for the forts standing down without further attrition, it will have its full remaining force intact to invade and hold Ravenstrike."

Peemla swallowed, then stepped away from Essa and straightened her shoulders. "What do we do to get my son back?"

"Which way did they go?" Arya asked Arken.

"North, along the main road. The nazal and its raiding party were mounted, but we have to assume they'll diverge off the road into the foothills and then up into the mountains where its army is encamped. I've got a battalion preparing to deploy. We'll follow Laskin's trail and—"

Arya shook her head. "You won't catch up before they reach their army or disappear into the tunnels under the Diamondfang."

It would have to be her.

Arya closed her eyes, fighting back the instinctive dread that tightened her stomach at the thought of facing a nazal. Her hand trembled where it rested on the hilt of her sword.

Tomin's voice whispered through her mind. *"Your injuries are not only physical, Arya."*

No! She *would* master this. Curling her hands into fists, she buried every trace of the aunt afraid for her nephew, of the mother afraid for her son, and instead let that white-hot Stormrider rage take over until it burned away every remaining trace of doubt.

Kill this nazal and Anji would be safe. Kill it and there would be one less creature to hunt Kirin and her *cairdre*. Kill it and she'd be stronger when facing the one that could tear into her mind.

"Elendryl?"

His snarl reverberated through her fury. *"We hunt."*

Peemla saw the change come over her face. "Arya, what are you going to do?"

She bared her teeth. "Bring Anji home safe."

"I'm coming," Essa said instantly.

At her side, Chiarn hesitated, paling. But after a moment he nodded. "Me too."

It was on the tip of her tongue to refuse them, but she reconsidered. They were her *caidre*. Her strength. And Essa had wanted this, had *asked* it of Arya. And Arya had to be absolutely sure she was not overcome and captured by the nazal. So, she settled her gaze on her friend and nodded. "You fight back this time, Lord Inkweaver."

Her mouth tightened, fierceness flashing in those green eyes. "*We* fight back."

Arya turned to Arken. "Keep this place locked down, double guard on the walls, just in case."

He gave a reluctant nod. "If you need anything—"

"I will ask," she promised, then looked to Peemla, hand on her heart. "I'll bring your son back to you. My word on it."

Spinning, Arya ran from the room, straight for Elendryl.

"Chiarn!" Essa shouted as she reached her wyvern, reaching up to grab the two packages she'd brought with her. She tossed one to him and started unwrapping the other. "Put this on before we go."

"I'm not waiting," Arya shouted. "Follow as fast as you can."

Elendryl's wings were already spreading as she swung herself onto his back, and together they launched into the sky.

***

"Find Laskin and his shield. The snow is deep—there will be a trail where they left the road," Arya told Elendryl as they crested the walls of Heathrock castle.

Her stomach dropped as her wyvern plunged towards the road, flying inches above its surface, wingtips brushing the trees on either side. Elendryl spotted it before she did, the broken snow on the verge where multiple horses had veered off into the trees. He went almost vertical, banking sharply and bringing them above the treetops, but still low enough they could make out the trail below. Her blood thrilled at his speed and agility, the way the cold air cut over her skin, her body shifting with Elendryl's movements in perfect instinctive harmony. Her mouth bared in a snarl. *Nothing* felt more right than this.

They were born to hunt together.

The nazal's raiding party had pushed their horses hard, leaving a trail of trampled foliage and broken tree branches. The Raiders on their tail only worsened the destruction.

"I'm not sure we'll be able to defeat a nazal in a stand-up fight, so we'll aim for surprise. If we can get it on the back foot, we grab Anji, get him clear, then attack and kill it before it can gather itself."

"Fast," he echoed fiercely. *"Strong."*

Elendryl crested a rise and Arya spotted Laskin and his shield ahead, galloping recklessly through the forested terrain of a narrow valley. A mile ahead was a group of mounted Nightblades. Even as Arya took all that in, the Nightblades reached a snow-covered plateau at the top of the valley wall. There they dismounted, grabbing bows and arrows.

Laskin's shield was catching up, so they were going to ambush it.

Beads of sweat broke out on Arya's forehead despite the cold, and fear licked at her. Her ribs and wrist ached with the memory of what the Night-stalker had done to her, how physically helpless she'd been. Gritting her teeth, Arya forced the memories from her mind.

"Faster, Elendryl."

Elendryl put on a burst of speed, flying in low over the treetops before dramatically swooping upwards toward the plateau where the raiding party lay in wait. She glanced down as they swept over the Raiders, recognising Charlin's curls, Wattin's beard, Laskin in the lead, grim resolve on his face.

They were riding to their deaths, and they knew it. But they were riding anyway.

"That plateau is sizeable, but not big enough for you to manoeuvre, and while their arrows can't hurt your scales, your wings will be vulnerable on the ground," she sent *"You'll have to let me down and support best you can from above."*

Assent shivered through her mind, edged with his hunger for enemy blood. She and her wyvern were simmering in a blinding rage, and she worked hard to keep enough control over it to maintain focused thought.

The ambush area jutted out into open space and provided a commanding view of the valley below. Elendryl landed as the soldiers were still dispersing to ambush positions, rearing in challenge as his taloned feet crashed into the snow. His head snaked out, snapping at any Nightblade close enough. Arya leaped to the ground, sword already drawn, and Elendryl launched back into the air, his waving tail taking out two soldiers within range.

She dropped into a fighting crouch, magic ready, her gaze going straight to the mounted nazal directly opposite her, to the small child it held in the saddle. The monster was making no attempt to look human—under its voluminous hood she caught snatches of papery white skin and terrifying red eyes. The rest of the Nightblades moved into an encircling position, but made no immediate move to attack.

"Anjurin?" she called out.

The toddler looked up. Tears streaked down cheeks that were flushed red, but he seemed unharmed. She saw Kirin in the boy's blue eyes. For a moment her rage blinded her, and she barely held back from launching herself, screaming, at the nazal. Instead, once she had herself under control, she took a careful step forward. "It's going to be all right, Anji. I'm going to take you home."

She couldn't be with Kirin. Couldn't keep him safe herself.

But she *could* protect her nephew.

"Lying to a child." The nazal's voice hissed out, sibilant and gravelly. "Bad form, Raider."

Anjurin screamed at the ear-splitting sound the nazal's voice made. Arya stilled, watching as the sharp claws on the nazal's left hand inched closer to the boy's throat. She reached for Essa and Chiarn—they were still some distance away, their wyverns smaller and not as fast as Elendryl.

Her awareness of Elendryl flared as he sent her an image of Laskin's shield quietly moving up the valley wall towards the plateau. The nazal was watching her carefully, almost smiling. "It seems we're at a stalemate," she said, stalling. "How about you hand over the boy, and I'll let you go."

The nazal hissed. "Kill her."

"Or not," Arya said, as the Nightblades moved at the monster's command, converging on her, swords drawn. Elendryl swooped out of the sky, jaws closing over one of the soldiers before tearing the man in two. Those nearest him quailed as hot blood sprayed, their attention shifting to the wyvern rather than Arya.

She took advantage of the distraction, lunging at the nearest Nightblade before he knew what was coming, and killing two more before they could defend themselves. By then the rest were closing in from all directions, and she fought with desperate speed, sword flicking and barely managing to hold them off her.

And then Elendryl let loose his wyvern's cry.

Her wyvern was close to full grown, his cry mature, and the nazal threatened his family.

The sound *roared* through the peaks and valleys. Snow cascaded to the ground from shaken trees. All around Arya the soldiers quailed, their instinct to hide, to run, to cower, fear dripping through their bones. Many dropped their swords. Some even loosed their bowels.

And Arya cut through them all.

Then, just as she felt like she was winning, the howling of shadowhounds ripped through the afternoon and a pack came streaming through the trees.

"Raven's balls!" she swore.

A glance at the nazal showed it still sitting its horse, clawed hand on Anjurin's throat. Arya sheathed her sword, focused her mind, and drew on her magic. With an almighty shout she let loose a powerful burst of magic. It tore the remaining soldiers to shreds, so fast they didn't even have time to scream. Blood and gore splattered her. Gasping, weary, she picked up the sword, turned to face the shadowhounds.

And saw the nazal turning its horse to retreat, leaving the shadowhounds to hold her off until it could reach the safety of its army. If the monster made it, he'd have Anjurin somewhere she couldn't reach.

But Elendryl had seen the same thing. He swooped out of the sky with another challenging cry, snapping his teeth at the nazal's horse. The poor creature screamed in terror and reared spectacularly before bolting. The nazal toppled into the snow, taking a terrified Anjurin with him.

Arya lunged towards them, but the shadowhounds streamed into the space between her and the fallen nazal, which was already getting to its feet. "Shit!"

One of the shadowhounds was already leaping for her, teeth bared … only to drop to the snow with a whine as an arrow drove into its throat. More arrows hissed, bringing down the creatures before they could get to her.

Arya glanced over her shoulder. Laskin's shield had arrived.

Her shoulders relaxed. She trusted her old shield with her life. So, ignoring the shadowhounds, she went straight for the nazal. Her boots sank into deep snow as she ran, ignoring the snarls and snapping teeth of the shadowhounds, her entire being focused on getting to Anjurin. Terror that he was hurt struck her, desperation lending her speed.

Gathering more magic, she sent a powerful burst toward the nazal before it could get all the way to its feet, forcing the creature to defend itself with an answering flare of dark energy.

"*Protect the boy!*" she sent to Elendryl, raising her sword and placing herself into the space between Anjurin and the nazal. Elendryl's scream made the ground beneath them shudder. He dropped from the sky, one taloned foot gently picking up Anjurin before he launched back into the air.

"Laskin, get back to your horses!" Arya bellowed as she scrambled to keep herself between the nazal and the edge of the plateau where her shield was. The shadowhounds were all down, either dead or injured. "Elendryl is bringing you Anjurin. GO NOW! Get him safely away."

It was only then that she felt the dark tendrils closing over her mind, seeking entry, willing her to let them in. Deep, instinctive terror flooded her at the same moment as the nazal hissed in fury, pushing back the hood of its cloak.

Nain.

Chapter 32

Nain had joined the nazal leading the Nightblade army. Or replaced it.

Arya staggered back, fighting off the monster's magic in her head, refusing it access to her thoughts. It was easier than it had been that night in Gateport, *far* easier. Tearing the Nightstalker's bond away *had* made them safer.

Yet, standing across from the creature who had murdered Thiara Raven-strike ... Arya's mind flashed back to the moment when she'd run her cazaix blade through Nain's chest without effect. The nazal's magic had felt overwhelming in its potency. If he got into her mind now, he'd see where Kirin was.

No. No more fear and doubt. She had made her choice to save Anjurin, and she would make that choice again. Even so, her heart pounded, her palms slick with sweat inside her gloves.

You have Elendryl and Chiarn and Essa with you this time.

As if summoned by her thoughts, two wyvern cries echoed through the mountains. She didn't dare take her gaze away from Nain, but felt her Sky Lord bonds shiver as Essa and Chiarn arrived on the plateau, the gusts of air washing over her as Asandryl and Alletryl circled above.

Chiarn swore softly as he got his first proper sighting of a nazal, and even Essa's trepidation trembled through their connection. Nain looked like a creature drawn from nightmares. Reddened eyes gleamed with hate, darkness swirling in their depths, bright against pasty white skin. Four needle-thin fangs were visible behind thin, white lips. Even as they watched, deep shadow descended over the clearing, swirling around the monster.

The darkness was alive, full of menace, just like that night in Heathrock city when it had almost found her.

"You ready for this?" she asked her *cairdre*.

"Not even a little bit," Chiarn muttered.

Arya managed a grin. "Stay behind me, let me do the fighting, but keep your fire at the ready, and be wary of it trying to break into your mind. Only jump in if I need it. Essa, you got those knives of yours out?"

"They won't miss," Essa promised.

"Good. We're going to—"

The nazal gave a shriek and *flew* at her. Arya held her ground and swung her sword. The monster's magic wrapped around her and the blade, turning it aside at the last moment. With a sibilant hiss, it sent her flying across the clearing. She hit the ground hard, and the sword fell from her grasp. Pain flared in her recently-healed ribs, and she swore.

The nazal didn't give her time to get back on her feet. It came at her with a series of powerful blows aimed to hammer her back into the ground. Worse, it was able to match her speed easily, and when she tried to send her magic flowing along the cazaix, the monster deflected it with apparent ease.

"*Arya!*" A shiver of warning from Elendryl, seconds before another shriek sounded, louder and closer. She risked a quick look upwards, only to see a dark, winged creature swooping out of the sky. It looked almost like a bat, but too big, larger than Elendryl and with a wingspan almost twice the size of the wyvern.

"*Can you deal with it?*" she asked her wyvern. Already the nazal was attacking again, trying to drive her toward where its creature was swooping. "I'm a little busy here."

"*Dead.*" Elendryl snarled.

A flash of gold, a challenging cry, and Elendryl attacked from above. Alletryl and Asandryl were there seconds later, their screams of anger deafening as they engaged in battle.

Arya was still recovering when Nain adjusted and drove his blade straight at her chest. Arya didn't have enough time to bring her blade around, but tried desperately anyway. Metal rang loudly as blades clashed, Essa sliding in front of Arya to counter the nazal's sword and save Arya's life. The Inkweaver bravely engaged Nain with a pair of flashing knives, giving Arya the moment she needed to recover. She staggered to her feet.

Snarling echoed nearby, and more shadowhounds streamed out onto the plateau. Raven's balls! Had the nazal called them here somehow? Asandryl and Alletryl broke off fighting the bat creature and swooped to engage the shadowhounds, teeth snapping, as if instructed to by Elendryl. Could he do that?

"Elendryl?"

"Fine." He assured her, bloodthirsty glee in his mental voice.

"Chiarn, we're going to need your help." Arya called. "Judge your moment."

"Okay," the Flamewielder called, voice shaky.

Sparing a quick look for the bitterly fighting creatures in the sky above, Arya hefted her blade and stepped up to Essa's side so that they fought as a pair, attacking Nain with everything they had. But the nazal was simply too quick, aided by magical speed and strength. At one point, it shoved Essa aside and slashed at Arya quickly enough to get through her guard. His sword caught her mail with a screech. Essa immediately leaped in front of Arya, but alone she was quickly on the back foot.

Arya's bond with Chiarn meant she felt him circling behind them, unsure how to help, afraid but managing his fear. "Ess, disengage, now! Chiarn, you're up!"

Essa immediately threw herself backwards, and in that same moment the Flamewielder wrapped the nazal in a wall of flame. It lit up the clearing. Essa and Arya scrambled to their feet, backing away.

The nazal stepped through the flame, unharmed, the fire dissolving, smothered by inky shadow. And then he *flew* at Chiarn, sword raised. The musician scrambled backwards, hands lifting helplessly, fire sparking but smothered each time. Arya lunged, sliding under the nazal's sword as it came down, taking the blow on her gauntleted wrist, bellowing in pain at the force of it, but managing to thrust her own sword at the monster. It spun away, leaving her a moment to breathe through the agony in her wrist.

There was no wound, the gauntlet had saved her, but the blow would leave bruising, if not a broken bone.

"You know you can't beat me," Nain taunted. "I'm just like you, only more powerful. He *made* me more powerful."

Scanning the plateau, Arya saw that the two wyverns still fighting bitterly to keep the shadowhounds off them, while above Elendryl tangled viciously with the nazal's mount. As her breathing settled, she felt new energy trickle through her body, enough to ignore the throbbing in her arm. The Etherean magic in Essa's armour.

Arya raised her sword. "You're nothing like us," she said, hoping that if she could get him talking, it would give them all a moment's rest.

"Wrong," he hissed. "I'm exactly like you."

"You might have been born as Sky Lord potentials, but you're twisted now. You're monsters."

"When he found each of us, he gave us a choice," Nain said in his hissing, wheezing voice. "Allow him to make us more powerful, more magical, and work at his side. Or die. Not a difficult choice."

"The coward's choice," Chiarn flung the words at the monster, voice rich with contempt, and Arya looked at him in astonishment.

Essa spoke clearly. "We choose to resist the Nightstalker."

Arya dashed forward and re-engaged the nazal. For the next few minutes, she fought it with every inch of skill and strength she had. He turned aside every attack she made, and while he clearly worked harder, he was still besting her. Not giving up, Arya kept at him, battering at his defences with every bit of skill she possessed.

Above them, Elendryl and the bat dived and swooped through the sky, screaming aloud each time one of them scored a hit. Arya was desperately worried for her wyvern, but had no focus spare to help him. In her peripheral vision, she caught glimpses of flashing copper and green as Alletryl and Asandryl fought the shadowhounds.

Eventually, despite Arya's best efforts, Nain regained the upper hand. He began forcing her towards the edge of the plateau. Her muscles trembled with exhaustion. Sweat ran into her eyes, blurring her vision. The chain mail she wore suddenly felt unbearably heavy, slowing her movements.

The doubt she'd successfully pushed away began to creep back. She could feel through the bond that Essa was as exhausted as she was. Her movements were slowing, and her reaction times were longer. Nain looked unaffected by the battle, still going as easily as when it had begun.

They were going to fail. Dunidaen would be lost. The nazal would get inside her head, find Kirin, and she would be dead, unable to warn Kulan in time. Arya's shoulders bowed, feeling more exhausted and despairing than ever before.

Nain's terrifying features curved into a smug grin. He knew he was winning, had known it from the start. He leaped forward suddenly, barrelling into Essa and sending a burst of magic that sent her flying backwards. The Inkweaver landed hard some distance away and lay still. The nazal went after her, sword raised, snarling in anticipation of a kill.

And Arya lunged.

They hadn't lost yet. And Arya Stormrider, when her most true self, *never* gave up, no matter how bad things seemed.

She collided with him just as he slashed down at Essa's neck. They fell to the ground, Arya sliding in the snow. Dark magic engulfed her as their bodies rolled together, making her cry out in horror. The nazal twisted, raking his blade along her arm as he disengaged from her and screeched his triumph.

Arya struggled back to her feet, dimly noting bright red dripping from her arm into the snow. She backed up, breathing hard and raising her sword defensively in front of her until Essa managed to get back to her feet. "Are you alright?" she asked.

"Just winded," she panted. "Your arm."

"It's fine."

Arya lunged forward to engage again, and as she did, Essa moved, drawing her knife from its sheath at her waist. A moment later, the knife flew through the air towards the nazal; he moved just in time to avoid it, and the blade ploughed into the snow. Nain came at them again, and Arya was too tired to react in time as he brushed aside her sword and lunged out with a kick. The force of the blow hurled her backwards. Pain exploded through her abdomen as she fell hard, and wet snow chilled the back of her neck.

Laughing with an eerie, hissing, sound, Nain turned on Chiarn, who was white with terror. Arya felt him try to use his magic, then saw the fear that flashed across his face when Nain stifled it again. The nazal raised his blade and prepared to attack for the final time.

"No!" The sound tore from Arya's throat.

She stumbled to her feet and raised her right hand, palm outwards. A bolt of pure blue energy shot towards the nazal. Unbelievably quickly, he dropped his sword and spun around, hand raised to counter her. A whisper of shadow leaped from his hands and met hers mid-air. The darkness of the nazal's magic writhed around Arya's bright blue light, seeking to contain and destroy it.

Arya felt the nazal's magic push against hers. Gritting her teeth, she stood her ground and refused to budge. "No," she gritted out. "I will *never* succumb to you."

Nain increased the amount of power attacking her magic, and Arya dug deep to hold him off. Her blood heated, and her Sky Lord magic roped painfully through her. Just when she thought she would explode from it, a hand pressed against her shoulder, and her magical strength almost doubled.

Essa.

"Remember the lake at the mine camp?" her Inkweaver murmured in Arya's ear.

A smile spread across Arya's face as she remembered that night, what she and Essa had done together.

They were *cairdre*.

Their combined magic swept through Arya, and together they battled the nazal's darkness. Where the two magics met, sheer energy sparked and hissed, struggling for ascendance. Arya felt the nazal probing them for weakness, nibbling at their strength, using his superior skill to defeat them. Each time he reached a vulnerable point in Arya's attack, Essa's magic would sweep in and bolster her.

Carefully, quietly, she reached for the thread between her and Chiarn, the one that had deepened over months of fighting together, and she asked a question. A shiver of assent came back to her.

An agonised shriek reverberated in the sky, making Arya wince. A moment later, a flood of weary triumph swept through her from Elendryl, and then a thud that made the ground shudder under her feet as something heavy crashed out of the sky.

"*Dead,*" Elendryl flashed into her thoughts. The wyvern was close to exhaustion, but he gave her what he had left. Smiling grimly, Arya grabbed more tightly onto Essa's magic and kept battling the dark tendrils of nazal magic as it fought to tear hers apart.

A movement flickered in Arya's field of vision. Slowly, Chiarn was inching towards the nazal, determination etched on his face. By now, Arya was pouring enough power into their magical battle that Nain was completely absorbed by it. He'd forgotten about Chiarn.

Confidence suddenly surged in Arya, flooding through the bond she shared with both of her *cairdre* members.

They had this.

The Flamewielder inched closer, drawing his dagger—the cazaix dagger Arya had gifted him, made of the metal that could kill Sky Lords and nazal—with a white-knuckled grip. When he moved, it was like a striking snake.

The musician who'd never been a warrior didn't hesitate for a second.

Nain's magic broke off abruptly as Chiarn's cazaix dagger, wreathed with the entire force of his flame magic, drove deeply into his neck. For a brief moment fire exploded out from the knife, blinding all of them. The nazal let out a blood-curdling scream, and when she could see again, Arya watched its cloaked form crumple into the snow.

She allowed her magic to dissipate and fought not to sink to her knees from utter exhaustion. "Is he dead?"

"If not, he soon will be." Chiarn extended an arm, and the cloaked body became engulfed in white-hot flame. All three of them stood and watched as the body burned to ash right before them.

Arya limped towards Chiarn, reaching out to grip the young man's shoulder. "You did good, Lord Flamewielder."

He smiled at her, pride in his blue eyes. "I did, didn't I?"

"We all did." Essa smiled. "Together."

Arya leaned on her sword for support. Her left forearm throbbed alarmingly, and she cradled it against her chest, hiding a wince. "Are you both okay?"

"My entire body feels like one huge bruise, but I think I'm alright otherwise." Chiarn said.

"I'm not hurt either. I just feel like I've been running for six months straight." Essa gave her a tired smile.

Arya looked up as their wyverns landed. Their wings drooped, and all three were splattered with blood and gore. Elendryl's scales were scraped raw in several places from claw slashes, Asandryl had a torn wing, and Alletryl bled from a nasty gash on her leg. A short distance away, the dead body of the bat creature lay fallen in the snow, dead shadowhounds scattered around it.

Arya limped over to her wyvern and wrapped her arms tightly around his neck. "Anjurin?"

Elendryl sent her an image of the boy sitting in Laskin's saddle as the shield raced back to Heathrock. One of the veteran's arms was wrapped tight around the boy.

"Anjurin is safe," Arya told Essa and Chiarn. "Laskin and the shield are taking him back to Heathrock."

Essa's shoulders slumped in relief.

"You know what?" Chiarn said eventually, standing as close as he could to Asandryl.

"What?" Arya asked.

"We just defeated a nazal, and Thiara Ravenstrike's murderer to boot," he said. "All these years of them hunting us, and we finally killed one."

A slow, tired smile crossed Arya's face as his words sank in. Pride filled her; she faced down the nazal and won.

She'd avenged Thiara Ravenstrike's murder.

"You know what else?" Essa said dryly. "We now have a very short window of time in which to defeat an army ten thousand strong."

"Right." Arya straightened, feeling the burden of leadership settle firmly on her shoulders. And for the first time in a long time, she welcomed it. "We'd best get to it, then."

As Arya looked up, both Essa and Chiarn gasped in astonishment. "What?"

"You look different," Essa said in wonder.

"Has exhaustion made you delusional?" Arya said. "What are you talking about?"

"Here." Chiarn bent and concentrated over a large pile of snow. It melted slowly, forming a wide, clear puddle of water. "Look."

Frowning, Arya kneeled and looked down into the puddle. Her features swam into focus, but they were much different from what she was used to seeing in the river.

"Chiarn, it's not just Arya. Look at you!"

Arya heard Essa's words dimly as she stared at the picture in the water. It was as if the entire structure of her face had shifted slightly. Her cheekbones were more sharply defined and arched up under her eyes. Her gaze was brighter, sparkling with magic. Arya's face glowed with something other; it was the face of a Sky Lord, and it gleamed with power.

Astonished, she glanced across and saw Chiarn peering into his own puddle of water. He looked up and over at her, the same astonishment written over his face. He'd changed, too, cheekbones just as arched as hers, and eyes now flecked with flashing copper and leaping with magic. He looked older, more assured, and ethereal. Beautiful. When she looked up at Essa, she saw the same changes, though they'd not had as much of an effect. Essa had always been stunning.

"If you're finished staring at yourselves, we have to go," Essa chuckled.

Arya hesitated, gaze narrowing as she looked at the puddle Chiarn had created, then looked up, to the snow peaks looming around them. Then, a blinding grin spread over her face, despite her exhaustion.

"I know that look," Essa said. "Arya's got a plan."

Arya straightened her shoulders. "I'm going to make sure Anji gets home safe. Chiarn, I need you to go to SheerRock Fort, and Essa, you to Windfall. Here are my instructions."

Chapter 33

Arya and Elendryl caught up with Laskin and his shield well before they reached Heathrock; she trusted Laskin with her life, but she was determined that her nephew would get home safely. The shield reined to a halt when Elendryl landed ahead of them, relief flashing over their faces.

"The nazal is dead," Arya answered Laskin's unspoken question as she strode towards him. Anjurin was curled against Laskin's chest, sobbing himself into a frenzy. "Is Anji okay?"

"Terrified." Elendryl noted.

Laskin looked uncomfortable. "He's not hurt, far as I can tell, but I've no idea what to do with a crying child."

Arya reached out to touch the boy's golden curls, affection washing over her as she did. "Anjurin? It's me, Arya. Everything is okay now."

He looked at her uncomprehendingly, eyes red from crying, breath coming in panting gasps. She smiled in what she hoped was a reassuring way, thinking about how in those few moments she'd held him, Kirin had seemed to like being rocked gently on her hip. Moving slowly, she lifted Anjurin out of the saddle and settled him against her. Her heart broke at how similar it felt to holding her son, and she cradled Anjurin with all the love she couldn't show Kirin. "Elendryl and I killed the monster, Anji. I'm going to take you home now. How does that sound?"

Her words seemed to calm him. The sobbing stopped and a tentative smile spread across his chubby features. "Aunty Ayah?"

"That's me, kiddo. Would you like to come for a ride on my wyvern?"

Anjurin glanced over her shoulder at Elendryl, then looked back at her. He seemed to consider her for a moment, then reached up with his little hand. Smiling, she closed her free hand around his. As their skin touched, a small thrill of power rippled between them.

Arya's eyes widened in shock and Elendryl gave a surprised snort. "*Valheran.*"

But how?

"You're going to be a Sky Lord one day, Anjurin Ravenstrike." She spoke the words without even thinking, and they rang with foreshadowing.

He nodded, eyes soberly fixed on hers. "Mama?" he asked hopefully.

"Elendryl is going to take us to Mama, Anji. It won't be long now."

***

They came slowly through the clouds, Elendryl flying smoothly so as not to alarm Anjurin. She held him close against her, one hand resting on his curls, biting her lip and trying to hold back tears. As terribly glad as she was that Anjurin was safe, she couldn't help but wish it was Kirin she held.

As soon as he spotted the Raiders gathered in the courtyard, his mother waiting with them, a beaming smile spread over Anjurin's tear-stained face. Arya smiled with him, and they raised their hands and waved.

Peemla came running, Raiders trailing her. Arya passed the boy down to his mother, who took him with a cry of relief and joy. Arken stood a short distance away, and as Arya's eyes fell on him, he bowed deeply, hand over his heart. Around him, every single Raider in the entry yard followed suit.

Suddenly swamped with weariness, Arya slid down from Elendryl's back, and leaned against him for support. She'd done too much to her still-healing body.

But she'd do it all over again without hesitation.

This was who she was.

She hadn't lost. Things hadn't ended badly. The relief that came with that realisation was overwhelming.

"Arya? Are you okay?" Peemla was looking at her with that shy smile she remembered so well, gratitude and concern warring in her eyes.

"I'm all right, just a little tired." Arya said, wondering, as she looked at Rorin's wife, remembering what had passed between her and Anjurin. Who *was* Peemla that her son was a future Sky Lord?

"I don't know how to thank you."

"Don't." She raised a hand. "I would have done anything to bring him back." Arya turned to Arken. "General? Laskin's shield is on his way back. Will you send a shield out to meet them, help any injured and make sure they get back here safely. Their trail is easy to follow."

"I'll send a shield at once." Arken nodded.

"Once you've done that, meet me in your office. I've got an idea. It's a little on the risky side, so you're going to fight me on it for a bit. But I think it could work."

His eyes gleamed. "Very good, Lord Stormrider. I'll see you there."

"Arken?" she called as he moved off.

"Yes?"

"I hope you've been practicing the fast deployment of Raiders Desomer had us learn all those years ago."

"I'm really not going to like this plan, am I?"

She winked. "You'll get there."

"Come inside, Arya." Peemla cradled Anjurin. The boy's eyes were sliding closed. "I can make sure you have somewhere warm to rest and get a good meal and some willow bark tea into you."

"Have the food and tea brought to Arken's office. But the rest will have to wait, I'm afraid." Arya told her. "We've got an invading army to defeat."

***

Fortified by Peemla's tea, a hearty meal, and a robust discussion with Arken, Arya and Elendryl were winging their way back to Icecliff within a couple of hours. She'd gone to her old room before leaving, opening her closet and taking out the folded silken cape she'd left there.

She'd stared at it for a long moment, then, with a little smile flickering at her mouth, she'd unfolded it and put it on.

As they arrived at Icecliff, her wyvern opted for a dramatic entrance, landing with a triumphant cry and a shower of golden sparks in the entry courtyard.

The cry bought Taze and Rorin running. Taze caught sight of Arya first and stopped dead in his tracks. Rorin ploughed into him from behind, propped, caught sight of Arya and almost tripped again. Their reaction seemed to spread through those watching. Everyone on the walls and present in the yard had gone silent.

Arya felt the moment keenly. And decided to take advantage of it.

"I am Lord Arya Stormrider, descended from the ruling House of Andahar, and rightful heir to its throne." Her words were clear and sharp. "The nazal general is dead at my hand. I propose to destroy the remainder of the Nightstalker's army. Who's with me?"

A deafening roar swept over the fort as Raiders, Lances, and Firemen gave a resounding assent that could be heard in every corner of the icy stone walls. Arya grinned and dismounted, waving Rorin and Taze over.

"*You're covered in blood and bruises and cuts. You killed the nazal? Are you alright?*" Rorin signed emphatically. "*Are Essa and Chiarn all right? Where are they?*"

"All three of us are well, if not weary and sore," Arya reassured him. "Chiarn and Essa are doing a flyover of Windfall and SheerRock, but they'll be here shortly with the information I need."

Taze's face lit up with hope. "You have a plan, don't you?"

She smiled. "Can you bring me a map of the area around all three forts? As detailed as possible, including topography."

Taze snapped an order to a nearby Raider, and she ran off. He then turned back to Arya. "Hundreds of Etherean warriors descended upon us just before you showed up. I assume you had something to do with that?"

"*Yes, it's been fun,*" Rorin interjected dryly. "*Attempting to cram almost a thousand more people in here has sent Commander Sapontis into a furious meltdown.*"

"Lord Stormrider." A new figure stepped forward then, a familiar winged warrior. Cirilla bowed his head in salute. "We are at your disposal."

"Cirilla, I'm glad to see you. We're going to need every soldier in these walls to wipe out this army," Arya said.

Running feet sounded as Raiders reappeared, one carrying a rolled map, and two others a trestle table. Amius SparrowWing and Commander Sapontis followed in their wake. "I heard Arya Stormrider has a plan?" The SparrowWing heir rubbed his hands together in glee. "I wasn't going to miss that."

Together they clustered around the trestle. Cirilla bore the multiple curious glances stoically. Arya addressed them. "The nazal is dead, which means the invasion force is currently leaderless. We're going to take advantage of any disarray before they have time to steady themselves."

"How exactly?" Sapontis asked. "This isn't going to be like that time where you decided you could break a siege of Icecliff with a single shield of Raiders, is it?"

Arya flashed a grin at her. "This might be *similar* to that time."

Two wyvern screams washed over the fort, causing a series of winces and muttered curses. By the time everyone had dropped hands from their ears, Essa and Chiarn were making their way over.

"You got what I needed?" Arya asked them.

Chiarn gave her a showy salute. Essa rolled her eyes at him, then nodded.

"Right." Arya drew everyone's attention back to the map. "The main concentrations of soldiers and wraiths near Icecliff are here, here, and here." Arya stabbed the points on the map. "Essa, Chiarn, show me the numbers and concentrations around the two sister forts."

They pointed, explaining what they'd seen. Each fort was surrounded. But as Arya had hoped, the entire invading force was clustered around one of the three forts. And in terms of numbers, the nazal had drawn the bulk of his force to the main encampment near Icecliff—which made sense if its intent had been to exchange Anjurin for a Ravenstrike retreat.

"Good work. As soon as we're done here, you'll both fly back to Windfall and SheerRock to issue my instructions. Chiarn, you'll stay at SheerRock. We'll need to ensure all three fort commanders coordinate their attacks."

"*What attacks?*" Rorin raised an eyebrow.

"We're taking the fight to them. At break of dawn tomorrow. Cirilla, are your warriors up to carrying heavily armed soldiers a good distance tonight?"

"You're going to flank them." Essa looked up from the map, eyes alight.

"Damn right I am. We're going to place a third of our fighting force at the known entrances to the underground road." Arya pointed on the map. "Our best archers, in fortified positions. The rest of us are going to empty the forts and take the fight to the Nightstalker's soldiers and force them to break and run. When they do, they'll run right into our archers."

"*You empty the forts and we're done if they overwhelm us out there.*" Rorin pointed out. "*And I don't like to disagree with you Arya, but we don't have the numbers to win without the protection of these walls. They'll overwhelm us fast, no matter how hard we fight.*"

"You're assuming we have to fight thousands. Here at Icecliff, it's going to be more like hundreds."

His gaze narrowed in suspicion. "*How exactly are you going to accomplish that?*"

"You'll see," she promised.

Sapontis looked to Rorin, who looked at Arya. She gave him a little nod. "*All right, we're in.*"

"Good." Arya leaned over the map again. "Here's how it's going to go."

Once she was done, they scattered to their various tasks. Arya reached out to hold her brother back. "I need a word."

"*Something wrong?*" her brother asked.

"Not anymore," she assured him. "But there's something you should know. The reason the nazal is dead ... he took Anji from Heathrock. Likely to ransom him in return for abandoning the defence of the forts."

Rorin turned sheet-white, and Arya hurried to reassure him. "Anji is safe home with Peemla. They're both okay. I swear it. Laskin and his shield are keeping a close eye over them both."

He stared at her with tear-filled eyes. "*You got him back?*"

"With help from Essa and Chiarn, yes."

Rorin lifted a shaking hand to his mouth. "*Peemla must have been so scared. I'm scared, even though I know he's safe.*"

"She *was* scared. But she was also brave, and tough." Arya settled a hand on his shoulder. "We need to talk about Anji sometime soon. But for now, let's concentrate on winning this fight, okay?"

He nodded, swallowing. "*I wish I could see them both.*"

"You will, soon. My word on it."

As Rorin left, Arya found Chiarn and Essa lingering, waiting to hear what she wanted them to do. Quickly and succinctly, she explained her plan.

By the time she finished, Chiarn had paled. "Arya, I know they're the enemy, but you also know many of them are conscripts. They're forced to be here."

"And they're still climbing those walls every second day trying to kill us." She let out a breath. "I don't like it either, but if we don't win this now, a lot more people are going to die. Ess, can you do it?"

"If I start today while there's still light, yes." Her eyes were shadowed, but her voice steady. "I wish there were another way."

Arya simply nodded. "Chiarn, can you do what I need at SheerRock?"

"If I can use some of your strength, yes."

"Okay, good. Then you'd best get flying." She glanced up at the sky, taking a deep breath of the cold mountain air.

Tomorrow she was going to end this invasion. One way or another.

Chapter 34

As dawn's blue light first appeared in the sky the following day, every open space inside the fort was filled with mounted warriors. A skeleton force manned the walls to give the appearance that all was normal. Arya wondered if the Nightblade army realised their general was dead yet.

She and Essa stood atop the outer wall facing west, the mighty mountains looming over them. The pinpricks of light from the Nightblade campfires seemed to fill the forest and mountainsides everywhere they looked. An overwhelming force. Chiarn's words from the day before came back to her and she tried to stifle her doubts. A glance at Essa's expression showed she wasn't having much luck doing the same.

"We have to give our soldiers a chance, Ess," she murmured. "There's no other way."

A sharp nod. "Then let's get it done."

Essa unrolled a large piece of parchment, placed it on the battlement before them. She'd drawn it the previous afternoon; it was an outline of the mountains and terrain looming to the west of the fort, the shapes drawn with exquisite detail, but not filled in. Not yet. The Inkweaver placed three sticks of charcoal beside the parchment, then picked one up.

Arya sought Essa's free hand, closing her fingers around her friend's chilled skin, and opening the bond between them. She reached for Chiarn then, and the connection between the three flared to life. A questioning came from Chiarn, still laced with reluctance, and after one look at Essa, Arya sent a firm sense of assent. He should begin.

"Take whatever you need from me," Arya murmured.

Essa took a deep, steadying breath, lifted the charcoal towards the parchment, and began drawing, swift, skilled strokes. It wasn't long before Arya felt a tug on her magic, and she sent magical strength along the thread between them, part of her in awe at the terrible beauty of the drawing taking place before her.

The first sign of the Inkweaver's power was a tortured creaking somewhere high up on the slopes, followed by a long, deep groan.

Then a snapping sound, another groan. Essa's speed picked up, filling in more and more detail. Arya swallowed at the sight of what was taking shape on the parchment. It was the mountains as she'd looked upon them day after day.

Except they were destroyed.

Essa drew on more and more of Arya's power, until, with a final shuddering groan, the slopes disintegrated. It was the best way Arya could describe it. There was pristine snowy mountainside, and then there was ... destruction.

Essa kept drawing, unhesitating, shaping the avalanche as it cascaded down toward them. Cries of fear and shock spread throughout the fort as the waiting soldiers watched hundreds of tonnes of snow, rock, and ice thunder down on top of the invading army.

Swallowing them whole.

Arya swayed as Essa drew upon a final burst of strength, drew a final piece, then dropped the charcoal and stood back. The thundering cascade stopped clear of Icecliff's walls, leaving the main road clear as well.

Debris settled into a thick, horrified, silence that weighed over the morning.

It held ... and then it was shattered by the shouts and screams from the Nightblades encamped to the east of the fort—they'd been left untouched, protected by the walls. Some ran to see if they could dig out comrades, others tried to rally those that still survived.

"You okay?" She squeezed Essa's hand.

"No."

Arya drew her close, kissed her forehead. "Rest, Inkweaver. This next part is mine to bear."

Heart heavy at the hundreds of deaths she'd just caused—despite the fact they were the enemy—Arya turned and walked the couple of steps to look down over the inner wall, where Dunidaen's soldiers waited.

She drew her sword with a loud, clear ring. Using a touch of magic, she sent blue sparks shooting up into the sky. Elendryl swooped to land on the battlement behind her, magnificent golden wings spread wide.

Arya took a breath, dispelled her guilt, and filled her voice with the fierceness her troops needed. "Let's run off these bastards and end this today! Who's with me?" she bellowed.

The ground shook as the waiting Raiders, Fireman, Andahari, and Lances roared their agreement. At a nod from Arya, the Raiders on the gate winch started opening them up. As soon as they stood wide, Ravenstrike's Raiders—Rorin and Taze riding at the vanguard, cazaix blades gleaming—streamed out of the fort and wheeled around to crash into what remained of the Nightblade army. Behind them came the Lances.

As Arya had hoped, their attack was entirely unexpected, and the Nightblades were in complete disarray. The Raiders and Lances drove deep into their ranks, swords flashing.

And then, the moment battle was engaged, hundreds of Etherean warriors swooped from the skies above, raining down a hail of arrows into the wraiths and shadowhounds that came boiling in. The Firemen left the fort last, spreading out into a wide cordon that acted to mop up any Nightblades or creature who slipped though the lines.

Arya turned to Essa. The Inkweaver was white and drained, sitting slumped against the wall in exhaustion. "I'm alright, Arya."

"Good. Get something to eat, then keep an eye on Rorin. I'm off to Sheer-Rock."

Grim-faced but determined, she nodded. Arya offered her a reassuring smile, then leaped onto the battlement and scrambled onto Elendryl's back.

As Arya and Elendryl flew swiftly south for Windfall, she reached out to Chiarn. He was focused, too focused to respond properly, but she sensed enough to know he was well, nothing had gone wrong at SheerRock, and he still had reserves of magic left. She sent him a reassuring shiver, then withdrew, conserving her own magic for what came next.

Within a half hour Elendryl was swooping down over the besieged SheerRock Fort, screaming his wyvern's cry.

With no way to coordinate the time to attack exactly, Arya had worried that the delay in her being able to reach Windfall from Icecliff would lead to its Raiders being overwhelmed before she could arrive. Though roughly two thirds of the nazal's force had been clustered around Icecliff where it guarded the highway, the numbers that surrounded the two sister forts were still overwhelming compared to the Raiders still alive and able to fight.

She and Arken had come up with a counter.

Ravenstrike's general had sent orders for the thousand Raiders stationed at the barracks in Aren—the port city nestled beneath Windfall—to slip out under the cover of night and march on the fort to be in position for a dawn attack.

It was a move General Desomer would never have countenanced—a thousand Raiders did not substantially change the large discrepancy between the forces, and it left a critical port city undefended if the battle went the Nightblades' way.

But Arya was banking on the surprise of the attack, combined with the flanking manoeuvre, would allow the Ravenstrike forces to hold long enough for her to arrive.

By the time Elendryl soared over Windfall fort, the two forces were heavily engaged in battle. Arken's uncle, the fort's commander, had emptied the fort at the same moment the Aren Raiders had launched their attack, and a bitter battle was taking place in the snowy terrain around the walls—the Nightblades sandwiched between the two attacking forces.

The Raiders were still heavily outnumbered, so the fighting was bitter and bloody, but Arya's arrival on Elendryl had the very effect she'd hoped. The wyvern tore through entire units of Nightblades while Arya used controlled bursts of magic against the largest concentrations of soldiers, breaking them into smaller units easier for the Raiders to pick off. She stayed long enough to see the tide of the battle turn, and the Raiders start pushing the retreating Nightblades towards where the hidden archers awaited them before flying to SheerRock.

The forest surrounding SheerRock was aflame, fire crackling and popping. Chiarn had used walls of fire to force the Nightblades encamped around the fort into narrow corridors of movement, chokepoints, that could be picked off by the Raiders riding out of the fort to attack. Even as she arrived, another wall of flame roared into existence, forcing the fleeing Nightblades along the highway towards the underground road. Raiders rode in pursuit.

The Flamewielder rode Asandryl to the east, copper hair glinting in the sun. He turned, sensing her arrival, and lifted a hand. She returned the wave and reached for him at the same time. He was weary, but okay. She sent a shiver of gratitude along the bond, then banked Elendryl to the north and away.

From all three forts, the Nightstalker's army fled west, some using the road, some through the forest, all heading for entrances into the underground road. And when they got there, they were met by a hail of arrows. The pursuing forces of Raiders, Firemen, and Lances hit them from behind and from there the battle for the three forts was all but over in Dunidaen's favour.

Arya stayed aloft until the end, Elendryl flying swiftly between each underground entrance, ensuring the Dunidae forces didn't get overwhelmed, and offering a blast of magic or Elendryl's snapping teeth when things looked precarious.

Finally, as the sun began to lower, the mountains turned quiet. Arya landed on the highway towards the pass, not far from one of the tunnel entrances. Rorin and Taze were both there, bloodied but well. The forest was scattered with bodies, Nightblade and Ravenstrike alike. Etherean warriors were still aloft, keeping an eye from above, just in case. Alletryl was up there too, watching over Rorin for her rider.

Raiders, Lances, and Firemen were withdrawing back to the road, Taze calling out sharp orders to get them organised for the ride back to the fort.

As Arya dismounted, all the weariness of a day-long battle crashed down over her in a wave. She leaned against Elendryl for a moment, hand stroking his scales in affection, before she pushed herself to her feet and walked down the road to meet Rorin.

"*We've won the day,*" Rorin signed, but there was no excitement in his movements, only a grim relief. He was splattered with blood and ichor, most of it not his, though she eyed the roughly bound gash on his left side with concern.

"*It's fine.*" He waved off her worry before she could say anything. "*It's shallow.*"

Taze joined them. Like Rorin he was a bloodied mess, but his worst wound seemed to be his blackened left eye.

"*SheerRock and Windfall?*" Rorin asked.

"Both are secure. The remnants of the forces surrounding them have been destroyed. The remaining Raiders are heading back to the forts as we speak. The Firemen cordons preventing Nightblades fleeing east into Ravenstrike are unbroken."

Taze let out a long breath. "A decisive victory, Arya."

"Captain, may I?" The nearest Lance captain had heard Taze's words, and now unhooked a small horn from his saddle and lifted it questioningly.

"You may."

He raised the horn and blew a loud, ringing, note out into the mountains. From every other location where Lances had fought, answering horns echoed, announcing the victory. Weary cheers erupted. These men and women had been fighting relentlessly for months. Arya understood their joy and relief. But it had come at the cost of many lives—many who'd only been here in Dunidaen because they were forced to be. Lives of *her* people, even if that was in name only for now.

She couldn't celebrate that.

***

Arya, Taze, and Rorin led the weary Raiders and Lances back to Icecliff Fort. She'd dismissed Cirilla and his warriors back to the citadel, with much gratitude. "Please pass my thanks to Elder Salyarin. You and your warriors were critical to our victory today."

Cirilla bowed. "I will leave my healers with you to tend the wounded. Until we meet again, Lord Stormrider."

Rorin stiffened in surprise as they approached Icecliff Fort and saw the walls bristling with fresh Raiders. He turned to stare at her.

She grinned, finally finding a spark of joy. "If we'd lost today, the invading force would still have had to deal with three fully manned forts."

Rorin was still gaping at her when they rode through the gates to find Arken waiting for them. He saluted sharply.

"Well done, General." Arya said, genuinely impressed.

"All three forts are fully manned, Warlord, Lord Stormrider, though the Aren and Heathrock barracks have been entirely emptied." A look of dawning hope flashed over his face. "You won?"

"*We did.*" Rorin signed. "*But if we hadn't, you would have saved us, General. Thank you.*"

"It was a gamble," Arken replied, glancing at Arya. "But one I was confident in making, Warlord."

Essa appeared from inside, still pale and drawn, but walking well enough, alerted through the bond of Arya's arrival. Soon after, Asandryl's call reverberated through the skies, and everyone moved aside to make room for him to land. Chiarn looked as exhausted as Arya felt. None of them would be in a condition to use their magic for a time.

"Rorin, I should have said this earlier," Arya said. "Your parents have been avenged. Nain was the nazal we killed."

He looked at her, tears forming in his eyes. "*You killed the creature that murdered my parents?*"

"No, actually." Arya's mouth quirked. "That was Chiarn."

Rorin's eyes widened in astonishment. "*Chiarn?*"

"It might have been me that drove the dagger into that foul creature's neck," Chiarn said. "But it was the three of us together that killed him."

"*Thank you,*" Rorin said. "*Thank you, all of you. I will never forget what you've done for me.*"

"You know I'll always protect you, Rorin." Arya squeezed his arm.

"*Same goes, sister,*" he murmured, before pulling her into another hug. Then he stepped back, looked at Taze and Arken. "*I'd like to ensure the wounded are treated, then talk about sending out fresh shields to patrol.*"

He spoke with a warlord's authority, and Arya stepped away, leaving them to it. They'd need to manage cleanup now, and she was glad Arken was here with fresh eyes and energy to help manage that. Essa went with them, and Arya left her, knowing the woman would feel better by helping.

Visions of eating a massive meal and then sleeping for a month flashed temptingly through Arya's mind and she turned for the mess.

"Arya?"

Chiarn's voice stopped her. "What is it?"

"When we fought the nazal, you saved my life. It had me on the ground, and I couldn't move. That sword was coming down on my neck until you threw yourself at him." Chiarn's head lifted. "He might have gotten your wrist, but Arya I was underneath you and I saw his sword was a hairsbreadth from your throat. You threw yourself at him, knowing he could have killed you, and you did it anyway."

Arya nodded. "You said you wanted to be worthy, Chiarn, but you already are. I knew if I didn't do something, he was going to kill you. And that will never be something I will stand by and allow to happen."

Tears glittered in Chiarn's blue eyes. "Thank you."

"Don't thank me." She slung an arm around his shoulders. "You had my back in that fight too. It's what *cairdre* do for each other."

"I suppose it is." He smiled. "I'll definitely be composing a heroic song about you after this."

"No, you won't," she warned.

"Oh yes, it's going to be epic," he said. "You just wait."

"Chiarn, you write a heroic song about me, and I'll stab you somewhere painful."

"No, you won't." He grinned. "Now, where can we find food?"

***

Hours later, too wired for sleep despite her physical exhaustion, Arya sat on the eastern battlement, back leaning against the rough stone. She'd discarded her cape and mail some time ago, and now sat comfortably in her scuffed and dirtied blue tunic and breeches. She clasped a mug half-full of ale in one hand, and her other rested on bent knee. Below her in the main courtyard, a raucous celebration was going on. It had started hours ago, and was getting progressively rowdier as more ale was consumed.

Arya wished she could share in the joy. Above it was a clear night, and stars sparkled throughout the sky. Her thoughts, loosened by the few mugs of ale she'd consumed, turned to Kirin, wondering what he was doing at that moment. What would the Nightstalker do next? Would he leave off searching for her son to deal with the threat she now posed? Arya hoped so, but worried that he had the power and resources to do both at once.

Leanir was still out there too, furious at her. His last words had promised revenge of some kind. And Mathas Crowtalon was still High Warlord of Dunidaen. He wouldn't relinquish that without a fight, and there was no way of her winning Dunidaen in a formal alliance until that happened.

Still, she could hope this victory had bought her some time. She looked up as Rorin and Taze approached.

"Good ale, this," Taze dropped beside her.

Arya swallowed the remainder of her mug. "You're right."

"*So, what's next?*" Rorin asked.

"You have to take your remaining forces south to meet Dar and Spar-rowWing and help them hold the borders against Mathas."

"I *do? What about you?*"

"I have a plan to help you, but there are a couple of people I need to see first."

Rorin reached over and squeezed her hand. "*I'm so glad to see you back to your plan-making best.*"

"I'm glad too," she told him softly.

Arya took a deep breath, looking up at the stars in the night sky. She felt like herself again. She just hoped it would be enough.

Chapter 35

Arya left with Chiarn early the next morning, just ahead of Rorin, Taze, and Amius SparrowWing. Rorin would ride straight to Heathrock to check on Peemla and Anjurin, then head south with Warlord SparrowWing and his uninjured Firemen.

"I will leave Peemla and Arken in charge of Heathrock, and our State, while I am in Gateport," Rorin signed. *"I worry for Anji, but I have a feeling if danger comes, it will be in Gateport. I don't want my son anywhere near Mathas Crowtalon."*

Arya agreed. "The north should be temporarily safe. Arken will make sure of it, and the Etherean have agreed to patrol the Diamondfang on our behalf. Essa will travel with you as protection until I can join you."

"Where are you and Chiarn going?" he asked.

"I'll let you know if it works out." She grinned.

The air grew warmer as Elendryl and Asandryl flew south-east, the sky a cloudless blue around them. Spring had finally arrived in Dunidaen's north. By mid-afternoon of their second day out from Icecliff, Arya's sharp eyesight spotted her destination below and she motioned to Chiarn. The two wyverns circled lower, above a wide highway that meandered through a lush valley of green fields leading to a lake to the east.

Darulan, the seat of Hawkesdale, was a picturesque sight, sitting along the eastern shore of the glittering blue lake. Arya had to repress a smile at the looks on the faces of two farmers staring up at them, agape, as the wyverns flew over their field.

They followed the road towards a large walled estate southeast of the city, before landing on the tree-lined road leading to the main gates. Four

Longbows clad in the Hawkesdale green and brown appeared on the sandstone wall. Their reaction was no different from that of the farmers, and there was a long pause before Arya and Chiarn were addressed. One went so far as to draw an arrow. "Can we help you?" he shouted down, a quaver in his voice. The other three remained occupied staring at the wyverns, agape.

Elendryl had grown big enough now that Arya barely had to look up to meet the Longbows' gaze. "Could you please tell Warlord Hawkesdale that Lord Arya Stormrider is here to see him?"

Arya and Chiarn shared a small smile as all four Longbows vanished, their shocked voices carrying as they ran to alert their captain. It wasn't much later that footsteps sounded on the other side of the gates, and they swung inwards, revealing a huge, pebbled yard surrounded by lush gardens that rolled away in every direction. Arya and Chiarn dismounted. Elendryl levelled a warning growl at the Longbow who ushered them inside. The poor man jumped violently.

The gates closed, and Arya didn't miss the Longbows watching carefully from the walls. Before them was a large, sandstone villa. The yellow walls gave the entire place a soft, welcoming air. It seemed to have been built haphazardly, three stories at its highest point, but sprawling out in all directions. She liked it.

The front doors opened, and Gelfrey Hawkesdale appeared with his daughter and two more Longbows in tow. He looked surprised, but his bearded features were creased into a wary smile of welcome. "This is unexpected."

"Greetings, Warlord Hawkesdale," Arya said politely. "I apologise for intruding without notice. This is Lord Chiarn Flamewielder."

"Warlord Hawkesdale, Lady Hawkesdale, it's a pleasure to meet you." Chiarn inclined his head, every inch the charming minstrel.

"Another Sky Lord, is it?" Hawkesdale asked, crossing his arms over his chest. "Well, you'll have to forgive my unease at having two magic-wielders show up at my home, unannounced and uninvited, and riding wyverns."

Arya grinned. "You're not uneasy, Warlord. You've got at least twenty elite archers pointing arrows at my heart as we speak."

He huffed. "Come on in then. I don't want to stand out here all day."

"Actually, we can't stay," Arya said. "I apologise, and mean no offence, but Chiarn and I have little time and many things to do."

"What can we do for you, then?" Illia asked, stepping forward to link her arm through her father's. Her sharp features were alive with curiosity.

"I'm sure you know that the High Warlord's Defenders are currently encamped on the Crowtalon-SparrowWing border," Arya said. "His intent is to invade Crowtalon, SparrowWing, and then Ravenstrike and remove their warlords."

Hawkesdale gave a disgusted snort. "My scouts tell me Defenders are heading my way too, no doubt hoping I'll give them access to attack SparrowWing from the east. If I don't, I suppose Mathas will take my position as well. What do you want of me?"

Arya shrugged. "I want you to join Ravenstrike, Crowtalon, and SparrowWing, and force Mathas to call an impromptu State Council in Gateport. If my understanding of Dunidaen law is correct, a Council vote can be forced at the demand of four or more warlords."

"Oh, *that's* all you want?" Hawkesdale barked a laugh. "What's Andahar's interest in this?"

Arya shrugged. "We don't want Mathas Crowtalon as High Warlord any more than you do."

When he hesitated, his expression giving nothing away, Arya continued, "Warlord Ravenstrike and I have defeated the first wave of the Nightstalker's invasion. But you can be sure he will try again, and he'll come himself next time, on a wyvern double the size of the two outside your gates right now."

"Because he wants *you*," Hawkesdale said pointedly.

"Because he wants *more*. Hunting me is merely an excuse." Arya paused, cocked her head. "I'm sure your general and your chief advisor have already told you that."

"I hear you," Hawkesdale made an impatient gesture. "Now, if you're not coming in, then make yourselves scarce and leave me time to consider your request."

"Thank you, Warlord. We very much appreciate your time." Arya smiled at both him and Illia, then she and Chiarn returned to their wyverns.

***

From Hawkesdale, Arya and Chiarn flew directly north and over the Dunidaen border into the Icelands. Once in Icelands territory, Elendryl angled north towards the village where At'eir's tribe returned to when winter eased into spring. This far north, snow still lay thick on the ground, and Asandryl and Elendryl were buffeted by a strong, icy wind as they landed.

Figures emerged from the huts, and Arya recognised At'eir's tall, broad-shouldered figure straight away. His eyes widened in surprise as he took in her and Chiarn. "Lord Stormrider."

"Er'fin At'eir." She smiled in greeting. "It's good to see you. Allow me to introduce Lord Chiarn Flamewielder."

At'eir gave a polite bow of his head. It was then that Arya saw the bandaging on his right hand, the warrior leaning heavily on a crutch nearby, and no sign of At'eir's cousin and second, At'near.

"What's happened?" she asked, voice turning sharp.

At'eir's welcome smile faded. "The Ce'Garn rode on our capital, Is'heim, and launched an attack on my mother's leadership. I was required to lead her forces against the challenge. I've only just returned to my tribe, so your timing is fortunate."

Arya frowned. "The queen is all right?"

"As testy and sharp as she was twenty years ago, and At'near remains at her side to ensure her safety." At'eir assured her. "Ce'Garn was a fool."

"Now a dead fool, I take it?"

"Indeed." At'eir looked even more troubled. "Arya, I now believe the nest of wraiths we stumbled across before winter was here to carry messages to the Ce'Garn. They were in his territory, you remember, and I do not believe he suddenly decided, for no reason, that attacking the queen was a good idea. I've known him a long time, and he was always troublesome but not a gambling fool."

That news crashed into Arya. "You think the Nightstalker was behind it?"

"If a puppet held our throne on behalf of Lucius…" At'eir lifted his hands in the air, he didn't need to spell out what that would mean. "We heard of the invasion of Dunidaen. How do you fare?"

Arya gave him a quick rundown. "I've come to ask the Icefolk to stand by Andahar in ridding Mathas Crowtalon of his position."

At'eir frowned. "The queen will be hesitant to influence the leadership of an allied nation. She would not stand for it happening here."

Arya said simply, "You have seen what happened to Dunidaen under Crowtalon's leadership. I'm sure I don't need to point out to you that Dunidaen holding firm against Andahar is in the Icelands' best interests."

He shook his head. "Even if my mother agreed, by the time I reached Is'heim to speak with her, and then left for Dunidaen, we would not reach Gateport in time for the vote, not if it needs to be done as quickly as you say."

"It is spring, so the storm channel will be opening. Elendryl and I will fly you to Is'heim and we'll be there in hours. You could speak to the queen and be on a ship for Gateport with an appropriate entourage the day after. You might even beat the rest of us there."

An anticipatory smile flashed over At'eir's face as he conceded. "What man could say no to flight on a wyvern's back? I will speak to my mother, Lord Stormrider."

***

Arya returned to Heathrock to find Niallin and his four hundred rebels barracked at the castle. The man himself emerged from the castle with Peemla to greet her after Elendryl landed. He wore her blue uniform with the grey lightning bolt emblazoned on the front of his tunic.

"Lord Stormrider." He bowed low. "Elder Salyarin asked his warriors to carry us here. He felt our presence at the citadel placed his people in too much danger."

"Oh, he did, did he?" she asked dryly. She supposed that was fair enough—they were her people, her responsibility, not Salyarin's. "Peemla, I apologise. Is there space at Heathrock to accommodate them?"

Peemla waved a hand. "It hasn't been a problem at all. Those that are fighters remained here to train with your personal shield, and the others we've found lodgings for in Heathrock city."

"You're amazing," Arya said gratefully, before turning to Niallin. "I suppose it's time you rode with me. You know we have a long and difficult road to walk?"

"I'm here to walk it with you, Lord Stormrider," Niallin said. "All of us are."

Arya's smiled widened as she pointed at Niallin's uniform. "And you've been extra busy, Peemla, I see."

"It was nothing. Not after what you did for Anji, Arya, I can't ever—"

"Enough." Arya stepped forward and swept her into a warm hug. "We must march tomorrow, but first, I want to see my nephew and give him a kiss. Will you take me?"

Peemla squeezed back fiercely before letting go. "He'll be thrilled to see you."

Arya turned back. "Niallin, find Laskin. Tell him he's to have your people and his shield ready to march at dawn."

Niallin hesitated.

She stopped. "Is there a problem?"

"No, Lord Stormrider. I'll find him at once."

***

Arya and her little army reached the southern Ravenstrike border after a week of hard marching, then angled south through SparrowWing. Another week of pushing the pace bought them to where the borders of Hawkesdale, Crowtalon, and SparrowWing converged.

They pulled up at the top of a small rise, looking over the rolling plains below. Seelan sprawled to the east, smoke curling into the sky from its hundreds of homes and businesses. It was a starkly different sight compared to the haze-filled and ash-coated city she remembered from that fiery summer all those years ago.

To the west of the city, the once empty plains were covered with tents; the black and violet, gold and brown, and dark red of Crowtalon, SparrowWing, and Ravenstrike covered at least half the area, spanning miles of acreage before the southern walls of a SparrowWing fort. Arya estimated a combined force of thirteen thousand warriors.

Across a wide, sluggish river splitting the plains before curling away to the south of Seelan were the white and gold tents of the High Warlord's Defenders. These numbered roughly seven thousand, but Arya spotted at least three thousand blue Aggressors in a support position behind the High Warlord's army.

Arya whistled, impressed. While both armies had access to the river and its fresh water, the three rebel warlords held the high ground around the fort and, by taking the northern side of the river, Darmanin's Lances had managed to cut off the city from the Defenders, which meant only the rebel soldiers had access to supplies from Seelan.

"Not bad," Laskin remarked beside her.

"Not bad at all," she agreed. "Let's camp here. See the Andahari settled, leave Allicen in charge, then come after me. Bring Chiarn too."

He saluted and wheeled his horse, already issuing orders.

"Elendryl, you and Asandryl are staying well back?"

She got a grumpy harrumph in response. A chuckle escaped her. She could sense Essa's presence at the fort, though they'd seen no sign of Alletryl. Arya urged her stallion into a fast gallop. She'd been chafing at the slow pace of their march and was eager to find out what had developed in her absence. Their arrival had been noticed, and a rider on a gleaming bay mare emerged from the gates, racing toward them.

Darmanin.

They met in a flurry as both horses half-reared to avoid hitting each other.

"Arya!" Darmanin greeted her. "We've been waiting for you."

"Sorry I took so long. There were some people I had to see." She gestured to the positioning of the armies. "I like what you've done with the place. Very impressive."

"I aim to please," he said, that little smile tugging at his mouth. "We've heard all about your victory on the border. Rorin can't stop talking about how magnificent you were."

She laughed. "He's exaggerating, I promise you."

"I doubt it." Darmanin sobered. "You *look* magnificent."

"I'm glad you approve."

"I do. Very much." His face sobered, voice lowering. "You still want to do this?"

She gave him a single nod.

Darmanin looked over her shoulder as the thunder of hoofbeats signalled the arrival of Laskin and Chiarn. "Lord Flamewielder, General Carter," he said formally. "The warlords are waiting to greet you. The situation is at a stalemate. Now you're here, we need a plan to push things forward."

"Lead the way," Arya said, eager to get started.

But before they could move, warning shouts echoed across the fields where the allied warlords' army camped. Arya's hand was halfway to her sword as she wheeled her horse, but a few minutes later, highlighted against the late afternoon sun, rows and rows of green and brown-clad Longbows marched over the rise. Riding at the head of the force was the bulky figure of Warlord Gelfrey Hawkesdale.

Darmanin looked at her wryly. "Visiting people, was it?"

Arya grinned smugly.

The marching Longbows halted and dissolved formation to begin setting up camp. Two riders emerged from the ranks, angling toward them when Arya and Darmanin lifted their arms in greeting. Gelfrey Hawkesdale and his daughter Illia.

"Good party you've got going on here, Crowtalon. High ground, supplies cut off. A nice bit of tactical strategy." Gelfrey's eyes twinkled as he rode up. "We could take Mathas by force if we had a mind to."

"It's good to see you, Warlord, Lady Illia." Darmanin inclined his head. "Rorin and Helden will be glad to see you also."

"As soon as Mathas spots your Longbows, he'll be calling for parley by first light," Arya said. "You can then force a State Council vote."

"That's the whole plan, isn't it?" Gelfrey grumbled. "The reason I had to leave my nice comfortable villa, rouse my army, and march hundreds of miles to this blasted hot State?"

"Now, Father," Illia said lightly. "Don't pretend you don't love being on a war march."

He glared at her. "Children should be seen and not heard."

"I'm your heir now, you *have* to listen to me."

Darmanin smiled. "Please allow me to escort you in. Quarters will be set aside for you all. I hope to hold a war council tonight before my father calls a parley. I want to ensure we have a unified response prepared."

Darmanin rode ahead with Gelfrey, Chiarn falling behind them. Arya had watched the challenging, yet affectionate look Illia had given her father, the way he'd grunted in acknowledgment, and decided she liked the young woman very much. It prompted her to bring her horse alongside Illia and say, "I'm glad the Council confirmed you as heir."

Illia's smile was genuine. "I think after *your* appearance, Lord Stormrider, confirming a female heir was the least controversial part of the entire session."

She winked. "Glad I could help."

Laskin cleared his throat, loudly.

Arya glanced over her shoulder. "What?"

He scratched his beard. "Nothing."

Illia chuckled and tossed a smile at Arya. "Your general reminds me of my father."

Arya burst into peals of laughter.

***

Once at the fort, Arya was shown to a sparse room in a narrow wing that had been set aside for her entourage. She made quick work of scrubbing the grime of travel from her skin, then dressed in her Etherean tunic and breeches, matching leather weapons' belt and boots. She emerged from her room soon after with the intent of searching for Rorin and Essa. A little humming on the thread between her and Essa gave her a general direction to head in.

The sound of murmuring voices floated into hearing, and Arya paused at the top of a wide stairwell, not wanting to interrupt if someone was having a private conversation.

Darmanin stood in the landing below with Illia Hawkesdale. He said something which made her laugh. Arya let out a breath. Illia would be such a good match for him—smart, but also confident enough in herself to cut through his silent reserve when necessary. Not to mention it would get him Hawkesdale's vote for High Warlord.

And while part of her ached at the thought of Darmanin marrying Illia, it didn't crush her either. Not like the thought of ... ugh. Emotions were tricky, annoying things. The truth was, Darmanin would probably be happier with Illia. He'd have the life he wanted. And maybe that's why she felt okay about it. Because she wanted Darmanin's happiness more than anything. Or maybe it was because she still didn't really know what *she* wanted when it came to Darmanin.

Movement in her peripheral vision had her turning to see Rorin, fingers flickering in greeting. "Rorin." She grinned in relief at the distraction. "It's good to see you."

"*Can we talk?*"

He led her out onto a small balcony which looked out over the grassy plains surrounding the fort. She welcomed the warm afternoon air on her skin. Rorin faced her with a smile. "*You're well?*"

She gave him a suspicious look. "What? You have that look on your face you wear when you think I'm being dense about something."

"*Busted.*" He beamed, but then shifted closer, a sober expression closing over his face. "*What's going on with you and Dar?*"

Arya stared at her brother, then snorted a laugh. "What do you mean?"

He crossed his arms and gave her a *you heard me* look. *"Dar and I are closer than brothers, Arya. He keeps things hidden deeply, but I've always known how he feels about you."*

Sibling rivalry had Arya unable to help needling him. "Oh, you know it all, do you? Did you know that he wanted to marry me?"

Surprise flared over Rorin's face.

She couldn't help a chuckle. "Your 'closer than a brother' didn't tell you about going to your mother to ask permission to marry me, then?"

"No." He looked glum. *"And neither did you."*

She shoved his shoulder affectionately. "That's because as much as we both love you, it's our private business. You never spoke to me about Peemla, remember? Essa, but not me."

"I'm sorry."

"I'm not angry about it," she assured him. "So don't apologise. I loved you, but I would have sided with your mother, and I would have been wrong."

He huffed a breath and settled more comfortably against the stone edge. *"You know, if you succeed in what you want to do, you're going to be queen of Andahar. I'm not sure if you've really thought about what that means. Being a leader is a lonely life; even I've experienced that. You outrank those around you, and they must obey your commands. It's not easy."*

Rorin had changed so much from the boy she'd grown up with, and she wondered that she hadn't noticed how much until now. Rorin had Matte Eaglesoar's features and build, but his mother's wisdom and intelligence shone from his faded blue eyes. His persona of sparkling merriment hid it well, but he'd grown into a strong warlord.

She gave him a serious answer. "I haven't thought about anything but defeating the Nightstalker. That is such an impossible task that imagining what comes after seems foolish."

"Fair enough." Rorin shifted, as if trying to parse his next words. *"I suspect I know what you've truly wanted for a long time now. And I also know that you've*

accepted it isn't possible. But have you considered that someone else could be that for you?"

"Raven's balls, Rorin, you're talking in circles and giving me a headache." She waved a hand between them. "Is this what we're going to do now? Discuss our romantic entanglements."

"We're each other's family. Who else would we discuss them with?"

She considered him for a long moment, before letting out a sigh. "In that case, the situation with Dar is complicated."

"Because he knows you, and he's not after being your temporary bed partner," Rorin said, arching an eyebrow.

"That's not..." Had that been what Darmanin thought she was offering that night on the lake? *Had* it been what she was offering?

"Then what is?"

She wanted to tell him so badly, share the burden of her fears with her brother, the one she loved most in the world after her son. "I'm carrying a lot, Rorin." She gave him as much of the truth as she dared. "I've accepted that I can't protect those I love by hiding and running from the Nightstalker. But openly facing him carries so many risks, and always I worry about whether my decisions will result in what happened to your parents. That fear is constant, and it leaves little room for any other feelings."

Rorin glanced away, troubled. *"Dar's not going to get what he wants, is he?"*

"I wish it were otherwise, but he's a Sky Lord, whether he likes it or not. As stubborn as he is, I don't think he's going to be able to escape it forever." Arya pushed off the wall. "Come on, we should get inside for the Council."

***

The fort's council room was almost full by the time Arya and Rorin arrived. Helden and Amius SparrowWing sat with Gelfrey Hawkesdale at one end of the table, chatting companionably. Darmanin was near them with Illia. Essa sat beside Rorin's empty chair, and Chiarn on her other side with Taze. Laskin sat at the opposite end of the table. Also in the room were SparrowWing and Hawkesdale's generals, and Andrian Crowtalon. Darmanin's older brother waved a cheerful greeting to Arya, who returned it before taking a seat next to Laskin.

"Let's get on with it, then," Hawkesdale barked as soon as everyone was seated. "What are we planning to do here? Force a State Council so we can get rid of Mathas and put someone in his place?"

There was a beat of silence—most attendees discomfited by the blunt stating of their aims—but then Rorin shrugged and nodded, Taze once again translating. "*That's pretty much it, Warlord.*"

"Right, so who are we putting in his place?" Gelfrey asked with a shrewd look. "Crowtalon's son?"

Arya hesitated for only a fraction of a second, refusing to let herself glance in Darmanin's direction. This had to be done. If she wanted Dunidaen's army, then she needed a High Warlord who would help that happen. "Warlord Hawkesdale," she said crisply. "Andahar supports only one candidate for High Warlord of Dunidaen. Rorin Ravenstrike." She caught Darmanin's expression as it turned hard with anger, but deliberately looked away. "The Icelands stand with Andahar on this. Er'fin At'eir will be present in Gateport for the vote and the queen has given me her proxy until then."

"And what have either of you got to do with who we choose for High Warlord?" SparrowWing asked. "You have no vote among us."

"Dunidaen does not exist in isolation, as you well know, Warlord SparrowWing," Arya said calmly. "If our three countries are to be allies, then—"

"Allies? You don't even *have* a country," Hawkesdale pointed out.

"Er'fin At'eir and his mother most assuredly do have a country, Warlords," she said. "A country which, if I understand correctly, is currently negotiating fishing concessions off your eastern coast."

"Hold on." Illia Hawkesdale's voice lifted about the hum of restive muttering. "All we need to agree upon now is forcing Mathas to call a State Council and a leadership vote for a new High Warlord. Once the Council is in session, the normal voting process will apply as to who becomes High Warlord. Am I not correct?"

Arya glanced at her, impressed. The warlords seemed to realise the sense of her words too.

"Right you are," Hawkesdale barked. "That's our position then. We demand a formal State Council to vote upon a new High Warlord. Mathas gives us that or we take his army by force?"

"Agreed," SparrowWing said decisively.

"*Agreed*," Rorin signed.

"Agreed," Darmanin gave a tight nod.

Arya sat down, let out a breath.

One step at a time.

***

After the impromptu council concluded, Arya grabbed a bowl of stew from the kitchen, and carried it through to the library, where Rorin sat with Essa and Taze, already beginning their planning for a State Council. Dark clouds had moved in, and rain sheeted down the glass, the fire in the hearth giving the room a cosy glow.

"Don't tell me," Arya grumbled, throwing herself into a chair and avoiding Rorin's glare. "More endless dinners and lunches and social events with vicelords and generals in Gateport, courting votes, etcetera, etcetera."

"It won't be so bad this time." Essa chuckled. "We'll insist on holding the vote within a week of all warlords arriving in Gateport—because of the threat from the west, we can't afford to wait for all vicelords to travel there. Only those who can get to Gateport in time will be able to vote."

Arya frowned. "Won't that put you at a disadvantage? Ravenstrike vicelords have the furthest to travel."

Rorin began signing but Taze cut over him. "It will, but in terms of numbers, between our four States, we have the advantage to make sure the vote doesn't go Mathas' way."

Essa gave Taze a warning look. "As long as we don't take for granted that all the vicelords will vote with their warlords."

"*Yes, yes*," Rorin said in exasperation. "*But that's not—*"

"Just keep your lists away from me," Arya warned.

"*Enough!*" Rorin signed sharply, pinning her with a glare. "*Stop blathering about lists and explain yourself. You couldn't have given me a heads up you planned on insisting that I be High Warlord?*"

"I'm glad she did," Essa said promptly. "You're the best choice for the job."

"Couldn't agree more." Taze leaned back in his chair, hands linked behind his head.

"*Traitors!*" Rorin stared at them all. "*This is my life you're all talking about.*"

"Rorin." Arya leaned forward. "Your mother wanted more than anything to be High Warlord of Dunidaen. I robbed her of that chance. If you truly don't want it, then I will stand down, but your mother deserved this, *you* deserve it." A niggle of guilt wriggled in her stomach. That was the truth, but it wasn't the full truth. She needed him to be High Warlord for her own purposes. For Kirin, she had to be ruthless with her own brother, and part of her hated herself for it.

His surprised gaze stared at all three of them. "*You all really think that I'm the best choice? What about Dar? He's so much stronger than me.*"

"I love Dar, and always will," Essa said softly. "And he would be a strong, competent, High Warlord. But the compassion in your heart, Rorin, *that's* what Dunidaen needs. You could bring about real change."

Taze nodded, reaching out to grip his friend's shoulder. "I would serve happily under you or Dar, but my vote will *always* be yours first."

It was Essa's words that had captured Rorin's attention though. He had that thoughtful look on his face as he looked at his chief advisor, the same look he'd worn after the Dreadwater run, when he'd told them he didn't want his voice to be healed—that he wanted to prove that he was just as capable as anyone else. So that others with a disability could see that and know they were capable too.

His gaze shifted to Arya. "*The power to make things right.*"

"Exactly." Arya held her brother's gaze, and when she spoke the next words, they were more honest than anything she'd ever said. It felt *good.* "Let's change the world, Rorin, you and me together."

Rorin's blue eyes lit up, mouth curling in a fierce grin as he held her gaze. *"You and me, sister."*

Chapter 36

Arya rose from her chair, started pacing. It was late, rain still pattering against the glass. She'd mostly been listening while Essa and Rorin planned, joining in occasionally, but otherwise bored by the minutiae of politics. She stopped by the window and reached for the threads linking her to Darmanin and Chiarn. Both seemed well. She paced back to her chair, sat down, then promptly leaned forward, rolling her shoulders.

Essa looked at her sharply. "You're uneasy."

Arya met her gaze. "Yes."

"*What's making you uneasy?*" Rorin asked.

"It's probably nothing," she said, then. "*Elendryl?*"

He sent an image of dark ground and trees; he was miles away over the isolated western plains of SparrowWing, hunting sheep with Alletryl and Asandryl. Arya shook her head and stood up again. "I'm going to go and ride the boundaries of the camp, make sure."

"I'll come with you." Essa put down her quill.

Arya held out a hand to stop her. "If there *is* danger lurking, then it's best you and Chiarn stay here to protect Rorin and the other warlords. I'm probably just being paranoid, but with Mathas Crowtalon so close, I want to be sure."

"In that case, *I'll* come with you." Taze rose from his chair, ignoring her scowl.

***

Arya and Taze collected their horses from the stables and rode out into darkness and driving rain, Taze making no complaint about either, gaze watchful. Arya was abruptly glad he'd come. She'd forgotten how much it had always made her feel safer, having her oldest friend at her back. A storm hovered in the distance, and intermittent flashes of lightning lit up the landscape.

"*Come?*" Elendryl asked.

She hesitated, then, "*Yes, I think that's a good idea.*"

A swift assent came back.

"Where do you want to start?" Taze asked.

Arya considered for a moment, then spurred her horse into a canter towards an area of woodland north of the fort. Although it was patrolled like the rest of the camp perimeter, it was the only area that offered cover. Thunder rumbled overhead, and her horse shied. Into the silence after the thunder, she and Taze heard a single, stifled cry. They glanced at each other and pushed their horses into a gallop. In the next moment, a flash of lightning lit up the dark sky. The light illuminated several battling figures and two riderless horses at the edge of the trees.

Arya leaped from the horse's back as they approached the fight. Rain had turned the ground under her feet into a quagmire, and she almost slipped twice as she ran, drawing her sword. Of the two Raider sentries who'd been patrolling, one was down, unmoving. The second was backing away, one of his attackers coming at him fast and hard, sword a blur in the darkness. He got through the Raider's guard before she could reach him, and he went down with a gurgling cry.

Furious, Arya pushed herself, sprinting forward to engage the attacker and send the sword flying from his grasp. She kept the momentum going, swinging her cazaix blade hard enough to take her adversary's head clean off.

A grunt sounded behind her, and she spun, sword lifting—

To see another adversary slump to the mud, Taze's sword between his ribs. Lightning flashed on the dagger in his hand that had been about to bury itself in Arya's back.

"Thanks!" she said.

"It's what I'm here for."

Without a word, she and Taze moved back-to-back and faced the remaining three attackers. The fighting was bitter, the skill of their adversaries surprising, but she and Taze formed an unbreachable wall. Once they were all down, Arya kept her sword ready, searching the darkness for any more enemies hiding beyond the trees. Rain tapped against leaves. All else was still. She glanced at Taze. "Watch my back?"

"Always." He nodded, gaze already scanning their surroundings.

She went to the nearest body. The man's clothes were dark, unremarkable, and there was nothing identifying on the body. He had the circular brand on his face given to magic-wielders, though. The sight of it made her ill. "Thoughts?" she asked Taze after passing that on.

"They took out two mounted Raiders easily and without raising the alarm—not an easy thing to do. And they were highly competent swordsman. Add that to no identifying marks or items on the bodies, and my bet is Shadeweaver assassins. The branded one confirms it."

She expelled a breath. Her thoughts exactly. "Mathas."

"We know he's used them before." Taze pointed at tracks in the mud, presumably left by the assassins. Together they began following them.

"If it's Mathas, who's he after? He can't surely think that murdering warlords will allow him to keep his position?" Arya murmured as they moved, squinting in the darkness.

Taze shot her a grim look. "Not unless he murders *all* of the rebel warlords."

"Surely Eaglesoar and Falconcrest wouldn't stand for—" Arya froze as they reached a large clearing in the trees. There were more tracks in the mud here, two large prints with long talons that she recognised instantly. "Raven's balls!"

Arya reached for her Sky Lord bonds, brought alive the thread to Leanir with a burst of furious magic. He was far closer than he'd been last time she'd checked, when she'd assumed he'd returned to Gateport, but he was moving away rapidly, presumably on his wyvern. She tried to yank on the bond, compel him to return to her, but he was already too far away for that to work. A shimmer of vicious smugness came back.

She muted the bond. She'd deal with Leanir once this was over, but she didn't want him sensing her coming when she did.

"Arya, what is it?"

"Leanir was here." She swore loudly and fluently. "We have to get back to the fortress now!"

Arya was already reaching for Essa and Chiarn, lighting up their threads with urgent warning. She shared it with Darmanin, who had been asleep but woke rapidly at her tug on their bond.

"You think he drew you out here while he was inside?" Taze asked as they ran.

She swore. "It's what I would have done."

As soon as they were astride, Taze and Arya galloped through the encampment, Taze bellowing orders as they rode. "Alert! Alert! Captains, rouse and arm your shields. Rouse and arm your shields!"

With every hoofbeat, Arya tried to work out who Leanir would have gone for. Rorin? One of the other warlords? Had the assassin been contracted, or was Leanir going rogue again? Had more assassins penetrated the fort? They dismounted inside the gates. The Fireman guards looked calm and relaxed.

"There's nothing out of place, sir." One answered when Taze asked, looking confused. "It's been a quiet night."

"Two sentries were just killed by Shadeweaver assassins on the northern camp border," Taze spoke, calm, in charge. "Alert your captains and get a double guard on the walls. Now!"

He and Arya ran for the main building. The closest entry was to the kitchens. Arya was a step behind Taze as he went through the door, her gaze going straight to the shadowy figures slipping through the hall beyond. Arya leaped forward and shoved Taze out of the way as metal gleamed and a knife flew through the air where his head had just been. They hit the ground and kept rolling until reaching the cover of one of the kitchen benches.

Almost as soon as they stopped, Taze was scrambling back to his feet and drawing his sword.

"*Help?*" Elendryl demanded. He was closer now, flying fast, barely minutes away.

"*Shadeweaver assassins are going after the warlords. I'm fine. Alert the other wyverns and get them to tell their riders to warn the fort if they haven't already, then eat anyone who tries to escape,*" she said tersely.

The answering snarl that ripped through her mind was truly fearsome.

She couldn't help a fierce grin. "*Leave at least one alive for questioning.*"

Two masked figures rounded the bench as Taze and Arya scrambled to their feet, forcing them back towards the unlit cookfires. Taze leaped forward, sword moving quicker than a blink, killing one before engaging the other. By then, two more were rounding the other side of the bench to come at Arya. She raised an arm and sent a burst of magic straight towards them. Blood sprayed as she ripped them to pieces.

Alarm bells started pealing.

Arya looked at Taze, dread settling in her stomach. If Leanir had already been here… "First priority is making sure the warlords are all safe. Darmanin is awake and well, he'll be fine. You go to Rorin, he should be okay with Essa. Both of you stay with him and sit tight. I'll check on my people and Hawkesdale, then head for SparrowWing."

"Aye." Taze took off at a sprint towards Rorin's quarters.

Arya took the stairs up two at a time, her sword lit with blue magic and lighting the way, following her link to Chiarn. Two dead Lances lay at the closed entrance to the corridor where her and Laskin's quarters were. As she ran, she kept her link to Essa alive, ensuring she and Rorin were not under attack. She skipped over the bodies, then shouldered through the door.

On the other side, she stopped dead at the sight of Laskin and Chiarn running her way. Laskin had his sword out, and Chiarn his shield. Relief cascaded through her. Leanir hadn't gone for Laskin. Dead bodies littered the hallway behind them, some of them badly burned. They both slid to a stop, relief filling their faces at the sight of her. She felt the same to see them unharmed.

She waved them after her. "Shadeweaver assassins are crawling all over the place. Rorin is fine, I'm going to check on the other warlords."

Laskin kicked one of the bodies. "I've never seen them operate with such a large force before."

Arya frowned. "True. Come on. Rorin and Dar are alright but we need to check on the others. Hawkesdale's closest, then SparrowWing."

A pitched battle was going in the corridor outside Hawkesdale's guest quarters. Gelfrey Hawkesdale was calmly ordering a row of Longbows to fire into the assassins battling it out with Amius SparrowWing and a handful of Firemen. Illia hovered behind her father, knife clenched in a white-knuckled grip.

Arya, Laskin, and Chiarn crashed into them from behind, killing a few before they were even aware of their presence. Hawkesdale drew his sword with a bellow, and waded in, taking two with one sweep. In seconds the fight was over.

"Appreciate the help," Hawkesdale grunted. "You okay?"

"We're fine," Arya said. "Amius, where's your father?"

"In our quarters, I think. I was here for a late supper with Illia when the attack started."

Arya turned and ran. Her legs burned as she pushed herself, already knowing it didn't matter how fast she was. As she turned the corner into the right corridor, she slid to a halt at the sight of several Lances standing guard and Darmanin emerging from Helden SparrowWing's room, a grim look on his face.

She sagged, breath coming out in a gasp. "Not Helden?"

"Clean kill, execution style." Darmanin confirmed. "No trace of any of the assassins when I got here a few minutes ago."

Arya swallowed, grief rising up in way that made that difficult. She'd *liked* Helden SparrowWing. Respected him. He'd risked everything to ride to her brother's aid. And now he was dead.

Running footsteps heralded Amius's arrival. He looked frantic, gaze shifting from Arya to Darmanin. "Where's my father?"

"I'm so sorry, Amius." Darmanin told him heavily.

Breath sobbing, Amius ran, pushing past Darmanin into his father's room. A moment later his cry of anguish echoed through the doors. Arya's heart clenched. She'd been in Amius' position before. She knew exactly how he felt.

Anger came on the heels of grief.

She locked gazes with Darmanin. "It was Leanir. He drew me outside while he was in here killing SparrowWing, then fled on his wyvern."

His eyes darkened at her words, and he didn't need to speak for her to know exactly what he was thinking.

More bootsteps thudded, and a fully armed and helmeted Andrian came running up the hall with a shield of Lances. "We've got Lances and Raiders combing the halls for any Shadeweavers that remain. Warlords Ravenstrike and Hawkesdale and their people are safe in the dining hall. The battalions surrounding the fort are on alert—every shield dressed and weaponed." He trailed to a halt as Amius stumbled out of Helden's room, face tear-streaked. "What happened?"

"Our father ordered this," Darmanin said grimly. "No doubt seeking to stop us before we forced him to parley. We send a message tonight. He decamps and marches for Gateport first thing tomorrow for a State Council or we attack and destroy his entire force."

He strode off, fury in every line of his body.

"There will be a reckoning for this," Arya promised Amius, then she turned and followed Darmanin.

***

Essa and Chiarn went aloft to patrol the skies, make sure the plains surrounding their army remained free of threats. It took several hours, but finally every corner, hallway and room of the fort was searched and found free of assassins. They then dragged the assassins' bodies into the entry yard and set them alight in a great burning pyre. The pyre was Arya's suggestion—let Mathas Crowtalon see what happened to his attempt to wipe them all out.

Arya sought Taze out in the crowd standing by the fire, speaking quietly, "Thanks for having my back out there. That knife would have gotten me good if I'd been alone."

"If you'd been alone, you wouldn't have left your back exposed." He smiled. "I was there, so you knew you could. I'm always going to have your back."

"And I'll always have yours, Taze Nameless," she promised. "Always."

They fell silent, each staring into the crackling flames and thinking their own private thoughts. Arya bit her lip as the stillness let her grief rise again. There was guilt too. Leanir was her Sky Lord, and she didn't have him under control. Worse, she'd made him an enemy by betraying him. SparrowWing might still be alive if she hadn't.

This time, though, Arya didn't let herself dwell on that. She'd decided to protect her son, and she stood by it. Wallowing in guilt would only hamper her, and if she was going to avenge Helden, she couldn't go back to the shell of herself she'd been until recently.

"You really think Crowtalon ordered the hit?" Hawkesdale broke the silence. He looked haggard, the death of an old friend hitting him hard.

"Who else benefits from the four of us being killed, Gelfrey?" Darmanin snapped. "Ranier didn't suddenly decide to take out half of Dunidaen's leadership for no reason."

"*There's no sign of alarm or alert in the army across the river,*" Rorin added, Taze translating. "*So, no assassins went after Mathas or Warlord Falconcrest.*"

Amius said noting, staring white faced into the flames. They'd bury his father properly in the morning. A grim silence descended. Arya left them to it, Darmanin falling into step with her as she walked back towards the fort. "I'll make sure my father answers for this."

"Leanir will answer too. I leave for Gateport in the morning." She looked at him. "It was a lot of Shadeweavers to send on a hit. They usually work alone, but I counted almost thirty bodies out there."

Darmanin stopped by the doorway. "My father is getting desperate."

"Maybe." She frowned.

Or maybe something else was going on with the Shadeweavers.

Chapter 37

Nobody slept that night. The rebel warlords' demand was sent to Mathas Crowtalon in the early hours before dawn and received a terse reply of concurrence. Raider scouts reported movement from the High Warlord's forces almost immediately, and as dawn broke over the horizon, most of his soldiers were already marching in the direction of Gateport.

Arya was awash with restlessness. Anger at Leanir beat at her self-control and she was hard pressed to ignore the urge to fly straight to Gateport. Except that was what he would no doubt be expecting. Best to let him sweat a little. Besides, she couldn't let revenge overshadow her goal—getting Rorin voted in as High Warlord and then winning the Dunidae as formal allies. She *had* to have their army behind her. For that, Arya needed to arrive in Gateport in proper diplomatic fashion. Not in a furious frenzy hunting a Shadeweaver assassin and terrifying everyone in the process.

Once that was done, she could focus on figuring out how to access the Inkweaver knowledge and build a functioning *cairdre*. Easy, achievable tasks. Arya huffed a bitter laugh and tried to fight off despair.

By tacit agreement everyone gathered in the fort's kitchen for a quick breakfast and a final hurried conference before departure. Darmanin was on his feet, clearly as impatient as she was to be gone. "We'll have to be careful arriving in Gateport," he said. "Mathas will try and set the residents against us—who knows what he'll tell them to make sure they're hostile towards us when we arrive. He'll be doing his best to poison the vicelords votes too."

"Not to mention sending more assassins after us," Hawkesdale said, his ebullient manner muted, his gaze on where Amius sat, eyes glassy, bowl of food untouched.

"I will sort that quickly," Arya promised, anger leaking through into her voice. "To that end, I'll be fast-marching to Gateport to get there ahead of all of you. By the time you arrive, you won't have to worry about Shadeweavers."

"I don't even want to ask." Hawkesdale grumbled.

Amius cleared his throat, some life coming back to his features. "Darmanin's point stands. The last thing we want is a fight on the streets of Gateport. Avoiding innocents getting hurt must be our first priority."

"It won't be my father's," Darmanin warned.

"Which is why we're forcing him out," Gelfrey grumbled as he rose to his feet. "Young Warlord SparrowWing is right. See you all in Gateport."

Darmanin followed Hawkesdale without another word.

Rorin made a face at Arya across the table. "*He's still angry at you, then?*"

"I think so." Arya sighed, then swiped a sweetbread from the table and dropped down beside Chiarn, chewing. Darmanin hadn't been anything but terse since she'd put her support behind Rorin for High Warlord.

"Arya, I wanted to show you something." Essa turned towards her, rolled up her left sleeve.

She gasped in surprise, tentatively reaching out to touch the whirls of ink on her friend's skin. The art was beautiful, running from her wrist to her elbow along the inside of her forearm.

"The story of our fight against the nazal," Essa murmured.

Arya smiled. "In your blood and bone. *Our* story now."

"It felt like the right time to start." Essa rolled down her sleeve and sat back.

Gaze lingering on Essa's arm even though the tattoo was now covered, Arya stole another piece of sweetbread and shot to her feet. "Come on Chiarn, Ess, we'd best go make sure Laskin has the army ready to start marching."

She stopped behind Amius's chair, squeezed his shoulder, and murmured. "You're going to make a great warlord, Amius, one that will honour your father's memory."

His shoulders straightened a little. "Thank you, Arya."

"See you in Gateport." Taze waved.

Arya smirked, looked between him and Rorin, trying to bring a little levity to the grim atmosphere of the room. "I look forward to discussing the lumber concessions you're going to offer me in return for my formal alliance, Ravenstrike."

"*We'll talk about fishing concessions when you have an army stronger than four hundred, Stormrider*." Her brother promptly signed back.

"Hilarious. Now get off your ass and start helping me change the world, little brother," she called over her shoulder as she left.

"Changing the world, is it?" Chiarn grumbled at her side, but then brightened. "Ooh, I could write a ballad about saving the world."

"No ballads, Chiarn. That's an order."

***

With each day that passed, Arya's urge to get to Gateport grew stronger. She distracted herself by focusing her full attention on her fledgling army.

She and Laskin roused the Andahari at dawn each morning, spending the hours pre and post march teaching them formation fighting—usually while Chiarn and Essa slept in. It made for long, exhausting days, but Arya found them all to be willing and hardworking. One of the discussions that repeatedly came up was whether to horse the rebels and turn them into a more mobile force like the Raiders.

"I don't think it's feasible, Lord Stormrider," Niallin said, not for the first time, as they watched drill one morning. "The only mounted Andahari warriors are the Horselords. It's been that way for generations."

"There are no Horselord rebels?"

"There are not, Lord Stormrider." There was a faint hint of something in Niallin's voice that made her curious. She thought it might be disdain. She filed that away for later consideration.

Laskin remarked, "Everyone can learn to ride, and this lot seem willing to do whatever we ask of them."

Niallin's face tightened, but Arya spoke before he could. "He's right, Niallin."

"Yes, Lord Stormrider, but learning to ride takes time, not to mention developing the skills to be able to ride and fight capably in the midst of a battle."

"That's also true," Arya said, her attention catching on two of the sparring Andahari. One was a woman her own age. Her short blonde hair was tied at the nape of her neck, and her face was a mask of concentration as she faced off against a bigger male opponent. She seemed vaguely familiar.

"If we're settled on an unhorsed force for now, I'll reach out to some old contacts among the retired Aggressors in Gateport," Laskin said. "We need trainers that are more familiar with fighting from the ground. I've been cavalry all my life."

"Good idea," Arya murmured, watching as the blonde woman dispatched her opponent. "Niallin, who's that?"

Niallin sighed. "Esdee Aurelian."

Arya started. "I recognise the name. Is that the same Esdee who was with the conscripts we freed on the road to Darkclaw?"

"That's right, Lord Stormrider. After I got the conscripts to a permanent safe house, she demanded to join us. She's desperate to prove herself and too reckless with it."

"She might need discipline, but she just defeated a taller, stronger, and more skilled opponent with relative ease," Arya said.

"Yes, without using proper style or footwork. She's lucky Antonn didn't take her head off."

Laskin stifled a cough. It might have been a snort.

"Wrong footwork?" Arya turned to Niallin. "What I saw was creative thinking employed to defeat a more skilled opponent."

"She got lucky." Niallin insisted.

Arya turned back to watch the woman. Even though the fight was over, she stood with a watchful air, hand clasped firmly around the hilt of her practice sword as if ready to use it again in a moment. "Laskin, if you're my general, you need an apprentice. She's it."

Laskin's eyebrows shot upwards. "What?"

"You heard me. Esdee is yours to train. If she can't make the grade, let her go, but I want her to have a chance."

He eyed her suspiciously. "And you're going to let me make that decision?"

"Just like Thiara Ravenstrike gave Desomer the latitude to kick me out," Arya promised.

"Works for me." Laskin saluted, nodded to Niallin, and headed towards Esdee.

Niallin turned to her, sputtering. "You can't just pluck an un-ranked girl out of her unit and make her apprentice to your general."

Arya watched Laskin speaking with Esdee, recognising the look on the woman's face as Laskin delivered the news. "On the contrary. That's exactly what I *can* do."

Niallin bowed his head peremptorily, tone curt. "We should end sparring for the morning and get moving."

"I agree. Go to it."

Niallin left, and Arya waited for Laskin to come over with Esdee. The woman's eyes shone, even though she was doing her best to hide it behind a mask of seriousness. She bowed. "Lord Stormrider."

"*Captain* Aurelian. General Carter has offered you a valuable opportunity. I advise you to take full advantage of it."

Esdee straightened, determination threading her voice. "I won't let you down, Lord Stormrider. I swear it."

"See that you don't."

Arya waited until she'd walked away, then looked at Laskin. "Niallin said the man she beat just now is named Antonn?"

"That's right, Antonn Eugenian. He's a quiet one. Haven't quite gotten his measure yet."

"Hmm. I'm going to keep an eye on him too."

"You do that." Laskin scowled. "How'd Niallin take the news about my new apprentice?"

Arya settled a look on him, recognising his tone. "What?"

He shrugged, scratched at his beard. "Nothing. I'd best go and deal with my new apprentice."

***

They made the distance to Gateport seven days after leaving Seelan, arriving as the mid-afternoon sun bathed the city. With only minimal training, Arya's Andahari weren't as sharp as Rorin's Raiders, but they looked impressive enough in their blue and grey. Arya wore her platinum chainmail over a blue, high collared tunic, and her silk Stormrider cape hung from her shoulders. Chiarn and Essa looked just as extraordinary, and Arya waved them to the front of the column. "Don't expect a warm welcome," she warned. Mathas, Falconcrest and their forces had been mounted, and would have arrived a few days ago. "No matter what reception we get, we stay calm and polite. Understood?"

"I've had tomatoes—and worse—thrown at me during a performance before," Chiarn said dryly. "I think I can manage whatever Mathas' Defenders or the Gateport residents try."

Essa smiled. "We'll be fine."

"Laskin, that goes for the army, too," Arya warned him. "I hold you accountable for their behaviour."

He scratched his beard. "I've given strict orders. I suppose we'll soon know how good they are at following them."

A breeze kicked up as they trotted towards the city gates. Arya's cape blew back from her shoulders, and the cool breeze rifled through her hair. She moved slowly, making sure the Defender guards on the gates had time to see them coming. She also wanted to take a good look at the place as they approached—wary of ambush. But Elendryl had soared over the city in the light of pre-dawn and seen no troop buildups or anything out of place. And now, as far as Arya could tell, there was only the usual complement of Defender guards patrolling the walls.

She reined in before the Defender captain that stepped out of the gate-house to greet her. He wore a grim and unwelcoming expression, saying nothing as he waited for her to announce herself.

"Lord Arya Stormrider of Andahar, with Lord Essa Inkweaver and Lord Chiarn Flamewielder." She thought she caught the man's mouth twitching as she reeled off the names, *definitely* spotted two Defenders peering out through the gatehouse windows. "I also have my general and twenty shields with me." That was well below the battalion allowed.

The captain sniffed, looked warily up at the sky as if searching for a wyvern, but then said. "Guest barracks have been set aside for your warriors." He gave terse instructions. "You and your Sky Lords will need to sleep there or find your own accommodations."

"Such a warm and welcoming host is your High Warlord," she remarked.

He merely spat and returned to the gatehouse.

Arya glanced over her shoulder, grinned at Laskin's scowl, then urged her horse through the gates and into streets far busier than Arya had ever experienced before.

Gateport was a busy city, always with lots going on, but the main street leading in from the main gate was *packed* with people. And they were all staring and pointing at the Andahari delegation.

"Oh shit," Chiarn muttered. "I think we're about to get stoned."

"No." Arya didn't get any sense of hostility. Just curiosity, and maybe a touch of wariness. "Laskin!" she snapped an order.

He immediately brought his horse up alongside hers. "Yes?"

"Pass the word down the column, *quietly*, that they're to smile, look friendly. Even wave a little."

"Right you are." He wheeled his horse.

Essa came alongside her then, keeping her voice low. "This crowd is here to see us, but for some reason they're not afraid or angry. You can work this to our advantage."

"Damn right I can. Chiarn, do that flirting with your smile thing to anyone who makes eyes at you. We're going to seduce this crowd."

He tossed back his head and laughed aloud. "Finally, Arya, you ask something of me that I'm good at."

Arya grinned, urged her horse forward again, keeping the mare to a trot, and bringing an easy smile to her face. At first, when she met someone's staring gaze, they immediately looked away, eyes going to their feet or the person next to them. But more times than not, their gaze swung back, and she smiled and nodded her head.

Occasionally they even nodded back.

And then Chiarn unslung the lute over his shoulder and started playing a merry tune—one of his most popular ballads that never failed to have feet tapping on the floor. A glance back showed the marching Andahari smiling from ear to ear, shoulders straight and a snap in their step. She heard a few '*May the waters you travel always be calm*' from her warriors to those waving.

Residents continued to duck out of shopfronts and inns, lining the sides of the streets. None tried to impede the passage of the Andahari. No insults were shouted. It was utterly unbelievable to Arya.

"Could they have heard about us defeating the invasion in the north?" Essa suggested. She too was smiling and waving—her genuine smile, the one full of her light and life.

"They've heard something." Arya said. "And I'd really like to know what it was. But I'll take it."

They made it to the barracks that had been set aside for the Andahari delegation without incident. The gates closed behind them, shutting out the crowds. With obvious relief, Laskin began getting the soldiers organised.

"Keep them in the barracks for now." Laskin was telling Etan as Arya dismounted. "That reception was better than I'd expected, but we can't rule out trouble."

"There are likely to be Aggressors and Knights about the city as well," Etan agreed. "Arya will have our heads if we let them provoke us into a fight again."

"Yes, she will," Arya said, making them both start and salute sharply. "Laskin, you and your warriors did an excellent job just now. Well done."

The grizzled veteran's habitual scowl dropped for a whole breath before reappearing. "Permission for a thorough search of these barracks before I let them all in?" he asked.

"Permission granted. I trust you to look out for them as you think best." Arya glanced at her Sky Lords. "Chiarn, Essa, and I will be at the Ravenstrike residence if you need us."

Leanir was going to hear word of their arrival any minute now.

***

Again, Arya encountered no trouble as the three of them rode through the darkening streets to the Ravenstrike townhouse, despite their appearance clearly marking them as magic-wielders. Once there, they left their horses with grooms in the stables and made straight for Rorin's study, where they gathered. Arya stood in the centre of the room, taking a deep breath.

She sank into her magic, brought to life the thread between her and Leanir. He was in Gateport, close enough for her to reach him and feel his snarling response. Ignoring it, she took hold of the bond and *compelled* him to come to her, using enough magic that he literally had no ability to refuse.

Then she opened her eyes, looked at the other two. "He's on his way."

Chapter 38

Arya knew Leanir was there before he soundlessly slid up the study window and slipped into the dark room. She spoke into the shadows, "Coming to kill *me* this time, Leanir?"

His soft snarl was the only sign he was disconcerted by her awareness of his presence. Flame flared and multiple lamps in the room lit up, filling the space with light and revealing the assassin one pace beyond the window. Chiarn stood at the door, Essa by the now-crackling hearth.

"Don't." Arya warned when the assassin made a move towards Chiarn. "He'll light you up before you get within ten paces of him."

"I warned you *never* to use your magic on me," Leanir's hand was on his knife, dark eyes glittering. Sweat slicked his skin, and his breath came fast. He'd fought hard against the compulsion, then.

"You lured Darmanin into a fight with the nazal and abandoned him to die. You murdered Helden SparrowWing. How did you think I was going to respond?" Arya kept her tone even, holding her anger and grief at bay.

"What do you *want?*" The words ripped from the assassin's mouth, vicious yet frustrated.

Arya couldn't help a flicker of empathy. Leanir was accustomed to having full control over every inch of his surroundings, who saw him, and who didn't. Yet with her he was vulnerable—he stood in a room where someone else held all the cards. It must be terrifying. So rather than taunt, she simply asked what she wanted to know. "Who contracted you to go after the warlords? Or was it your idea?"

"I don't know what you're talking about."

"You were there." When Leanir stayed silent, she let out a breath. "I need to know what you know, and I'll do whatever it takes to get it."

He bared his teeth. "Do your best."

At the doorway, Chiarn lifted a hand, and a ball of flame crackled into existence, spinning idly above his palm. Leanir glanced in his direction. The musician smiled. The fear with which he'd once regarded the Shadeweaver was gone.

"You've tried killing me before," Leanir sneered, looking back at Arya. "It didn't work."

Arya drew her dagger, quick as thought. Leanir, always faster, lifted his knife, but Arya reached for the thread between them and *stifled* him with ruthless ease. Her senses swam as he tried to use his magic on her, but she stifled that too. A moment later she had him pressed against the wall, her dagger at this throat. She pressed the tip hard enough against his skin to draw a pearl of blood. "I *can* kill you, Leanir," she murmured in his ear. "You can't best me anymore."

"I am owned by nobody," he spat, strong and determined to fight her.

"Wrong," she said quietly. Part of her hated what she was doing, hated using her magic to subdue him, but the rest of her remembered the sight of General Desomer falling of that horse, the arrow in his back. The feeling of Darmanin's life slipping away. Helden SparrowWing's canny mind and rigid honour. "Tell me what I want to know."

He writhed, but eventually bit out, "Some of the assassins are no longer under the control of the Shadeweaver leadership."

Arya's gaze narrowed. "What does that mean?"

Leanir smirked. "An anonymous entity has been trying to recruit them for some time. Ranier crushed their overtures, but when he vanished there was nobody strong enough to stop those that wanted to defect."

"Was it this *anonymous entity* that sent the assassins after the warlords in Seelan?"

A single nod. Fear and frustration and violence seethed in Leanir's brown eyes as he glared at her. The thread between them roiled with his emotion as he uselessly fought her domination. It made her sick, forcefully subjugating another human, the way the Nightstalker had dominated her. But her anger was bright and hot and part of her *wanted* Leanir to hurt. "Is it Mathas Crowtalon?"

"No." Leanir grated out. "It's Lucius Nightstalker."

Arya's eyebrows rose in genuine shock. She let go of her hold on the bond between them and stepped away, lowering her knife.

"Seems like maybe the Nightstalker wants Mathas Crowtalon as High Warlord," Chiarn drawled.

That was the most obvious conclusion. Arya wondered why. There *was* more to Leanir's story. He'd told her only the bare bones; she'd sensed him leaving things out, deliberately crafting his words. She tried to summon her resolve to force him again, but Essa spoke first.

"What do you know of Mathas' plans, Leanir?" Essa asked. "We'd expected a lot more hostility than we got when we arrived this morning. What's he up to?"

The assassin shrugged insolently, but couldn't help his gaze flickering to Arya's dagger. She sheathed it, then lifted her empty hands. "I will use force if I must. Now, the information Essa asked for will cost you nothing."

Leanir took a single step away from the wall. "Initially, it was the shortages. No wood coming from Ravenstrike, less wheat from SparrowWing. People were beginning to grumble, and rumours began spreading through the city that the shortages were due to an invasion in the northwest."

"And then?" Arya asked sceptically, sensing he wasn't telling the full story.

Leanir's jaw tensed, as if he was going to refuse, but she sent a warning shiver along the bond, and he capitulated. "Warlord SparrowWing started sending his injured Firemen for treatment in Gateport's healing centres. They were more than happy to talk about the invasion and how the Sky Lords were helping them fight, and win. The Firemen were *so* happy to talk that one gets the idea they were specifically ordered to do so."

"He was a canny old man, SparrowWing," Chiarn muttered in admiration before sadness flittered over his face. Essa's eyes sheened with tears at the mention of him.

"Keep talking," Arya snapped around her own grief.

"It didn't take long for Mathas to realise what was happening and lock down the hospitals with his Defenders, but by then it was too late. It didn't help that he's been away from the city so long. If he'd tried barring you entrance to the city today, he might have had a riot on his hands, and he knew it. He's in a vulnerable position," Leanir said.

"Ah, so that's why you went for Helden first. Mathas wanted revenge." Arya's voice shook with bitterness as she glanced at Essa and Chiarn. "We thought Mathas was vulnerable once before and look how that turned out."

"One might argue that his vulnerability combined with the Nightstalker controlling the Shadeweaver assassins seemingly on his behalf makes Mathas even more dangerous," Chiarn said, the ball of flame still spinning in his palm.

"Am I done here?" Leanir snapped.

Arya spun back to him. "No, you're not going anywhere. Where is the Nightstalker right now?"

Something flickered in Leanir's gaze.

"Are you *working* with him, Leanir?"

The assassin hissed. "I *told* you that you would regret betraying me."

Silence fell across the room as the full import of Leanir's words hit.

"You lured Darmanin into an ambush," Essa said in horror.

"I went there with him to kill the thing so it would stop hunting me. But it overwhelmed us. Darmanin was badly hurt, maybe dying, and I was next. So, I got into its head, convinced it I would help it and its master if it let me go."

"You handed the assassin cadre over to the Nightstalker," Arya said, realising what he'd been holding back. "And orchestrated the attack at Seelan on his behalf."

"You gave me up! I did what I had to do to survive." Spittle flew from Leanir's mouth. He seemed crazed, like a trapped animal, for the first time since Arya had met him losing his self-control.

"Where is the Nightstalker right now?" Arya asked again.

"He doesn't send me messages with updates, and you killed the nazal that was able to reach my mind." Leanir snapped, but Arya pulled tight on the bond, forcing him to say more. "I dream-walk the remaining nazal, a way of keeping myself safe. One of them is with him now."

"Where?" Arya demanded.

"Khadini. He has a purpose there." Leanir slumped, gasping, "I don't know what it is, so demand all you like, I can't tell you."

Arya froze. Khadini. Kirin. Somehow the Nightstalker knew Kirin was in Khadini.

In a burst of fear-fuelled panic, she grabbed Leanir by the arm and hauled him after her, using a combination of strength and magic to drag him down the stairs and into the kitchen cellar. "You try and escape, I'll kill you."

She slammed the door behind him, locked it, turned to Chiarn and Essa. "I have to go. Stay on that door until I send some Raiders here to watch it."

Essa ran after her. "Arya, what's going on?"

Arya's heart was beating too fast, sweat slicking her skin, panic pounding in her chest. But enough reason remained to realise that Essa could help. She leaned down, murmured the words so quietly nobody could hear. "Kirin is in Taskari."

Essa paled, but quickly her expression firmed. "Arya, you can't go."

"I *have* to go."

"You don't think the Nightstalker, Mathas, the Shadeweavers, have someone watching you here? Watching all of us? If you go, if you send *anyone*, they will know for certain Kirin is in Khadini. They'll know where." Essa grabbed her hand. "Hear me, Arya. You must stay still. It's the only way to protect his location."

"How did he find out, Ess?" She ran her hands through her hair. "Nobody knows."

"If he knew exactly where Kirin was, he wouldn't have bothered seeking the emperor's help. He might not even be certain about Khadini. It could be a ploy to draw you out. He could even be there for an entirely different reason to what you're assuming."

Arya paced, backward and forward, backward and forward. "Essa, I can't just *sit* here."

"You have to," Essa said, frowning in thought. "What if we distract the Nightstalker somehow, turn his attention from Khadini before he finds anything?"

Arya swore. Fear and worry gripped her chest so tight she couldn't think straight. "I need to *kill* Lucius Nightstalker, not distract him, but to do that, I desperately need an Inkweaver to teach me what I need to know. His weaknesses, his magic, all of it."

Essa placed a gentling hand on her arm. "All we need to do right now is distract him from hunting for Kirin."

The words and touch combined to calm Arya enough to take in a deep, steadying breath. An idea came to her then, one that fit nicely with the last resort plan she'd quietly been putting together for months. "You're right, we need to draw the Nightstalker's attention somewhere else. To *me*. I'm the greatest danger to him. I'm the one with magic and a wyvern, powerful enough now that I killed one of his monsters. So, we draw him to me. And then we ambush him."

Essa's eyes went wide. "You want to attack the Nightstalker *now*?"

"He has all the advantages over us. Strength, knowledge, power. Those aren't going to change, not anytime soon. We don't have time to wait and grow strong enough to face him. Therefore, we'll manufacture an advantage. Surprise."

"How?"

Arya stopped pacing. "We use Leanir. And we play Mathas Crowtalon at his own game."

Chapter 39

After a night spent pacing before her window in the barracks, thinking, planning—fighting terror at the thought of the Nightstalker so close to Kirin—Arya headed to the drill yard. But even the exertion of running laps failed to take the edge off her barely repressed fear. She couldn't stop worrying about whether the impromptu Council session to overthrow Mathas would happen soon enough, before the Nightstalker found anything meaningful in Khadini. And if it didn't, would Kulan see him coming in time to get their son out?

She had to keep repeating Essa's warning over and over, and it was just barely enough to hold her from flying straight to Taskari. To hold to the plan she'd sketched out overnight and already put in motion.

"Care for a sparring partner?"

She looked up, surprise flashing at the sight of Darmanin approaching. For a moment her worry vanished. "It's good to see you. You've just arrived?" If he was here, the other warlords would be soon, too, which meant the High Warlord vote would not be far off.

He nodded. "I wanted to check in with you, make sure you hadn't experienced any problems with my father?"

There was no smile, and his voice was more reserved than usual, but he'd come immediately to see that she was okay, and Arya took heart from that. "It's only been a day, but no issues so far," she said. "You?"

He let out a confused breath. "I deliberately arrived at dawn to avoid any unpleasantness, but the Defenders on the gates were polite, and none of the people we passed in the streets looked upset at our presence."

"We got crowds turning out to see us when we marched in, and there were no jeers or insults. Even the occasional wave." Arya grinned as his eyebrows shot skyward, and then explained what Leanir had told her. "It was a clever move by SparrowWing."

Sadness softened Darmanin's usual grim expression. "He is a great loss. I miss him, funnily enough, even though we never spent a huge amount of time together."

Arya looked away, chest tight. Darmanin frowned. "Everything okay? You seem on edge?"

"Aren't you?" she deflected. "Four years ago, we were in almost this exact same position with your father, and look what happened."

His eyes were bleak. He remembered all too well. "I left two battalions of Lances a few hours' march out of the city. I thought it would be wise to have soldiers close by in case of trouble. Rorin and Amius planned to do the same."

Arya lifted her blade, tried for a smirk, but mostly failed. "Since you're here, I could use a distraction. Up for it?"

He shifted into a fighting stance. "Last time was a draw, if I recall correctly."

"I was easy on you."

His mouth curled into the smile she loved. "I was easy on you, too."

They moved at the same instant, blades leaping out and crashing together with a loud ringing. Arya disengaged, dodged to the side and swung her blade at his head. He brought his up to counter, and the cazaix crashed together again. This time Darmanin disengaged first and lunged at her with a dagger in his left hand. Knowing she wouldn't be able to dodge it in time, Arya used a touch of magic to stop his thrust. Surprisingly, he countered her magic with his own, and she was forced to use a surprising amount of effort to stop the blow. They broke off and circled each other.

"I learned some things from Essa while I was recovering at the citadel," he said. "I thought about asking Elder Salyarin, but he didn't seem to like me."

"Show me," she challenged.

Only Arya's experience and more advanced training allowed her to hold out against Darmanin. She had to fight with every scrap of skill she possessed, and even then she was astonished to find that he was slowly overwhelming her. This realisation sparked her competitive nature, and she re-doubled her efforts, trying to regain the upper hand. Their magic clashed, again and again, blue sparks meeting inky blackness, neither giving way to the other.

The deadlock was broken by the rustling of wings in the sky above. When Arya saw four Etherean, Salyarin and Cirilla among them, her mouth dropped open in astonishment. Quickly followed by dread. After what she'd set in motion the previous night, this was the last place they should be.

"Etherean in Gateport," Darmanin murmured in similar astonishment.

Arya sheathed the sword and went to greet them. With Salyarin and Cirilla were two heavily armed winged women. She assumed they were bodyguards. "Elder. Commander Cirilla. I'm surprised to see you. Gateport is still not a safe place for Etherean."

"Lord Stormrider. Warlord Crowtalon. We understand the risk." Salyarin let out a breath, as if expelling a heavy weight on his shoulders. "But with you taking up the mantle of heir to Andahar, events across our lands are moving quickly. It's time for us to reengage with the world—and the Dunidaen leadership vote is critical for our safety and our future. So, I decided to attend."

Darmanin spoke, "I shall arrange a meeting of our allies at my residence this evening, if that suits you? It will allow you to meet them all in person."

"I would appreciate that," Salyarin said stiffly. "Lord Stormrider, I must ask a favour. May Cirilla and I and our guards stay in your barracks while we are in Gateport? I would avail ourselves of your protection."

"As my allies, you have my protection always." Arya bowed her head slightly. "But my advice would be to leave. I applaud your intentions, but Mathas Crowtalon cannot be trusted, and I'm not confident I can guarantee your safety."

"Our safety is not your responsibility. We do as we must," Salyarin said with quiet dignity.

Arya swore under her breath. The Etherean had never taken her warnings seriously. "Then of course you may stay here in the barracks."

"Thank you." Cirilla said, genuine relief crossing his face.

Darmanin cleared his throat. "I will see you this evening."

"Thanks, Dar." Arya smiled at him.

He gave her his little smile, bowed to the Etherean elder, and strode off.

Arya turned back to Salyarin, still smiling, but the elder's expression had turned strangely cold. She turned to Cirilla. "If you take your two guards through that door there, one of my captains will see you to comfortable quarters."

Cirilla and the two guards peeled off towards the barracks, and Arya waited until they were out of earshot before speaking. "I'm not sure exactly what your problem is now, Elder, but I can see you have something to say."

Salyarin's voice was as cold as his expression. "You've become his lover, haven't you?"

Arya choked on a laugh. "What? Why would you think that?"

"He is descended from the Nightstalker," Salyarin said. "He has the instability of that monster's magic running through his blood."

"Darmanin is a good man. He is not his grandfather."

"He is powerful enough to defeat you!" Salyarin insisted. "Why can't you see that? He is your weak point, the chink in your armour. One wrong step, and he becomes that which will destroy you. And he loves you, which makes him even more dangerous to you."

"One wrong step?" She stared at the elder in disbelief. "He would *never* hurt me."

"You can't know that."

"Yes, I can. Lucius Nightstalker did not become an evil monster just because he loved a woman and lost her. He was obviously ambitious, and powerful, and I suspect there was always a touch of madness in him. He made choices to become what he is now. It didn't just *happen* to him," Arya said heatedly. "And you know nothing of how Darmanin feels about me, just as you know nothing of what I feel for him. You were the one that told me, when I was only sixteen years old, that I had to protect him. You told me that was more important than anything."

"So?"

Arya's temper snapped. "What did you think would happen when you threw together a lonely boy and a girl desperately wanting a family? Of course we became close. It was never my idea, Elder, it was yours." She met the Elder's gaze firmly. "I have faith in Darmanin. Nothing you say will change that."

"I don't think you understand."

Arya raised a hand. "We are allies, not master and subordinate. I have much greater concerns taking up my attention right now, Elder, and Darmanin betraying me isn't even close to the top of the list. Now, I will fetch my general and then we can leave."

She spun on her heel and stalked off towards Laskin's quarters, fury still simmering in her veins. She was sick of Salyarin's accusations.

Darmanin would never betray her. *Never.*

***

When they arrived at the Crowtalon residence that evening—the icy silence between Arya and Salyarin on the way causing Cirilla and Laskin to share multiple wide-eyed looks—Arya pulled Darmanin aside. "Is there somewhere we can have a quiet word? You, Rorin, Taze, Chiarn, and Essa. Laskin too."

He frowned. "Everything okay?"

She let out a shaky breath. "There's something we need to discuss."

"It might be best after dinner, once the others have left, if you want it to be discreet?"

"Thanks, Dar."

Arya made an attempt at eating her meal, but her stomach was in knots, and she barely tasted anything. Hawkesdale, Illia, and Amius seemed fascinated to meet the Etherean, though perhaps a little put off by their chilly politeness. Rorin and Andrian kept the conversation flowing easily, however, and Arya hoped none noticed her quietness.

Finally, it was over, the warlords and Etherean trickling out—Darmanin sending a shield of Lances to escort the Etherean safely to the Andahari barracks—leaving Arya with Rorin, Taze, Laskin, and her *cairdre*. Darmanin led them downstairs to a basement level. A single, low-ceilinged hall led to a thick stone door. Inside, a single table stood in the centre of a medium-sized room, with the only other furniture a scattering of chairs.

"The walls are thick stone, and once the door is shut, you can't hear through it, so nobody can spy on us," Darmanin explained. "Andrian will be upstairs and make sure nobody—"

Boots echoed outside and Andrian himself appeared. "Sorry to interrupt, but the Icefolk prince just arrived. Their ship docked earlier this evening, apparently. Your dinner invitation was awaiting him at his residence."

Darmanin glanced at Arya, question in his eyes. She hesitated, biting her lip, "Send him down."

While they waited, Rorin glanced around the room wide-eyed, signing. "*You Crowtalons really are a grim lot. Was this once a dungeon or something?*"

Darmanin smiled slightly. "Not in my time, but very possibly in the past. I wouldn't have put it past my father to lock people in here. Let's take a seat."

At'eir appeared a few moments later, snowy braids barely fitting below the doorframe, his fierce features creasing into a wide smile at the sight of Arya. "Lord Stormrider. I am glad to see you here and safe."

"Er'fin At'eir." She held her palm out, waiting for him to press his against hers before bowing her head. "You didn't have any troubles sailing the storm channel?"

"It was bumpy but fine. I'm sorry we didn't arrive in time for your dinner, Warlord Crowtalon." His gaze took in the room. "What are we discussing?"

"Please, have a seat." Arya took the chair beside Laskin, Essa, and Chiarn on her right. Rorin and Taze arranged themselves next to Andrian. At'eir sat opposite. Her leg jiggled constantly until Rorin gave her a concerned glance and she forced herself to stop. Darmanin took the final chair.

"I asked to speak with you tonight because there's something you all need to know." Arya took a steadying breath. "The immediate future is uncertain, and now that I've declared myself to the Nightstalker, he will come for me, and there's a better than decent chance I won't survive it." She didn't mention that she was actively trying to bring that about. Dread climbed up through her bones. She swallowed the fear away. Keeping Kirin safe was everything.

"That's all very morbid," Chiarn drawled, but the rest of the room looked sober.

She swallowed, clenching and unclenching her sweaty hands. Once she did this, there was no going back. But it was a calculated risk, one she'd gone over and over and judged necessary. "I need to clear up the matter of my succession. The Stormrider claim on the Andahari throne is tenuous at best, and should I die, all hope to dislodge the Nightstalker would die with me."

"You are right," At'eir said gravely. "What do you propose to do about it?"

"I haven't named an heir because it was too dangerous to do so. It still is, but the days ahead grow only more dangerous. I cannot guarantee my survival, and so you, those I trust with my life, need to know my chosen heir. This way you can protect them if the worst happens."

"How can you name an heir?" Darmanin asked, echoing the looks of puzzlement around the table. "There are no other living Stormriders, and only a Stormrider with Sky Lord potential could hope to successfully challenge for the Andahari throne."

Arya met the eyes of all those gathered. "There is another Stormrider. My son, Kirin."

A stunned silence descended on the room. Essa was the only one who didn't look completely and utterly dumbfounded. She gave Arya a little smile of support.

"*A son?*" Rorin asked wonderingly. "*How? When? Why did you never tell us?*"

"I couldn't. The threat that faces him..." Arya steadied herself, forced the words out around the fear collapsing her chest. "The Nightstalker knows he exists, but not where he is, and that's because until now, only four other people knew of his location. If I die, then you must find him, keep him safe and protected, but otherwise he stays out of all of this."

A chair scraped against the stone as Darmanin pushed back his chair, then stood and walked from the room, the door slamming closed behind him.

Arya flinched, then swallowed. "Kirin is still young. If the worst happened before he is old enough, then Essa Inkweaver is my chosen regent. I want all your agreement—that if I die, you follow Essa until Kirin is of age."

Essa gaped at her. Shock and horror and pride all reverberated down the thread between them.

"I agree." Chiarn spoke first.

"*As does Ravenstrike,*" Rorin signed.

"I am your ally, and I will follow your wishes." At'eir inclined his head.

"Laskin?"

He smiled sourly. "Nobody's going to get to you before getting through me, so it's a moot point. If you die, it'll be because I'm already dead."

"He's as maudlin as you are," Chiarn grumbled. "Is that a pre-requisite for becoming a member of your inner circle, Arya?"

"If only four people know of Kirin, how did the Nightstalker learn of his existence?" At'eir asked.

"It's a long story, and unimportant," Arya said tiredly. "But I'm doing everything I can to ensure he never learns Kirin's location. Or destroy him before he can learn it."

"*That's why you decided to do all this.*" Rorin signed with muted gestures, gaze full of understanding. "*Take the throne, destroy the Nightstalker? For Kirin.*"

She have a sharp nod. "He'll never be safe while the Nightstalker lives."

Essa glanced at her across the table, looking troubled. Arya hadn't told them her plan to get the Nightstalker out of Khadini, to try and ambush him, and had asked her friend to keep it quiet. For her plan to work, none of them could know what was coming. Arya let out a sigh. "That was all. Let's disperse before someone wonders what we're doing down here so long."

Everyone nodded, and began standing, trickling out of the room, a grim mood weighing down the atmosphere.

"*Arya, a moment?*" Rorin asked as the others left.

"What is it?"

"*I won't ask questions, because the less I know the safer Kirin will be. Just know that I can't wait to meet my nephew, so please hurry up and destroy the Nightstalker.*" Fear and pain flashed over his face. "*But if anything happens to you, I will protect Kirin as I would my own Anji. My word on it.*"

Tears welled in her eyes as she threw her arms around him. "Thank you."

"*I love you, Arya.*" Rorin signed. "*I'll always be here for you.*"

Essa waited in the hall outside. Rorin gave her a smile as he passed her, leaving them alone in the dim space.

"I'm sorry, Ess," Arya said immediately. "I know I promised you your cottage, but if anything happens to me, Kirin will need someone to rule for him. It's only until he's of age, and then you'll be free. I swear it."

Essa merely stared at her. "You truly think *I'm* the best person to be his regent?"

"Without a doubt in my mind. He needs to learn to be a good ruler, smart and compassionate and strong. That's you, Ess. I know if I leave Kirin and the Andahari in your hands, they'll be fine. Better than fine."

Essa moved suddenly, wrapping Arya in a hug and whispering, "Please don't die."

"I'll do my best not to." Arya held her tightly.

***

Arya went from the Crowtalon residence straight back to the windowless room in the Andahari barracks where she'd moved Leanir. Carrying a tray of food from the kitchens with her, she opened the door, placed it on the ground before him, then closed the door behind her.

"I already did as you asked. What do you want now?" Even now, none of Leanir's defiance was gone. His teeth were bared, violence glittering in his brown eyes.

"You want to survive, and I can give you the best chance of that." She pushed the tray closer, sat down cross-legged before him. "You and I are going to come to a new deal. And then I'm going to open that door and let you walk free."

Chapter 40

A day passed. Two. Three. Then the day of the Council finally dawned. The hours dragged unbearably. It felt too much like the same night four years ago for Arya's comfort. Once again, she was trying to turn the tables on Mathas Crowtalon. It made her skin crawl. She'd failed last time.

The streets were quiet as dusk fell, and then almost empty by the time night settled over the city. The High Warlord's Defenders patrolled in large numbers. All the warlords' soldiers were confined to barracks until dawn. Crowtalon, Ravenstrike, SparrowWing, and Hawkesdale were on high alert. A signal system of torches had been set up across the city so each could communicate with the other if the need arose.

As evening approached, Arya dressed in every bit of finery she had, then paced her room before the windows, unable to sit still.

"Arya, you ready?" Laskin called through the door as he knocked. He frowned when she opened it. "Something wrong?"

"It's nothing." She shook her head. "Let's go."

Downstairs, Chiarn and Essa waited. The two Sky Lords were glowing in their full Sky Lord mail and capes. Laskin looked dashing in his blue general's cloak. And then, a shadow slipped through the door. Laskin didn't see anything, but both Chiarn and Essa glanced that way.

"You came." Arya was surprised, despite herself.

"I gave my word," Leanir bit the words out, and Laskin started and swore. "Any update?"

Leanir's mouth tightened. "They're doing as you hoped for."

Arya took a deep breath, trying to settle her nerves, then strode out into the yard, Laskin beside her, the others falling in behind. "The High Warlord only prohibited the States' forces from leaving barracks tonight, correct? He didn't impose a curfew on any of the foreign warriors?"

Laskin scratched his beard. "Technically, no, but it was heavily implied."

"Understood," Arya said, gaze shifting to Esdee, who waited at the gates. The woman came over quickly when Arya gestured. "Ready our warriors and have them prepared to move to the Council chamber at speed."

Esdee saluted. "Consider it done, Lord Stormrider."

"If anything happens tonight, and I sound the alarm, I want our entire force running for the Council chamber. You are to ignore any commands from the Defenders, and fight through them if necessary."

"Nothing will prevent us coming to your aid," Esdee promised.

"Good." Arya's shoulders relaxed slightly. At least now she had some contingency if things turned badly. "We should go."

***

The domed State Council chamber was ringed with Defenders when Arya's retinue arrived. She could still feel Leanir's presence nearby, but he'd melted away as they approached the lit grounds of the Council enclave. A Defender shield captain came up to demand their identities.

"I am Lord Arya Stormrider of Andahar," she said coolly. "Lord Flamewielder and Lord Inkweaver accompany me."

"Of course, my Lord," he stuttered and stepped back with alacrity.

"*Stay out of sight but be ready,*" Arya instructed Elendryl as they dismounted.

"*Close,*" he promised.

"This feels just like last time," Laskin muttered as they walked up the steps.

"Your skills of observation astound me, old man."

"She likes to do risky, foolhardy things," Chiarn chimed in.

Essa stepped up to Arya as they paused at the entrance, one of her hands unconsciously resting on the hilt of her knife. "Are you sure about this?"

"It's too late to back out now, Ess," Arya murmured. "Laskin, you'll stay out here, watch our backs?"

"Always." He nodded.

"Here goes nothing," she said as they walked into the domed chamber.

***

A long table for the warlords sat on a low dais at the far end of the Council chamber. Torches lining the circular walls glimmered orange against the polished oak floor. It looked almost identical to the night Arya would never forget, so much so that nausea curdled in her stomach. Rows of chairs to accommodate all the vicelords lined up before the dais.

The warlords and many vicelords were already there and the hall bustled with attendees. Arya entered first. Her Sky Lords trailed with Laskin. A quick glance showed At'eir with six of his warriors seated on the right side of the room. Salyarin and Cirilla and their guards sat with them. Clerks of the Council were present to take notes, and several Defenders stood at each of the three exits.

Sweat slicked her skin under her clothes. She was gambling with so much. Could she figure out some way to get the Etherean and Icefolk out of the chamber before Mathas made his move? Because she had no doubt in her mind he would make a move.

Arya took a steadying breath. It was different this time. *This* time she'd engineered what was coming.

But that didn't mean she could handle it. Or that everyone here would survive it.

Arya focused Kirin in her mind. Keeping him safe. This was the only way.

"Mathas Crowtalon," Arya arrived at the dais, refusing to bow her head or use his title. None of the warlords were yet sitting. The muttering and conversation had faded as she made her way through the room, all the attention turning to the front.

His face tightened. "You will show respect in this forum and address me by my title."

"I don't recognise you as High Warlord of Dunidaen," she replied coolly.

There was an immediate outcry from Falconcrest, and even Eaglesoar muttered angrily under his breath.

"I am here tonight to demand that Mathas Crowtalon be removed from his position, and that a vote be held for another to take his place," Arya continued, speaking to the group of warlords, voice pitched loud enough the vicelords nearby could hear too.

"A foreign leader has no voting right in this Council," Falconcrest blustered.

"No, but I do," Darmanin said. "Crowtalon formally puts forward a motion to have Mathas Crowtalon removed from the position of High Warlord."

"*Ravenstrike seconds that motion.*" Rorin stood also, Taze translating for him.

"Let the record state that Er'fin At'eir of the Icefolk also demands the resignation of Mathas Crowtalon." The Icelands prince came to his feet, his imposing height only adding to the effect he had on those in the room.

"As do the Etherean of the Diamondfang," Salyarin said, wings flared to make himself bigger and more imposing.

"This is absurd." Eaglesoar sounded disgusted. "None of you have any say in how Dunidaen is run. And you, Ravenstrike and Crowtalon, should be ashamed of yourselves for allying with such people."

"Such people?" Darmanin raised an eyebrow. "I prefer to treat our foreign allies with respect, Warlord Eaglesoar. No matter what you might think of them, they are here today to help us."

"Enough," Surprisingly, it was Amius SparrowWing that spoke up. His face was gaunt, tired from grief, but his father's steel shone in his eyes. "Four warlords have called for a High Warlord vote, and so by Dunidae law we must hold one. Let's not pretend we all didn't know this is why we're here tonight. It was what we agreed to in Seelan."

Silence fell over the chamber as everyone looked towards Mathas. His face was composed, though anger flashed in his sunken eyes. "You're right, of course, SparrowWing. We may as well begin proceedings. Guards, the doors please," he said.

The Defenders moved to place heavy bars on all three doors leading into the chamber, preventing anybody from the outside gaining entrance. Or anyone inside leaving.

Gelfrey Hawkesdale growled. "Planning to keep us all locked in here until we change our minds, Mathas? It will make no difference; the majority of the warlords are against you."

"*He's right. We face too great a threat in the north to waste time with a High Warlord who refuses to defend our borders,*" Rorin signed, Taze translating for him as always.

Mathas said nothing. He simply gave them all a small smile. Arya got the impression he was waiting for something. She braced herself. The torches lining the hall flickered, and half of them died with a puff of smoke.

Something moved at the far end of the circular chamber, in the shadows by the unlit torches. Arya's hand fell to the hilt of her sword. A figure stepped into the light, slowly making his way toward the dais.

Lucius Nightstalker.

Vicelords, clerks, they all scrambled backward without a word, the aura of power surrounding the Nightstalker a physical presence that effectively *repelled* them. He was tall, with powerful shoulders and neat, slicked-back raven hair. With every step, a shadow swirled, and Arya could feel the man's magic, and his sublime control over it. Doubt surged. What had possessed her to think she could do this?

"*Elendryl?*"

"*Danger?*"

"*Speak to the wyverns. Tell them to tell their riders to do nothing.*"

Resistance.

"*Tell them that I order them, as their leader, to do nothing until I tell them. Essa knows what to do. They must protect the warlords and the others. Do it quickly, Elendryl. The Nightstalker is here.*"

A flare of fear, then a confused image. "*Xaphistryl?*"

"*I don't know where she is, so be wary and stay out of sight.*"

"Rorin, Taze, get the warlords and vicelords out of the way and then try to get those doors opened," Arya said tightly, eyes on the approaching form of the Nightstalker. He seemed to her like a venomous snake ready to strike at any second. "Quickly now."

She stood before the dais, trying to hold the Nightstalker's attention, while behind her Rorin and Taze did as she asked. Eaglesoar demanded to know what was going on, but Hawkesdale snapped at him to shut his mouth and move.

In her peripheral vision Arya saw Rorin and Taze begin herding the attendees into the shadows along each side of the chamber. Essa and Chiarn moved to stand protectively in front of them, but made no attempt to join Arya. Her gaze shifted into the shadows of the balcony directly above, where her magic told her Leanir crouched, bow drawn and ready. Would he hold to his word?

Only Mathas remained on the dais now, Arya standing before it.

Lucius Nightstalker halted, his presence reverberating deep in her magic like a blight. Boots sounded, and the ring of a cazaix blade sounded beside her. Darmanin's presence dispelled some of her fear, and she drew her own blade.

"Do as I ask, Darmanin. He doesn't know who you are, and we need to keep it that way," she said in a low voice. "Trust me, please."

She felt his hesitation in the silence that followed, but then he stepped away to join Essa. Arya had her full Sky Lord *cairdre* in the room with her for the first time ever.

That had to count for something.

The Nightstalker cocked his head, silver eyes amused. "Arya Stormrider. Well met. I must say, you look better than the last time I saw you. Less broken. Much ... shinier."

His voice was smooth and edged with magic, his words cutting easily through the cavernous room. She said nothing, simply watched him, waiting for his move. His gaze narrowed, and one of his fingers twitched. The great table on the dais rose into the air, flew through the room and slammed into the wall of the Council chamber. In quick succession the seven chairs followed, most splintering on impact. Arya could almost taste the fear leaking from the gathered warlords and vicelords at the Nightstalker's display of magic.

"Impressive," Arya said dryly, trying to give herself time to plot the right course. Of all the things Mathas could have pulled, bringing the Nightstalker here, into his own city, was despicable. Yet she'd been banking on him making that decision once Leanir got into his head, amplified his fear, planted the suggestion of calling upon the Nightstalker for help. "Did you come here just to throw the furniture about like a child?"

He smiled. "I'm here to kill you, the rest of your paltry *cairdre*, and finally your child, and end the Stormrider name forever. Your High Warlord helpfully promised to lure you here in return for keeping his power and his country."

"He did, did he? That's not a surprise. Mathas Crowtalon is a traitorous snake." She cocked her head. "But who do you think planted that idea in his head? I've been expecting you, Lucius."

Something rippled across his face. It was fast, so fast she wasn't sure she caught it. And then he was laughing softly. "I'm not afraid of your *cairdre*."

Arya attacked, leaping at him with her sword aimed at his heart. The Nightstalker blocked it without any apparent effort, then employed his magic to send her flying across the room, just as he'd done with the tables and chairs. Arya hit the wall hard, ignored the pain shooting through her back and leaped straight back to her feet.

Lucius followed up his attack with a bolt of black lightning.

How...?

A sharp tug in her chest—Essa—shocked her out of stunned stupor at the sight of the Nightstalker using what had to be Stormrider magic. She managed to dive to her left just in time, and it passed by inches from her, crashing into the wall with an electrical hiss.

Instead of following with another attack, the Nightstalker watched her, a small smile on his face, like a cat toying with a mouse. That smile was so familiar it made her stomach turn. For the first time, she was truly aware of Darmanin's link to this monster.

Arya's thoughts raced. She had to lull him into a false sense of security, make him think she was weakened. She came to her feet, slightly exaggerating how hard it was, and hoping her *cairdre* continued to do as she'd asked. They were her trump card. Another bolt of lightning came for her. She leaped to the side, hitting the floor and rolling away. More dark lightning followed. She smelled sulphur.

Arya rolled to her feet as another blast came, this one too quick to avoid. Instinctively she raised her sword, catching the lightning on the cazaix blade. With a well-practised move, she spun the sword and tossed it away, sending the lightning with it. Continuing her motion, she leaped directly at the Nightstalker, pulling her dagger from its sheath.

He was too fast. Just as she reached him, he drew his own dagger and stabbed upwards into her chest. It caught in her mail, not getting through, but winding her with the force of the blow. Arya hit the floor, and he sent her flying across the room again. She slammed into the wall, banging her left shoulder badly.

Arya swore, cradling her shoulder. This wasn't going to work. Little tendrils of despair started to spread through her. The Nightstalker began laughing, a low, menacing chuckle. Could the Sky Lord be genuinely mad? "And this is all I am confronted with? I had expected better from the scion of House Stormrider."

The contempt in his words sparked Arya's temper. As always, anger gave her strength, and she struggled determinedly to her feet, picking up her sword. Soon she was facing the Nightstalker again. "You can't compel me anymore, can you? You haven't tried, which tells me you no longer have power over me." She spat the blood from her mouth. "I'm not dead yet, Lucius. Far from it."

"Is that so?"

Arya's instincts tingled, but before she could react, an arm wrapped around her chest from behind. In the next breath the edge of a blade pricked against the skin of her throat.

Mathas Crowtalon hissed, "Don't move, or I'll slit your throat wide open."

Arya turned rigid. Her skin crawled at the sensation of Mathas Crowtalon's breath on her neck. The Nightstalker laughed again. His mouth curled into contempt. "Kill her and complete our deal, High Warlord. Dunidaen will be all yours."

"Kill her and you both die!"

The words thundered through the room, full of enraged fury. Arya risked turning her head just slightly enough to see Darmanin had stepped forward, sword raised. Cold anger was etched in every line of his face and body. And his magic—his magic *vibrated* from him, unmistakable to anyone looking his way.

He'd just revealed himself as a Sky Lord to everyone. For her.

Lucius spun, a triumphant hiss coming out of his mouth, silver eyes wide with triumphant delight. "Ah, my young heir finally shows himself, just as I'd hoped. I have been searching for you for some time."

"Let. Her. Go." The words were pure ice.

"*Join me, and I will let her go, I promise you.*" Arya winced as the words speared into her mind and Darmanin's, Lucius' magic seductive and compelling. "*You have power, I can feel it. If you joined with me, we would be an unstoppable force.*"

Darmanin didn't blink. "Let her go, or I will kill you."

"*Join me, and you will be free to have her,*" Lucius continued. "*I know what it's like to fear losing something you love more than life itself. I know the blackness that consumes you at the mere thought of that loss.*"

Darmanin's expression didn't change. Arya was impressed by his control at the same time as she wondered how much of an impact the Nightstalker's words were having. In a flash of inspiration, she reached for the thread between her and Darmanin. She couldn't talk to him directly, not with words, but maybe she could...

Darmanin blinked. A shiver returned across the thread. Confusion. Arya swore. She was terrible at subtlety, and they hadn't worked on this enough. She tried again, hoped that it worked. Ignored how much of Darmanin's fear she'd also felt in that moment of connection. Then she tried to draw the Nightstalker's attention. "Leave him alone," she snapped, ignoring the feeling of Mathas' blade biting into the skin of her throat.

The Nightstalker didn't even turn her way. "Join me, and you save her. Join me, and you never have to fear for her again." Speaking aloud, his voice was utterly compelling, seductive, as he focused his entire attention on Darmanin. "Refuse me, and she has to die. I have no other choice."

Darmanin flinched. It was miniscule, but they all saw it. His grip on his sword became white-knuckled.

"*You can have her forever*," Lucius whispered into their minds.

Darmanin's eyes closed, and it was a long moment before they opened again.

"*Come Darmanin, this is what you want more than anything. I know it. I can see into your heart.*"

"You know nothing," Arya shouted.

"You *are* nothing," he dismissed her.

"*Arya!*"

Elendryl filled her thoughts with a quick flash of images. It took her a mere heartbeat to process what he was telling her, and then, she reached for her *cairdre*, bidding them wait, just one more moment.

Then, with the strength of her wyvern's presence flooding her, she *finally* thrust her elbow deep into Mathas' chest before wrenching herself away from him. At the very same moment, the hand holding the knife at Arya's throat burst into flames. Mathas screamed in agony and stepped back as white-hot fire engulfed his arm. In a matter of moments, his entire body became wreathed in flame.

"Now!" Arya bellowed.

Chiarn stepped forward, arms spreading wide, letting loose an almighty shout. A wall of flame encircled the Nightstalker and bore down on him. The Nightstalker raised his own hands, spread them wide, and the flame halted progress.

The Flamewielder and Nightstalker strained against each other.

An arrow whistled through the chamber, cleared the flames, then was pushed aside with magic an instant before it hit Lucius. Concentration narrowed the Nightstalker's expression, but he was still holding Chiarn back easily enough. Another arrow, another deflection. And another. Arya felt Leanir's frustration pulse through their bond. He'd *never* missed a target before.

Arya pulled on her thread to Chiarn, felt his assent, and leaped for the Nightstalker. Chiarn dissolved the flame as she swung her blade at the Nightstalker's throat. Another arrow flew through the opening.

Lucius parried her attack, stepped aside from the arrow, and dropped back into fighting stance. His speed and magic were incredible, far more than she'd imagined. How could he have so many abilities, wield them so seamlessly?

Flames crackled as Chiarn brought it back to life, their heat slicking her skin with sweat. Arya hefted her blade to try another killing blow, but the Nightstalker's power wrapped her, holding her still as he hissed inside her head. *"I'm going to have Dunidaen soon, Stormrider, especially now the Khadini emperor has agreed to ally with me. Once that happens, your child can't hide from me for long. You can try all the ambushes you want, but you and your* cairdre *don't have enough to defeat me. You know that as well as I do."*

Arya froze with shock. He *hadn't* been in Khadini looking for Kirin, he'd been negotiating with…

He laughed, venom and smugness both. *"Oh, dear, I let that slip didn't I. Yes, I have a new alliance. Just a little measure to ensure my success sooner. Until next time, Stormrider."*

With that parting note, a great thunderclap almost deafened her, and the Nightstalker vanished into thin air.

Arya heaved in one breath, then another.

Horrified silence fell over the chamber.

What had once been Mathas Crowtalon was now a pile of ashes on the marble floor. Chiarn's wrist flicked, and all the unlit torches roared back to life, bringing light back to the room.

"He's gone?" Essa asked. "Just like that?"

"Xaphistryl?" she asked Elendryl.

A shiver of unknowing came in response. He still hadn't seen her.

Arya swore long and fluently, her gaze searching for Darmanin. He hadn't moved, though he'd lowered his sword to his side, gaze still on the spot where the Nightstalker had stood. Arya went straight to him, searching for and catching his gaze. "Are you alright?"

"I'm alright, Arya."

There was that little smile she loved so much, and her shoulders relaxed completely. She reached out and took his free hand, squeezing it tightly. He squeezed back, entangling their fingers. "We did good."

"We did."

Suddenly she wished they were alone. So she could kiss that smile.

Then the sound of muttering and movement broke out. The spell of shocked silence broke and vicelords and warlords moved in groups from the shadows into the centre of the chamber, talking loudly and over each other, many demanding answers. Arya stepped away from Darmanin, wincing as her shoulder throbbed in tune with her bruised chest. Chiarn and Essa joined them. The entire room was looking at Arya and her *cairdre*, expressions ranging from afraid to horrified to disgusted, to vaguely impressed. Loud knocking came from the other side of the main doors, a muffled voice sounding like it was demanding to know what was happening.

"Why did he vanish like that? He had the upper hand," Chiarn asked, pale and sweaty.

"I don't know."

Two loud clangs sounded as Defenders hefted the bars away from the main doors and dropped them to the ground. As soon as they did, the doors flew inwards and more Defenders ran inside, eyes wide and panicked. Behind them strode the Defender general, gold glinting on his shoulders. He halted, seemingly uncertain of who to address when he couldn't find Mathas among those standing.

"What is it, General Dyon?" Hawkesdale barked.

"A mass of flying creatures heading for the city, my Lords. Hundreds of them. Led by another monster riding some kind of bat. They'll be over the walls in moments." The poor man sounded like he couldn't believe the words that were coming out of his mouth.

"*In the air! You and all the wyverns!*" Arya snapped the command to Elendryl. "*If that's a nazal leading the force, you all steer clear until I'm with you. But attack the flying creatures if you can and delay them.*"

Elendryl's snarl rippled through her mind. "*Hunt!*"

Gelfrey Hawkesdale spoke into the shocked silence. Those gathered were still processing that Lucius Nightstalker had just battled Sky Lords in their Council chamber and didn't seem able to process that their city might be under attack. "We need someone to take charge temporarily, until a proper vote can take place. Ravenstrike just pushed back an invasion in the north. My vote is for him."

"Crowtalon agrees," Darmanin said, nodding at Rorin.

"SparrowWing for Rorin Ravenstrike," Amius echoed.

Rian Eaglesoar merely shook his head, white faced. "Fine. Eaglesoar for Ravenstrike."

Nashdar Falconcrest snapped furiously. "I will not vote for Rorin Ravenstrike, even on a temporary basis."

Hawkesdale growled, lifted his sword. "You're outvoted, Nashdar."

Nashdar's lip curled in helpless fury.

General Dyon turned to Rorin. "Warlord Ravenstrike. What are your orders?"

"*Get all Defender archers up on the walls to kill as many of the flying creatures as possible,*" Rorin signed crisply, Taze translating. "*Put shields of swordsmen up there with them to make sure they're protected.*"

They all turned as another Defender commander ran in, blood splattering his white and gold uniform. "These things are breathing fire, my Lords. The city is going up in flames."

"*Amius, get your Firemen out to control the fires.*" Rorin spun. "*General Dyon, send a shield to make sure he gets to the barracks safely.*"

Amius sprinted for the door, some of his vicelords close behind.

"Chiarn, go with them and do what you can," Arya snapped.

The Flamewielder was already moving, acknowledgment rippling through their bond.

Arya stepped forward. "Rorin, Dar, you all left a secondary force encamped near the city in case of emergency. Did Amius leave Firemen among them?"

"*A battalion of them.*" Rorin signed.

"Essa, can you and Alletryl fly there as fast as you can and get them marching here?" Arya asked.

"Consider it done." The Inkweaver ran.

Arya reached for the thread between her and Leanir and tugged hard. "*Go with her and keep them safe.*"

A hard shove on the bond was all she got in response, but a shadow rippled above as Leanir moved.

"If that's a nazal leading the attack, it will overwhelm your non-magical defences." Arya swept her gaze across the warlords. "I'll take it out, or at least distract it while your armies defeat the force of fire-breathing creatures and quell the fires. Are we agreed?"

Rorin and Darmanin wisely remained silent, even though Darmanin's hands were curled into fists of tension at his sides. The warlords had to accept her formal offer of help—if they did, and she succeeded in helping them, the beginnings of a true alliance was born. She hadn't forgotten that she needed to win these men to her side.

"Agreed." Hawkesdale grunted.

"Works for me," SparrowWing said.

Eaglesoar gave a terse nod.

After a hesitation, Nashdar added, "Whatever it takes to stop talking and actually get out there before Gateport burns down around our ears."

Rorin spun into action, signing crisply. "*Taze, you're in charge of the Raiders. I want them deployed to the southern half of the city. Hawkesdale, your Longbows will be invaluable on the walls, I'll leave it to your experience to distribute them as you and your general see fit; Eaglesoar, set your Knights to protecting the Longbows. Falconcrest, deploy your Aggressors to the northern half of the city. Darmanin, what do you suggest for your Lances?*"

"We'll operate as a roving force, filling in wherever it looks like these creatures are starting to overwhelm us."

"And the Defenders?" General Dyon asked.

"I want runners sent across the city. Tell people to stay in their homes, and in basements if they're built from stone or brick. Tell them to get buckets of water prepared in case fire breaks out."

Everyone seemed to move at once, striding quickly for the doors, voices mingling as they coordinated their forces.

"Arya." At'eir materialised, and she blinked in surprise. She'd forgotten all about the Icefolk and Etherean. "We'd like to help too."

Her gaze sought out the Etherean elder. "Go to my barracks and hunker down there. Keep the Etherean safe. This is not your battle to fight, Er'fin."

He showed teeth. "Icefolk do not sit out a fight, Lord Stormrider."

"I doubt you'll be sitting out anything. These creatures will probably hit the barracks too. Elder Salyarin has no protection here. Keep him safe."

"As you wish." He nodded tersely. "Stay alive, Arya Stormrider."

"You too, At'eir."

Chapter 41

Arya emerged from the Council building into a nightmare.

Defenders who'd been on duty outside the Council chamber fought desperately against nightmarish shapes that swooped from the sky. The creatures were the size of huge lizards, with the same scaly, leathery skin, but with fearsome fangs and talon-tipped wings and feet. As Arya watched, one of them opened its mouth and breathed fire.

And then she saw blue uniforms among the Defenders battling the creatures—her Andahari. Laskin caught sight of her emerging and ran over, Esdee with him.

"Report!" she snapped.

"When the attack began, I left half our force under Antonn and Niallin to defend the barracks and brought the other half here." Esdee spoke fast. "I figured someone would need to help Defenders hold the centre of the city and protect Dunidae leadership, and we were the closest and quickest to respond."

"Thank everything for that," Arya said. "Or we'd be lost already; slaughtered as we left the Council chamber. What are these creatures?"

"Firedrakes," she said. "They live in the Horn, like the wraiths and shadowhounds. They're vicious but they can be killed by normal weapons. If you can get them on the ground, they can't manoeuvre very well."

"The defensive lines are breaking," Laskin said calmly. "What do you want us to do?"

"Pull our warriors in closer and tell them to hold their positions," Arya said. "If they stay together, they have a better chance. You'll soon have reinforcements. Longbows and Aggressors. Can you hold until then?"

"Absolutely," Esdee said, earning a scowl from the general.

She couldn't help grinning. "Laskin, once the centre is secure, leave the defence of this area to the Defenders and get all our warriors back to the barracks. Er'fin At'eir and Elder Salyarin will be sheltering there. Your priority is keeping them safe. Clear?"

"Understood." He saluted.

"All right. I'm going after the nazal. Keep yourselves safe."

"*I come.*"

Wind gusted as Elendryl dropped from the sky, snapping at a firedrake as he did and tearing the creature in two, his powerful tail smashing two more out of the sky. As soon as she'd scrambled onto his back, Elendryl spread his wings and leaped into the night sky.

And they went nazal hunting.

***

Arya and Elendryl soared high over the city, making no attempt to hide themselves. Reaching for the thread linking her to Chiarn, she quickly spotted him and Asandryl swooping low over the eastern edge of the city, where spot fires were dotted everywhere she could see.

Raven's balls. Half the city was built on wood. If they didn't stop those flames from spreading, it would be a catastrophe. Thousands of lives lost and even more homes and livelihoods. How had the Nightstalker even gotten his damned firedrakes to Gateport? Surely, they hadn't flown the distance from the Diamondfang. Arya swore again.

That wasn't her fight.

Instead, she turned her attention to the skies, looking for the bat creature carrying the nazal, she and Elendryl fully linked and sharing their senses. Part of her dreaded spotting Xaphistryl instead. A battle with the Nightstalker and his massive wyvern wasn't one they'd walk away from.

She heard a scream from the south at the same time as a ripple of bloodlust went through Elendryl. Arya's gaze snapped in that direction and there—a winged creature flying low between the ships moored in the narrow harbour, and then, as it flew over the city, its nazal rider let out a scream and wind gusted, fanning the flames there into a conflagration.

Arya sucked in a breath. This nazal had once been from House Wind-Dancer.

"Hunt!" she snarled to Elendryl.

He was already dropping into a steep dive, his wyvern's cry roaring from his throat, a deep, soul-tugging scream of challenge that had the bat creature shrieking in response. Elendryl roared again, louder, deeper, the sound reverberated through Arya, shaking the buildings beneath them.

And then the two creatures crashed together, Elendryl's talons clawing deep into the bat's underbelly, his roar of anger shaking the very sky around them. Arya held tight to his back, gaze searching out the hooded nazal, timing it just right.

She leaped, slamming into the nazal and sending them flying through the air. It screamed in fury, but they hit the roof of a dockside building before it could attack, Arya on top so that its body broke their fall.

The slats underneath them cracked and broke, and Arya fought to stay atop the monster as they fell through and down onto an empty warehouse floor. The impact was jarring, and she grunted as pain rippled through every bone in her body. But she ignored the pain and rolled off him, climbing to her feet in one smooth movement, drawing her cazaix blade ... and then she was shifting forward, swinging for the nazal's head as it, too, got to its feet.

The creature hissed, and wind gusted around them, strong enough to force Arya to stumble backwards, her swing going awry. She summoned her own magic and sent a furious blast of cracking energy at the thing's chest. The wind changed shape, flinging her burst sideways so that it hit the wall of the warehouse. It exploded, gouging a huge chunk from the wall and sending wood splinters everywhere.

Arya cocked her head, swung her blade. "Nice trick."

It *screeched* at her, mouth wide to reveal its pointed teeth, madness and pain and anger in its glowing red eyes. But its sibilant hiss, the horrifying visage, none of it scared Arya anymore.

Because she could destroy this creature.

"You can't kill me," she told it, the words fierce and taunting. "No more hunting. No more fear."

After a quick check in with Elendryl—he was battling the bat creature but doing fine—Arya summoned her magic, lighting up her sword with it.

"I am your superior." She roared the words and then went at the nazal, fast and deadly. "And you will die at my hand."

Her magic forced the nazal off balance, distracted it, and despite the wind screaming around her, the darkness of shadows tugging at her feet and balance, Arya's cazaix blade sheared clean through its neck.

She bared her teeth as dark blood splattered her face and chainmail. "Two down."

Then, as the nazal's head was hitting the ground, its bat creature came crashing through the hole in the roof, landing beside its master, dead.

Elendryl's triumphant cry shook the very foundations of the city.

Arya took one moment to savour the sight of the dead nazal at her feet, then headed for the door.

There was more work to be done.

***

Back astride Elendryl, Arya flew high over the city, trying to get a picture of how the battle was going. It didn't take long.

Her heart sank.

Half the city looked like it was on fire.

Hundreds of firedrakes swarmed the sky over the city, swooping down and attacking at will. Wherever flames caught from a firedrake burst, the fire spread quickly through the preponderance of wooden buildings. In the north, Aggressors fought fiercely, but they'd been scattered into small units that were slowly being overwhelmed—none were trained to fight creatures attacking them from the sky.

In the south, Raiders fared better as they fought from horseback with more experience and superior training, but they didn't have the numbers to hold half of the city and entire blocks were up in flames. Lance shields rode from one vulnerable point to another, but were spread too thin. Amidst all this, SparrowWing's Firemen were heroically fighting back the fires engulfing the city while firedrakes focused their attention on picking off the men putting out the fires.

Arya thought quickly, trying to figure out how best to help turn the tide of the battle.

"Zaphirdryl," Elendryl sent suddenly.

Arya turned as Darmanin and his wyvern approached, wyvern and rider blending with the shadows of night so that they were barely visible. Blood splattered Darmanin's dark tunic, but he looked uninjured. "The city will be ashes by morning if we don't do something," he said grimly, clearly having made the same assessment as she had.

She scanned the city roofs below. "We need to get those damned firedrakes out of the sky. If we can stop new fires being created, we can put all our resources to saving the rest of the city."

"How do you plan on doing that? The Longbows are overwhelmed."

"Such little faith in us, Dar?" She lined her words with a challenge.

His grey eyes glowed.

"Watch our backs from above?" she asked. After all, Xaphistryl could still be out there.

"We've got you."

Elendryl started diving as Arya began sinking into her Sky Lord magic, reaching for the thread between her and Darmanin. His magic surged to join with hers.

The rush of power swept through her, heady and electrifying.

This was what it meant to be a Sky Lord.

The firedrakes were flying low, the fire they breathed unable to travel a large distance, so Elendryl brought her down to their level. As they reached what Arya judged to be roughly the centre of the city, right over the Council grounds, she sat up straight, bringing her palms together.

Elendryl levelled out, wings spread, keeping her steady.

Then, using every inch of magic now at her disposal, Arya ripped her palms apart and sent a shock wave of pure energy exploding outwards. Tinged with blue and silver, it spread in an ever-expanding circle, sizzling and crackling as it destroyed any firedrake that it touched.

A mist of blood, bone, and gristle rained down over Gateport.

Magic drained from her like water flowing out of an unplugged bath as the shock wave expanded across the city, then winked out of existence as her reserves emptied. Arya slumped over Elendryl's neck, panting. Weariness throbbed through her. A brief touch of her thread to Darmanin revealed his matching exhaustion. She'd drained them both dry.

He circled down from above, Zaphirdryl coming as close as she was willing to Elendryl. Arya gave him a weary smile. "Thanks for the assist."

She saw only a few scattered groups of firedrakes left in the skies—those who'd been too far away to be caught in her shockwave.

"Any time," Darmanin said, his gaze scanning the skies. "If the Nightstalker was planning to make an appearance, now would be the time."

"Let's try not to worry about that unless it happens," she said. "Will you take point in the north of the city—organise the Aggressors and Lances, get them doing a street-by-street clearance, working from the walls back towards the Council compound and taking out any firedrakes they come across? I'll do the same with the Raiders from the south. We'll make sure the Firemen and Chiarn have enough breathing room to get those fires under control."

He nodded. "Once I've got the shields moving, I'll find Amius and his general. If we can coordinate moving the Firemen into areas after they've been cleared of firedrakes, it will keep them safer, and make the firefighting more efficient."

"Great idea." She grinned, despite her weariness. "I'll meet you in the Council compound when we're done. Ten silvers say I'll clear the southern half first."

"Ten *gold* pieces I clear the northern half first, Stormrider." He gave her his little smile, then Zaphirdryl banked right and dropped down towards the city. Arya sent Elendryl winging to the south, asking him to land in a street where the biggest concentration of Raiders had just finished killing a firedrake that had escaped her shock wave.

"Commander Derrin!" She recognised the man leading them. "I've got a plan. Care to hear it?"

He grinned through the blood and grime on his face. "Whatever it is, we're in."

She explained what she intended to do, saw a series of enthusiastic nods, then bellowed for the first time in too, too long. "On me, Raiders!"

Chapter 42

Throughout the night, Arya and her Raiders methodically swept through the smoke-filled streets and alleys of southern Gateport. Every time they came across a Raider shield, Arya issued orders, and soon she had ten shields spread out, working methodically north towards the Council building and clearing streets as they went.

Occasionally, her shield ran into Firemen struggling with the fires, and stopped to help when they looked overwhelmed. Her magic reserves were entirely gone, but her sword arm was still perfectly fine. Elendryl swooped overhead, helping where he could, covering the Raider shields, making sure none of them were blindsided.

Even so, it was dangerous work. Their numbers decimated, the firedrakes had taken to hiding in unlit streets and alleys, curled up and attacking when unsuspecting Raiders came too close. And every time they breathed fire, wood caught alight and spread. It made for painstakingly slow progress, and impatience wore at Arya.

Hours later, as the blue light of pre-dawn lit up the sky, Arya's muscles trembled with fatigue; her movements growing sluggish, her reaction times slower. One firedrake—curled in the shadows of the roofs above a narrow street—got through her guard as it swooped down from directly above, giving her a deep slash along her left bicep before she killed it. A short time later, Derrin only just knocked aside one of his Raiders before she got her head taken off. After they killed it, he looked at Arya. "We need rest. It's getting too dangerous to keep going."

"I'd agree with you if these damned creatures weren't still starting fires. We have to clear them out if we're going to save the city, and the lives of the people living in it." Somehow, she managed to summon the strength to lift her blade again. "Come on."

Eventually, every street they moved through was empty. Elendryl reported the same from the other Raider shields moving steadily towards the Council building. The sky was lightening above them too, early morning sunlight leaving less places for the firedrakes to hide.

Arya shoved loose tendrils of sweaty hair behind her ears as they turned into another street and began carefully moving along it. She felt grimy. Her tunic and breeches were damp with sweat. Dried firedrake ichor was spattered all over her mail and cloak. Her body was heavy with weariness, and she wasn't sure how much longer she would be able to keep upright. "Nearly there," she told the tired Raiders behind her. "Let's keep moving."

The sun had fully risen above the horizon as Arya reached the large open square containing the Council chamber and the smaller administrative buildings around it. To the south, the harbour glittered in the morning sun. A few merchant ships were still on fire. Others were charcoaled hulks.

At first, Arya was thrilled, despite her exhaustion, to see that she'd beaten Darmanin, but then frowned as she realised it wasn't just him and the Aggressors and Lances that weren't present. The area was empty of anyone but Rorin and Taze and Rorin's personal Raider shield hovering protectively around him. They stood near the entrance to the domed building—Rorin signing to the captain of his shield, Taze translating. Once he'd given the orders, half the shield peeled off, heading for where their horses were tethered a short distance away.

"Derrin?" She turned to him. "Find out where the Defenders and their general are. And when you do, tell them to get here immediately." There should be at least a few shields of them guarding the centre of the city.

"Aye." He saluted and rode off.

"Hold here," she called to the rest of the shield. "Set up a blockade along this end of the square and don't let anything past. As more Raider shields arrive from clearing their sections of the city, use them to bolster the blockade. We don't know if the Lances and Aggressors have fully cleared the northern half of the city yet."

Leaving them to it, Arya started crossing the square towards Rorin, pleased to see two shields of Aggressors accompanying their warlord appearing to her right, turning towards the Council building. Maybe they'd have an update on how things were going. Rorin spotted her and waved. He walked towards her, Taze pacing protectively at his side, the remaining Raiders of Rorin's personal shield staying where they were at a gesture from their warlord.

Arya rolled her eyes. Rorin was too cavalier with his safety sometimes—although she supposed the shields of Aggressors approaching meant he didn't need to have the Raiders too close.

"Ware!" Elendryl bellowed into her mind. *"Behind!"*

A second after her wyvern's warning, the Raiders behind her shouted in warning. Arya spun.

Six firedrakes, flying low, from an area of the city that hadn't been cleared yet, heading straight for the Council building. Elendryl, who'd been covering a shield of Raiders blocks away, flew in pursuit, his size dwarfing the creatures, golden wings spread wide as he moved as fast as he could. His roar was full of frustration.

He wasn't catching up fast enough.

Arya lifted her sword, dropped into a fighting crouch. She noted the Raiders urging their exhausted horses towards her, but the firedrakes were going to get to her before...

...they flew low over her head, bypassing her entirely...

...and aiming for Rorin and Taze. The two men were halfway across the square, exposed and vulnerable. The Raiders of Rorin's protective shield saw what was happening at the same time Arya did and sprinted for their warlord. Warlord Falconcrest saw it too and snapped an order to his Aggressors. Arya saw the captain hesitate briefly, but Falconcrest repeated his order, and the Aggressors launched into a run, swords drawn.

But they weren't running to help Rorin and Taze.

They moved to intercept the Raiders coming to his defence.

A battle broke out as the Raiders roared in anger, desperately fighting to get to their warlord, but they were heavily outnumbered. Arya stared with helpless fury, momentarily frozen with shock at what they were doing.

Then panic spread through her.

"Rorin! Taze!" she screamed. Forgetting her exhaustion, forgetting everything but the danger her brother was in, she began sprinting, running as fast as she could.

But Taze saw what was happening too.

He spun and shoved Rorin as hard as he possibly could. Rorin flew backwards and fell to the ground, hard. He lay still where he fell, clearly dazed. Taze drew his sword and sprinted forward to engage the firedrakes before they could reach Rorin.

"*Elendryl!*" she screamed for her wyvern.

His cry roared out, followed by an echoing cry from Asandryl, who sounded even further away. A part of Arya sensed her Flamewielder flying to her aid.

By the time she reached Taze, the firedrakes were on him, and he'd disappeared in a cloud of leathery wings and snapping teeth. Arya slashed and hacked with desperate abandon, trying to get to him at the same time as she tried to stop any of the creatures breaking off to go after Rorin. Her world became a cloud of biting teeth and a pungent, earthy scent. One slashing talon opened her cheek. Hot blood flowed down her jaw and soaked into her tunic, but she barely noticed it.

Time slowed to a crawl. Arya couldn't kill fast enough. Bodies piled at her feet, and she sustained another wound to her left leg. Desperately, she tried to summon her magic, to use it to blast them away, but it was no good, her reserves were gone.

And then Elendryl was there, screaming his anger, his mighty jaws tearing a firedrake apart before snapping at the next, his spiked tail waving furiously. And hooves clattered, swords clashing as Derrin's shield arrived, half riding to surround Rorin, the other half remaining to help fight the firedrakes.

Once help arrived, it wasn't long till all the creatures were dead. Arya's breath rasped in her chest, and her leg threatened to collapse under her. But her searching gaze went straight where Taze stood. He was on one knee, covered in blood, swaying as he stared at her.

"Taze!" Arya's heart clenched as he fell.

Elendryl landed behind him, wings spread wide to protect Taze from any further threats. Her wyvern made a sound she'd never heard before, a low keening.

Arya's leg gave out as she reached Taze, and she collapsed to the cobblestones. He was covered in bloody wounds, and red soaked through his shirt and tunic. His skin was white and clammy, his breathing shallow.

She slapped his cheek. "Come on Taze, stay with me."

Taze's eyes flickered, open, then closed, then—too slowly—open again. "Too late," he whispered.

"Get me a healer!" She screamed the words to anyone who was listening, gaze not leaving Taze's. "Taze, NO! You stay with me. That's an order, Raider. You stay with me."

"A healer is on his way, Arya!" Derrin called out, but she didn't tear her gaze away from Taze. "The warlord is safe."

Another wyvern cried—Asandryl—and then Chiarn was running towards them. "Arya, are you okay? All I could feel was distress and terror and … oh no."

She ignored him, her attention fixed entirely on her oldest friend. "You're going to be okay," she whispered, forcing him to hold her gaze.

A ghost of a smile crossed Taze's face. "Thank you … Arya … everything. Best…"

"Taze, please. No…" she begged.

It was no good.

As Arya watched, his eyes closed and his head slumped, lifeless, against her.

She screamed.

Elendryl screamed in echo, head raised high in the sky, grief filling his cry.

Strong arms wrapped around her middle and pulled her away. She fought, not wanting to be separated from Taze. The arms were stronger, though, and relentless.

"Let me go!" she snapped, realising it was Darmanin who held her.

And then Rorin was standing before her, eyes glazed, signing, *"Arya, he's gone."*

Her brother was the only thing that could break through her haze of anger and grief. His arms wrapped around her, and she gripped his tunic with both hands, clenching the leather with a white-knuckled grip as she shuddered from the wave of grief that threatened to swamp her. His body trembled against her, silent tears streaming down his face and onto her neck.

Eventually, Arya mastered herself. She let go of Rorin and stepped back, scrubbing at her face. Darmanin was a short distance away, his expression like stone as he stood protectively by Taze's fallen body. His voice was short as he directed Raiders to carry Taze into the Council chamber.

Arya fell in behind the Raiders carrying Taze, unwilling to leave him alone, and Rorin walked at her side, his hand in hers, shoulders slumped. Darmanin followed them wordlessly.

But when her gaze fell on Warlord Falconcrest standing with his Aggressors, watching them, something inside her snapped. Darmanin must have sensed the change, because he reached out a second too late to stop her. Arya broke away from Rorin, drew her sword, and marched towards the Aggressors, towards the man who had caused the death of one of her dearest friends. Fury crystallised in her veins.

"Arya!" Darmanin's voice called out a warning.

The Aggressors must have seen the blind anger on her face, because two of them moved to protect their warlord. Darmanin planted himself half in front of her. "He is a Warlord of Dunidaen."

She halted her movement to snarl, "And he just murdered Stormrider kin. I will not let that go unanswered."

Darmanin took her arm, trying to pull her to a halt. She turned and shoved him as hard as she could, sending him stumbling backwards. Her cazaix blade gleamed blue in the morning sunlight as she approached the Falconcrest warlord.

Nashdar Falconcrest pushed aside the Aggressors who'd moved to protect him, and faced her down, arms crossed, a smirk on his face. "You don't dare touch me."

"Oh, I fucking dare." Arya swept her sword in an arc, neatly decapitating the warlord.

Then, sprayed with fresh blood, she sheathed her sword and returned to Rorin, oblivious to the outcry behind her as she followed the Raiders carrying Taze Nameless into the Council building.

Chapter 43

After getting their wounds seen to, they gathered inside one of the many ante-rooms in the Council building. Darmanin and Arya sat at the opposite ends of a couch. Chiarn stood before the fire, his back to them. Occasionally, he flicked a finger, and the flames flared, crackling and spitting. Rorin sat in a chair, staring unseeing into the flames with reddened eyes.

Arya's bandaged leg and arm throbbed in time with the ache in her bruised shoulder and the stinging on her cheek, but she barely registered the physical pain amid the unbearable constriction in her chest, fighting a never-ending battle with the tears that wanted to fall. She remembered with perfect clarity the first time she'd met Taze, when he'd been hiding in that alley in Aren, still with yellowing bruises all over his body from his father's beating. The image of his dark, flashing eyes, untidy hair and warm grin kept entering her thoughts. As a bodyguard to Rorin, Taze had been thorough and unflinching, and was one of the finest Raiders Arya had ever served with.

And he'd been her friend. Her family.

Magic tugged in her chest, and she sat up. Essa and Leanir were approaching Gateport.

"What is it?" Darmanin asked. He was stiff, cool, and she wasn't sure whether it was from grief, or whether he was angry with her. It was probably both.

"Essa and Leanir will be here soon."

"Good, we desperately need those extra Firemen," Chiarn said. He'd finally been forced to stop helping once his magic drained completely.

A short time later, the doors opened to admit both Sky Lords. Essa took one step into the room and froze. Behind her, Leanir frowned.

"What's happened?" Essa demanded. "Rorin?"

Rorin stood and went to her, saying nothing until he was standing in front of her, then he signed, slow and halting. "*It's Taze,*" he said, broken-hearted. "*He died saving my life.*"

"Oh, Rorin, no." Essa's eyes filled with tears, and a hand lifted to her mouth. Grief surged white-hot along the link Arya shared with her Inkweaver, powerful enough to make her wince and bit her lip, hard.

Leanir raked the room with a glance. "A quarter of the city still looks like it's on fire. Warlord SparrowWing is deploying the fresh Firemen as we speak."

Essa's voice was shaky. "Hawkesdale and Falconcrest are looking for you and Darmanin, Rorin."

Rorin looked haggard as he nodded. "*I'll go and speak with them. We need to make sure we've properly deployed our forces around the city, get those fires out, and then organise the High Warlord vote sooner rather than later.*"

At a look from Arya, Essa touched his arm. "I'll come with you. I'm sure you could use a chief advisor right now."

"I'm feeling a little better after food and water," Chiarn visibly straightened his shoulders. "I'll go back to helping with the fires."

"I'm leaving now," Leanir said pointedly. "My part in this is done."

"On the contrary, Leanir, this is far from over." Arya forced herself to her feet. "I need to go and make sure At'eir and the elder are safe back at my barracks. I'll come straight back."

"I'll walk you," Darmanin said shortly.

She opened her mouth, closed it. She didn't have the energy to fight him on it.

***

He was quiet as they walked, and Arya couldn't bear the silence, so she started talking, the words spilling miserably out of her. "I keep thinking, if

I hadn't sent Essa with Leanir to fetch the Firemen, then maybe she would have been there when the firedrakes ... or if I hadn't told the Raiders to hold back and blockade the square, they could have helped me get to Taze quickly enough. Maybe we could have saved him."

"It wasn't your fault. You made two sound tactical decisions. Without the fresh Firemen to help put out the fires, the city would still be burning right now, killing hundreds and destroying even more homes. And leaving the Raiders to guard the square was a decision any good commander would have made."

"But what if I could have saved him by making a different decision?" she whispered.

Darmanin paused mid-stride, halting her with a light touch. A look of realisation filled his face. "This is why you've been so hesitant these past months. You're afraid your decisions could kill someone else you love. That's why you ran away after Thiara Ravenstrike's death. Why it took you nearly four years to come back."

She avoided his eyes. Left her silence to answer for itself.

"Arya, I was terrified last night."

At his whispered confession, Arya felt her heart clench. "I know."

"And I only just arrived in the square earlier when I saw you wading into the firedrakes attacking Taze ... if you had been hurt or killed ... I literally don't know what I would have done."

"I promise to do my best not to die on you, Dar." She smiled, trying to lighten his mood.

"But you might," he said, eyes dark.

She had nothing to say to that, so they walked on, a less stiff silence falling between them. It was Arya who broke it again as the barracks appeared in the distance. She kept her voice low. "Dar, I don't think the Nightstalker truly wants me dead."

His gaze pinned her. "Is that instinct, or do you have evidence for that theory?"

"Mostly instinct, but he could have had me last night. He disappeared instead."

"If that's true, then..." Darmanin's expression turned thoughtful.

She smiled, nodding. "It might work."

"I personally hope it doesn't come to that," he said, a grimness hanging from his words.

"I understand why. I'm sorry, Dar."

"No need to apologise."

Darmanin peeled off as they reached the barracks, and Arya went looking for Laskin. He was in the mess, where a subdued air hung over proceedings. At'eir and his warriors and the four Etherean were there too, and her shoulders relaxed in relief. The Andahari were clearly pleased to see her and offered waves and nods.

Laskin sat with their old shield. All of them wore black armbands.

Taze had been one of them. Just like her. A small family of soldiers posted together at the edge of the world, looking after each other during the most dangerous moments of their lives. The relief that shuddered through Arya at seeing them all still alive was so strong she had to take a seat before her legs gave out. She didn't think she could take losing another of them.

"We pulled through well," Laskin reported quietly. "Six dead, many injured but none life threatening. A few of the creatures attacked the barracks but the walls are stone, so the fire didn't threaten us. We held them off easily enough."

"Thank you, Laskin." She looked at the others. "Do you mind giving us a moment?"

"Need some sleep anyway," Charlin grumbled, grabbing his tray and standing.

"You need a shave first," Allicen said.

"See you later." Kait sketched a wave.

Once they were gone, Arya settled a look on Laskin. "We need to talk."

He scowled. "Nope."

She took a breath. "I'm going to release you from my service, Laskin. It's the last thing I want to do, but Dunidaen needs you."

"Arya—"

"I'm sorry," she interrupted, voice firm. "If Rorin is voted in as High Warlord, Ravenstrike needs a warlord, and until Anji grows old enough, someone needs to rule for him. Rorin needs you."

Laskin's scowl deepened. "I can't be warlord. I'm not even of noble blood."

"You'll technically be a regent, not a warlord."

"There's no guarantee Warlord Ravenstrike will even become High Warlord."

"But if he does, he will need a man he can trust to run Ravenstrike for him."

"Arya Ravenstrike Stormrider!" he barked at her, causing multiple heads to swivel their way, eyes wide. "There is a far better solution to your problem than me, and if you got out of your stubborn head for a second, you'd have already realised it."

She stared, mouth falling open. Laskin had *never* spoken to her like that before. Which meant ... Arya's gaze narrowed as she thought through his words. And then groaned. "Yes, yes, all right. I'm an idiot. Let's go."

***

When Arya and Laskin returned, the Defenders on guard informed Arya that Rorin could be found with the warlords in the main Council chamber. She entered to find Rorin pacing, running a hand through his messy blonde hair in agitation. Essa stood nearby with Chiarn, both looking warily at the table where warlords Hawkesdale, SparrowWing, and Eaglesoar sat with Darmanin. Every person in the room looked exhausted and in desperate need of a bath and fresh clothes. They also looked mad.

"Has something happened?" Arya ventured.

Rorin spun at her appearance. "*You may not have noticed, but half the city burned down last night. The fires are finally out, but many storehouses were hit, which means there isn't enough food to go around until we can get supplies in. Hundreds of people don't have homes anymore.*" He took a breath, continuing his pacing. "*Dunidaen doesn't have a warlord for Falconcrest, and we're going to need their army to meet the invasion that's coming now the Nightstalker has apparently allied with Khadini. On top of that, the surviving warlords are up in arms because an Andahari Sky Lord assassinated one of our number without even a 'by your leave'. Hawkesdale and SparrowWing are demanding furious punishment and want assurances it will never happen again."*

"I certainly hope you don't expect me to give those assurances," Arya said, taking in everyone at the table with her glance. "I won't apologise, and I won't promise not to do it again."

Darmanin winced, while Rorin threw his hands in the air and collapsed into a chair.

"You are not a Dunidae warlord," Hawkesdale barked. "You don't have the right to execute our citizens."

"We can't have a High Warlord who will tolerate that either," Amius added, mouth tight as he avoided Arya's gaze.

"If I may suggest something?" Darmanin spoke, then continued at a nod from the others. "Perhaps if the Sky Lords were to do something like this in the future, Dunidaen would revoke their diplomatic rights and bar them entrance into Dunidaen. We could also increase tariffs on any future trade with Andahar and arrest any Andahari citizens residing in Gateport and ship them back home."

Arya stared at Darmanin in affront, but both Eaglesoar and Amius nodded with grudging approval. Hawkesdale just looked angry. "You'd be one of those Sky Lords, right, Crowtalon?" he barked. "You ever plan on telling us that?"

Darmanin's mouth thinned. "I am the warlord of Crowtalon. I am not a member of Arya's *cairdre*. I flew my wyvern and used my magic last night only because it was needed in the defence of my country, Dunidaen."

Rorin eyed Arya for a moment, then nodded firmly. *"Arya, you're family and I love you, but do that again, and we will do everything Dar suggests,"* he said. *"All of you here know that I plan to nominate for High Warlord, and my first priority must be the interests of Dunidaen."*

"Do as you must," she said. They could talk about this later.

"We need to deal with Falconcrest State." Helden said. "Nashdar had no heirs, confirmed or otherwise."

Hawkesdale grumbled. "He was a traitorous coward. What he did to that young man was reprehensible."

"If I may?" Essa spoke. "You're not entirely correct, Warlord SparrowWing. Nashdar has an older sister—Dahlia. Rorin, you'll remember we met her at a dinner during our visit to Gateport two years ago."

Arya's eyes widened slightly when, apart from a few disgruntled looks, none of the warlords protested the idea of a woman replacing Nashdar.

"*We'll send for her at once so she can be confirmed as warlord,*" Rorin said. "*Fortunately, the Falconcrest vicelords are already here for the High Warlord vote, so we can hold it as soon as she arrives. In the meantime, let's turn our minds to managing the fallout of last night's attack.*"

"You might not have time to wait for Dahlia to arrive," Arya interjected. "You need every minute at your disposal."

"When we want foreign advice, we'll ask for it." Eaglesoar waved her off.

Arya bristled, but didn't push it. She ignored the pointed looks saying 'I told you so' from Rorin and Darmanin too. Instead, she and her Sky Lords remained quiet as Eaglesoar suggested a brief break so they could confer with their generals and get a status update. While the warlords dispersed, Arya approached Rorin.

"Have you thought about what you're going to do about Ravenstrike if they vote for you as High Warlord?"

Rorin sighed. "*There's so much to do, I can't really think that far ahead right now. It might not even happen.*"

"Rorin, you've just led them through an attack on Gateport. They'll vote for you," she told him. "You need someone to be warlord in Heathrock until Anjurin comes of age. I think you should appoint Peemla as your regent."

His eyes widened. "*The warlords would have a fit. She's not of noble blood.*"

"What does that matter? She's your wife and the mother of your heir. And even if she was neither of those things, Rorin, the woman is brutally efficiently and clever. The household both adore *and* respect her. She'd probably do a better job as warlord than you."

A laugh escaped him, eyes lightening. "*You're not wrong.*" Then he rubbed at his face when Darmanin came back in to take his chair. "*What about Darmanin in all of this? He might win the vote.*"

"I think—"

The doors opened suddenly, and a Lance captain strode in. He carried his helmet at his side, and his hair was rumpled, jaw unshaven. Darmanin leaped to his feet and snapped, "Captain Felder. Aren't you stationed in Anduil? What are you doing here?"

"My shield rode from Anduil as fast as we could, Warlord," Felder reported, an undercurrent of tension in his voice. "The day we left, word came from the barracks in Tamrin of an invasion force—fifty or more Khadini and Andahari ships— landing on our eastern coast. The message reported they were marching inland toward Anduil, razing everything before them. Commander Roion immediately sent me to bring you the news. Anduil's defences were being prepared when I left."

A shocked silence reverberated through the room.

Arya swore loud and fluently as the pieces fell together in her mind. "While Etherean scouts watched the Diamondfang for another invasion force, the Nightstalker instead sailed his army south. There to join with his new Khadini ally and attack where we least expected."

"What could he have promised Emperor uq-Danresan that he's willing to invade us without cause?" Darmanin asked in disbelief.

"*We can worry about that later. I'll get Hawkesdale and the others back in here.*" Rorin gestured for one of the guards standing by the door. "*We'll need to start marching west immediately, with or without our full armies.*"

Arya nodded. "I'll go to the elder and Er'fin At'eir. Ask them to do what they can to bring fighters quickly to help you. Elendryl and I can get the er'fin home within days."

"Chiarn and I could fly west, see if we can slow the pace of the invasion, give time for the Dunidae army to catch up." Essa offered bravely.

"You need to—" But Arya's words died at a sharp tug on the thread that connected her to Leanir, and then the assassin himself was flying in, face pale, dark eyes bleak. Dread filled her at what might have driven the composed Shadeweaver assassin to walk openly into the Council chamber.

"What is it?" she demanded.

"Xaphistryl is coming," he said. "The Nightstalker leads his army this time, one of the nazal at his side. I've been dream-walking it. With his help, they've already crossed half of Crowtalon and they're a few days' march away from Gateport."

A few days.

The Dunidae army could never gather enough strength in that amount of time. The Nightstalker had planned this to perfection, using his firedrake attack to thin out the Dunidae forces before his real attack. Arya had tried to outwit him, but he was two steps ahead of her. She didn't have enough to catch up. Not yet.

Arya swallowed, a sick certainty settling in her chest. She forced herself not to look at Darmanin. "Then we have only once choice."

"*Which is what?*" Rorin asked.

"If the Nightstalker is coming in person to take Dunidaen," she said. "Then only one thing can hope to stop him."

Darmanin sucked in a breath, his face granite.

Rorin signed, "*Arya, you told me you aren't fully trained yet, you told me you are years away from being able to confront the Nightstalker and win.*"

Ayra searched out Chiarn, Essa, met their gazes. Asked a silent question through the bonds between them. Felt their response.

Then she turned back to the room. "Tell me what other choice we have?"

Only silence greeted her.

Chapter 44

Arya spoke into the grim silence her words left, turning to her *cairdre*. "If we can defeat the Nightstalker, Dunidaen's armies will have a chance."

"Then we need to pick the place for this fight, give ourselves as much of an advantage as possible," Darmanin said.

Arya shook her head. "Dar, you're not coming with us."

"What?"

"You said it yourself, you're Warlord Crowtalon. You don't want to be a member of my *cairdre*."

"That's ridiculous," he said. "Even if I'm not with your *cairdre*, I can still help you."

"No, you can't," she told him firmly, pitching her voice loud and clear. "You're needed here, to help fight for Dunidaen. You know I'm right. This is what you've always wanted, and this is where you should be."

"And what about you? You expect me to do nothing while you fly to your death?" He was furious, eyes alight.

"This is what you chose." She held that furious gaze. "You stay here."

"*Arya, you can't do this,*" Rorin protested. "*You'll all be killed.*"

"Rorin, it's this or we all die anyway when the Nightstalker gets here," Arya said. "And don't even try suggesting that I run and hide while he takes Dunidaen and kills hundreds in the process."

"Have some faith in us." Essa tried for a smile, failed.

Rorin looked anguished. "*My family is about to fly away from me into dire danger. How am I supposed to feel?*"

Arya smiled for him. "If I die, not all hope is lost. You will still be alive. Kirin too. Do you understand?"

"You're planning to die?" Darmanin said incredulously, voice lifting in volume.

"Of course not," she snapped. "But I know my chances aren't good."

"They're non-existent," he argued. "You couldn't best him in Andahar and you couldn't last night. What is different now?"

She had no answer to give him.

Darmanin stared at her bleakly. "You know you're not getting away alive, don't you?"

"I don't want to die," she said clearly. "And I will do my best not to. I promise you."

He nodded, looking away for a long moment. When he spoke, his words were distant and cool and her heart broke. "I suppose this is goodbye, then. Good luck, Arya."

Then he turned and strode out, the door slamming behind him.

Arya turned to her brother, not letting herself watch Darmanin go. She hugged him tightly. "We'll do our best to come back, Rorin, I promise you."

Rorin stepped back, running a hand through his messy hair. *"The warlords and I will get our forces moving as quickly as we can."*

"We'll be waiting," she said, throat closing over. She hated lying to her brother.

Her eyes drank in Rorin and her Inkweaver as they hugged tightly, and then let go so Chiarn could shake Rorin's hand. Arya would make sure they had the chance to see each other again.

But she knew, however the coming battle went, she wouldn't be coming home.

Unable to watch anymore, she turned and left, planning to wait in the hall outside. She found Leanir waiting for her.

"I gave my word," was all he said in response to her questioning look.

"You break it, and I'm going to do worse than kill you, Leanir. By now you know that's not an idle threat."

His jaw tightened. "I heard what you did to Falconcrest."

"Good," she said, then left.

***

Arya and her Sky Lord's flew west until nightfall, seeing no trace of an invading army or the Nightstalker and his wyvern. Knowing they were all exhausted after a night of fighting, she brought them down to make camp and get some rest. It was dark and drizzly, and Chiarn started a fire while Arya sat staring into the flames, thinking of Kirin, his bright blue eyes and chubby cheeks, of how far she'd go, how much she'd risk, to keep him safe.

Depending how the next day went, she might never see her son again. Arya swallowed down the stabbing pain of that thought, trying to reassure herself with the reminder that if the Nightstalker had been in Khadini to make an alliance with the emperor, then at least Kirin was safe for now. But the Nightstalker had been right when he'd taunted Arya the previous night. Once he had Dunidaen, and Khadini as his ally, it would only make it easier for him to find Kirin, kill her and her *caidre*.

Whatever it took. She'd make sure Kirin lived.

"Dar didn't look happy back there." Essa spoke from beside Arya.

"He's afraid one or more of us will die tomorrow."

"Aren't we all?" Leanir said.

"He's afraid *you'll* die," Essa said quietly, ignoring Leanir.

"He'll be fine, Ess."

Chiarn shivered. "Arya, I don't understand why you think facing him will work after he beat us so soundly last night. What has changed?"

"Nothing," she admitted. "But you learn something from every losing fight. Having said that, I won't force any of you to face him with me. You can leave any time you want."

Leanir said nothing, face tight and set. He hated her. She wondered if that hate was strong enough to let him break his word. If he did, everything would be lost. Shivering, Arya tried to come up with some way of facing the Nightstalker and beating him. If she could somehow avoid having to rely on the only card she had left to play in this game...

Essa squeezed her hand, held her gaze. "I said I'd stand at your side for whatever comes, and I meant it. I fight to the end with you, my friend."

Arya nodded, barely able to choke out, "I am sorry, if..."

Chiarn let out a heavy sigh. "Don't apologise. I too, choose to stand with you."

Arya's stomach clenched with guilt.

***

When she rose in the morning, having barely slept, Arya found Leanir awake and watchful, his gaze turned inward. "What are you thinking?" she asked.

"Nothing I care to share with you."

It was an overcast, drizzly morning. The light rain soaked Arya's face and hair as Elendryl led the way north to meet the Nightstalker, her *caidre* flying in her wake. She'd been able to sense his nearness from the moment they'd lifted into the skies that morning. Since the day he'd almost beaten her to death, she knew the feel of his presence like nothing else, and now she could sense his anticipation.

The Nightstalker knew they were coming.

Arya touched Elendryl's neck, and the wyvern slowed, allowing the other Sky Lords to gather around her. "He's waiting for us."

"Tell me you have a plan, Arya?" Chiarn asked her, his face pale with fear.

"I have a plan," she spoke confidently for their sake, even though she knew there was a million ways this could go wrong. "It's simple. We go down there and try to kill him. We stay in the air, that way he has to come to meet us, and he can't use his army against us if things go badly for him. And remember, your cazaix can hurt him *and* Xaphistryl."

"I suppose there's no point in waiting," Essa said, her gaze focused on the horizon.

"No," Arya murmured, turning her gaze back to the sky ahead of them. "I suppose not."

Soon after, they dropped below cloud cover, the wooded slopes of Crow-talon visible below, and then … the massed army marching through the fields, heading for Gateport. Khadini Rangers marching with black-clad Nightblades. It was an intimidating sight. The light was dim, sunlight blocked by the heavy clouds and drizzling rain making visibility limited.

A whisper across her senses, a shiver from Elendryl, and Arya looked west, where a dark shape flew through the clouds towards them.

The Nightstalker and Xaphistryl.

The wyvern was beautiful, her scales raven black, her wings the same. And she was so much bigger than Elendryl and the others, almost dwarfing them, her spread wings blotting out what limited light there was.

Arya drew her sword, holding it ready, her Sky Lords hovering close behind her, watching her back. The tight ball of anxiety in her stomach grew fiercer as they waited for the Nightstalker to reach them. Her grip on her sword was white-knuckled, and she fought hard to keep her breathing calm and her expression clear.

"Wait for him to make the first move," she shouted over her shoulder. "Let me take the brunt of the attack, and all of you move in support, just like we did against the nazal."

Xaphistryl flew closer, then banked, powerful wings keeping her hovering before them. The Nightstalker's voice rang into the skies. "Once again, you make things easier by handing yourself over to me."

"You won't find it easy to defeat a united *cairdre*, no matter how strong you are," Arya said.

"I only see four Sky Lords, not a full *cairdre*." He laughed that mad laugh of his. "I've defeated you twice before, Stormrider, and I doubt your Flamewielder or Inkweaver will be any harder. The Mindbreaker has no loyalty to you whatsoever. Without your fifth and most powerful Sky Lord, you will lose. Surely you already knew that?"

"I think you're bluffing. We've destroyed two of your nazal. We are not going to be easy to kill, and I think you know that. I think that's why you've rushed your invasion, to try and get to us before we're too powerful."

Lucius' smile only widened. "You're a fool, Arya Stormrider."

The Nightstalker lifted his hand in a 'come hither' gesture and another wyvern and her rider dropped out of the clouds above them.

Darmanin and Zaphirdryl.

Shock flared in Arya's chest, the emotion reverberating from her bond with Chiarn, and then shock *and* disbelief from Essa, and Arya's hands pressed harder against Elendryl's scales. He shivered beneath her, his teeth baring in Zaphirdryl's direction. She snapped at him in response.

Arya's gaze flicked between Darmanin and the Nightstalker. "You didn't," she shouted, staring at Darmanin. His expression was hard and unyielding. "Darmanin? Tell me you *didn't*."

"Didn't what?" Chiarn demanded, voice tight with terror.

"What are you doing, Dar?" Essa called out.

"My grandson and I have come to an agreement," Lucius said, balancing easily as Xaphistryl rode out an updraft. "Which regretfully means I cannot kill you today. It doesn't stop me, however, from preventing you all getting in my way."

"Darmanin, please tell me what's going on," Arya said, ignoring the Nightstalker to fix her gaze on him. "Tell me this is a trick. A plan to ambush him."

He said nothing, but she could read the answer in his face, in the flash of guilt and pain quickly hidden behind a featureless mask. Essa let out a cry behind her—pure despair. Her connection with Chiarn reverberated with terror. Leanir was still. Like a predator readying to leap away from a greater threat.

"The trick is on you, Stormrider," Lucius laughed, and again she heard the note of madness in it that chilled her to the bone.

"I will stop both of you if I have to," Arya said, raising her sword.

"No, you won't. You're not strong enough."

"Darmanin!" Essa called again, voice pleading. "What are you doing?"

"I think what I'm doing is clear, Essa," Darmanin spoke for the first time, his tone distant and cold. "Put down your weapons and come peacefully. Nobody needs to get hurt—I made sure of it. You'll be safe if you make no threatening moves."

Arya reached for her wyvern. *"Elendryl, tell Alletryl and Asandryl to flee, now. Tell Leanir's wyvern to do as I ordered. I will hold Darmanin and the Nightstalker long enough for them to get free."*

Affirmation from Elendryl, and then Leanir shouted. She sensed the flash of his magic, then the gust of air as one or more of the wyverns behind her turned abruptly and dived for the ground, ignoring their riders' cries. Snarling, the Nightstalker moved to counter them.

Elendryl dropped into Xaphistryl's path and Arya loosed her magic, sending a bolt of pure energy at the Nightstalker. He swung to avoid her blow, and the two wyverns collided, screaming in anger. Letting out a roar, the Nightstalker sent his knife spinning at her, a metal blade wreathed in the darkness of his magic. Arya hurled herself backwards to avoid it, but wasn't quite quick enough. The hilt of the knife caught her temple, and she felt pain flare through her head.

The Nightstalker reached out, quick as lighting, and grabbed her as she fell, both hands fisting in her jerkin. Elendryl screamed as he disengaged and wheeled away, fury and despair in his cry. Detached curiosity filled the Nightstalker's voice as he asked her. "Why come here like this and hand yourself over to me?"

She managed a bitter laugh. "Wouldn't you like to know?"

And then blackness clouded her vision and the last thing she saw before passing out was Darmanin, watching impassively from above.

Epilogue

I t was dark and raining heavily when Arya came to awareness again. It took a few moments for her to realise that she was in the back of a jolting cart. Water dripped through a canvas roof above her. She had just managed to sit up, pain thudding in her head, when the cart came to a halt. Before she could react, the canvas was thrown back and hands reached for her.

She struggled violently, kicking and yelling and scratching, but was inevitably dragged out. The heavy rain soaked through her hair and ran down her face and into her eyes. She tried raising a hand to clear her vision, but her arm was yanked forcefully behind her back as her wrists were chained together.

"Walk!" one of the men shouted.

Arya stumbled forward as someone pushed her hard in the back, and she staggered across slick cobblestones towards a cavernous entry in a dark stone building. Her skin prickled with discomfort. There was only dark open space to her left and right, and her captors pushed her towards the dark opening before she could get a proper look at her surroundings.

Belatedly, she tried to reach for Elendryl, but couldn't. Head hurting, she tried again, but hit only a blank wall of numbness. Arya stumbled again as she was dragged relentlessly. She fell into a puddle, the muddy water soaking through her pants. The guard yanked her back to her feet, and she was taken the last few feet inside the entryway. Here, a man waited.

"Welcome to Blackstone Prison." He spoke with a voice that was cold, emotionless.

Arya stared at him; he was a big man, with a thick black beard and dark brown eyes.

"You'll be here for a while," he continued. "I am Commander Luri, and I'm the warden of this prison."

She spat at him. "Let me go or I'll tear you to pieces."

He laughed aloud. "You are no Sky Lord in here. You may have already noticed that your magic won't work inside these walls, and you won't be able to contact your wyvern either. If it's even still alive."

Arya swallowed back the fear that swamped her at his words. Elendryl would be fine. He had to be.

Luri leaned closer, a thread of iron entering his voice. "Your Sky Lords are dead, Stormrider. Nobody knows you are here, and nobody will think to look for you here either. Nobody has ever escaped from Blackstone."

"I *will* kill you." She spoke the words with as much confidence as she could muster, but they had no impact on the warden.

"There will be plenty of time for you to try." Luri stepped back. "You'll be in here for the rest of your life. Guards, take her to her cell."

Arya fought bitterly, but it was to no avail. The sound of the rain faded behind her as she was dragged deeper into the prison. She kept fighting until they tossed her into a cell, the door clanging shut behind her.

And when they were gone, and she was alone in the dark, she let a little smile break through the fear and worry that consumed her—for what had happened to those she loved, how they might fare while she was gone.

Because this was exactly where she'd hoped to be.

It all went back to that conversation with Essa all those months ago. Defeating the Nightstalker, saving Kirin, it would happen one step at a time.

Time to try step three.

THE END...

***

The story continues in *The Unleashed Storm* - available now

The Dock City Chronicle

·

Want to delve deeper into the Archive?
Buried in the depths of the Inkweaver Archive is a prequel novella: *The Stolen Throne: a hidden Record from the Archive.*
Set decades before *The Nameless Throne*, this story follows a dangerous escape involving the fearsome Nightstalker — and it's yours free when you sign up for my monthly newsletter, **The Dock City Chronicle**.

·

Each edition *of The Chronicle* is filled with:
Insider updates on my books
Fantasy world news and hot takes
Hilarious book memes
My book recommendations
Exclusive sneak peeks

·

Sign up for *the Chronicle* at my website: lisacassidyauthor.com

~

Become an Inkweaver?

This is your invitation.

I'd love to welcome you into my **Inkweaver Community**—a private space for readers who love epic fantasy, found family, and all the feels.

.

Whether you've read *The Inkweaver Archive*, *A Tale of Stars and Shadow*, *The Mage Chronicles*, or *Heir to the Darkmage*, you'll find fellow readers who are just as invested as you are.

Inside my Inkweaver community, you can:

Discuss characters, moments, and theories

Chat with me directly

Access behind-the-scenes insights, sneak peeks, and the occasional spoiler

.

It's also a place to talk fantasy more broadly — to share recommendations, discover new favourites, and connect with readers who speak your language.

The adventure doesn't end on the last page.

Join me in the Inkweaver Community:

(https://inkweavers.mn.co)

About me

I'm a self-published fantasy author by day and book nerd in every other spare moment I have. I'm also self-confessed coffee snob (don't try coming near her with any of that instant coffee rubbish) but I am willing to accept all other hot drink aficionados, even tea drinkers. I live in Australia's capital city, Canberra, and like all Australians, I'm in pretty much constant danger from highly poisonous spiders, crocodiles, sharks, and drop bears, to name a few. As you can see, I am also pro-Oxford comma.

A 2019 SPFBO finalist, and finalist for the 2020 ACT Writers Fiction award, I'm the author of young adult fantasy series *The Mage Chronicles* and *Heir to the Darkmage*, and epic fantasy series *A Tale of Stars and Shadow* and *The Inkweaver Archive*. I'm currently working on a sequel to *A Tale of Stars and Shadow*.

As part of my writing journey, I've partnered up with One Girl, a charity working to build a world where all girls have access to quality education. A world where all girls — no matter where they are born or how much money they have — enjoy the same rights and opportunities as boys. A percentage of all my royalties go to One Girl.

You can follow me on Facebook and Instagram. I also have a fantasy reading community – The Inkweavers - where you can jump in and talk about anything and everything relating to books and reading.

I also have an author street team. I call them the *Wolves*, after Prince Cuinn's fierce personal guard in *A Tale of Stars and Shadow*. If you'd be interested in becoming a Wolf, you can email me at wolves@tatehousebooks.com. Everyone is welcome, and I'd be more than happy to answer any questions you have.

If you want to learn more about me and my books, head on over to my website at lisacassidyauthor.com

BORROWED FROM
The Inkweaver Archive